D1595791

GUS C. GARCÍA, TRAGIC HERO OF THE CIVIL RIGHTS MOVEMENT

FEET OF CLAY

A NOVEL

TCU Press

FORT WORTH, TEXAS

MILLIE ROSE DIAZ

Library of Congress Cataloging-in-Publication Data

Names: Diaz, Millie Rose, 1979- author.
Title: Feet of clay : Gus C. García, tragic hero of the civil rights movement, a novel / Millie Rose Diaz.
Description: Fort Worth, Texas : TCU Press, [2021] | Summary: "In the early 1950s, a Mexican American man named Gus has become a top Texas civil rights attorney-a climb that has been bedeviled by his competing obsessions with the law, la raza, the ladies, and Chivas Regal whisky. On the day he learns that his failed marriage has rendered him homeless, Gus hastily takes on a new client, a man accused of shooting and killing a man outside a bar in Edna, Texas. The case becomes one about equal representation when his associates uncover a disturbing fact: no minority or person of color has sat on a Jackson County jury in at least twenty-five years. Without funds, without political support, Gus and his team courageously pursue a demanding course that forces them to battle the system at every turn. The case and Gus himself are targeted by Symmetry, an elitist, ultraconservative secret society bankrolled by Texas oil barons. A representation of the many extant southern white supremacist groups of the day, the group engages Gus's longtime nemesis to stop the progression of the Hernandez case using schemes of persuasion and bribery. Gus finds occasional solace when he begins a relationship with the world's first female bullfighter, but his unresolved past threatens his well-being. The story also introduces a young Mexican American girl who learns the complications of being shades darker than her sister and struggles to find her voice. This is a fictional account based on true events."— Provided by publisher.
Identifiers: LCCN 2021036099 (print) | LCCN 2021036100 (ebook) | ISBN 9780875657936 (cloth) | ISBN 9780875657950 (ebook)
Subjects: LCSH: Garcia, Gus C., 1915-1964—Fiction. | Civil rights lawyers—Texas—Fiction. | Mexican Americans—Civil rights—Fiction. | Discrimination in criminal justice administration—Texas—Fiction. | Edna (Tex.)—Fiction. | BISAC: FICTION / Hispanic & Latino | FICTION / General | LCGFT: Novels. | Historical fiction. | Biographical fiction.
Classification: LCC PS3604.I184 F44 2021 (print) | LCC PS3604.I184 (ebook) | DDC 813/.6—dc23
LC record available at https://lccn.loc.gov/2021036099
LC ebook record available at https://lccn.loc.gov/2021036100

TCU Box 298300
Fort Worth, Texas 76129
To order books: 1.800.826.8911

Design by Preston Thomas

IN MEMORY OF MY BROTHER,
ROBERT DIAZ, JR.

Mexican American civil rights attorney Gus C. García poses for a picture in 1952 with a warm smile. Courtesy of UTSA Special Collections/Zuma Press.

Gus C. García stands in front of a courtroom, gaunt and tired, only a year later, in 1953. Courtesy of UTSA Special Collections/Zuma Press.

PREFACE

MEXICO AND THE UNITED STATES SIGNED THE TREATY OF GUADALUPE-HIDALGO in 1848, as a result of the US victory in the Mexican-American War. It recognized Texas as a US state, and ceded about half of the land in the Mexican republic to the US for the cost of $15 million. Upwards of eighty thousand Mexicans instantly became US citizens, bringing mixed reactions from all sides. More immigrants entered the US in the early 1900s due to a Mexican civil war, unsettling many US southerners.

Mexican Americans struggled to find a place in society, and the Fourteenth Amendment overlooked their ethnicity, stating there are only two races, white and black. Mexican Americans were considered white but didn't get the perks that came with the association.

This is the story of a group of Mexican American lawyers who took their case to the Supreme Court and fought for recognition of their race, and more particularly, of Gus C. García, an out-of-the-box character who led the group, and whose downs were just as dramatic as his ups.

Gus C. García understood his faults in King Nebuchadnezzar II's dream of a towering statue with a head of gold, chest and arms made of silver, bronze belly and thighs, iron legs and feet partly made of iron and clay tile. Curious about its meaning, the king approached Daniel for an interpretation, which can be found in the second chapter of his book within the Bible.

Daniel told the king: "When you looked at the statue, a stone which was hewn from a mountain without a hand being put to it, struck its clay and tile feet, causing them to break into pieces. The iron, tile, bronze, silver and gold all crumbled at once, fine as the chaff on the threshing floor in summer, and the wind blew them away without leaving a trace.

"As you saw the iron mixed with clay tile, and the toes partly iron and partly tile, the kingdom shall be partly strong and partly fragile."

1922

A YOUNG GUS INHALED THE SCENT OF VICTORY AND DEFEAT as his abuelo paid for their tickets to the bullfight, two dollars apiece. His heart quickened as a trio of glittering flags came into his view. The clash of man against beast in an arena spelled danger to the boy, and what could be better than that?

Mateo bought several beers in unlabeled bottles before leading his grandson in a walk around the outside perimeter of the arena, just beneath the highest part of the stands. "Bullfighting is an old sport. They built some of these places long ago," he explained. "Did you know some arenas have collapsed in the middle of a fight?"

The boy pumped his little legs to keep up with his abuelo. "Why?"

"Bulls pushing too hard from the sides, or too many people sitting in the same area." He pointed up. "Nobody cared to check for signs ahead of time." Mateo blew a puff of air from his mouth. "Then poof. Things deteriorate and crumble eventually, don't forget that. It's just a matter of time."

A trumpet blared out as they reached their seats, signaling the matador's march would begin shortly. Gus sighed happily as he looked upon the sea of copper-colored dust and waited for horses to gallop out. He noticed a girl seated several rows in front of him; she played with a wooden toy car and a small figurine of a matador.

"*Mijo*, stand on top of the bleachers so you can see every detail." Mateo looked him dead in the eye. "This is your first bullfight, Gustavo."

The boy held the stare, then intensified it. "Call me Gus."

The man matched his serious expression and gravely nodded. "Gus."

One look at matadors entering the arena, however, melted any maturity Gus tried to show. He burst into cheers with every ounce of strength his seven years could muster. "I wasn't expecting three bullfighters!" He didn't even mind their hot pink, knee-length socks and tasseled black shoes.

"Sí, mijo. The dance can be quick. Six bulls will die today, but some will not die fast." Mateo took a drink from his beer and gazed at the sky cryptically. "The swill tastes bitter today. That is not a promising sign."

Gus studied the men without listening to his grandfather. "I want to fight bulls," he declared.

"*Bueno*, then you must learn to dance."

The boy wrinkled his nose. "Dancing is not fighting."

"It is! Everything is a *bailar*, a dance, if you think about it." Mateo pretended to steer a woman into a salsa. "Finding a lady friend *mujer*, even if just for a night, it's all a dance. Surely you don't think with a bull it can be a fight. Even the strongest and fastest of matadors would be loco to think he can fight a bull and win. One must avoid contact with the bull until the last second."

Gus cocked his head sideways. "I could do it." He liked how a crowd erupted into cheers when a matador waved in their direction. "I can fight them all."

"You will need help. A bull weighs fifteen hundred pounds. One cannot fight a bull alone." Mateo pointed to the arena. "Those men on horses are *picadors*, and they will switch places with more men, the *banderilleros*. Both weaken the bull with their tools, each different from the other. The *toreador* enters at the end to kill it."

"So the matador wins."

"Not necessarily. The dance needs to be a spectacle to satisfy us, the people. A bull will die, but how? A matador must be fearless and cunning with his skill to please a crowd while avoiding the animal. He must show complete control over the bull by hypnotizing it until the moment of attack. If he takes too long, the audience is unhappy, but if he goes too fast, they still feel the same. The matador must be stylish, flawless, and all in the perfect amount of time."

"The audience must be hypnotized, too, then?"

The final trumpet sounded, leaving Gus's question unanswered. A bull rushed out of an opened gate and the picadors went to work, then the banderilleros. Finally the matador walked out, purposeful and full of confidence. His red cape, the muleta, fell from a two-foot-long thin wooden rod and draped around him like a cocoon. He approached the bull with a syncopated gait, and the animal glared with wild eyes, obviously annoyed and sensing his end might be near.

Gus watched intensely. "I want to do that."

Mateo drank more. "To fight with bulls you have to live with them. Do you think your mamá would allow that?" He waited for the image to sink in. "Besides, you'd be better as a bull."

Gus's grass-green eyes widened. "I can be the bull?" He glanced at the animal as it grunted loudly and charged into the cape. "No, they die. I'm a bullfighter."

"There are three of them, don't forget . . . and they can die, too."

"I'm the *winning* matador, Abuelo."

Mateo smiled. "Drink some of this cerveza, if that's true. It gives courage to face all sorts of *toros*." He leaned in closer. "If you don't like the taste, maybe you're not ready."

Gus yanked the bottle out of his grandfather's hand and eagerly drained it in a gulp. His throat put out tiny flames as the liquid traveled, and he winced at the aftertaste. Courage in a bottle.

Mateo laughed grandly, a sign of approval. He produced another bottle from his back pocket and twisted the cap off swiftly with his teeth before spitting it to the ground. After taking several gulps, he handed it to Gus. "Boy, are you happy?"

Beaming, Gus gazed at the arena, the colors, and listened to the noise of the crowds. "Yes, I am."

"Then mijo, can I trust you to be alone? I'm going to the bathroom, and I'll be a little while, my stomach is upset. Can you promise you'll stay here?"

"Yes! Do you see what's happening out there? I won't wander off," he squeaked out.

Gus watched as Mateo disappeared down into an exit. Just as the boy turned away, a heavy-chested woman wearing an orange blouse came into view, seemingly to wait for his abuelo, he thought. He glanced back to verify, and she turned into the exit, flashing a yellow ribbon woven into a braid of brunette hair.

For a time, the bullfighting went as expected. Gus drowned himself in the second matador's style as he sipped the beer Mateo left him. The man moved faster than the first, and more fluidly. His muleta followed him as an extension of his moves, rather than the thing propelling him. It looked like a spinning rose . . . and a dance, he noted.

Suddenly, it became a plucked rose. The bull dashed at the matador and connected. When the horn plunged into the man's side, the crowd went silent for an instant before reacting. A woman's wail broke the quiet and others joined in horror or approval, exalting at the sight of blood and mayhem.

Gus scratched into the unvarnished wood he sat on, and it splintered underneath his fingernails. Most of the crowd clapped and stomped their feet while yelling out words of encouragement . . . but for man or animal, he could not be sure. Some people appeared grief-stricken and felt pain for the matador. He imagined what the gash in his side might look like and how quickly the bloody sweat would seep through his clothes. What if he died? He looked for his abuelo to offer answers and found no familiar face.

The girl in front of him with the wooden car and the matador figurine crashed both into one another again and again.

Men corralled the bull, and other men carried the bullfighter away. The process happened seamlessly, but Gus couldn't stop thinking about the wounded matador, how people must be tending to him, and the sound of his howl. Consumed with the idea that the matador was dying, the boy decided to make his way to the area beyond the arena, but he didn't get very far.

Mateo immediately scooped him up at the exit. "Mijo, mijo, take a deep breath." He held his grandson's face. "The idea of death isn't new to this sort. Calm down, breathe. You are panicking."

Several minutes passed as Gus contained himself and picked up the pieces of his shattered expectations. "Abuelo, do bulls ever win?"

"Sometimes. Most crowds like that outcome best of all."

"Why?"

Mateo drank another beer as they returned to their seats. "A bull knows no rules, it only sees red. So, a matador must defend himself, and he can make mistakes. Bulls strike when they do, and people go crazy-mad with pleasure. But it's an honor in bullfighting, it's a decision made long ago. They pledge that their sacrifice will mean something."

Gus pondered on it and drank from the offered beer, successfully hiding his discomfort in the taste. "Abuelo, maybe I *am* the bull."

"You can be the matador and the toro when you need to, mijo, just make sure you aren't both at the same time." He drained his bottle in four gulps and pulled another from a back pocket.

"Have you seen a matador die? Have you danced with a bull? Is this why you know?"

Mateo's black eyes went darker as they skimmed the arena. He tapped his finger against his forehead. "I dance with this bull, every minute I'm not sleeping. I'm gonna die dancing with this bull."

"What do you mean? Fighting a bull in your head?" Gus tried to fathom the concept and his eyes scrunched up in thought. "How is that the same?"

"Are you kidding? The bulls up here," Mateo tapped again, "they come at you with a force you wish didn't exist. The bulls morph into other objects up there. But what does it matter, it's all in my head anyway. Everything is."

Gus stayed quiet, thoroughly confused.

"Like the scare from the bull. Once you overcame it, you realized being scared was just in your head. Everything is all in your head."

"Okay."

"Don't worry, mijo, you will understand someday. You'll realize if you want to be happy you will be, or you'll dance with the bulls until you die."

"Uh-huh."

Mateo reached out and tousled his hair. "You'll know what I mean before long."

CHAPTER 1

GUS GARCÍA GRIPPED AN ENVELOPE TIGHTLY TO HIS HEART. A familiar cursive script spelled out his name; the letter even smelled like her, an intoxicating mixture of vanilla and cumin spices. He sank into his office chair and swiveled it until it whined.

Squeee-squeee.

Rather than use the letter opener within arm's reach on his desk, he chose to rip the paper sleeve at one end. As he reached inside to pull out a single page of text, it cut the inside of his forefinger and left some blood beside his wife's signature at the bottom. He smeared the drop with his thumb and as he did, a question caught his eye, nestled among others: *Don't you feel something nearing?*

A knock at the door interrupted his thoughts. An elderly Mexican woman then hobbled in wearing black polyester slacks, a simple black button-up cotton shirt, and a white embroidered shawl covering her head.

"Señor García? Gustavo García?"

Gus shot up in his seat, glancing once more at his letter, starting from the top.

My love... Gustavo...

I'm in love with you forever, you need to know. Life is short, but the hours between us can be long.

Not off to a good start. "Here! I am Gustavo!" As the elderly woman neared him, he took in her state and his smile dropped. "Madame, you are crying!"

The woman's tears turned into sobs. "Señor, *lo siento*, please forgive me. I stopped my tears when I entered the building, but your office was difficult to find. My anxiety increased." She cleared her throat. "My name is Lenora Hernandez. I'm from Edna, and my family needs your help. My son, Pedro, needs your help." She tightened the shawl under her chin and covered her face to cry into her hands.

Gus circled his desk and consoled her. "No crying, Señora, my heart hurts as if I saw mi mamá weeping before me. Sit, sit." He coaxed her into a spongy, bright blue chair. "Let me get something to dry your eyes, and I will attempt to ease your troubles."

"Gracias. I have tissues in my purse." She pulled a bundle out and peeled a single tissue away from the clump. Loudly, she blew her nose. "You are the lawyer, sí? Gustavo García?"

He nodded proudly.

Lenora dried her eyes and studied him. Outside, a cloud passed and sunlight fell through the window, gleaming on his slick hair. "A *suavecito*," she commented, "and handsome."

Gus placed a hand over the left side of his chest like a pledge. "You called me Gustavo, and it rang the bell of nobility within me. What can I do? Would you like a drink? Un momento, por favor." He pulled out a bottom drawer of his dark brown walnut desk to reveal a clean crystal tumbler and a new Chivas Regal whisky bottle with a red bow around the neck.

Lenora stood suddenly and began pacing the room. "Drinking is what started all of this! Drinking is what has brought me here to you." She stopped in front of him, placing her hands on the edge of his desk to lean in closer. "Is that what sort of man you are, too?" She pulled out a piece of paper from her purse and waved it in his face. "Tell me now, because I can go to the next lawyer on this list."

Gus exhaled. "Madame, por favor, *sientate*." He took another peek at his own piece of paper before continuing. "I'm all sorts of man, the good kind and the bad."

I've not seen you at home lately, so I thought mailing a letter to your office would be the easiest way of reaching you. Talking to you in this manner is actually freeing, and easier for me. We all know how you love to monopolize the conversation.

A tiny smile formed on his lips as he looked up. "Lenora. Señora Hernandez. I can't imagine what it's like to currently be in your position, but I do have a mother as passionate as you. No drinks, just talking." He opened his mouth to launch into a rehearsed speech about his area of expertise, then thought of his tendency to "monopolize the conversation," and stopped himself. "Now, tell me about Pedro. Or Pete." He rolled the *r* in Pedro's name.

Lenora tightened her grasp on the rosary and inhaled deeply. "My oldest. Lives at home and helps me with his brothers and sisters. Takes care of me. He's loyal. Hard worker. Harder drinker. Picks cotton. Emotional. Carries a short temper. He limps on a clubbed foot, and it makes him bitter at the world."

"When did that happen?"

"Childhood, six years old? He jumped off the house, thought he'd bounce like a ball. Broke everything. The foot gnarled." She gave him a tired smile. "I didn't say he was smart. My daughters are, but my sons, not so much."

Gus glanced downward again.

I need to speak to you about our daughters. They've hit puberty, and they crave my full attention in a way you don't anymore. They miss you and wait for you most days, as I do. Sometimes I lie to them for you. Disappointment and longing shouldn't be served with dinner three times a week.

"Well, who's to say we all can't be stupid once in a while? That's not a crime." A bitterness filled him. "Did he react more to this as he aged?"

Lenora nodded. "He grew angry at every turn, throwing tantrums and all the like." She shook her head. "I always thought it would get the best of him someday and something horrible would happen." She fingered the rosary cross between her forefinger and thumb, and tears began rolling down her cheeks. "He's a good boy."

Gus patted her hand. "What's the reason for you sitting before me today? What happened?"

Carlita and Teresa are old enough to know when you're lying. A girl shouldn't grow up thinking excessive excuses from a man are excusable. Thinking like that leads both parties to do regrettable things.

A familiar guilt slid over Gus like slime. Talking about their daughters was Irene's way of fighting dirty, and it worked. He knew where this would end.

Lenora didn't notice the struggle on Gus's face. "Last Friday night he went to a beer joint with his *primo*." She began drumming her fingers on his desk and stared at the floor. "I asked him to stay home because they'd been drinking already, but his primo teased him about listening to me. The house quieted and hours passed. I fell asleep. Suddenly Pete came stomping through the house. I heard him mumbling as his shadow walked past. A door opened, slammed, and the shadow went by my room again. Sleep came to me when I heard the back door." Tears fell. "They said he killed Joe Espinosa outside of the bar. Police threw him in jail." Using her rosary, she lightly touched her forehead, her chest, her left shoulder and the right: the sign of the Cross. More tears. "He's never learned to protect his emotions. Like his father."

"Your husband? Where is he?"

She shook her head. "Left with another woman years ago."

Gus paused to contemplate the bitterness in her words. "Do you believe your son is guilty?"

"Oh, he is, he'll tell you so. He's nothing but honest, even when he does dishonest things."

"When is his indictment?"

"What's that?"

"It's when they call his charge and set his bail."

"No bail."

Gus exhaled. "I can wait no longer." He produced the Chivas from his desk and gestured to Lenora for a drink, but she denied him for a second time. He poured two fingers for himself before continuing. "He's been indicted then. Mrs. Hernandez . . . Lenora . . . why did you come to San Antonio? Why not find a decent lawyer closer to home?"

"Not one with a last name like ours."

His eyes veered to Irene's letter as he took a sip.

I know so much of your time is taken up with work, don't get me wrong, you work hard and I want you to continue that. I want the girls to know it's worth it, no matter what. Your future is nipping at your heels, I can feel it. Don't you feel something nearing? You will fight cases to make us proud, damn proud, as long as your misdeeds stay to a minimum.

Her support gave him guilt. "Who else have you visited?" The guilt gave way to paranoia. "Carlos Cadena?" He shook his head and straightened his posture. "Don't answer that."

Lenora hesitated, glancing down at her lawyer list and back at Gus. Ignoring his question, she asked one of her own. "Have you worked with him? This Carlos Cadena?"

"We attended law school simultaneously and shared a practice for a short time, but our habits didn't match. I'm two years older than him." He coughed, embarrassed. "That's not important; I apologize." He adjusted his tie knot. "This is . . . unprofessional. Cadena is a scholarly man who knows every facet of law by heart, but our approaches differ. He's subtle; I'm not."

"They say you do daring things," she said. "You are not scared to fight."

"They?"

"People, newspapers," she stopped. "Are they wrong?"

Gus stood and walked to the window. He took a sip, then sipped again. A sense of obligation started up in him, a familiar feeling. *What perfect timing,* he thought, *something to occupy time.* "Señora, I will make sure they are not. A lack of subtlety helps in these situations."

"Lines divide Edna, and it's best we keep to ourselves," she said. "Who will understand our problems better than one of us?" As Lenora regarded him, sunlight shined through the window, illuminating him. She took it as a sign from God. "Pedro will like you," she decided.

"It is done." He raised his glass before downing the remainder. "I want to learn more about Edna and the men and women who inhabit it." When he returned to his desk chair, he lost an inner battle and looked again at his wife's letter.

There are other nights though, I'm certain you're not working when you say you are. Aren't you exhausted from fabricating lies? It's exhausting to hear you say, "I'm sorry." You must be tired of coming up with new ways to apologize, no?

Lenora dried her eyes, straightened her posture, and released the shawl from her head. "I think I'll have that glass of whisky now, Señor García."

He obeyed quickly. "There's nothing that doesn't feel better after a couple of drinks. It's medicine most divine."

She cupped the drink with both hands. "You said you've visited our town before."

"It's been a long time, and it was only a pause for food or gas," Gus admitted. "As a child mi abuelo would take me every year to a bullfight in Mexico." He winced. "I'll admit, I don't know very much about the town."

"You will visit us then," Lenora offered. "The people will be nice." She sipped again and raised an eyebrow. "Maybe too nice."

"Señora?"

"People of a darker color are hung from trees by people of a lighter shade." She returned the glass to his desk, nearly full, and pushed it towards him. "The ones who do the hanging, they pretend people our color are ghosts even though we are dark enough to see, but they are the dark ones." She touched his hand. "We sew their clothes, tend to their fields, make their food, clean their houses, even raise their children, and they believe they're thanking us by not stringing us to a tree."

Gus shook his head, mouth open. "That still happens there?"

She nodded.

The unmistakable call of duty rang out in him, and energy surged through him. "I will fight for both you and Pete as if my last name was Hernandez," he pledged. He held out a hand, and she clasped it. "I will fight for all of us. Mañana, I will go to Edna."

Lenora shrouded herself with her wrap again and clutched it at her chin. "Yes. You will be our hero." The rosary dangled from her hand as she repeated the sign of the Cross. "May God bless you." She pulled out scraps of paper from her purse. "Here is my phone number and address, plus where my son is located."

They hugged before Gus walked her out of the building. As she disappeared down the parking lot, he dashed back inside and ran up the five flights of stairs before taking the elevator the rest of the way. Making a beeline for his wife's letter, he read more.

I'm tired of wondering where you are most nights, and I'm broken without you. My heart is tired like the rest of me. If we left, I doubt you'd notice. Since you're rarely at home, I need you to permanently continue in that fashion. Stay away. I would do it for you if you asked.

Her request hit him like a car and ran his heart over. He staggered slightly and sat down in the swivel again. *Squeee-squeeeeeee*, it squeaked back at him. A dull pain thumped in his chest as he read the last words.

Be strong and remember: the lawyer you will become is who you were meant to be. Keep fighting and you will live on in people's hearts. Always yours, Irene.

The pain strummed out again, an emptiness where she should be, his Reenie. Her request didn't come as a surprise. He knew she'd become unhappy with him in the past year but hoped she wouldn't take it that far. The letter, complete with his blood, symbolized an ultimate failure. It became something he vowed to fix.

No more melting into their bed beside her curves after a tough day; no more nuzzling into her neck and drowning deep into her sweet hair that tumbled down her shoulders. No more would her arms wrap around him as he drifted on the edge of too much drinking or thinking, and no more making semiconscious love to her languid body at dawn.

Suddenly, he didn't want to drink alone, or more honestly, *be* alone. The International Building contained his office and a number of other independent offices, but Gus knew no one else would be interested.

When he first moved into the building, others invited themselves inside his office to say hello, but exited quickly when they learned his last name. His skin color fooled some; they thought him to be a different ethnicity. For that reason, he opted his name be left off the door. His pale skin and leafy-green eyes kept them guessing.

I will get her back, Gus swore to himself. *My guilt will be my motivation. She will still be devoted only to me.* He gulped the remaining whisky and held it in his mouth a moment before swallowing. It gave him the sting of punishment he searched for.

He allowed himself one more drink before kicking off his shoes, leaning back, and lifting his feet. His brain snuggled into a fluffy whisky pillow with a sigh. *Squeeeee*, his chair agreed. Irene's words came to mind once more.

Can't you feel something nearing?

Yes, Gus realized, he could feel something nearing, but he didn't have the faintest idea what.

CHAPTER 2

THE FOLLOWING DAY, GUS PARKED IN FRONT OF THE JACKSON COUNTY COURT-house in Edna, a small town south of San Antonio, and took in his surroundings. A wide walkway led to the front door with a manicured garden full of bluebonnets and Indian paintbrushes on either side. A few sprawling oak trees shaded the lawn and blocked the sun's rays. Across Main Street, a stretch of shops sat side by side on the block, and William's Pharmacy and Soda Shop caught his eye. A sign perched in the window with scribbly writing: Fryday hamburger spechul, 15 cents.

Though meeting Pete Hernandez and obtaining court papers topped his list of things to do, an empty stomach disagreed. Just as he crossed the street, a teenage girl with blonde ringlets stopped on the sidewalk to adjust her dress. As she reached for the door handle Gus stopped her and pushed it open for her. A bell dinged their entry, and a soda jerk popped up from behind the counter, a boy not out of high school.

Loudly, he squeaked out, "Welcome to William's!" His voice deepened when he saw the girl. "Oh, hey Lucy," he said, and pointed to a table where another girl sat, who could've been Lucy's twin.

"Hiiiiiieee, Ben." Lucy gave him a little wave.

Ben then ignored her to acknowledge Gus. "Hello there, sir! Find a seat and I'll be with you on the double."

The William's Soda Shop portion faced outward to the street, with the pharmacy directly behind. The patrons in the shop totaled eight: three graying men drinking root beer floats who sported farmer tans and blue jean suspenders, a conservatively dressed mother eating ice cream with her young son, and Lucy sipping on a soda with her clone.

Gus tilted his charcoal fedora toward the adults. The men nodded at him while the woman smiled congenially before looking to her son. Gus chose a seat at the counter as Ben approached him.

The personification of an all-American boy, he looked as if he'd never experienced a bad day. Curly blonde hair poked out from a crisp, white paper hat outlined in cobalt blue that matched his eyes to a tee.

"The name's Ben," he straightened his white bow tie. "What can I do ya for?"

Gus laughed at his clothes. "Ben, your hat is the only thing that stayed white! I see stains in every color: faded orange, pink, and brown blobs, plus green and blue too." He leaned over the counter. "No, your shoes are black."

Ben shrugged. "Boss said white shoes scuff too quick."

"Yours are polished to a shine like mine. Did you do it yourself?"

"Na," he rolled his eyes, "my ma. I tell her no one will notice, but I guess I'm wrong now!" The corners of his mouth curved up into a grin. "You're dressed nice today; my grandfather would say dapper. What can I get ya?"

Gus glanced down at his slate-colored suit. He chose a white linen shirt to go underneath, a subdued combination he hoped would make him inconspicuous. "Thank you, thank you. Do you recommend a Friday special?"

"Naturally," Ben said. "It's all fresh."

"Sold!" Gus gestured to the wall of colorful liquids in bottles with pumps at the top. "What kind of sodas do you offer?"

Ben rounded the counter. "This one is strawberry, that one chocolate, and the orange is, well, orange. I can make you a soda, a milkshake, or a float."

"A float?"

"A soda AND a milkshake," He grinned again, showing pearly whites. "Do you like root beer soda?" He continued without waiting for an answer and pulled out a tall glass mug from underneath the counter. Using one of the two soda fountain spigots sticking up between them, he filled it halfway with root beer. "Here comes the fun part. First, I put in a little bit of vanilla ice cream, a half scoop, and stir it in with a straw, like so. See how the soda fizzes up?"

"Impressive," Gus indulged him. The ice cream lightened the soda from brown to tan, and bubbles fizzed out.

"Then, top it off with a full scoop of ice cream and add a soda spoon." Proudly, Ben handed Gus the mug between the spigots. "The ice cream floats on top . . . it's a root beer float!" He clapped. "Your burger'll be ready in a jiffy."

Gus sipped the float and thought it overly sweet. He gave Ben the thumbs up sign. "This is damn good!"

A ding at the door presented a brunette girl with low pigtails and pale skin wearing a perky knee-length asparagus-green summer dress. She nodded her head at the adult patrons with surety and climbed onto a barstool next to Gus. She removed a small black cross-body purse, crossed her legs, and showed two fingers to Ben. "Two strawberry sodas, please." She enunciated each word carefully.

Ben leaned on the counter and cupped his hands underneath his chin. "Are you planning on drinking both of those, little lady?"

Her leg twitched and began to bob. "Nooooo," she replied.

"Well, how about I make you one and we'll start there?" Ben pivoted to the wall without waiting for an answer. He chose a highball glass and added flavoring. "Have you ever wondered why straws aren't in strawberries?"

Lucy giggled at his joke, but Ben didn't look at her; instead, he pretended he hadn't heard and focused on the little girl in the green dress.

"You didn't laugh." Ben lowered his head to meet the girl's gaze and pouted his lower lip dramatically. "It wasn't funny?"

She limply shrugged her shoulders, but Gus noticed her leg twitch.

Ben responded in kind and began to yank on the soda fountain handle until carbonated water pumped from the tap.

Her leg twitched again and bumped Gus's leg. "Sorry."

"It's okay." He noticed gray, splotchy sandals on her feet, an accent less polished than her other garments. After longer scrutiny he realized the splotches were scuffs on once-white sandals. Her leg twitched again, this time bumping his briefcase, a mocha-brown leather bag his two daughters pinched pennies to purchase the previous Christmas for him.

"Sorry," she said again, averting her gaze.

Gus waited until her eyes met his. She reminded him of his daughters, with long eyelashes and eyes a deep, dark chocolate brown. "It's okay," he said calmly, and nodded his head.

The doorbell sounded off again.

As Ben turned to the wall to add flavoring, another brunette girl entered meekly with her head down. Gus assumed her to be the second strawberry soda. A faded cherry-red dress hung heavy on her like velvet drapes and nearly touched the ground. Two baggy pockets spooned outward as if too many hands had tucked themselves inside over time. A man in suspenders nudged another man when she sat beside the girl in the green dress. One of the girls nudged Lucy as well.

Gus watched them all and knew the reason why: her skin was brown.

Ben spoke to the wall with the same greeting he gave Gus. "Welcome to William's! Take a seat–" In mid-sentence he spun around smiling, but the smile dropped from his face when he saw the girl in the baggy red dress. He glanced at the men in suspenders, who began whispering to each other with raised eyebrows. This dictated Ben's next move.

He sharply blurted out, "You gotta go." The glass clinked on the counter when he set it down and gave a finality to his statement. His chest puffed out.

The girls traded a look before the red dress stood from the stool, dropped her chin, and headed back to the door. She lifted the dress off the floor with both hands, long enough to show an identical pair of splotchy gray sandals.

Gus gasped. "They're sisters."

"Wait a minute. Why are you telling her to leave?" The girl in the asparagus-green dress stood from her stool.

Ben's chest deflated for a brief second, then he lifted his chin in defiance. "You know why." He crossed his arms. "I won't serve her."

She mirrored his arm position and raised her chin disobediently. "No, I don't. I'm ten years old. Tell me why," she demanded.

Most patrons perked their ears and caught on to what unfolded before them, but Lucy had watched from the start. Soon the entire parlor, adults and students alike, lifted their head at the girl's noncompliant tone and Ben's aggressive one. Everyone grew tense, but for different reasons.

The mother gasped and darted a hand out to shield her son's face, though she knew it was more about what he heard. She looked to the door and noticed the smiles on the men in suspenders, the ones who looked hog-happy at someone else's tragedy.

The men knew the owner, Ben's father. One wrong move and they'd mention it to him straightaway. Ben knew it. Their eyes turned to slits as they hooked their thumbs under their suspenders. They didn't care he denied service to little girls, in fact, they expected it.

Lucy kept watching.

Ben narrowed his eyes at the girl before answering. "For the same reason other sorts might not receive service. Don't act like you don't know."

"Umm-hmmm," one man piped up.

"Be strong, boy," another chimed in.

"She's not *black*," the girl in the asparagus-green dress flatly stated.

"But she's not *white*," Ben popped back.

"I'm her sister," she loudly announced and pointed. "She's my sister." With extra caution for her green dress, she picked up the strawberry soda and tipped it over, spilling its contents on as much countertop as she could, starting with the right side and slowly making her way towards the left. Pink liquid dripped from the counter and splattered on the linoleum floor.

"What the . . . what is wrong with you? Are you nuts?" Ben scanned the parlor at the others. "Is she crazy?"

Lucy gasped in delight.

Gus blurted out a single laugh at the girl's daring.

"Let's go." The first girl scooped her sister's brown hand into her own pale-colored hand, and they intertwined fingers. "You won't serve her, so you shouldn't serve me. Clean *that,* soda *jerk.*"

The door dinged their exit.

One of the men in suspenders clucked his tongue. "How dare she?"

"How *dare* she?" The mother mocked him and glared at the man. She pointed to Ben. "How dare *he*?" She and her son left.

"How was I supposed to know?" Ben pointed outside to the sisters. "Do they look the same? They don't look the same." He submerged two white towels into the pink liquid and cursed as more spilled to the floor.

Lucy stood up, her eyes wide with shock. She grabbed her friend's hand to leave, and paused in front of Ben. "You just broke my heart not serving those girls. They're just *girls.*"

"I wouldn't take that sort of behavior from wetback girls like that," a man said loudly in agreement to his friends. He snapped a suspender strap. "I'd follow them outside and give them a piece of my mind."

"Eh," another said, "not worth it." He clapped for Ben. "Good for you son, not stooping to their level."

Disgusted, Gus pushed his root beer float away and stood, placing his fedora on his head. He headed for the door.

"Heyyy, hey!" Ben called out. "Don't you want your burger? I haven't started it yet."

Gus pivoted towards him, and the people. "Not from here, no thanks. You wouldn't want my money anyway." Whispering loudly, he added, "My last name is García. I'm one of *them*. Shhhh."

"You need to go set them straight," a man huffed to Gus. He glanced at his friend. "It's better to have their own kind do it."

Gus whirled around to the trio of men. "I will do no such thing. I will congratulate them for standing up for themselves."

He eyed the Jackson County Courthouse as he exited. The sound of a girl's giggling rang out and he followed it around the corner to see a twirling asparagus-green dress in the middle of the street.

CHAPTER 3

AMELIA DIDN'T WANT TO BUY A STRAWBERRY SODA AT WILLIAM'S WITH HER sister. The trip seemed like a waste of time. Her money priorities aimed at higher goals. Recently they pointed to an item of more importance: a chip of a diamond ring at the local jeweler three doors down from the drugstore. She'd been saving money from picking cotton the moment she laid her eyes on it, and it motivated her like nothing had before. Besides, she didn't have access to the new green dress that day. Her sister, Delia, wore it. Their mamá promised Amelia could wear it next time.

She finally agreed when Delia offered to buy the sodas.

Amelia didn't care for Ben the soda jerk, nor the prejudice his comments exposed. He hurt her feelings, and her anxiety reached unbearable levels as people stared at her in the shop. Their own kind. Her own kind. The soda jerk's attitude was exactly why she avoided places like William's. Her anxiety didn't skyrocket when she stayed at home.

But Delia always beckoned her to experience new things, and this time Amelia complied. The two couldn't be more different, but they kept each other in line. The more rebellious one dressed in frilly garments often, leading Amelia to feel soiled and dusty in her play clothes. She considered Delia the prettiest of the Cruz family and had a sneaking suspicion her sister felt the same way about herself. Plus, Delia's skin happened to be much lighter than her own, naturally leading to more positive experiences in the outside world.

When Amelia heard the man stand up for them, it surprised her somewhat. He didn't know them, and as they exited, she heard him talking back and standing up for them. It renewed her spirit, but at the same time, it put her in an odd predicament. Mexican elders taught young girls of the family to always listen to white people and never talk back. Stay quiet, keep your head down, and respond with yes ma'am or sir. Those rules guaranteed someone of a higher status wouldn't talk down to you or respond with a look of disgust.

So it simultaneously horrified and electrified Amelia when Delia poured her beverage over the counter and called Ben a jerk. An act deliciously forbidden. The soda jerk deserved it, though Amelia worried he'd come running after them.

Not Delia. The exchange tickled her pink, and she hoped Ben would chase after them. She wanted to see what he would do or say. Not much, she assumed. She giggled uncontrollably as she spun herself round and round until her green dress rippled out.

This stressed out Amelia further, afraid her sister's underwear would show and someone would see. "Delia, this isn't funny, none of this is funny. Please stop laughing," she pleaded.

"Who cares! Lighten up. Seriously Amelia, it's not that . . . serious."

Amelia's eyes kept darting to the corner they had turned, expecting an adult to appear and head toward them. "You're going to get in trouble. Someone will, will. . . "

"Will what? Call mamá?" Delia stopped spinning and gave her a baffled look. "What do you think will happen if they follow us outside? Grip our ears and drag us home? Or to the police station?" She clapped her hands. "I'd like to see them try," she said with a sly look.

Gus turned the corner with his jacket slung over one arm and his fedora tipped slightly to one side.

Amelia noticed him and pointed. "He might . . ."

Delia whipped around. "Shit." When he waved at them, she reciprocated. "Please come here," she requested. "Mister, you're not gonna tell on us, are you?"

Amelia's eyes widened with fright. "Please don't. We don't want to be in any trouble."

"No, no, I'm like you. My last name is García." He put a palm to his chest. "Or Gus. Call me Gus."

His tone dispelled Amelia's panic. Curious, she took a breath and focused on this man. He could pass for a fancy white man, she noted, the sort who wouldn't give two shits about girls being denied service. She searched for red flags telling her not to talk to him but could find none. No impending doom overcame her; quite the opposite, actually.

A warm kindness emanated from him, a magnetism that pulled her closer to him.

Apparently, Delia didn't feel the same. She hooked her arm into Amelia's and pulled her away. "Let's go," she urged.

Amelia didn't budge. "No," and pulled her arm back. "My name is Amelia Cruz," she told the man.

"Fine, then," Delia said. She propped her hands on her hips. "I'm Delia."

Gus bowed at the girls. "I'm a lawyer. I'm going to be trying a case here in Edna." He squatted down to their eye level. "You girls didn't get your strawberry sodas. Are you still thirsty?"

Both aware they shouldn't be talking to strangers, they traded looks and Amelia nodded sheepishly.

Delia shrugged her shoulders. "S'okay, it doesn't matter."

"I think it matters. How about I pop over to a store down the street and pick up a couple of sodas? I'll be back in a jiffy."

The girls traded looks again.

Gus let out a hearty laugh. "You two remind me of my daughters, their names are Carlita and Teresa. They look about your age. They don't trust carelessly either." When he received no response, he continued. "You two wait here, okay? I'll be back. If you don't want the sodas you don't have to wait."

As he hurried off, Delia offered her thoughts. "He's not coming back."

"Why do you say that?"

She shrugged. "He doesn't have a reason to come back."

"But he said he'd bring us a soda."

"Yeah, but why? For what? We can walk down to the store, and I'll buy us sodas like I was supposed to in the first place," Delia wrinkled her nose. "First you don't trust him, and then you do?"

Amelia frowned. "You always trust everyone, and now not him?"

Delia shrugged. "This isn't like you."

"You can leave," Amelia said bravely. She didn't want her to leave but didn't want to ask her to stay. "We're going to get what you wanted . . . strawberry sodas. And you don't have to pay."

Delia shrugged again and played at balancing herself on the curb.

"You don't think he looks nice?"

"I dunno. Didn't need him to be nice to me."

Amelia frowned at this.

"You're always so needy for attention," Delia said. "So quiet and agreeable. Wait a second," Delia reached out and touched Amelia's arm. "Do you have a crush on him? Do you liiiike him?"

"Don't be crazy." Amelia pushed her slightly, still annoyed at being called needy, and annoyed that Delia implied it again.

Delia lost her balance and stuck her tongue out. "Don't get *mad.* He's cute for an older man."

They said nothing more until Gus returned with a small paper bag. He pulled out two strawberry sodas and one root beer, all in glass bottles.

"They're not opened," Delia pointed out. "Are we supposed to use our teeth?"

"Hold on, hold on," he said, and pulled out his car keys to reveal a bottle opener.

Delia studied him carefully. "Are you a drunk?"

"What the . . . I just bought you a soda. Here!" He handed it to her with a smile.

"Thanks, mister." She sighed. "My mamá says anyone who carries an opener on their person is a drunk."

Gus laughed heartily and handed Amelia her soda. "Is she right? Is that what your mother says?" He pulled straws out of the bag.

She gave him a wide smile. "She says a lot of things."

He knelt down again and dropped the smile. "Never accept anything to drink—even water—from someone you don't know. If you do, make sure the top is sealed. That's very important for little girls to know. You never know what someone could put inside."

They nodded with serious expressions.

"I told my sister I didn't think you'd come back," Delia challenged. She blew bubbles into her soda.

"You don't let up, do you?" He looked at Amelia for verification. "What about you?"

She nodded happily. "I knew you'd be back." She sucked in a mouthful of soda and held it. It tasted vaguely of strawberries, but mainly sugar, which she didn't mind. The bubbles fizzed and bounced off the roof of her mouth. She held in the liquid until it calmed, then swallowed, burning slightly as it traveled down. She sipped it again.

"How'd you know?"

"You looked us in the eye." Amelia blew air into her straw and watched the bubbles gurgle and gather at the bottom of her bottle.

He sat on the curb.

Delia spoke. "Okay, Gus, tell us more about you."

"I'm a lawyer who's going to be fighting a case here in Edna really soon." He pointed at the courthouse across the street. "Over there."

Amelia perked up. "Smart people work there. Papá told us that."

He gave them a thumbs up. "That can be true. What else did your dad say about that place?"

"A lot of white people work there," Delia said flatly.

"White people? What about brown, or black?"

She shook her head. "That's not the way things go around here. It's white or black."

He laughed. "You've heard of the saying before, yes? There're only two sides to a story, black or white. It's a sentiment I don't agree with, but a saying nonetheless."

Amelia cocked her head in confusion.

"There's always more than two sides, and there's more than black or white. Like the way that soda jerk treated you both earlier; it's not only about what you two experienced and what he did, the other people inside the shop experienced something, too. Has anything like that happened before today to either of you?"

Delia shook her head staunchly; Amelia shook her head slowly. She knew lying to the man wouldn't help, but she couldn't help it.

He narrowed his eyes. "You're not telling me the truth."

Suddenly Amelia felt sick to her stomach and wanted to upend the soda in her stomach on his shoes, but kept it in. "I've been called a brown bitch before, at school, but I didn't understand what he meant until our older sister explained it to me."

"How did that make you feel?"

"I wasn't embarrassed until she explained it, like today. I didn't know what he meant." She glanced up at Gus and her sister, and seeing the anticipation in their eyes made her uneasy. Once she began, her words tumbled out quickly, like the soda over the countertop. One drop turned into a waterfall. "My face flashed with heat like it'd been shoved into an oven. I thought everyone stared at me, at us, because of the soda jerk. It was as if he'd shoved me to the ground and laughed at me."

Delia's mouth began to widen as she listened to her sister until she gawked with an open mouth.

Amelia raised an eyebrow. "Why are you looking at me like that? What?"

"You've never talked like that."

"It moved me," Gus said. "Both of you, look at the color of your skin."

They obeyed.

"Now tell me, what color do you see?"

Delia spoke first. "A caramel color, a golden brown."

"A burnt caramel color," Amelia commented on her own skin.

He nodded. "Neither of those colors were simply brown, or white. Or black for that matter."

Wide-eyed, the sisters traded glances once more. They didn't speak a word.

"I experienced an epiphany watching that soda boy's prejudices play out on you two. Behavior like that is taught, it doesn't come from within." He placed his right hand over his heart. "I want to change all that; I want the people in this county to see color for what it is and recognize there's more than one race in this country. I don't want you two to experience again what you did today. I want people to look at things in a new light." He smiled at Amelia. "I want to speak up so shy little boys and girls will find their own voices."

Delia rolled her eyes. "That's a lot. I think we really gotta go. Come on Amelia."

But Gus's words paralyzed Amelia, and paused her mind. As she allowed her sister to forcefully pull her away, she memorized his face and waved a hurried goodbye. Her faded cherry-red dress flipped in the wind, a curtain ending to their encounter.

Gus walked straight across the street to the courthouse and filled out a notice for a request of information regarding Pete Hernandez. Beside the line asking the requestor's name in reference to the defendant, he wrote: hired counsel.

CHAPTER 4

"DO YOU THINK YOU'RE UP FOR THE CHALLENGE, SON?"

Donovan Kincaid wondered the same thing that evening, a question he asked himself at every pivotal moment of his thirty-five years. As a child, he spent nights eavesdropping on his father talking business with wealthy men and impatiently waiting for the day he would be in their position. Now he stood here, finally being challenged for a task, and he didn't know what to say. Some of those same men he remembered from childhood circled around him—Livingston, Dorrance, Lowell, Rothschild, Armstrong—their eyes full of inquiry and doubt.

Donny, Donovan's older brother, spied on them from behind the staircase and wondered the same thing.

"With all due respect, I'm not entirely sure I understand what I'd be doing and who I'd be doing it for," Donovan said uneasily. "I grew up under this roof understanding secretive behavior unfolded from time to time, but I never grasped the entire concept. If you could go into a little more detail . . . "

The men chuckled knowingly at his confusion while Preston Armstrong took a step forward. "I'll give you the short version and let your father fill you in on the rest. Call us Symmetry, a group we've kept running longer than the mockingbird has been our state bird. Interests focus on anything or anyone threatening all that is holy and right in Texas, so it's a wide range of topics. Politics, business, oil, schools. Our goals depend on who's on the board. We're a project working on various projects."

"Symmetry," Donovan repeated, "and you want me to . . . "

"Halt a case on our radar in Edna, or flip it into our hands," Armstrong filled in. "One involving a man named Pete Hernandez."

Donovan's inner voice asked, *how in the hell do I do that?* He wanted to be told what to do.

Saturday nights in Austin meant a dinner party at the Kincaid manor, if they considered you worthy of an invitation. The tradition began in the 1900s in the very home where they stood. A porch wrapped around the entire bottom floor like a buffer against bad taste, and pairs of rocking chairs peppered all sides, giving a country feel to high-society meetings. Nothing about the manor did people consider to be subtle, which was the intention. Just like a Kincaid.

The family believed every man and woman who carried the name carried the necessity of keeping said name in the upper Texas echelons. Thus began Symmetry, first talked about in the wee hours of the night after too much bourbon. What would be the harm in creating a private group with private interests? The group's goal aimed toward eliminating or deterring anything threatening the morals and values that built the state of Texas. Members peppered the area, but the overall number stayed small.

They met after the Kincaid parties to trade updates and general reports when other couples went home for the evening. In doing so the Symmetry spouses developed their own inner circle once they understood what the men spoke of in the library. Donovan's mother, Cordelia, led the group and made sure the other ladies carried themselves with classy elegance.

Being accepted into the circle meant being a made man wherever one went, no matter what. Donovan's attributes and age synced up to make him a desirable for the group, and imminent success pulsed through his Kincaid veins. His motto matched Symmetry's: Honor and pride will lead you.

Donovan's physical and facial attributes already gave him a leg up on anyone. His features were all Kincaid, with a tall, lean, California surfer body and icy blue eyes peeking out through yellow-blonde hair from root to tip. The look alone demanded all eyes land on a Kincaid when one entered a room, Donny included, but something about Donovan would lengthen a woman's glance into a lingering look, and then a stare. He carried enough youth and vigor to pique the curiosity of all ages.

The black sheep of the family, Donny wasn't motivated by social acceptance, as were the other Kincaid men. Adventure by way of breaking the law was as intrinsic to Donny's personality as his shaggy hair. It satisfied him all too much to ruin his parents' pride, yet he asserted his freedom to squander his share of the family fortune. He'd received an opportunity to be in Symmetry years back but lost it after some unsavory behavior.

The same opportunity now waved at Donovan. He turned his head to the left and saw his father, Don, joining them.

Armstrong repeated himself. "Do you think you're up for the challenge, son? Will you do everything humanly possible to halt the Pete Hernandez case?"

"I'd love to be given the chance," Donovan answered breathlessly. "I'll do whatever it takes to succeed for the group."

"Naturally, the reward for your success is an offer to join us. Our monies and clout are at your disposal, as long as it's within reason. We wouldn't want you renting women of the night." Armstrong cleared his throat. "Unless she knew some very important secrets!"

"When the cause for celebration arrives," Rothschild said, "—when we've regained our rightful place in history, we will celebrate."

Symmetry murmured in agreement.

"Donovan, go enjoy yourself, and I'll speak more on your tasks shortly," Armstrong said.

"Yes, sir. If you'll excuse me gentlemen, Father, I'm going to refresh my drink."

"We'll use the chance to voice our opinions about you," Don said wryly. Though Don assumed the head of Symmetry, Armstrong doubled and tripled the sum of Kincaid money on a regular basis striking oil, so Don allowed for him to preside over certain matters.

"Kincaid, must you be hard on your youngest?" Armstrong playfully chided.

Don gave a half smile. "Our safety makes it my duty to be difficult, especially on my own blood. Come, men, let's have a cigar on the terrace before dinner. Cordelia is dying for me to show off the new renovations on this money pit."

"Now, now, Kincaid," Lowell said. "We all know you can afford it and then some."

Donovan watched the men retreat outside. He walked past his mother and the wives chattering on the couches and heard snippets of their conversation.

"Well, it's true!" Cordelia sipped her champagne, her wide blue eyes looking at her friends in earnest. "Don has said it since we met, but I finally understood it on a new level when we chose decorations for tonight." She smiled cordially at the nearest maid and lowered her voice. "They really wouldn't know better without us around to teach them."

The ladies surrounding her nodded in agreement.

Cordelia Banks understood what she entered into when she married Don Kincaid Jr. It took great skill to run a mansion, his mother lectured, and that much more when reaching the rank of manor, and housing a full staff. A young Cordelia jumped at the challenge and began hardening herself to show her worth. She bided her time, and not until she bore Donny was she fully accepted, which allowed her to make decorating choices reflecting her own style. She wanted to remind Austin that the Kincaids still held a place in society, while adding a postscript that a Banks sat at the helm, too.

Donovan frowned at his mother's comment and walked away as fast as his legs would carry him. Sweat sprouted on the back of his neck when someone in his family spoke in that manner. His father imposed those ideas early on, but he never chose to communicate his disagreement. Saying no to his father sat first on his never-ever list.

He reached the bar and opened his mouth to give the bartender his order, but a familiar voice interrupted him.

"My brother will have a Drambuie with two ice cubes, and I'll . . . make my own drink." Donny pulled out a flask from his front suit pocket.

"Turd, how you doing?" Donovan chose Donny's nickname because he was the third Kincaid.

Donny rebelled against their mother's dress code for drinks and dinner by letting loose his top three shirt buttons, sans tie. "I still loathe that name," he said, "and that face." He threw an arm around Donovan. "What are you doing here? There's nothing but old people here."

"I live here, dummy. When did you get in?"

"Moments ago," Donny said, ignoring his brother's non-answer. "Ran out of money."

"Figures." Donovan accepted his drink and sniffed it. The sweetness came through, but not to his liking. He hesitated to ask for extra honey because he didn't recognize the bartender.

"I can get the heather honey for you, sir."

Donovan turned to see Kiana, one of the regular maids at the Kincaid manor. "Did you just read my mind?"

Nineteen, petite, and subservient, Kiana kept her eyes on his shoes as she nodded imperceptibly. "You always add extra honey." She blushed momentarily before resuming her professional demeanor. "I'll return shortly." She curtsied and accepted his drink.

She personified forbidden fruit to Donovan, but he did his best not to show it. "Yes, please."

Donny took her place as she walked away. "Brother! I forgot how nice it could be still living at home." They watched Kiana head towards the kitchen. "The living art here is . . . buoyant."

Donovan shoved his brother lightly. "Stop. Father needs better behavior than that. Why are you here? I wouldn't have expected you at one of these parties again."

Donny shook his head. "Are they courting you? Did they give you a challenge?"

"Nah, just checking in. You jealous?" He could see it in his brother's eyes, the envy flashing.

"Don't be crazy. The way they circled around you . . . " he shrugged. "I'm just saying it looked familiar."

"What if they did?"

"Are you kidding me? You're a better fit." Donny leaned in. "Are you stringing them along or have you said yes yet? You're probably eating what they say with a knife, fork, and silver spoon."

"Should I not?" Donovan moved in closer. With vitriol, he said, "You and I are not the same."

"If you start screwing the help you're one step closer, little brother," Donny said. "Don't forget that."

Donovan tightened his fists but restrained himself from leaping at him. "Your advice is always appreciated." He spoke through clenched teeth.

Unaware, Kiana returned to them. "Donovan, sir, here's your Drambuie with extra heather honey added."

He replied without making eye contact. "Many thanks."

Donny watched Kiana walk away. "A little young," he commented, "but that's for her to decide. Gorgeous specimen. Smooth, dark maple syrup skin . . . I bet it's that sweet, too. As sweet as heather honey," he smirked.

Donovan imagined the feel of punching his brother in front of everyone. As children they rarely used fists, but it seemed like the perfect reaction now. Before he could think on it further, Armstrong's wide-shouldered silhouette appeared in the corner of his eye, beckoning him.

Armstrong raised his glass to Donovan as he joined him outside. "Donovan, my boy! Happy to have you."

Preston Armstrong suffered from delusions of grandeur, a king of kings. He found the oil industry lucrative because oil kings steered him toward their live wells. Manipulative and intimidating, he was the wrong man to cross and had amassed enough power to annihilate an enemy without leaving his armchair. Armstrong rewarded his allies for being on his side. He shared money, contracts, and business connections to inspire loyalty, and it worked. Penny, his wife, did the same with the women. They earned the majority of their relationships that way.

"Thank you for this opportunity," Donovan said.

"It's not an opportunity yet, we've challenged you. Success leads to an offer with us, and *that* leads to opportunities. It can be difficult answering honestly in front of a group of men like us," Armstrong said. "You'll get used to it. Can you imagine doing it consistently, month after month?"

Donovan said nothing.

"That's what it's like being a part of our group," he went on. "It takes tenacity, and if that isn't part of your fiber, you should honestly think about that. We're not asking you to extend past your capabilities, but we're asking you to search inside of yourself to see what's inherent and find out how far you can push it."

"What do you expect? What are you hoping for?"

"Pete Hernandez, a man in Edna, shot and killed a man in cold blood. His lawyers will be using the Fourteenth Amendment to fight it. We know this because the argument was used in another case last year but didn't gain much ground. Their second attempt will be different. We're looking for you to halt or suspend the progression of this case in any way possible, maybe even convince Hernandez to change lawyers."

"Who's on his team?"

"Gus García, out of San Antonio. I think he's with John Herrera's firm out of Houston. Have you heard of either man? Hell, maybe go through the murderer himself, see if he'll switch sides. He's in Edna right now."

Hearing Gus's name bristled the hairs on Donovan's body. He raised his hand and took a step back. "Mr. Armstrong, please, I don't want to make this personal."

"Call me Preston. Yes?"

The air in his chest whooshed out like balloon air. "Yes. Yes, sir, Preston. Gus double-crossed me in college, and I still carry some bad blood about it. I wouldn't want things to get . . . sophomoric."

Armstrong laughed. "Son, the politics from high school and college don't change much; the biggest thing that changes is our age. Probably our bank accounts, too." He put a hand on Donovan's shoulder. "Let me be blunt. The percentage of your success shoots up by half if you make this personal. You understand that, yes?"

"I'm sure you're right," he said, feeling uncomfortable.

"Of course I'm right. That's how this world turns. Your nemesis is the reason the case came to our attention. He can move mountains with his words, and it might come to that. Gus García makes everything personal, and people know his name because of it. That's where his passion comes from. Whether he wins or not, he will make a dent in history. If we can put our stamp on this case, then it'll be us making the dent."

Jealousy surged through him. "So what happens if I can eliminate Gus from the case? Who will take over?"

"That's not for you to worry about," Armstrong reassured him. "First things first. Try to make a move that sticks."

"I just . . . I just don't know where to start."

"Think of everything, that's what we do in our little group here. We think of all the possibilities and then go forward with the best choice. Like I said, you have our money at your disposal, so think big. Think of more than one avenue, because by golly, I think you're going to need it." He clapped Donovan on his back. "The fact that you went to college and law school with the man, can you imagine how far ahead you are on this task? Use everything you know. Think if we tried to put your brother on this, how long would it take for him to get near Gus?"

"That makes sense," Donovan said thoughtfully.

"Do you have anyone who can aid in this endeavor?"

"Horace, we've been friends since childhood. He's an assistant to the attorney general. I'm not sure how I can use him, but he'll support me in any way he can. We're meeting up tomorrow for our biweekly fishing."

"Wimberly?"

"Yes, sir, that's his last name."

"I'm aware of him but don't know much about his family. He doesn't come from a superb pedigree, but you're right, his position could help you. Plus, I hear he can be quite a prick, which can be of some use. Like your father." The men smiled at each other. "If you succeed, expect great things from our small circle, know that. Just relax and get into it, you're tailor-made for this. Get dirty." Armstrong shook his hand and turned to walk back inside.

"Sir," Donovan squeaked out. "Can I ask you one more question?"

Armstrong executed an about-face. "Anything to help you do your job easier."

"Um, I'm not sure if there's a better way to ask this. Why are we, or the group, Symmetry, why is this the goal?"

Armstrong nodded and returned. He gazed out into the night. "Always, we must hold on to everything we have. Make it precious, and hold it tight. Sometimes, we have to take what we know is ours. It's like marriage vows, to hold and to take. None of it is tangible, you see, I speak more of power, the upper hand, the knowledge. Survival of the fittest."

This left Donovan wary. "You speak of we, but as opposed to whom? Poor people? Other races? I'm sorry if I'm overstepping bounds."

"Whoever opposes us," he said in a deep voice. "Usually it slots itself into rich and poor, but not necessarily. If my butler inherited ten thousand dollars, it would mean an elevation in his society, but not in ours. It wouldn't mean he knew more than me, or understood the plight of life better than I. We'd still be in two worlds. A world of opposites. We know what's right because our people made this world, and it's up to us to keep it in the right hands. Does that make sense?"

"Uhh, sure, I think." Though he didn't mean to, Donovan scratched the back of his head.

"Trying to take this case into our hands is a small step toward keeping our future intact. We work in small ways, which collectively work toward big outcomes. It's all very upstanding work," Armstrong said with a wink.

Donovan's heart sank, but he didn't let it show. "I understand, it's about having the upper hand."

"Exactly. Now, if you'll excuse me, I'm going to retrieve my wife."

Donovan contemplated everything that transpired so far. His future called to him, he knew that much for sure. It could begin with the success of the mission, and lead to acceptance into Symmetry. Plus, and possibly the most delicious thing of all, he could enact some revenge on Gus. Finally.

Something plucked a heroic string in Donovan. This was a chance to put some shine back onto his family name—to fix some of what Donny tarnished. He desperately wanted to answer the call despite the vaguely unsavory nature of the group's ultimate goal, and despite having no idea what moves he should make. It was his duty to elevate the family name into the future. The Kincaids could rise to greater heights, and it could start with him.

Armstrong assumed Donovan embraced the group's ideas, but it didn't matter right now. Donovan was still too low in the ranks to worry about it. Completion of the task was paramount, and he believed adopting their outlook wouldn't matter as long as he executed the challenge.

Failure wasn't an option. The more he thought on it, the more he believed his success was inevitable. Soon Donovan couldn't imagine his life without the backing of Symmetry. He simply needed to figure out a way through.

Donovan got to their normal meeting spot on the Colorado River banks before Horace arrived. They favored the area as teenagers, and over time, the river had turned into a third friend. When joking ceased and topics became serious, they spoke to the river instead of having to look at each other; it helped their honesty flow.

Donovan spent some time clearing his mind from the previous night and listened to the quiet. The sun's rays were reflected by the sparkling water. Suddenly he heard his last name being called out by a familiar voice. Donovan turned to greet his friend.

Horace Wimberly struggled down a small hill wearing a floppy tackle hat and waddling in rubber fishing waders. He stopped a few feet from the water's edge. "Kincaid. You're not dressed for bass. Isn't this a fishing day? It took me an hour to wriggle into these," he snapped the rubber against his leg. "How could I forget?" They fished every other time they saw each other.

Donovan tried not to laugh. "You look smashing though," he faked a British accent. "Those boots accentuate your hips when you walk."

"Shut up. Don't make fun of me because I'm weight-troubled." Horace yanked off his hat and allowed his thinning blonde hair to whip in the wind. He shoved his glasses back up the bridge of his nose. "I can't wait until it starts getting cooler."

"You'll be cooler if you take off those waders. Or keep them on if it's good for weight loss."

Though the two could be described as an odd couple, their friendship's biggest strengths came from their dichotomy. Donovan stretched two feet higher, while Horace's belly stretched twice that far in circumference. The Kincaid reputation helped Donovan play the cool, laid-back one, while Horace was uptight. Coming from parents on the opposite ends of the financial spectrum, they taught each other how to survive in each other's world. It would be a theme revived by day's end.

They met at age nine through a local baseball league, a sport neither wanted to participate in, but did so for their parents. The Wimberlys wanted Horace to lose weight, and the Kincaids wanted Donovan to gain the competitive edge he lacked. Both sets of parents banked respectively on their sons' width and height for powerful drives into the fence, and both received a fat wad of whopping nothing. Except for the boys, who warmed the bench long enough to become friends.

Neither possessed the courage to share with parents their hatred for the sport; they avoided it by pretending they liked to play, which brought more problems. Horace developed anxiety over not being able to run fast enough, and Donovan tended to dodge balls rather than catch them. The coaches kept them on the team far longer than either expected, thus cementing their bond further.

"I'm not joining you out there, I'm liable to tip over," Horace staunchly said. "Damn, I told my boss I'd bring in leftovers tomorrow."

"You're wearing the gear to still come through with your promise," Donovan pointed out. "To be honest, I need so much help today I wouldn't mind catching you a fish or two just to get your thoughts. Let's sit on the bank, and I'll tell you my dilemma."

Horace smiled in anticipation and removed his eyeglasses once they sat in the grass. "You need some advice, do you?" He leaned back and shut his eyes. "Before you start, Kincaid, do you want the attorney general's

Horace, or the ruthless one?"

"What do you think?"

Armstrong had been correct about Horace's unsuitable pedigree, but working as one of two assistants to the state attorney general made him appealing in circles like Symmetry. Horace knew it himself. His pet peeve held him in limbo; he didn't like the idea of being rich because it seemed to be more trouble than it was worth. Status and power, yes, but having money gave him an uncomfortable feeling.

Other people's wealth, i.e., Donovan's, Horace had no problem with. He grew up assuming he'd been slotted into the wrong caste of families, so he felt at home with the Kincaids. It pumped up an already formidable ego, enough to get him through law school and out into the real world. Donovan didn't mind. He understood his friend's duty to elevate his family's reputation.

"Ruthless," Donovan decided. "All the way."

"Perfect."

"My dad's group wants me."

Horace sat up. "Symmetry?"

"How do you know what they're called? I didn't even know that."

He leaned back again. "I know that because I listen closely to people. I doubt they refer to themselves as such when they gather. They move mountains, you know."

"Huh," Donovan said blankly. "We've never spoken on it."

"It's not something you talk about."

"Huh," he repeated. He explained his task. "They call it a *challenge*."

"What about your job at the counsel? What kind of sway can you get to help back you up with this?"

"Absolutely nothing. They can't know about anything. Being sneaky is the name of the game." The Chief Disciplinary Counsel hired Donovan three years prior, the office to visit when filing complaints, hearings, and punishments for the state lawyers. He took the job for the behind-the-scenes perks.

Horace narrowed his eyes.

Donovan noticed. "What? Out with it. Let me guess, you're incredibly jealous of me, but you don't think I'll follow through with it."

Horace gave him a thin smile. "Exactly. They should be asking *me*, but I don't have your last name. Instead, I will help you in the hopes of you dropping my name to them later. I'll steer you right for both our sakes."

"I already have."

"I'm honestly surprised," Horace said. "Tell you what, Kincaid. You wriggle into these thigh-high boots, catch me a fish for my boss, and I'll give you every angle on your subject I can think of." He clasped his hands behind his head and executed an I'm-waiting face.

"I suppose I have no choice but to say yes. I'd love nothing more than to catch a fish," he said sarcastically. "You better make this worth it."

"Already at it. Now tell me, what does Symmetry want for admittance?" He lifted a chunky leg in the air. "Here, you're going to need my waders for this."

Donovan waited until he stood over Horace to share the next piece of information. "Squeezing the life out of a murder case. But it was the person who interested me." He paused until he yanked off both boots. "Gus-goddamn-García," he announced.

Horace shot up in the grass. "GGG?"

"The very one."

"The time has come! Oh, this makes me splendidly happy."

Donovan stuffed each foot into Horace's waders and wriggled into them as best he could. He snapped the suspenders on his shoulders. "It's a case he's working on farther south. They want me to try and axe it. Horace, I promise you, I almost let out a sound when Armstrong said his name. It was . . . "

"Kismet," he finished. "No one knows more than me what this can do for you. Because it's Gus, you can pull out all the stops and not feel guilty about it. Although, we all know how you love to feel guilty, and that could get in the way." He leaned back again and tucked his hands behind his head. "This can finally be your time to enact some revenge. You look keen, by the way, despite the boots only reaching your knees."

"So, you too? You think I'm supposed to make this personal?"

"Why the hell not?"

"I thought it more noble not to, but Armstrong seemed to imply it would make my job easier."

"See, I knew this would happen. You're trying to attain a position in Symmetry, aren't you? Do it by any means necessary. Come on, Kincaid, you're getting permission to break the rules."

Donovan chuckled. "You'd be perfect for Symmetry."

"Don't I know it?" Horace's eyes glinted in the sun.

"I go back and forth about being professional or getting dirty," he weighed. "Can't I do both at the same time?"

"That's the goal." Horace snorted. "When you get to Symmetry's level, behaving that way will become second nature. Don't worry, your humanity will have diminished greatly by then."

Donovan winced at that and looked out at the water. "Accompany me to the edge, it shouldn't take long."

"Do I have to? I can still hear you from here."

"Do you want a fish or not?"

Horace groaned and got to his feet. "Just think about Gus stealing your girlfriend when you need motivation."

Donovan's body tightened. "It doesn't frustrate me like you'd think. It only infuriates."

"Still?"

"Always. Give me your fishing rod and get your bucket ready. I'll hook the worm. Shit, the worms." He went back and found them squirming in the corner of Horace's tackle box. "Get ready for your life's purpose, little guy." As he prepared the rod, Donovan supposed he might be the worm in the situation. Symmetry hooked him, and he'd be cast out soon, but he wondered whether he'd get eaten or sink under the pressure. *They have me squirming by the balls, just like that,* he thought. *Hook, line, and sink me.* He rejoined Horace. "Now talk."

Horace shaded his eyes from the sun. "To do this properly, someone would have to infiltrate San Antonio and watch his every move. Learn what he likes, what he does, what he eats, who he spends time with," he explained. "Be honest, how much of that do you already know?"

"We went to college and law school together, so we traveled in some of the same circles. How many of us never change after college?" Donovan waded out a few feet into the river as a small school of fish swam past him. "Regardless, I don't think it would take long."

"The basics don't change; we're fully formed by then. What were his weaknesses?"

Donovan thought for a moment. "The law, a neat glass of whisky, and a striking woman with thin ankles. He rarely eats when he's working a case, it takes over his life. Or it used to; I don't think that's changed.

Armstrong mentioned Gus would be pairing up with a firm in Houston, a Herrera?" He let the hook go and cast the line.

Horace shot up again. "Johnny?"

"That sounds about right."

"Are you kidding me? Kincaid, this is too good to be true." After not receiving a response, he went on. "Don't you know who that is?"

"No idea. Did you go to law school with a Herrera?" He waited for a fish to bite.

Horace revealed a greedy smile. "You know who Herrera is. You've heard of his father. He used to be a sheriff in Houston. If you don't remember the man who put your brother in jail, maybe you aren't cut out for this." Horace jabbed Donovan with his foot. "And yes, he and I took many of the same classes."

Donovan turned slowly. "His father is John Sr."

"The very one."

His life clicked into order. "Maybe the world waits until you've collected enough enemies and then gives you the rest of your life to make things right."

Donny had moved to Houston for a short time, and John Herrera Sr. became the first to throw him in jail and put his name in the system. Not only that, John Sr. wouldn't take a bribe, which infuriated the entire family. Donny's name became synonymous with police run-ins after that, causing him to move back home.

Donovan wondered out loud. "Could this be my chance to have purpose?" The water sparkled from the sun's reflection just as he felt a tug at the end of his rod.

"It most certainly is," Horace said. "I will do whatever I can to help, as long as you tell Symmetry good things about me."

"I can promise you that." Donovan agreed. "What about the Symmetry wives? Shall I let them know their daughters might have a suitor waiting in the wings?" He began to reel in the fishing line.

Horace shuddered. "Absolutely not, unless you're speaking of yourself. What would possess you to say something like that? I would not touch their daughters with *your* hands." He snorted a laugh. The thought of a wife made Horace uncomfortable. "You have lots of connections with this offer. This journey will cause you to change for the better, or worse, depending on your perspective. Are you ready to deal with the consequences?"

"I think so, but I'm not sure I entirely understand your meaning." The tugging turned into pulling on the line.

"You will need to be manipulative yet charming, pushy in your approach, conniving in your moves, and you'll probably need to fib about a few things." Horace chuckled.

"So, your advice is to behave more like you? Great," Donovan said with a flat tone. He yanked on the fishing rod twice.

"Basically."

"I didn't think there'd be an acting challenge," he joked, then grew quiet at the statement's truth. He hoped he didn't have to go to the extremes Horace spoke of. "What should I do first?"

"Let's start with a list of the people you could go through to deflate the case. List anyone and everyone, then revise it for importance. Who has common interests, where do loyalties stand? As much as I'm sure you'd like to give Gus a visit first, I'd hold off and start with his client. The mother is probably the one who hired him." He snapped his fingers. "The client could change representation like that. Does he like Gus? Does he like money? Prepare how much you're willing to offer in increments."

Donovan took in what Horace said and watched his friend's eyes go wild and wicked. He turned his focus back on the fish. With his upper-body strength, he pulled it in with ease. It turned out to be a bass. "Right. Because that would . . . "

"Help you figure out your approach when you visit him. What did you think you'd do?" Horace scoffed. "Throw a bunch of money at him and demand he do what you say without any finesse?"

"Sort of," Donovan laughed shakily. He unhooked the bass and studied it struggling and gasping, clearly unable to deal with the requirements of its new surroundings. He wondered if his desperation would show in the same manner to the members of Symmetry. *Father would surely smell it,* he thought. *Don Jr. misses nothing.* For the moment Donovan threw his fears into the bucket with the bass. He sat next to Horace and flopped out on the grass.

Horace looked to the sky. "Help him, Lord. This man does not know what he does. Send him a sign that this is the right thing to do, or give me the strength to push him aside so I can be in his place!"

In that moment, two women in skin-tight swimsuits water-skied past them, waving and laughing. The men saw them as a sign but interpreted the meaning differently. Horace believed it to be the sign he asked for, and Donovan took it as a sign to circumvent brooding and find a wife, or at least a woman for a night. He thought briefly of Kiana and the night before. "Have you wondered why they tasked me with this?"

"I thought we answered that question already. It's because you're tailor-made for the task."

Donovan eyed him sideways. "No, not that." He paused. "If you'd heard the way Preston described the group's main objective . . . to me, it all appeared a bit elitist. Or racist? I can't decide which. Both? They want to stop a case focused on equal rights for Mexican Americans. What about that needs to be stopped?"

Horace shook his head. "Don't look at it like that. They requested something from you, and are willing to give you something in exchange for success. No need to question it further." He shrugged. "Keeping people down who are 'less-than' means keeping our own heads above water just a little longer."

"That sounds rather elitist to me."

"I don't see that."

Donovan groaned and threw down the fishing rod. "Not you, too. Must this outlook be something I adopt?"

"Not necessarily, but you're crazy not to. What's your motive here? You need to keep reminding yourself why you're doing what you're doing. It's the bigger picture."

"That's easy." The answer came without thinking. "Gus."

"So, use that. If the client in jail is loyal, don't talk badly about Gus. Find the man's weakness, which I'm sure is money. Tell him we—errr, Symmetry—has more resources and money at their disposal than Gus's team could ever offer. If he's not loyal, list all of Gus's questionable qualities. Does that make sense?"

"When you say it like that it does! I need to make a map." Donovan shook his head. "Five minutes more and I would've still been in the water for those two women."

"No distractions. You'll need to prepare and practice." Horace waved the idea of them away. "Hearing no isn't an option. You get one chance. Go into that meeting knowing the client will fire Gus, and say what you need for the yes. It's like being a salesman. Know your rebuttals." He paused. "Those women could've run you over."

"I've never sold anything to anyone." Donovan looked out to the river. "I'm willing to do anything to make myself a cushy spot in that group. I care so damn much about what they think of me, this could be to my detriment."

"Don't we all . . . " Horace suppressed an urge to give his full opinion. "Your mental outlook needs to toughen up. Hand to heaven, I will do what I can. The Kincaids have done so much for me, and I'm not going to let their son down after all these years." He cleared his throat. "Start with a timeline of the events you know, then use it as a countdown for what needs to happen."

Worry formed into a knot behind Donovan's left shoulder blade when he thought of the work up ahead, but the idea of being responsible for Gus's demise supercharged him past the initial stress. He decided to behave as if he had everything under control and hoped the rest would fall into place. "I don't know what I'm doing."

"It's okay, you'll figure it out. Kincaid blood runs through you."

Donovan said, "I believe you," and meant it.

Horace added a postscript. "I don't mean to ruin the party, but at some point, you'll need to figure out whether your views match their own. It doesn't matter now, but it will in the future." He nudged him and grinned widely. "Now, re-hook those rubber boots and hook one more bass for me before we call it a day."

CHAPTER 5

GUS SHOVED OPEN THE DOUBLE DOORS OF LA MANCHA, HIS FAVORITE LOCAL bar in San Antonio. A hole-in-the-wall bar, it grew popular for its cheap drinks and colorful, gaudy decorations. Red, blue, orange, and green *sarapes* billowed from the ceiling and sombreros hung on the walls for customers to wear. Inexpensive *alebrijes*—fantastical multi-colored creatures with body parts from various animals—sat on the bar and tables for customers to appreciate and inspire conversations.

A bartender popped up from behind the bar. "Gustavo!"

"Petee! The one who never judges me."

"What brings you here on a Tuesday afternoon? Did you have a pleasant walk?" La Mancha was located a block away from the office.

"I needed somewhere to think." Gus told Petee about Irene's letter, Lenora's visit, and the service denial he witnessed against the Cruz sisters in Edna. "I made my decision right then and there to take the case. That act of discrimination, those two random girls, they hand-delivered me a little joy in that hopeless moment. My home wouldn't feel like home if I buried my head and ignored what I saw. Those girls certainly didn't feel at home. The minority will stay silenced if I don't do something."

Petee chewed on a toothpick as he listened and served him a Chivas Regal. He kept an extra bottle behind the bar specifically for Gus. "Unfortunate. It could've been worse. At least the entire shop didn't join in with the men yelling at them to leave. At least a man didn't try to follow them out to kidnap them and defile them in some forest. Maybe because you followed them out and protected them by default."

"I guess so, and I know you're not lying," Gus agreed. "It's just . . . to see it unfold, it made me sad."

"Sundown town." Petee pulled out a pack of cigarettes from the sleeve of his white semi-clean tee shirt and offered one to Gus.

"For men like you and me . . . "

"What town in the Deep South doesn't become one when the sun sets?" Petee shook his head. "I couldn't live like that, scared to leave my house once it turned dark. That's why I moved here."

Gus snapped his fingers. "Voices silenced just like that." He gestured for another pour. "So, I skipped the burger and crossed the road to the courthouse to fill out a notice requesting information. I called myself the hired counsel."

Petee slid the bottle over. "Help yourself. I see some people about to come inside."

Gus pulled out a stack of papers from his briefcase. "I'm going to do some work."

"My office is yours," Petee called out.

Gus read that a number of people clearly witnessed Pete Hernandez shoot a man dead outside the Chinco's bar in Edna. He stared at the indictment list as he sipped his whisky and scanned the last names over and over again: Horton, Schroeder, Simons, Smith, Larkin, Winstead, Drushel.

Not getting anywhere, he reached for the alebrije nearest to him, a creature ten inches tall with a purple and pink speckled dragon body and tiny yellow butterfly wings, a lion's head, and a green unicorn horn. The mouth stretched wide with claws for teeth, and a green tongue flopped out with an arrowhead end. Gus mimicked the animal's expression while he reread the paperwork again. He wished a clue would jump out to guide his next steps.

Petee rejoined Gus. "Do you want another alebrije? I have one shaped like a frog with bat wings."

"What's the time?"

"Nearly five o'clock."

"How much would it cost you to install more lights in this bar?" Gus peered at the paper in front of him.

"What's that now? More lights?"

He pointed to the ceiling. "Lights, my friend! Why not add more lights? Lights are golden and lead us to truth!"

Petee hiked himself over the bar top and whispered. "You do know people drink alcohol here? Drunks don't want to see other drunks seeing them clearly." He grinned and dropped back behind the counter.

"You could have one put in that suspends just above my seat."

Petee lit his cigarette. "I'll ask the owner."

Gus laughed and held the indictment list away from Petee's lighter. "I need to find something here, but I don't know what. We already know man shoots man in cold blood. It's not disputed."

He took the paper. "What exactly? A word? A phrasing?"

"That's just the thing. I'll know it when I see it." Gus poured himself another drink.

"You're looking for a way in. A loophole," Petee filled in.

"I'm searching for a back door. When they gloss over race and hang anyone who isn't white simply for being who they are, I know something will be there."

Petee exhaled a cloud of smoke. "Is that how the law works?"

"Don't kid yourself, good man," Gus said. "Anyone who's different—"

"Can make a difference," Petee cut in.

Gus scoffed. "Actually yes, that's how the law *can* work. It's all about the loopholes and what you can prove." He widened his arms as if asking for a hug. "But hey, I'll be the first to admit it. My people inhabit San Antonio in larger numbers, so much that we're a force. They may not string us from atop a building, but even here, if we're caught alone and vulnerable, we're as good as dead. I've got to fight for people who don't know how to fight for themselves."

"I'm sold," Petee said, and glanced at the list once more. "You know what?"

"Tell me."

He tapped at the paper. "Right here, there's women on this list. That surprises me. Who are these people?"

"Commissioners on the jury who brought him in."

"So, your guy is guilty?"

Gus frowned. "Did I not say that?"

Half-smiling, Petee eyed the almost-empty glass between them. "Come on, you're the minority lawyer."

"A lawyer for minorities or a minority lawyer?"

"Both."

Gus flipped a thumbs up. "You get a healthy tip." He poured himself a generous portion.

Petee scanned the list again with disdain on his face, then flicked at the piece of paper as if a mosquito landed on its edge. "Why else would you be staring at a bunch of white names if the man wasn't guilty, no matter the crime. How long did it take?"

"For the verdict or the crime?"

"To bring him in. Unless arrested on the spot," he countered. "I know this isn't a gender thing, but when are women called in for something like that?"

"It happened overnight," Gus straightened his posture, "and you're right, this isn't a boys' club," he pointed. "Schroeder and Drushel are women. Why didn't I notice it before?"

"What kind of names are those . . . German, or Polish?"

"Exactly!" He downed his Chivas in three gulps. "This isn't a gender issue, but it can be a racial one. I gotta run, Petee my man! Thanks for the talk, I know who to call now!"

Gus ran the distance from La Mancha to his office building and took the elevator up. He double-checked the names once more before dialing an old friend in Houston.

CHAPTER 6

JOHN HERRERA STOOD IN THE KITCHEN OF HIS HOUSTON LAW FIRM, SCANNING the refrigerator top for spices. "Love, you've got to let me edge in a word so I can tell you my plans for the evening." He threw his tie over a shoulder and exhaled noisily. "I know it's late, but I need to stay at the office for another hour or two more. LULAC wants me to think about a higher platform, and I haven't had a chance to think until now. I need time, *mi amor*."

John liked to keep the peace. Though he made his name as a tough-as-nails lawyer fighting for his clients, being national vice president of LULAC, the League of United Latin American Citizens, made him even more popular in the Latino community. LULAC—a group over twenty years running—already took up a huge but happy space in his life. Now his peers suggested he run for national president.

He stood surveying his ingredients: tomatoes on a vine, green peppers, garlic, cilantro, and onions. Before he could choose, the phone rang. He wanted to ignore it and let his mind wander, but the ringing crept into his skull and banged against his brain. He opened a drawer, chose a knife, and then answered the phone.

"Herrera here." He exhaled a raggedy breath.

"And García is here!" A laugh boomed through the phone. "Aye Johnny, I'd ask why you were in the office on a Friday night if I wasn't calling from my own!"

"Gustavo," John said. He pulled the tomatoes first and removed three from their stems.

The two worked together over the years, most recently winning an education case with Bastrop ISD two years prior. The verdict granted Latino children equal rights in the school system by allowing them to attend a local Anglo school. Officials turned around and passed a law saying the students had to speak English in order to take classes. Many children were turned down because they didn't speak enough of the language. It singed the men's egos, to be sure, but where John could move on from disappointments, Gus could not.

John quartered the tomatoes and did his best to match his friend's tone. "My brother from another mother, how the hell have you been? I'm in my office kitchen making salsa. I'm a little hungry."

"Doing some heavy thinking, are you?"

"You know me well." John started to tell him about his dilemma but held back. Gus tended to make things about himself, and he didn't want to fan the flame. He scooped the tomatoes back into the bowl.

"I do," Gus said. "Listen, tell me about the Aniceto case."

"Gustavo," he growled. "Don't think you can start without some niceties. How are the girls? Irene?" He diced a green pepper while his train of thought went in and out.

John galvanized people, a trait he learned from his father. Gus passed for the James Dean rebel, and John the homecoming king, the tamer of the two. Both towered over others like redwoods. The two met through LULAC and advised over the same kinds of cases, like civil rights and education. They rarely butted heads, and both liked to drink, thus sustaining a true friendship.

Gus clucked his tongue. "You keep me living an honest life. The girls are healthy, but I'm not living at home right now. Things aren't well between Irene and me; apparently I can't help but continue to be a scoundrel. How's Olivia?"

"She's great, a little frustrated at me for still being at work." John jammed the knife into the onion and halved it. He put one half of it inside the refrigerator. "She understands when I'm busy; I'm not in the scoundrel category. I'm sorry to hear about you and Irene. How can you make it better?" The sulfurous onion fumes wafted up into his nose and eyes.

"It needs some time; she'll come around. She'll miss me sooner or later." Gus let out a chuckle. "What I am I saying, Johnny? She may not miss me anymore, but she might. I'd miss me."

He shook his head and chose a bulb of garlic. "How very . . . full of yourself, that's the Gustavo I know well. Just keep trying. Maybe she's looking for persistence."

"We haven't spoken since she asked me not to come home. The next time I see her, I'll know whether she intends on allowing me back at some point. If not, I would be wasting time trying to change. Futility is a mighty demon. In the meantime, I'll get by. Living out of my office eases the morning process. I don't know why I hadn't thought of it before."

John smiled at his friend's bravado and the touch of desperation in his voice. "I'm sure you will." He wondered what Gus could've done to upset Irene enough to ask him not to live at home. Was there another woman? Usually, the answer was yes, but Irene never kicked him out. More than one woman? Who had the time for that? Work took up the majority of his time. "I sacrifice lots for the firm, but you can't shortchange your family on the important stuff, especially the kids. You know Irene will be happy if you make your girls happy. You know, basic stuff. Hold on, loud noise." He smashed the garlic bulb against the cutting board, removed the skin, and minced the remainder. Again, LULAC passed through his mind as he added the garlic to the mixture and stirred.

"Yes, well, thank you, doctor. Let me ask, has enough time passed that I can ask about Aniceto again?"

"Always the impatient Gustavo . . . what is it you want to know?"

"How long have you been working on the case? When's the verdict?"

John chuckled at his friend's eagerness. "Aniceto Sanchez. We're still waiting for a verdict. Earlier this year, in April, we filed an appeal in the Texas courts." He salted and peppered the salsa twice. "Forgot the cilantro," he said, and pulled several green stalks to cut into bits and add to the mixture.

"Will you and your guy take it to the Supreme Court if the decision isn't overturned?"

"The guy's name is DeAnda." He viciously stirred the salsa and pressed the fork against the tomatoes to release more juice. "We're to tackle the subject if it becomes a possibility."

"Mmm-hmmm."

John opened the cupboard for tortilla chips. "*Que*, Gustavo? I can hear your mind ticking from two hundred miles away. I know how your mind works. What do you want to know?"

"How long ago did Aniceto shoot that Czech man? Was there a question of him being guilty?"

"No question about it. But the man is a *Mejicano*, though his last name is Czech. Or was, his name was Smershy."

"Smushy?" Gus laughed. "Apologies, I'm a little delirious."

"Smershy. He and Aniceto worked side by side in the Imperial Sugar fields." He tested the salsa with a chip. "Ay, Dios mío, that's tasty."

"Last year was the murder?"

"Sí, April 1950, but the trial wasn't until March of this year."

"How long for the indictment?"

"They moved fast, very fast. About a week."

"Huh! Now you're making me sit up. Tell me the argument."

"Lack of proper representation by his peers. James DeAnda gathered the proof—hell of a researcher, that boy, received his law degree last year—he dug into jury lists for Fort Bend County going back thirty-five years."

"What were the numbers?"

"What numbers? Not one Mexican sat on a jury in all the years he checked, and Richmond is in the middle of the state. We thought it was a drastic assumption to think it, but it paid off. We crafted the 'same race yet distinctively different' argument and have the numbers to prove it." John paused for Gus to pick up the conversation, but the silence lingered. "Whatdya got? Wait, before you answer that, let me switch the phone line into my office."

"Not sure. You think it's the same for other towns? No Mexicans on juries?"

"I do, and I'm sure it's in the books to prove it."

Gus exhaled through the phone. "I've got the same situation over here, I think. It's still new, still in the womb. But you'll be the first to know."

"Hot damn!" John slapped his leg. "Are we going to work together again? Bastrop ISD, round two?"

"Something like that . . . this could be another chance. Our case started the curve with schools' educational systems, this one could connect the dots and extend the line into a circle. Johnny, back then, do you feel like they toyed with us?"

After their win against Bastrop ISD, officials constructed a new school law to circumvent it.

"With the language deficiency law?" John scooped another chip. "I know what you want to say, but we have to expect moves like that. We're trying to do exactly what I'm doing now with this salsa: mix the colors of our culture enough to integrate them into the rest of society." He spread flour tortilla chips on a paper plate. "The green, white, and red of our ancestors' country—our families—they deserve that."

"I don't want the same thing that happened in Bastrop with this. They say 'Yes, Mexican children deserve the same education as the others, but, oh wait, if they don't speak clear English—if they're deficient in our language—then it's not a good idea. Let's relegate them back to their shitty schoolhouses, keeping them separated is easier.' Loophole!" He banged his fist on his desk. "I feel like a patsy, a pawn. A patsy pawn."

John deepened his voice, sounding fatherly. "Ya, Gustavo, calm down. I know you like to get up in arms about this, but now isn't the time."

"Education is my platform, too; it's not just yours. No one was more angry than me. They knew what chess moves led to checkmate. They knew it from the start." Gus began to scowl. "The loopholes ended up being a matter of semantics, and they set them up like back doors in case they needed an easy out. I need to find one and expose it."

"We need to be smarter and think farther ahead," John countered. He waited for a response as he scooped salsa. Most of the contents spilled out. "We'll need money. The process will be arduous by itself, and running out of money could stop the process no matter how smart our arguments are."

Gus growled into the phone. "The money will take care of itself."

"You say that now, but you don't think that far down the line."

"This isn't about money, Johnny! This is about the issues and the people, our race. I can't believe you, talking about money."

"You know this as well as I; don't circumvent. It doesn't cross your mind because you're not the one who takes care of the money or tries to get people to part with it. Michelangelo didn't find David in that stone with one swipe. Did Irene say yes to your advances right away? I, myself, know she did not. You had to wear her down, little by little, smile by smile, boast by boast." He crunched into the phone.

Another growl, louder this time, but a laugh followed.

"That's how we attack discrimination, the blatant types and the polite," John continued, "by chipping away at it little by little. We'll find our own loophole, we'll get there." He crunched more.

"We must," Gus agreed. "How can we not?" He repeated the question again, this time more softly. "How can we not?"

"Don't let that desperation hang over you, amigo. It's not mistletoe, so it will never give a favorable outcome." He drummed his fingers on his office desk and threw caution to the wind, finally giving in. "I'd like your advice on a topic."

"Yes, please, distract me with other thoughts."

John exhaled loudly. "This could be a big deal. Some LULAC men approached me about running for national president next summer, and I'm tossing the idea around. Your thoughts?"

Gus let the question hang a moment too long before answering. "Who did? Who asked you?"

John hung in the moment, too, and felt the implications. He cocked his head back at Gus's questions. "Some of the council." Instantly he regretted mentioning it. The newness of the idea made him blurt it out without thinking about the possible reactions Gus might have.

"Enrique? Who else?"

"Yes, he was among them." John squeezed the phone. "Why, do you wish they'd ask you? There's still time."

"Nonsense, just curious." Another silence passed between them. "I'd be proud to support you," Gus said, his voice more energized. "What brought this on?"

John knew Gus's tension increased with every passing minute. His information incensed the spoiled boy in Gus, and he never responded well to others receiving more praise than he. John knew that. "It's time to get some momentum going. I don't want my firm to be the only thing I've done with my life. There's more up ahead, I can feel it. I need more."

"Then do it. I'll help in any way I can," Gus said, enunciating every word. "We'll talk in a few days then. I'm going to Mexico *con* mi abuelo. Manolete, the great bullfighter, will dance."

"Two greats in one day! Until then," John said. He hesitated to speak more. "Don't dwell, Gustavo, it's not good for anyone, much less you and that mind of yours. It can be the worst thing for you."

"Dwell on what?"

John heard the phone click before he could respond and followed suit. He chided himself for telling Gus about his news when he'd initially planned on not sharing. He wondered, *does my competitiveness run deeper than I think?* A voice inside said, *No matter*, and he brushed the thought away. *The time for big moves has arrived*, it said, *and no looking back*.

CHAPTER 7

BEING IN AN ARENA AFTER SO MANY YEARS SWARMED GUS WITH A LOAD OF undecipherable emotions and fragmented memories. How long had it been, ten or twenty years? He felt Mateo's presence first on one shoulder, loving yet heavier than he expected, then quickly on the other shoulder, squeezing tighter and tighter. All of his memories suddenly felt unresolved and heavy. A pit started to open in his stomach—was it grief?—and then tears took over his sight. The sensations became so overpowering he could hardly catch his breath.

Find a seat, a voice said within him. He obeyed, merely to stop whatever seemed to be attacking him. As he sank into a seat he made a mental note to explore the reason for his shake-up.

The announcer's voice came through the arena speakers propped up on poles throughout the arena. "Señors y señoras, ladies and gentlemen, let the games begin! May I take a moment to introduce the world's first female matador sitting in our stands, Patricia McCormick! Patricia, can you stand up and give us a little wave?"

As his eyes landed on her, it was as if a spotlight lit her up at the very same moment. A striking woman, her hair was an equal mix of brunette and blonde strands that brushed her shoulders and framed a face with small, girlish features. Even from far away, Gus could see the hardness beneath her girlish appearance, no doubt what she tapped into for fights with bulls. He honed in on her pimento-red linen top and decided to approach Patricia McCormick like a bull.

By the end of the first fight he'd reached her side of the arena and chose a row behind her without attracting much attention. He used the spare moments to watch her focus as she studied man and animal.

Gus realized he'd stared too long when her head and spine suddenly perked and straightened. She turned around and found him instantly. Her eyes did not break from his.

He gave her a small wave and a soft look. When she smiled back he gestured for her permission to approach. She nodded and allowed him to ease over the row and slide nearer to her.

"Hello," he said. A lock of black hair wilted down over his forehead like a kiss-me-quick.

Patricia eyed him carefully, sizing him up. She scooted a few inches closer to him. "Hello," she reciprocated. "Have I truly become that compelling for you to be here in front of me?"

He noticed the raspiness in her voice, with a touch of smoothness like fresh honey. "Your voice, madame," Gus responded, "I've never heard anything like it before." He held out his hand and knelt on the wooden floor. "Madame McCormick, my name is Gus . . . Gustavo . . . I'm honored to be in front of you."

"Patricia," she smiled with playfulness in her eyes. "What sort of voices have you heard before?"

He briefly touched her hand, then returned to the seat beside her. "Thin, abiding voices with a lilt. Statements that always sound like questions, as if looking for my approval."

She chuckled and leaned in closer to look at his face. "I apologize for my forwardness, Gus Gustavo, but you are breathtaking."

Gus blushed. "I am not sure whether to laugh or cry. Pick one or the other," he pleaded. "Gus Gustavo is not my name, but you can call me anything you want." His posture straightened. "Gus. I prefer Gus." The smile wiped from his face as he remembered requesting the same from his abuelo three decades ago. A sadness cloaked him instantly.

Patricia didn't notice. "I will choose Gus." She studied his face and his exposed skin, his arms and legs. "You're not from Mexico, are you? You're too pale."

"Mi abuelo always said my color would be a camouflage." He mimicked an old man's voice. "'Mijo, your skin is a gift and a weapon, don't forget that,'" then returned to his normal voice. "But right now it seems I'm not doing a good job with either." He puffed his chest out. "I'm from Texas, born and bred."

"As am I." A pause hung in the air. "Gus, Gustavo, I think I like Gustavo instead."

He nodded with a smile in his eyes. “Whatever you decide.”

“My new friend, the great Manolete, is about to perform, and I would like to watch him without distractions.” She placed a hand on his leg, a bold move. “Are you planning on leaving anytime soon, or would you like to stay by my side for the evening? Do you have plans?”

A sheen of warmth slid over his face like sunshine as he gushed, “Unequivocally, and without reservation.” He scooped her hand into his. “I will wait by your side. I am nothing but a bull tamed by your beauty.” He wanted to be near her, and unsure why that force felt so strong.

“Your eyes are very green,” she blurted out. “I like looking at them.”

He nodded. “Let’s watch Manolete in silence, and we will speak about our evening afterward.” She didn’t pull her hand away until the matador stepped into the arena.

Over time, Manolete became a very popular figure, and known to be one of the best bullfighters in the sport. As he entered the ring he yanked the cape from his shoulder in one swoop and let it spin around him.

Gus decided against watching Manolete and stared at Patricia instead. His eyes lingered on the smoothness of her cheekbones and traveled to her lips and neck. Her eyes stayed alert and watched the dance unfold.

Patricia put her focus back on Gus after Manolete bested the bull. She gave him a sly look. “Once you find a target you have tunnel vision, don’t you?”

“Like you wouldn’t believe,” he answered. “How long have you been fighting bulls?”

“A little over a year. My first official dance was yesterday.” She smiled proudly, showing two perfect rows of gleaming white teeth. “I’m getting the hang of it, but I only fight young bulls right now, less than two years old.”

Hearing Patricia call bullfighting a dance brought another rush of sadness Gus found himself unprepared for. Grief crashed into him like a heavy wind and the pit returned to his stomach.

“You don’t look well, is there anything I can do?”

Gus returned to reality with a downcast look. “Lo siento, mi abuelo used to call it a dance. It brings back memories.”

“Happy ones I hope!” Patricia looked deep into his eyes. “When did he pass?”

"Two decades ago." He touched his heart and gazed out into the arena. "But he's here always." His breathing began to quicken uncontrollably and he did his best to make it unnoticeable.

Her eyes turned forward. "I call it the dusty sea. When you sit at the top row and look down, that's what it looks like." She angled herself back at him. "Gus Gustavo, I've been invited to dine with Manolete and his people this evening. Would you like to join us?"

The pit melted away when he looked at her, he noticed. "I would love nothing more."

She narrowed her eyes. "Are you with anyone today?"

"No lady in waiting, aside from the one in front of me." Gus reached for his heart again. "Y mi abuelo."

Patricia smiled warmly and reached out her hand. "Come then, we leave now, the restaurant is just down the street. Manolete likes to have a room full of fans waiting for him when he enters La Villa."

Gus held out his arm when they reached the street and Patricia hooked hers into it. They walked several steps in silence. The sun gave its final shine before preparing to set, turning the sky a warm blue reflected from the gulf. He looked at her face and beamed.

She noticed. "You're not intimidated by me, are you?"

He shook his head. "Why would I be?"

Shrugging, she said, "Many look at me and see only the first female bullfighter, an oddity."

"More like a specialty." He winked, then explained his profession. "Some might say I'm a specialty myself, others might call me bullish."

Her eyebrows raised. "Well, you know that changes things for me. You will be something—an animal?—that I must overcome. Are you satisfied with that?"

"Madame, more than you know."

They laughed together. "We're almost there."

Two members of the La Villa staff waited for them through side-swept curtains of ivy and ushered them to a back room where mariachi singers strummed guitars in the corner. Family pictures shaded in gray hung in frames on the walls surrounding them. Tables formed a small square in the middle of the room full of people drinking and talking.

Gus saw Manolete dressed in black, seated among the patrons. He had a slim face and pointed chin, large eyes and a wide nose. When he saw Patricia, he stood tall with open arms. "The rarity enters!" He looked at Gus. "Welcome hermano! Join us."

She laughed and embraced him. "Manuel, this tradition you have of wearing black to mourn the bull, I still do not know what to think of it."

"Ask me again in five years when you've shed enough life, you might be more surefooted in your opinion." He shook Gus's hand. "Call me Manuel. Manolete is just a stage name."

"Gus. She and I met at the arena and I've been unable to tear myself away."

He laughed heartily. "All strong men feel this way. Come sit next to me, and drink some wine, or whisky?"

"The latter." A server nodded.

The wine and whisky flowed for hours as the group drilled Manolete about his mindset during his fight and asked Patricia questions. They critiqued other matadors and ate steaks, molé, and fish with peppers and crispy vegetables while talking about the essence of a bullfight.

When the conversation began to quiet, Gus jumped up, tipsy from the whisky, and unfolded a red tablecloth he'd secretly acquired from one of the servers. He spun the material over his head and Manolete began to clap, causing the others to join in readily.

With a flourish Gus performed his best bullfighting veronica move. He finished with his hands poised over his head. "Olé!" Everyone cheered.

Clearly delighted with him, Patricia lifted her wine glass. "Do we have a novice in our midst?"

A glass of whisky waited for Gus at his seat. "I've dreamed about being a matador since I was a little boy. Even after I saw a bull plunge his horn into a man's side. I was seven, I think." His stomach flipped as if to ask, shall we replay the memory again? He ignored it.

Patricia leaned in. "What happened?"

He shrugged. "The bull came through and the matador made one mistake. Down he crumbled. Mi abuelo . . . " he trailed off.

"After you've shit your pants!" Manolete bellowed to his neighbor. "The close calls in the beginning feel that way, and being heroic is the last thing on your mind. More like staying alive. Gustavo! Why do you want to meet a raging bull?"

The question brought him back. He fantasized. "To look a bull in the eyes and feel the warm air from his snout, or his horn grazing my hip, I would feel like the most heroic man alive. I've imagined it's akin to dancing on a fire's flame."

"The fear, the victory, what could've happened, none of that is tangible until the attack is over. Survival, and surviving brilliantly: those are paramount in the moments before a kill."

"I must try it someday. I will."

"What do you fight, Gustavo? In this world we must all fight something," Manolete said.

Myself, Gus thought, but swiftly answered, "Injustice. Inequality." He glanced up at the people with a surprised look, as if he'd forgotten they sat there. "I'm sorry, I don't have stories filled with daggers, bulls, and swords; my courtroom tales are full of words spoken by *gringos* wearing fancy suits."

"And all the better for it!" Manolete boomed out. "My good man, these people hear of bulls so much it has turned into bullshit. See, they do not correct me," he smiled. "I use every move in the book to sidestep a bull, every spin and flick, while you rearrange nothing but words to stun and trick your opponent. You save lives and I end them. Who is the true hero?"

By night's end the two hugged and hung onto each other's shoulders in brotherly acceptance. An assistant entered the room with Manolete's cape and the matador stood to get the room's attention. "Gustavo, I want to give mi muleta to you for practice until you face your own bull. Until then, use it to distract your courtroom bulls. Your call to action for equal rights is inspiring. Use your words and charm to take them by surprise so they cover you with wins as I am roses." He stood and bowed to Gus. "Look, I have made him speechless for the first time tonight!"

At the end of the night, Gus privately asked Patricia if she would like to continue their evening elsewhere, and she said that she would.

Gus dreamed of a crumbling bullfighting arena with sounds of people crying for help and a bull shrieking. Off to the side, a little girl repeatedly crashed a wooden toy car into a matador figurine, but did so playfully without noticing the destruction in front of her. He awoke.

When he saw nothing familiar, a panicked sweat overtook him. A cheaply made bed jerked when he sat up, and it bumped a small table nearby. An empty bottle of wine clattered to the floor.

Patricia's head appeared around a doorway Gus assumed to be the bathroom. "You're alive," she commented. "We drank too much."

"My head."

"Yes. It will be time for me to say adios soon. I hope we will meet again."

He fell back to the bed and closed his eyes. "It smells like a burly animal in here. Surely that isn't me?" Suddenly he felt the weight of something soft and heavy drop on top of him that brought an awful stink with it.

"Don't you remember?" She giggled.

Suddenly, he did. "Manolete's muleta!" Gus jumped out of bed and attempted to whirl it about, but no matter which way it landed the weighty folds fell at his feet and gathered like a curtain. He marveled at the cloth, fingering one of the larger rips in the cape. "A bull's horn tore through this!"

"Is it heavier than you expected?"

"Very much so. Majestic." He closed his eyes and imagined a quiet arena waiting for him to begin. He mimicked the stance and began practicing the veronica he'd performed from the night before and tripped into the folds. As he fell, blips of memory returned to him. He recalled himself undressing Patricia and seeing her lean body highlighted by the bathroom light. She thrilled him when she woke him for more. He thought of La Villa, Manolete, the wine and whisky, and something else, what was it? Something, something pulling at him insistently, deep from his stomach.

He took in their surroundings. Darkly stained wooden slats covered the floor and walls. A familiar-looking bed from deep in his past. The silly attempt at an end table. "Where are we? I know this place . . . don't I? How do I? How did we get here?"

"You didn't black out, did you? Maybe you did." Patricia sighed. "We found a bar to drink more, and you paid the bartender to let us take that bottle with us. You led me here as if you'd been here before."

"Hotel Evitarse." The moment the words came out of his mouth the pit returned. He looked at her, shocked. "Evitarse is where mi abuelo and I would stay on long bullfighting days. He would drive hours from Laredo and then drink too much."

"Tell me more," she begged.

"I can't remember, it's fuzzy. Which is funny, because they're some of the best memories I have of him." Gus blinked at the bed and saw his child self with legs dangling from the bedside, waiting for Abuelo to wake up from his stupor. "I did mention last night about seeing a matador injured at my first fight."

"I noticed you went quiet."

He shook his head. "I always thought that moment to be traumatic because I saw someone get hurt, badly. But now I remember it became traumatic because mi abuelo wasn't there when I needed him . . . " A flash of a yellow ribbon woven into a brunette braid offered a plausible answer. "I think he was with a woman . . . " He went silent for several minutes.

Patricia nudged him and nodded toward the cape. "That does smell something awful. In some places worse than others."

Gus straightened his back. "I do not want to talk about mi abuelo. Tell me about your cape. What does it look like? What does it feel like?"

She exhaled loudly. "It's sad, but I don't have enough money yet for a real muleta like Manolete's, mine isn't even a cape. It's a blanket of my grandfather's," she said. "My muleta is a blanket he used in World War I."

Gus gasped. "How absolutely splendid. Miss McCormick, with every moment we spend together, you become more intriguing."

She rewarded him with a kiss. "What's your cape equivalent?"

He thought for a moment. "My clothes. My words? Both. My suits give me confidence and I'm judged by them before my mouth makes a move. My words keep them moving and distracted though, like muletas are meant to do."

She glanced at the sun through their window. "The time is quickly approaching for me to depart. Now listen, if you'd like, I could leave a number for me back in Texas. Unless you like meeting on foreign ground."

"Mexico isn't foreign to me. Which is why I'd like that very much." He watched her dress and fought back the urge to coax her into staying. "Is it plausible for a non-matador to be put in a practice ring with a bull? Or would I have to engage in months of practice for it to be possible?"

She shrugged. "Depends on how far you want to go."

"I desperately want nothing more than to whip a muleta around and catch the attention of a bull. But in all actuality, I want to feel the rush of air go past me as a bull runs by."

"We'll see." She leaned in to kiss him, and he pulled her back for another.

"A rarity is quite the perfect word to describe you."

As she exited he quickly discovered how unprepared he was to be alone. The solitude awaiting him on his drive home seemed endless. Herrera's news popped into his head. *Some LULAC men approached me about running for national president next summer, and I'm tossing the idea around. Your thoughts?* Gus groaned.

His thoughts ran rampant. Johnny would make a good president, but why not ask him, too? Did they find something wrong with the way he presented himself to LULAC? Gus knew he would ultimately be the one lacking, but he couldn't help asking such questions.

Jealousy clutched him. *First, Johnny opens his own firm,* Gus thought, *and now he wants to run for national LULAC office. The gall!*

Ironic enough, it was Herrera's words that came to him.

Don't dwell.

He decided the time had arrived to get home to business.

Gus dressed and gathered what few things he brought with him, including Manolete's muleta. He headed downstairs, hoping he'd run into Roberto, the owner who opened the hotel in the 1920s. Mateo taught Gus to see Roberto as family, and it caught on quickly.

As he neared the desk, sure enough, he could see the top of a man's head, but instead of the black hair he remembered, the fringe of this man's hair was graying, and behind the periodical that blocked the reader's face Gus could see his bald spot. The man lowered his paper to reveal a pair of black plastic eyeglasses. It was the same face, but aged.

"Roberto! Buenos días! Are those glasses on your head?"

Roberto pulled his glasses down a touch and stared for a moment. "No. No! Gustavo? I know that voice . . . my eyes do not lie! How can I forget that face?"

Gus embraced him. "I hoped to see you before I left," he said, then lowered his voice, "once I remembered where I'd spent the night." He glimpsed the hotel's side lobby in the corner of his eye, and it became hard to catch his breath.

Roberto laughed and returned the hug. "Some things never change, do they? Turn around, let me look at you. Ah, Mateo would be so proud."

"I hope so." Gus pulled his wallet out of his back pocket and cracked it open to reveal a handful of dollar bills. "I don't have much, but how much do I owe you?"

"Nada, mijo, don't worry about the money. You are a son to me." He leaned forward and whispered. "That woman who came down the stairs, that was the famous bullfighter, sí?"

"Patricia McCormick," Gus said proudly, "the world's first, and currently only, female matador."

"I thought so." Roberto removed his glasses and closed his eyes in serenity to the sky. "Gustavo, the way she walked down the stairs, so graceful and strong, I will never forget it. If you bring her here again, tell me so I can see her float down my stairs in the morning, that will be payment enough." He sighed. "A 1930s beauty, no?"

"Plus, she tousles with bulls! One must be the ultimate man to be with her." Gus shook his head. "I am eclipsed."

"Ah, so that's why you're attracted to her . . ."

"One of the reasons," he winked. "Regal yet rough: it's a new concept to me. I don't know how far I'll be able to get with her, but we'll see. We only met yesterday."

"Off to a great start, you old dog. It is I who feels in debt to you now." Roberto sighed. "I can barely imagine what it'd be like to stand beside her, much less," he swayed slowly, "*dance* with her."

"Sí, but breathtaking looks cannot pay the bills. You would be the perfect example." Gus pulled out four dollar bills and rolled them tightly until they resembled a cigarette. On the counter, a slender pen holder carrying a few pens caught his eye, and he slipped the money roll inside. The bills flared out underneath the lip of the holder. "There! I know it will take some time to get that out, and by then I'll be gone."

Roberto shook his head and looked down into the pen holder. "No, mijo, you bring her around the next time you visit and I will be a rich man. You don't have money coming out of your eyeballs, I know that. Fish that money out and take it with you."

Gus pretended to ignore him by glancing the other way and used the opportunity to glance into the lobby once more. "As far as I know, Patricia and I were your only patrons last night. If one were a lawyer it could be deduced that your business is failing."

"You stop! We've been around since before you were born, business will always be fine. Besides, I'm aging too quickly these days. My eyesight is leaving me, my back goes out every month, and I wonder what will fall apart next." He winked at Gus. "Maybe the next time you visit your lady friend should bring me a friend, too. Or you could share."

"Who's the dog now!" Gus brought his face in towards Roberto's. "I will be the only bull in her pen when I'm in her presence. If I cannot be found, I bid you good luck."

"You know a woman like her wouldn't notice a man like me." A wistful expression came across his face. "Think if Mateo was still alive, would she wave her muleta at him?"

"Ah, sí, if Patricia hadn't invited me to dinner, mi abuelo would've been victorious, no matter his age. With his rugged looks beside my clean-cut image she would've undoubtedly chosen him first. He embodied the ultimate manly man." He took another look at the lobby again.

Roberto tilted his head. "Have you thought about him lately?"

Gus smiled miserably. "Why do you think I'm here?"

"Aye, mijo. These things are hard. I remember the last time you were here, I didn't think you'd ever come back to life again."

Gus wondered what he meant by that. "I came here to clear my head and be with the bulls, but I'm leaving with my head more full than when I arrived. I didn't expect that. Everything feels so unfinished, and I'm not quite sure why." Gus glanced around. "Let me be honest, it's actually making me a bit paranoid."

"You're more like Mateo than you realize." He patted his hand. "I hope you're dealing with things. Will you visit me a little sooner next time? It's been two decades."

"No, it hasn't been that long. Ten at the most." He winked.

"How quickly we forget," Roberto mused. "Hey, I thought I was the old one?" They laughed in unison. "I tell you what, I will accept your money. Every little bit helps."

"Good. I'll be sure to visit sooner next time."

Gus drove home thinking about Patricia and his uncertain future with Irene. An image of Lenora Hernandez crying in his office passed through his mind. What if she'd chosen a different lawyer's office? What if he hadn't read Irene's letter while Lenora sat in front of him and lamented about her son, would he have said yes so quickly?

The possibilities surrounding the Hernandez case opened up to him, and he daydreamed about making a name for himself by revealing new ways to fight in the courtroom. Surely, if he could execute an "improper representation" idea correctly, he would catch the attention of the state, possibly even higher up. The Supreme Court? Gus shivered at the thought and replayed Manolete's speech from the night before when he handed him his muleta.

He contemplated buying whisky on his drive home, but decided against it since his lengthy drive back to Texas had barely begun.

Once he arrived back in his San Antonio office, he noticed a brand-new bottle of Chivas Regal comfortably snuggled into the corner in front of the closed door. An unsigned note hung from the neck that said: *Have a drink on me.*

Without thinking further on it, Gus took this as a sign that a drink happened to be exactly what he needed.

CHAPTER 8

THE FRIDAY AFTER HIS RETURN, GUS CONVINCED JOHN TO MEET IN EDNA WITH him and Pete Hernandez, now their new client. John brought his assistant, James DeAnda, the lawyer who specialized in research at Herrera's firm. The three went with the goal of getting Pete's story and deciding how to move forward.

They waited in a small room until the sound of clanging handcuffs signaled them that Pete neared. Keys hit the other side of the door as it unlocked, and a guard escorted what looked like a limping Pete into the holding room and ordered him to sit down. The lawyers watched as the guard locked the chain of Pete's handcuffs to a fixture in the middle of a rectangular metal table they sat on the other side of.

Gus spoke first and introduced the room. As he did, he noticed Pete's body language: crossed arms, slouched posture, an arched eyebrow. This launched Gus into the task of making Pete comfortable using only words, a specialty in his arsenal he knew not everyone possessed. Within half an hour Pete started joking with the men. Another half hour passed and he opened up about what unfolded that night.

Pete's cousin nudged him out of the house to drink at Chinco's Tavern on the third of August, a Friday night. They joined other men they knew, all tired from a day of hard labor, who sat drinking at the bar. Joe Espinosa, a local, entered the bar looking for men who needed jobs, but became particular about who he asked.

Instead of merely passing over Pete, he teased him about his clubbed foot and how it made him physically weaker. One of the men, Henry Cruz, confronted Joe about why he didn't ask everyone if they wanted a job. Joe answered that only a few positions were open. He glanced at Pete and commented that naturally he wouldn't ask him because he walked in figure-eights, thus enraging Pete.

The two shouted at each other, and the tone changed when Joe asked whether Pete could please a woman. Pete threw a punch, and Henry stepped in and separated them. Pete walked home to retrieve his handgun, then he returned to the bar and found Joe still there. The two men exited the bar and fell into the argument again. Soon after, Pete shot Joe in the street, and police arrested him shortly after that. On early Saturday morning he was indicted hours before roosters crowed on farms.

Each lawyer listened intently, but took notes differently. James, ever the dutiful researcher, madly scribbled keywords on his notepad. The facts were most important to him. Gus hung onto Pete's every word and followed his facial expressions rather than taking notes. He used his mind to record his story, because emotion reigned supreme with Gus. All business, John used a mixture of their methods. He pulled out a tape recorder, allowing him to relax about the details and study Pete.

When Pete stopped talking, he looked back and forth at each lawyer as if following a tennis match. James stayed hunched over his notepad while John and Gus said nothing.

Pete filled the silence and assured the men they didn't want his case. He made direct eye contact with each one and expressed his absolute guilt and lack of remorse. James raised his head and looked at his superior. John cleared his throat, expecting Gus to fill in the blanks.

Gus stared at Pete, but said nothing, as if his soul hung elsewhere, despite John tugging at his jacket.

John explained to Pete the definition of a face case, the Fourteenth Amendment, and the lack of equal representation on the Jackson County jury. Pete rolled his eyes and expressed his indifference to the entire situation. John asked him if he understood, and Pete answered that he didn't care.

John asked Gus in passing why he didn't speak up. Gus said it suddenly felt like he'd lost the ability to speak, just for that moment. A cat got his tongue. A frog in his throat.

The truth he didn't admit: a seed of guilt sprouted within him while staring at Pete, something he couldn't explain. The tendrils of guilt grabbed hold of his soul and it became all he knew, and all he could feel.

The three agreed to have a drink in Edna after leaving Pete. No sign or marquee easily alerted the bar's location to patrons, only a small printed name on the door: Chinco's Tavern. Underneath the name hung a sign that said: Sprung's Grocery out back. Burnt grease and cigarette smoke met their noses as they entered. Three patrons sat in the bar.

John walked the perimeter of the room, inspecting the pictures in frames on the wall that hung among eggshell ceramic plates with colorfully painted flowers and birds on it. "James, what'll you have?"

Timidly, James glanced across the room to John. "Beer, whatever they carry."

"Don't worry, I don't bite! I'll get your beer, you find us seats." Gus stepped up to the bar and ordered the beer, a vodka, and a whisky, both neat. "Do you sell Chivas Regal?"

"No señor, we used to, but that is too expensive. We carry Philadelphia." The bartender, a young Mexican man with messy brown hair, lined up two glasses. "You three are dressed too nicely for a place like this! But no complaints, we need the business."

"Perfecto," Gus waved. He watched the young man pour and retrieve their drinks. "Do you like living here? How old are you?"

He pulled the bottles and poured. "Twenty-five. I'm saving to move up north. Somewhere the people are more accepting."

"Ever thought of San Antonio?"

The bartender's eyes brightened. "I have . . . what's it like?"

"Filled with culture, pride, and history. It's more integrated, and home of the Alamo. It's my hometown."

"Sí, señor. Do you need a tray for everything?"

"Sure, thank you," Gus held up a hand. "Why is Chinco's hurting for business?"

He shrugged. "Not making enough money."

Gus pressed on. "Is it because you aren't getting enough people in the door? Did something trigger this?"

"Cómo?" He retrieved a tray crusted with brown bits.

Gus stopped himself from correcting the man. "Is this where a man died recently?"

The man's eyes turned somber. "I'm not supposed to talk about it."

"Lo siento, señor," he placed a hand over his heart. "Were you here when it unfolded?"

The bartender shook his head and pushed the drink tray at him.

Gus delivered the tray to his fellow lawyers. They clinked glasses, but subdued moods reigned.

John spoke first. "So this is where it happened, huh?"

James chugged some of his beer. "That's what Pete said."

"The bartender verified it," Gus answered. "We should have dinner here."

The vibration of James's bottle hitting the table jarred the liquid in their glasses. "Why?"

"He just told me they haven't had any business in a week. Wonder why? They've lost money, and from the looks of this place, it's been happening for longer than just a week." Gus squinted at James, then John. "Where did you say you found him?"

James spoke up with a stronger voice. "I can answer that. The University of Texas, the same law school you graduated from, García."

"Earned his law degree last year on his first try, unlike me who took the bar seven times." John grinned widely. "Not that I'm proud of that."

"Well, well, well! I thought Johnny had picked himself up a dark-skinned white boy," Gus said, and swallowed some of his whisky. "With hazel eyes like those."

"I guess no more can be said of you, right?" James covered up his smile with the beer bottle. "Those green eyes."

"Thank the Lord, he has spunk, too. You are officially DeAnda now!" Gus smacked his lips and stuck out his tongue. "I've got to be honest, this whisky tastes like warm feet."

"You'd know how a pair of warm feet would taste in your mouth, wouldn't you, García?" John grinned.

"You know I would," he retorted, "in the trenches!" The men laughed. "Taste your vodka," Gus urged, "and tell me if it doesn't taste like an unfermented potato."

John sipped. "It's awful. Do we have to eat here?"

"Yes," Gus said. "No options." He went back to the bartender and asked for a menu, but was told they stopped making food after the shooting.

John nudged James. "Chug that. Finish your cerveza right now."

"I paid," Gus said, returning. "Let's go find something to eat."

They passed by a spot, Winn's Cafe, with a clearly posted sign that said: No Mexicans served. James scribbled in a notebook without a word. They parked at a place down the street named The Eatery, off Main

Street. Gus glanced in the direction of William's Pharmacy and Soda Shop, but said nothing.

A curly blonde-haired waitress met them at the door with menus and a thick southern accent. "Howdy boys, how y'all doing today? Take a seat where you like and I'll be with you in a sec. Call me Shannon."

John answered her. "Thank you, we will." They agreed on a table near the back of the restaurant.

Shannon returned with a hand-sized notepad and nubby pencil. "Haven't seen you fellas around here before," she began. "Y'all live in the county?"

"The chicken fried steak," John said. "With green beans and macaroni and cheese."

James chimed in, "The same."

"I'll have the steak with mashed potatoes and corn on the cob," Gus said. "Thank you, Shannon."

She frowned at her question not being answered, but collected their menus without asking again. "To drink?"

"Iced teas all around?" Gus asked. The men nodded.

"Sure thing." Shannon studied their clothing. "Day of working?"

"More like day of driving, huh boys?" John joked and nudged James's arm.

"Ugh, tell me about it," Shannon said. "I'm working a double. Where y'all work at?"

"Our offices," Gus winked at her.

Shannon scratched her head with her pencil point. "So you fellas new 'round here?"

"Nah," Gus placed his briefcase on their table. "Shannon, I don't mean to be rude, but we've got some things we need to discuss privately. Time is short. Do you mind?"

"No, no way. I'm sorry," she replied. "I'll go 'round the corner and put in your order, sounds good?"

"Sounds great," Gus said. "Thanks a heap."

Smiling sweetly, she left their table. They heard her call out their order and ding a bell shortly after.

"What do you think, Jimmy?" John glanced at Gus. "I call DeAnda Jimmy."

"I can do it," James said strongly.

"Jimmy, this time, we're really going to get after it. We've done all the work before. We know how this goes, we simply have to change names. We've got the stuff to move forward," John said. "So García! Aren't you glad Pete's mother didn't go to your little giant first?"

"Cadena." Gus cringed and let out a moan. Carlos had received the "little giant" nickname because of his small height and big achievements. "Lenora could've, she came in with a list of names in the San Antonio area and I'm sure Carlitos's name was on it."

John explained to James, "Naturally you've heard of Carlos Cadena. But did you know the two don't get along so famously?"

James tilted his head. "I thought you two had a firm," he said to Gus.

"For a short time," he replied, "and that's why you're lying, Johnny. It's not that we don't get along, it's that we don't work the same way, and we don't agree on much. It took us ages to agree on anything, but when we did, we were fire personified."

John scoffed. "I think given the chance, you two could do it again."

"Cadena and I cannot find much in common, but we get along great. I respect that man and what he can do, because it's not what I can do. Our personalities clash," Gus corrected himself again with a smirk. "He can't help but be the stick in the mud he is."

"I know you're going to hate hearing this, but I think we should ask someone else to be on board with us," John added. "We've got too much work on our plates."

"So you think it should be Cadena?" Gus's eyes widened. "Are you kidding me?"

Out of nowhere, Shannon appeared with drinks. "Here ya go, iced teas all around. Food will be out in a few minutes." She narrowed her eyes at them before exiting.

All of them noticed.

"Carlos is well-known for his thorough arguments," James timidly reminded him.

Gus blew a raspberry into the air as Shannon walked away.

"DeAnda and I plan to stay overnight so we can gather research on the county. He's made a plan of attack," John said.

"Wonderful," Gus responded, sipping his tea and looking around. "I'm hungry."

Six men walked into The Eatery—a suit, three overalls, and two policemen—and Shannon pointed them to the trio in the back room.

"She didn't 'howdy' anyone," James quietly commented, then cursed. "We gotta go."

"Too late," Gus whispered.

One by one, the men filed into the room, frowning. "Gentlemen," Gus acknowledged. "How are we this evening?" He stood. John and James quickly followed his lead.

An overalled man answered, "We'd be better if we knew why you three were harassing Shannon."

"Did Shannon tell you we harassed her? *Shannon*," Gus chided, "I hoped you were better than that. My, we minded our business. Actually, I recall myself asking *her* to let us mind our own business."

A policeman spoke up. "What business could that be? You three were seen leaving our courthouse earlier today," he accused.

"We were doing our job," John said indignantly. "Are Mexican men in suits a rarity around here? Do they plague your town often? Is this a rampant problem here?"

"You never know," said another overalled man. "That's why we stay on top of things. Playing it safe."

"Good for Shannon," Gus said.

"Bad for you," the third overalled man shot back.

The other policeman stepped forward. "Look, we don't want to cause any trouble . . . "

"Neither do we," James spoke up.

"Kindly speaking," the policeman went on, "we figure it best you all mosey on home now. Just so you're not on the road when it gets dark. Shannon will prepare your food to go."

Gus smirked at him. "I don't think so, you can keep your food. I'm not going to wonder if the cook dosed us a serving of rat poisoning. How about you boys go home and we'll do the same?"

The policemen waited on the sidewalk and waved to them as they drove away.

Gus drove around the block and waited until John and James joined him. "You two still going to stay here tonight?"

"I think we all know the answer to that," John said with sarcasm.

"Did anyone treat you this way when you first visited?"

"Nope, but they denied some service to a couple of Mexican sisters," he admitted. "I didn't hang around long enough to see how they felt about me. In numbers, we're more powerful . . . and we can use this to our advantage," Gus stated, thinking about the sisters in their red and asparagus-green dresses.

"Money will go quickly if we drive back and forth from Houston every day. But I'm not staying in this town overnight. Who knows what could happen to us if we stick around?" John pointed out.

"It's worth it," Gus stated. "Justice is screaming to be found in this town, and if not justice, at least equal recognition. We must fight, we must push back. Whatever we need to do is worth it."

With no more than a look, the three understood what they must do in order to get what they were looking for.

CHAPTER 9

DONOVAN STOOD IN THE LISBON HOUSE QUIETLY REMINDING HIMSELF WHY HE donned a bespoke suit that night: Gus. If not for him, the night would be nothing more than another party at a monumental home to celebrate something equally monumental. Donovan said yes to the UT Law reunion party because a Symmetry source reported it the moment when Gus called in his RSVP.

Donovan received his Drambuie from the bar and turned toward the door. He waved at Preston Armstrong, who had just entered the party. As Donovan waved, the person he least expected to walk in next, did. Gus appeared directly behind Preston and thinking the wave for him, waved back innocently.

Gus dressed in a navy blue overcoat with a matching fedora he spun on two fingers. Underneath he wore a navy houndstooth suit and a starched white button-up. After he handed his outerwear to a butler, he walked up to Donovan without pause.

"Good ol' Kincaid, is that you?" Gus stepped forward to give him a hug, but Donovan didn't lean in, sticking his hand out instead. "I thought you might act that way," he said. "Ah yes, Chivas, neat," he requested from a nearby serving girl.

"Gus, good to see you," Donovan said, unable to make his voice warm and inviting.

"I suppose we don't have to hug," Gus said. "Let's break the ice so we can move on. What have you been up to? I heard you work in the office that can get us all in trouble," he joked.

"Well, one can try." His entire body tightened as he squinted at Gus. "Why are *you* here?"

"I should ask you the same thing." He accepted his drink gratefully.

"I live in Austin; you don't."

"Yes, well, aren't we being prickly?" Gus smiled with a raised eyebrow as he took a sip. "I'm embarking on a new case and need all the advice I can get, and help, if I can get it."

At that, Donovan's body deflated, as if a needle pricked his skin. He wasn't there to settle a score, he was there for his future. If success came early, he wouldn't have to work as hard, he knew that. Preston walked through the room and gave him a penetrating look. "Ah, yes." Donovan sipped his Drambuie and abruptly changed his demeanor. "I'm here to provide some if you need some."

Gus's eyes turned to slits. "I'm not looking for opinions from the likes of you, especially with the way you welcomed me moments ago."

"Not even if it had to do with large amounts of money?"

He froze for an instant. "Mention money and it always catches my attention." Gus adjusted his tie, a mosaic of light green-shaded tiles in varied tones.

"It's important to men who have none." Donovan's blue eyes grayed for a moment before coming to reality. "Apologies. That's something my father used to say when someone in his circle said what you just said."

"Ah, condescending men speaking to greedy men," Gus said.

He laughed. "You're not wrong. Actually," he cleared his throat and glanced up surreptitiously. "I'm here to offer you a way to make you and your family comfortable."

"What is this, a trick?" He looked from side to side.

Donovan shook his head and kept going. "Why do you practice law? To help others? To provide for your family? Or simply, for the money?"

Astounded, Gus covered his open mouth with a hand. "Do you hear yourself? Let's skip ahead. You want me to abandon the Hernandez family and give this case to you, or who? Who do you work for? What's your endgame here?"

"You'd be guiding the Hernandez family to someone who can offer more options." He held up two fingers. "Both them and your family will be taken care of." He saw consideration in Gus's face, but it quickly dropped away. The feeling was delicious, Donovan realized, offering bribes to mold a situation into his liking, and then to watch his nemesis actually consider it. "Anything they need."

Gus frowned.

"Hello, guys," a voice announced. "How are we doing this evening?"

They turned to see Otis Milner, an old classmate of theirs, standing before them. Otis talked with a nasal voice, like he'd clipped his nose with a clothespin and never removed it. His specialties were butting into business uninvited and asking slightly shocking questions while staying blissfully ignorant of reality. He held a mug full of foamy beer.

Though both men went quiet when they heard his voice, neither went so far as to abandon the other alone with Otis. Gus spoke first. "How the hell are you?"

Otis turned his nose up toward the main room. "Trying to decide whether I made a good decision in coming here."

"Surely the answer is yes, amigo," Gus said loudly. "We get to see each other again!"

"Have either of you attended one of these parties? I wonder if any behind-the-scene deals are made at parties like these," Otis wondered out loud. His eyes widened when he looked at Donovan. "Maybe I shouldn't be asking in front of you, being that you work at a complaint office."

"What, you mean hiding in plain sight?" Donovan laughed off the comment.

"Oh, who cares? Why else attend a get-together like this?" Gus answered, eyeing Donovan.

Otis shrugged. "That's why I'm here, to see what I can catch, whether it's money or information to get money. When you start your own firm, it goes quickly."

Donovan nodded enthusiastically. "Does it? Tell us more. Gus here just mentioned starting his own firm would be the tops."

Gus glared at him.

"You should!" Otis grinned. "But make sure you rob a bank first. I tell you, the secretary's salary alone, not to mention incidentals around the office that need care. It can be a money pit." He produced a card from his coat pocket. "Take it, call me if you need any guidance." Jokingly, he said, "And let me know if anyone needs a hit man. I've got some wheeling and dealing to be done."

"Don't we all," Gus said.

"Is that Carlos Cadena I see over in the corner by the baby grand piano?" Donovan pointed across the room. "He's probably doing better than all of us."

"He's definitely smarter than all of us," Gus commented.

"You guys are too funny," Otis said. "I'm going to tell him hello, and I'll let you get back to whatever you two were talking about. Good to see you both!"

Gus's glare returned when he turned away. "Tell me exactly what you're willing to do and who you're willing to do it for."

"We all know you would sell your mother's house if it meant lifting your station in life, and that's why I'm choosing to talk to you. You don't have to worry about Pete Hernandez if you say yes. Your girls don't have to worry where their new dresses are coming from, or how full their bellies will be after dinner. The money I offer can take care of all of it. Someone more qualified will take over with supreme colors." Donovan used his last missile. "Besides, I heard you've been tossing around the idea of leaving the San Antonio school board. If you give up the case you probably wouldn't have to do that, don't you think?"

"You are a coward," Gus leaned in, "trying to filch a case for your father, I'm sure, because you don't have enough in your pants to start one on your own." He leaned in further and lowered his voice. "You haven't changed one bit. Don't think I don't know why you accosted me here instead of at my office, or even on the damn street. You waited to be surrounded so I wouldn't give you an uppercut."

Donovan couldn't hide his smirk, but also couldn't deny the truth. "You've just arrived, so we'll wait until you drink a few and then I'm sure you'd punch me either way."

"You know what, Kincaid? You couldn't have appeared at a more perfect time." He smiled one hundred watts worth. "I've been doubting myself. Asking myself: do I have the chops, the staying power? Am I worthy of taking this case to a higher level without it ruining me? What if given the opportunity to quit, what would I do?" He downed his Chivas. "Then you come along and change it all. This little charade you acted out tells me everything I need to know, and renewed faith in myself."

"Tell me how you really feel," Donovan snarked.

"Don't mind if I do. This case will turn heads, and make your people take notice. It will make me who I am, and you can't do anything about it."

"I think you should take your deal and shove it up your ass. Is that too honest? Take the insecurities bubbling through you right now and let my 'no' amplify them to a decibel level you can't ignore," Gus said triumphantly. "I know that part hasn't changed about you, Kincaid, I know you still jump at your own piss stream. I ought to knee you in the stomach right here, just for the fun of it."

"Don't." Donovan focused on a man standing close by with his back toward them: it was Preston. He'd heard everything. A pink-red blush took over his entire face and body, and he threw back his Drambuie. Had he heard everything? Would he tell the Symmetry board? His anxiety took over so strongly he didn't speak or move when Gus walked away.

Donovan wanted to shove Gus right then and there: all of their bad blood resurfaced when Gus denied him. The men had been friends in college, but their divide began when each started dating a woman named Eileen without knowledge of the other. Donovan fell hard for Eileen. Within the first few dates he dreamt about a future with her, and even purchased an engagement ring. But Gus was the first to learn she'd been juggling the two of them, and wooed her into sleeping with him. Then he mentioned to Donovan in passing "how hard it must've been for Eileen to make a decision between the two." Trying not to seem caught off guard, Donovan agreed, although he was shocked and upset he hadn't received the same attention from Eileen. He demanded she sleep with him. She denied Donovan publicly, broke his heart, and went back to Gus. To make matters worse, she and Gus split soon after that, which angered Donovan further. His charmed life hadn't prepared him for this. How could Eileen have tossed him aside so nonchalantly? How could his friend do the same? He vowed to himself that day he'd never be bested again, by women or men.

A voice brought him back to the present. "Sir."

He swerved around to see Kiana standing in front of him, lovely Kiana, wearing a facsimile of the maid's outfit she wore for the Kincaid manor. Donovan thought she'd never looked so warm and inviting, with her small smile and that irrepressible look in her mocha-colored eyes.

"Kiana." He exhaled.

"At your service," she curtsied.

"What are you doing here?" He held up a hand. "Don't answer that, I'm sure the Lisbon offered you a great deal of money to be here tonight. Unless my father paid you to follow me around and pick me up when I'm feeling down."

She blushed and curtsied again. "If he did, I wouldn't be wearing this uniform."

He exhaled again. "You are a sight to see. My dear, tell me this one thing: why are you always present at the worst parts of my day? Is it you bringing me the bad luck I encounter?"

Kiana lowered her head to look at the ground. "I don't like to think of it that way, Mister Donovan."

"Oh, you don't, do you? In what way do you like to think about it?"

"It's not my intention to look like I'm stalking you," she said quietly. "I think God put me here tonight so I can pick you up, sir."

"Kiana, I could pick you up right here and take you to my home."

She nodded daintily and scurried away. In that moment he searched for Preston and noticed he was nowhere to be found.

CHAPTER 10

AFTER HIS ENCOUNTER WITH DONOVAN, GUS DROVE BACK TO SAN ANTONIO AND visited his touchtone, his wife.

Her warm amber-brown eyes met his when she swung the door open, and his heart leapt at the sight of her. Irene. He wanted to drop to his knees, but resisted for fear of her thinking him pathetic. Her soft hair tumbled far past her shoulders in thick luxurious curls. Gus thought her the epitome of a woman and kicked himself for not coming home more often.

Irene welcomed him into their home. To his surprise, she didn't treat him as if she wanted him to become her ex-husband. He'd expected her to turn him away. Instead, she welcomed him.

"I don't think I can do it," Gus pouted. "This is too much pressure, I don't think I'm equipped to handle it." He gave her puppy dog eyes.

"Do what? Come in, sit down. Is that smell beer or liquor?"

"It's not much, I drove in from Austin just now."

"Aye, Gustavo."

She did what she always had—let his head languish gently on her lap while he vented. He told her about Lenora and her son Pete, about Edna and the Cruz sisters, and lastly, about Donovan's offer. "I didn't know things like that happened, I thought they only happened in the movies."

"If they think it's okay to bully you or anybody out of a restaurant, that's just the behavior you're trying to shine a light on, isn't it? This is the kind of stuff you've been training for, but you tend to get into your head, you know this." Irene sighed and looked down at him, her hair falling into his face. "You're more vulnerable when you drink in front of rich, snobby gringos."

Gus shot up and a pillow tumbled to the linoleum. "I resent that comment: I object. We were at a party, for heaven's sake." He thought of Otis and his comment about looking for under-the-table deals. "You notice that level of vulnerability?"

"I can always tell." She smiled without malice and with warmth that warmed him through. "You can object all you want, but this is not a courtroom . . . if it was, we're definitely arguing the wrong case."

"This isn't funny," he said obstinately. "My ass is on the line. I've not fought a murder case before. Nor can I go so far as to turn it on its head. That's what Johnny and James did with Aniceto. They should be leading this case, not me."

"Whose office did the mother visit?"

He buried his face in his hands. "Yes, okay, yes, but that doesn't have anything to do with anything. I have a race of people on my back. If I screw up, it means more than a fail for our counsel. If I screw up, it will suggest that anyone with brown skin is inept, that we don't belong in a society of our choosing. They'll all say we don't deserve equality."

Irene turned to him, allowing a wavy brown lock to fall over one eye like a curtain. It was a perfect half-moon of loveliness to Gus. He wished to shrink himself and use her curl like a hammock to hang in. Instantly his fears would dissipate, he knew it without a doubt. If only she would love him back. Her smile, the perfect almond shape of her eyes, all of her features were grace notes to her beauty.

"Gustavo," she said in a low voice. "Stop looking at me like that. I can see the love on your face, in your eyes, but that is not why I let you inside our house."

He inched himself closer to her on their couch and cupped her cheek in his hand. "I miss you. I miss the girls." He dared to say more, but held back. His hand stayed on her cheek.

Irene melted into his palm, but he saw it when she stopped herself. She looked down at her lap, but didn't disconnect from his hand. "My love, you are on a path, and you and I are both unsure where it will lead, but I think it is your destiny. If you're going to fail like you say, do you think the girls and I could go through watching you rip yourself into pieces again?" She cupped his cheek in her hand. "You do not handle failure well, but think of this. What if you succeed beyond your wildest dreams, will you be able to handle that? Would you be ready to lead us to the top, even if it meant tumbling down sooner or later?"

"If you stayed beside me to be my support, I could do anything," Gus pleaded. He grabbed her hand desperately, petting it wildly. "I just need someone to tell me it's going to be okay."

"It *is* going to be okay, but you have to learn how to do that for yourself," Irene said. "I've been your support through it all, and you've repaid me by missing dinners, our daughter's recitals, and the sight of a pristine pillow telling me you never arrived home from the night before." She took his hand and kissed it with honest love.

Gus reciprocated.

"Your grandfather will never leave your side. Mateo is cheering you on forever to be the bull in the courtroom. You hear his voice, don't you?" She couldn't help but laugh from the memory. "Mateo and his devil's advocate voice," she shook her head and smiled, "always doubting, always wanting proof of life. You are more than everything he ever wanted you to be." She nudged him playfully. "Do you feel him?" She nudged him again. "He's wondering why you're behaving like a scared spectator at his first bullfight, and that's no way to act like a matador *or* a bull." Another nudge.

Gus lifted his chin bravely, the way he did at his first bullfight. "I suppose I have nothing to lose." A flash of the little girl with the wooden toy car and the matador figurine passed through his mind, but he said nothing.

"Exactly."

When he launched forward to kiss Irene, she didn't back away. They shared a sweetness in their kiss with the tickle of a burned-out flame, but her eyes didn't convey the bedroom vibe he strove for.

She thumbed out to the back room. "I set out some of your best suits, assuming you will probably want to take it all. You need clothes, don't you? It's been awhile."

Gus's eyes rimmed with tears. "See, this is what I'm talking about. You take care of me; you fill in the gaps."

"I will always take care of you, this will never change. I'm not going to leave you behind in that respect," Irene kissed him once more, just a peck. "When you look in the mirror, know all my guardian angels are with you, and all of our leaders with spirits as golden as the sun. I am a part of you, and you a part of me, but we need to be apart right now."

"I understand," he lied, and leaned in closer.

When he gently separated a skein of her hair from an eyelash, Irene allowed her husband to kiss her one last time. They kissed, nuzzled, and whispered to each other for a few minutes, but she stopped it.

He knew his drinking increased the chance she would say no, but he was aroused, and suspended himself in the moment as long as he could.

He mumbled her words in a continuous loop the entire drive to his office. *We'll be a part of each other forever, but you and I need to be apart right now.*

At first he was unbothered by her rebuff, but the more he ruminated, the more it morphed into a full-on rejection. One minute he blamed her by letting it go too far; the next minute he angled the blame at himself for pushing too hard.

Why did she have to be so breathtaking? And sweet, diplomatic, why be these things? Gus wished she'd been caustic with biting words and bullets shooting from her eyes. On the way home he fed off ferocious emotions like a hot meal. Emotional support without physical intimacy was a foreign concept to him.

No matter which way he turned, a wall of self-doubt hit him hard and square in the jaw, thwarting his determination. If it wasn't Irene, it was Donovan's offer, the case, and Pete. He found so many reasons to drink. He thought of the men's faces in The Eatery, the disgust and fear melded together to make anger personified. Did he have enough courage to weather hateful behavior like that? How should he and his colleagues respond? Submissive with heads down, or stand up and fight back? Doubt flooded him as he headed toward his office building.

As he neared he noticed something leaning on his door. It didn't take long for him to recognize the object: a Chivas Regal bottle and a note. Gus believed God reached down and delivered him exactly what he must've needed when he needed it the most.

Many drinks came quickly after that, not to mention the second guesses, the voices Gus learned not to trust. It started with Irene first. He whispered her name out loud and it strummed his heart with a painful flat note. He recalled her anger, and he moved on to Patricia's memory, fishing for clear images. Would he see her again?

He thought of Pete. His time and work for the case could lead to eternal and satisfying results. He could be the hero of Edna's Mexican people, at least for a short time. Distractions must be at a minimum, and obsessive work at a maximum. "Keep an eye on the drinking," he said to the mirror.

"No problem," he answered himself.

His mind roamed and ended up on Donovan. The offer of a blank check danced in front of him, but the curiosity about why he offered it tickled annoyingly in his ear like a feather. Gus poured himself another drink and wondered what it would be like to have money to throw away, which quickly led to what it would be like to be accepted as an Anglo-American, and not a Latino in a white race.

He'd experienced that sort of acceptance before—due to his skin color—and held onto it as long as he could. His abuelo correctly called it a camouflage, a gift and a weapon, because the moment others viewed his name on paper, the acceptance disappeared. He struggled with being "just another white guy" when he allowed others to assume his heritage, then was still treated as an invisible when he chose to reveal his true colors. Gus always made sure to point out the "C" in his name stood for Charles, and not Carlos, as if the explanation accounted for his pale skin.

Gus saw the law in an artistic way. Just like one would dance, sing, write, play an instrument, or produce art: in order to execute accurately and beautifully, he needed the luxury of concentrating without outward stimuli. For his work to be present, true, and passionate, he found it difficult to be present in other capacities.

Willing to sacrifice it all to get to the top, he saw no turning back. This reminder renewed him: he'd promised he'd get to the top even if it killed him.

The next morning he woke up on his office couch, having used Manolete's muleta as a blanket, and he stank like a bull. When he finally wandered outside to his car, he found the front end ruined with a huge dent. It appeared that the car had run into the fire hydrant near his building.

Gus pieced memories from the previous night together and remembered thinking it would be a grand idea to take out his car. A woman's voice loudly refusing to sleep on his office couch rang in his ear, someone he tried to sleep with, and he recalled putting her in a taxi. Shame ran through him like tiny pricks on his skin.

He found the anonymously gifted Chivas bottle under his desk.

Less than half of it remained.

CHAPTER 11

ON THE MORNING OF THE PRE-TRIAL GUS DRESSED IN A PITCH-BLACK TAILORED twill suit he specially ordered in San Antonio. "As black as your hair," the tailor's daughter guaranteed, and she added a skinny grass-green tie to match his eyes. The color reminded him of Amelia's asparagus-green dress and inspired him on his journey that day.

He arrived early with John and James to prepare, and as the minutes ticked down to the appointed time, they decided to find a public bathroom in the courthouse square. They encountered a janitor who pointed them toward a set of stairs. "Abajo," he said, and held up one finger. "One flight."

Their dress shoes clicked on the linoleum floor toward the bathroom. Upon entering, they noticed two toilets, one considerably more grimy than the other. A sign, constructed out of a torn cardboard box flap, balanced against a cement block beside the dirtier toilet. It read: Colored Men, Hombres Aqui. Both John and James stood dumbfounded looking at each other, then at the sign.

"Do my eyes deceive me?" John asked out loud.

"My God," James said, "who would've left this out?"

Both men were furious, but not Gus. He yelped with glee, picked up the sign and lifted it up high. "Everyone spent so much time removing all the 'No Mexicans allowed' signs around town they forgot to check inside their own home." He smiled. "We're going to use this to our advantage. But first, I still have to take a piss."

John knew Gus well, and anticipated his next move. "Please don't steal the sign."

Gus ignored him. "What we're seeing here is meant to be. They dole out servings of polite, subtle discrimination here, and it's ours to broadcast.

More than subtle, blatant. This is getting me fired up! Should I steal the sign?"

James shook his head. "How is it polite?"

"Has anyone been outright rude to us? Even at The Eatery, the men who asked us to leave did it politely. They didn't say they were going to hang us by our toenails, they simply said leaving was the right thing to do." Gus zipped up his pants. "But I saw a pair of sisters denied service because of one's skin color. It shouldn't be happening."

When they returned, they found Lenora waiting for them and praying, a glass-beaded rosary that dangled from one hand. "What do you think will happen here today?"

Gus took a step forward. "It should be me to tell you the ugly truth, and I'm sorry you have to hear it in this fashion." He placed a hand on hers. "This will be an arduous process that's only begun. This is more than about Pete or who he shot, although it is still that. This is about something much bigger."

Her eyes widened. "What do you mean this has nothing to do with mi Pedro?"

John raised his hand. "Allow me. When a jury is chosen, Gus will say it is not a jury of Pedro's peers. They're not putting Mexican Americans on juries all across Texas, just like here. They don't because the Fourteenth Amendment says the law protects African Americans and Caucasians alike, and we are considered to be in the white race. This is something we know to be untrue, because discrimination happens in this town."

James spoke up. "I've searched thirty years of jury records to find when the last Mexican American served. The results matched what I found out in Fort Bend County for the Aniceto Sanchez case: for the past three decades, not one Mexican American has sat on a jury."

"Then it will be up to our side," Gus chimed in, "the defendant's, to prove that Mexican Americans aren't treated equally. This is bigger than us or Pedro because we're fighting for our entire ethnicity. We deserve to be represented."

She shook her head. "That is not right, we are not white! We're not treated the same. I may not be smart, but I know they're crazy if they think that."

"No madame, we are not white," Gus said. "We know we're not, and we have to show them we won't back down until we are acknowledged rightly for who we are. We will fight all the way to the Supreme Court if that's what we're meant to do."

"Did you win this case in Fort Bend County?"

"We didn't win, but that's why we're fighting this case here in Jackson County," John answered. "They discriminate everywhere, so we're going to keep going until we win. They will hear us someday, and that's the only thing we can do, is keep chipping away at it."

Gus took a deep breath and nodded. "Chip, chip, chip away."

In his mentor role, John steered the research in the right direction when James hesitated. John couldn't find significant swaths of time to spend on the case because of other cases his firm was handling, but did write parts of the brief. They expected their first motion to fail, opening the way to present the equal recognition argument. Gus finished the brief and practiced his oral arguments. He committed facts to memory and sprinkled his presentation with dazzling words and persuasive sentences.

As they reentered the courthouse, Gus glanced across Main Street where he met Amelia and Delia. He vowed to represent for them. As he turned back around he noticed how much attention the three lawyers garnered. The eyes of the locals stretched out wide and curious, a behavior John and Gus had become accustomed to, but not yet James.

James whispered to John. "Why are they watching us so intently?"

"We are not a common sight," John said. "Educated Mexican men wearing nice suits. It's like when you see a freak at the circus…"

Gus blurted out, "Or a death on the side of the road. One continues to stare long past the acceptable time limit."

"We're museum objects," John continued.

"Nonsense!" Gus flashed rows of teeth. "I don't know about you two, but I'm a rare bird in captivity, one people travel for miles to see. There are no oddities here, only specialties," he said, and gestured from head to toe. He wanted nothing more than to officially present himself and his work antics to Edna. "If I had feathers I'd preen them."

"Be careful with your words, Gustavo," John warned. "Dramatic flair works, but too much and it loses power. Be assertive, not aggressive; deferential, not arrogant."

"I will be respectful, but I will not appear meek, I refuse to do that," Gus whispered. "I will piss on their fine line!"

"Oh sure, that's exactly what I meant," John said sarcastically, and glared at James, who cracked a smile. "Don't laugh at him, you'll only egg him on. He's like a child in that way."

Gus patted John's back. "Just joshing, hermano. Don't worry about me, you know I can handle myself when it matters."

Pete stoically waited for them at the assigned table, his hands cuffed together. Lenora took a seat in the row behind him, and occasionally reached out to squeeze his shoulder.

Lenora didn't pretend to hide the absolute fear that gripped her. She clasped a black embroidered shawl around her shoulders and continued praying her rosary, rolling each clear glass bead between her fingers. A stream of tears glistened on each cheek.

When they reached the front of the courtroom the lawyers hugged Lenora and nodded to Pete. Gus and John traded looks that said: let's do this.

Frank Martin, the district judge, entered and called the court to order. His face crinkled like paper when he spoke, and a pair of thin spectacles enlarged his eyes. He acknowledged the court before landing his attention on Pete and his lawyers. The judge's gaze turned into a gawk when it landed on Gus, who still wore his fedora.

Gus counted on this; he considered his act a sign of disrespect and simultaneous aesthetic presentation.

"You there, Mr. García," Judge Martin gestured. He lowered his head to see Gus without his eyeglasses. "You and your team, will you need a translator for today's hearings? I don't see a request for a translator on today's sheet." He spoke slow and measured, like one might speak to a foreigner still perfecting a new language.

This was something else Gus counted on. *Showtime*, he thought, and puffed out his chest, first removing his hat. "Your Honorable Judge Frank Martin," he said crisply, "my colleagues and I do not need to be using such a resource. But I ask you: will *you* be needing a translator for the hearings to follow?"

At this, the judge's posture hiked up as straight as a raised spike. He peeled his wire-rimmed glasses from his face and squinted his eyes into slits. "Excuse me? What did you say?"

"Sir," Gus said, speaking louder and slower. "Your Honor, if it's you who needs a translator, perhaps one of my colleagues can translate." In the corner of his eye he saw John's spine kink before springing straight.

"Well, well, well," the judge replied, "it's apparent you speak English, so what are you referring to? Are you asking if I need a translator for the Spanish speak?"

"Judge Martin, I assume you wouldn't understand our nuanced Spanish language, for you are indeed still trying to master your own," Gus continued. "Hence my reason for asking if *you're* the one in need of a translator."

John leaned over and whispered to James. "We're screwed."

The judge perked in his seat at Gus's suggestion. "Well, we speak the English language in this courtroom, and it appears we're adept at it, so I suppose we can move on."

He overruled the motion to quash the jury panel and the indictment, and Gus and John prepared to prove discrimination happened in Jackson County.

They argued that all people of Mexican or Latin descent were treated differently from people of Anglo descent. The lack of Mexican American representation on juries matched the pattern of black people deliberately left off the same jury selections, so Pete Hernandez wasn't judged by a jury of his peers in early August when he was arrested.

To begin, Gus questioned the people on the panel who indicted Pete and chose a jury, a total of eleven. They ranged from business owners, workers, and men and women who knew which citizens paid their poll taxes and owned land. Overall, each person stated that no discrimination occurred in the county, yet it became apparent that the court called people they knew for jury duty, because those people needed to be in good standing with the community and be known by others to be reliable. The interviews took two days.

Thus began the defendant's rebuttal, and Gus brought in his colleague as his first witness. He straightened his jacket and stepped forward. "What is your name?"

"John J. Herrera." He sat quietly wearing a standard gray flannel suit.

"Are you a member of the Texas Bar?"

"I am."

"Where do you practice?"

"I practice all over the state of Texas."

Gus turned toward the members of the public. "Mr. Herrera, I will ask you whether you examined a list that I handed you with some sixty-three names handed to me from the Edna Independent School District that showed the graduates for the 1951 term from the Edna High School. I will ask you whether you examined that list?"

"I did," John nodded, and lifted the list of names to show the court.

"Is Spanish your native tongue?"

"Yes, sir."

Gus pivoted to face John again. "Did you learn it simultaneously with English or before you learned English?"

"Before."

"At home, did you ordinarily speak Spanish?"

"Yes, sir."

"Will you say you are well-versed with the Spanish language?"

"Yes, I would say so."

"Are you bilingual?"

"Yes, and I can read and write both languages, too."

Gus took a few steps closer to John. "Are you familiar with surnames that can be considered Spanish or Hispanic?"

"Yes, I am."

"Names like Herrera, and so on?"

"Yes, sir."

"Did you find on that list of sixty-three graduates any Spanish names?"

"Yes, I did."

"How many?"

John looked down at the list. "Two."

"Do you recall what those names were?"

"One was Victor Rudriguez. I believe the last name was more or less misspelled. The correct spelling would be R-o-d-r-i-g-u-e-z. I believe on the list the last name was that. And the other name was Chris Rosa."

"You found no other Spanish names?"

"No, sir."

"During the noon recess I will ask you if you had occasion to go back here to a public privy, right in the back of the courthouse square?"

"Yes, sir." John sat up straighter in his seat.

"The one designated for men?"

"Yes, sir."

"Now, did you find one toilet there or more?" Gus turned to face the jury.

"I found two," John lifted two fingers.

"Did the one on the right have any lettering on it?"

"No, sir."

"Did the one on the left have any lettering on it?"

"Yes, it did."

"What did it have?"

John closed his eyes momentarily. "It had the lettering 'Colored Men,' and right under it there were two Spanish words."

"What were those words?"

"The first word was 'Hombres.'"

"What does that mean?"

"That means 'men.'"

"And the second one?"

"'Aquí,' meaning 'here.'"

"Right under the words 'Colored Men' was 'Hombres Aquí' in Spanish, which means, 'Men here'?"

"Yes, sir."

The district attorney and counsel for the state, Wayne Hartman, stood to cross-examine John. The two men measured each other with their eyes.

"What list was that you were talking about a while ago?"

"The list I believe Mr. Winstead gave to Mr. García and Mr. García handed to me," John answered.

Wayne lifted an eyebrow in confusion. "I am sorry. I did not understand."

"I think a gentleman by the name of Winstead handed it to Mr. García and Mr. García handed it to me." John gestured to Gus.

"What was the list supposed to be?"

"Reported to me as being the list of the last senior graduating class of the high school in Jackson County."

Wayne nodded. "And you state there were two Spanish names on that list?"

"Yes, sir. I should say there were only two names that could be interpreted as being from a Hispanic or Mexican origin. There might have been more. Of course, sometimes they inter-marry," John said.

"You are not undertaking to say that there were only two of those graduates of Latin American descent, but only two had Spanish names?"

"Yes, sir."

"And of course, you are not undertaking to say there was any discrimination against any other Latin American pupils so that they could not have graduated?"

"No, sir." John shook his head.

"You are just down here on a visit?" Wayne stepped closer to John.

"Yes, sir."

"There was not a lock on this unmarked door to the privy?"

"No, sir."

"It was open to the public?"

"They were both open to the public, yes, sir."

"And didn't it have on it, 'For Americans Only,' or 'For English Only,' or 'For Whites Only'?"

"No, sir. I assumed that's who it was meant for."

"Did you undertake to use either one of these toilets while you were down there?"

"I did feel like it, but the feeling went away when I saw the sign."

Wayne cocked his head to the side. "So you did not?"

"No, sir, I did not."

"But you are not telling the court you could not have used the unmarked toilet simply because your name is Herrera?"

"No, sir."

Wayne nodded and returned to his seat.

Gus stood and replaced Wayne's position on the floor. "Can you tell the court that you were invited to use the one on the right?"

"No, sir."

"And the one on the left that had the lettering 'Colored Men and Hombres Aquí,' did you see a sign that said 'For Whites Only,' or 'For English Only,' or 'For Americans Only'?

"No, sir."

"Only 'Colored Men' and 'Hombres Aquí'?"

"Yes, sir."

Judge Martin asked John to step down and return to his seat. Gus then called James as a witness, because he'd been handed the census roll for schools in the Edna Independent School District in Jackson County to look over. He testified the roll contained 1,184 names, and of those names, 211 included Spanish or Hispanic last names. He also testified a large number of names were crossed out, and though he didn't count them in the total number, he couldn't help but notice the majority of last names that were crossed out included Spanish or Hispanic last names.

Only eleven jurors had been chosen through special venire at the conclusion of the day on October ninth, a day after the case was set to begin. Twelve jurors showed up the following day, and just as quickly Gus moved to quash that jury as well, objecting to the method of choosing.

Gus spoke on his motion to quash the array. "Defendant further challenges the array of talesmen and moves that said array be quashed and that they be dismissed on the ground that by virtue of the fact that no person of Mexican descent or other Latin American origin was summoned as a talesman. This constitutes additional evidence of the custom, usage and practice in Jackson County, Texas, of discriminating against persons of Mexican descent, and of classing them as a group separate and apart from groups of other races or nation origins, and that by virtue of that fact, the defendant, who is a person of Mexican descent, is being deprived of his constitutional rights, particularly those guaranteed him by the Fourteenth Amendment of the United States Constitution. As additional support of this motion to establish the custom, usage and practice of discrimination against persons of Mexican descent in Jackson County, the defendant offers the witness, Mrs. Chris Rosa."

The court swore in a Mexican American woman in her thirties, wearing a tailored skirt and blazer in periwinkle blue lined in white. With confidence, she smiled at Judge Martin and the entire members of the public after she sat down. She crossed her white-gloved hands in her lap and waited for Gus to begin.

Gus returned her smile before beginning. "Your name is Pauline, correct?"

"Yes sir," she nodded.

"You are a resident of Edna?"

"For twenty years."

"Are you a native-born citizen of the United States?"

"In Victoria County, twenty miles on the other side of Victoria . . . McFaddin."

"Are you married to a resident of Edna?"

"Yes, sir," she looked out towards her husband and smiled again. "His name is Chris Rosa."

"Do you have any children?"

"I have three."

"What are their names?"

"Chris Rosa, Jr., Esther Rosa, Alfred Rosa."

"Their ages?"

"Chris is nineteen, Esther is seventeen, and Alfred is fourteen."

"In addition to your three children, you have an adopted child?"

"Yes, sir."

"What is her name and age?"

"Mary Elizabeth Rosa, eight months."

Gus took a few steps away from Pauline. "Are you the owner of land in this community?"

"Yes, sir."

"You own real estate?"

"Yes, sir."

"A café?"

"Yes, sir."

"Is this Chris Rosa the same Chris Rosa who graduated from high school in Edna this year?"

"Yes, sir."

"In June, 1951?"

"Yes, sir."

"You speak English fluently yourself?"

"Yes, sir."

"Did you teach your children English at home or not?"

"I have spoken English to them since they were babies."

"Did you teach them English before you taught them Spanish or not?"

"We taught them both. I usually talk English and Spanish," she said.

"I will ask you whether or not you attempted to enroll one or more of your children in the school in which only Anglo-Americans went?"

"I attempted to enroll Chris Jr. in that school, but they would not accept him."

"When you say 'they,' whom are you referring to?"

"I talked to Mr. Hays."

"Who was he?"

"He was the superintendent."

"What year was that approximately?"

"The first year he went to school."

"How old was he?" Gus began pacing slowly and intentionally on the courtroom floor.

"Six."

"I will ask you whether or not Chris spoke English at the time?"

"He did, very well," Pauline answered.

"Did you tell the superintendent your son spoke English?"

"I did."

Gus stopped pacing for a moment. "And what did he tell you?"

"He told me that they did not accept any Latin Americans in that school."

"Where did you send your boy to school instead?"

"I sent him to the Latin American school and to the Academy."

"Why?"

"Because I did not want my boy to go to school in one room for those four years."

"At that time you say the school consisted of one room and one teacher teaching four grades?"

"Yes, sir. The teacher was Miss Lucille Linberg."

"Mrs. Rosa, do you know approximately how many children were in that one-room schoolhouse?"

"No, I really don't."

"I will ask you, if you know, was the majority of the Latin American boys and girls enrolled in the first four grades?"

"Yes, sir."

"The majority of the Latin American children in Edna?"

"Yes, sir."

"Did you attempt to enroll any other of your children in that school?"

"The girl."

"What is her name?" Gus paced once more.

"Esther."

"How old was she?"

"She was six."

"How old is she now?"

"She is seventeen."

"What luck did you have with her?"

"They did not accept her either."

"Whom did you talk to?"

"I talked to Mr. Hays."

"He was still the superintendent?"

"Yes, sir."

"At that time did they still have a house for four grades?"

"Yes, sir."

"Now, were any particular difficulties involved in getting the children into this one-room schoolhouse?"

Wayne Hartman stood up. "I object. That is too general."

"I sustain the objection," Judge Martin said.

Gus continued. "Will you describe what the condition of this one-room schoolhouse was?"

Pauline sighed. "They did not have any conveniences inside the schoolhouse, and they have a wood stove in there, and when it rained the kids did not get into the school. The teacher usually dismissed them when it rained because the water was so bad they could not get into school."

"I see. Did the Edna Independent School District provide transportation for children of Mexican descent?"

"They did not have a ride. Those that came in the bus, they did not accept them."

"I did not understand you," Gus said.

"I mean they hauled them in the—"

"They made him ride on a separate trip from the Anglo-American children and did not let them ride together?"

"Yes, that is what I mean."

"Now, you say you talked to Mr. Hays about getting your daughter in? I will ask you whether or not your daughter spoke English?"

"She did."

"When you talked to Mr. Hays what did he say?"

"He just said they did not allow Latin American kids in the school and they had a separate school until they reached the fourth grade," Pauline answered.

"Do you recall when the school became a two-room schoolhouse?"

"I really don't, because from them on I never did try to send my children there."

"Now, did you send your daughter to Victoria?"

"Victoria Academy. That is a convent."

Gus nodded. "How far did she attend the Victoria Academy?"

"Until she was in the sixth grade."

"Did you then send her to school here?"

"Yes, sir."

"You mean to Edna?"

"Yes, sir."

"You say Mr. Hays told you Latin American children were not permitted to attend this same school with Anglo-American children?"

"Yes, sir. Mr. Hays told me Latin American kids were not allowed in the school until they were in the fourth grade."

"Do you know when the Latin American school was abolished?"

"No, I really don't know."

Judge Martin spoke up. "Mrs. Rosa, these occasions you are talking about when your two children started to go to the school that you testified about, when was that? How long back was that?"

"Well, my oldest boy is nineteen."

"And when did he start school?"

"When he was six years old," Pauline said.

"That would be about thirteen years ago?"

"Yes, sir."

"And about twelve years ago for the girl?"

"Yes, sir."

"When was it that you talked to Mr. Hays that you testified he told you your children could not attend?"

"When I started the boy to school."

"That was twelve or thirteen years ago?"

"When he started to school, yes."

"The boy?"

"The boy."

Wayne stood up. "We object to this testimony and ask that it be stricken for the reason that it is too remote in point of time in the present case that is on trial."

"I will refuse the motion and I will let it go in for whatever it is worth," Judge Martin answered back.

At that point, Cullen Vance, an attorney for Jackson County, stood up for Pauline's cross-examination. "Mrs. Rosa, was there any question about teaching to your son by anybody?"

"Yes, sir."

"Was there any question about qualification?"

"She was not qualified, because she did not teach them all the time."

"Did she meet the state requirements?"

"She did, but they never...well, I don't know she met them or not." Pauline shrugged. "She just taught them some things."

"Her qualifications in this respect never were questioned?"

"I could not tell you, because my children did not go to school here."

"Didn't the students in the Latin American school get the same course of instruction as the children in the other school?"

"I could not tell you."

"You don't know about that?"

"No."

Cullen sat down while Wayne replaced him on the floor. "You are not undertaking to say that there was any discrimination against a person of Latin American or Mexican descent in the case we are trying?"

Pauline lifted her chin. "*I* think there was discrimination."

"Who?"

"The town." She looked out toward the public.

"Who?"

"The town."

"The whole town?"

"Yes, sir, they discriminated; the town."

"Who in the town? Can you give us any names?"

"I could not name just *one*."

Wayne stopped his questions abruptly and returned to his seat.

Judge Martin leaned forward. "Are there any more questions?"

"The State has no more questions," Wayne said.

"That is all for the defendant," Gus said.

"The State has nothing further," Wayne responded.

CHAPTER 12

AMELIA SAT AT HER FATHER'S FEET TUGGING AT HIS DIRTY WORK TROUSERS as he stood near the front door. He kept peeking out through the curtains with anticipation, and she aimed to find out the reason why.

"Daddy." She jerked his pant leg again, harder than before. Two clumps of once-caked on mud fell into her lap, along with a small shower of loose dirt. She sneezed.

Henry Cruz looked down. "Em," his nickname for her, "you scared me."

"Nuh-uh! You never get scared." She yanked again, this time in a cleaner spot. "Papá, what are you doing?"

He twirled her ponytail around his forefinger lightly and let go. "I'm waiting for some amigos."

"Oh!" Amelia pulled a small orange out of the side pocket of her shorts and smelled the citrus. "Those people from the flower club?"

"What?" He removed his head from the curtain and squatted down. "What are you talking about? What flower club?"

"You know," she handed him the orange to peel. "The lilac club."

He took it from her and thundered out a laugh. "You mean the LULAC club."

"Okay," she said. "Are those the men you're talking about?" She gazed at him as he peeled the rind in spirals. Pulling and pulling, it disconnected in one piece and she clapped.

Henry suspended the peeled fruit in the air and bounced it a few times before releasing it into her hands. "Are you spying on me?"

Amelia giggled, basking in her father's attention. "Maybe. Do you want an orange slice?"

"I do, and yes, those are the men I speak of. We're going to meet in the garage when they get here." He eyes veered back to the window and he stood up.

Juice shot out when she pulled the fruit into halves. Recklessly she freed the segments while more orange juice snaked down her wrists. She handed him three pieces. "What are y'all going to talk about?"

"Adult stuff . . . I want you to stay inside the house, you hear?" He shoved all three slices in his mouth. "No sneaking around corners."

Engine sounds brought four cars into their driveway. "They're here," Amelia sang out. She nibbled on an orange slice as she watched her father greet and lead them to the garage.

Not for a second did she intend to obey him. Once they settled in she planned to post herself underneath the open window. She'd just gotten to the garage when Jane, the oldest of the four Cruz sisters, caught her eye. She was jumping rope. Amelia watched her for a moment.

"Do you need something? I'm about to lose count."

Amelia nodded. "Will you help me move a ladder to the side of the garage?"

"Why?"

"I want to climb it."

Jane stopped jumping and put a hand on one hip. "What are you up to?"

"Please?" Amelia held out a fourth of a dripping orange as payment, but Jane didn't take it. "Okay, you saw the people, right? Dad said they're having a meeting, but he wouldn't tell me about what." Her eyes sparkled. "I want to find out."

Concern flickered over Jane's face. "What if we get in trouble? What if one of us gets hurt?"

Amelia recalled Delia's carefree disposition at the soda shop and thought about how vastly different her sisters were. "Delia would help me."

"Well, go find her then," Jane crossed her arms. "Guilt trips do not work on me. Try again."

"Come on," Amelia whined. "Live a little and help me. I don't have anything to do," she pouted.

She groaned. "Fine, but you're gonna owe me. Especially if I get my clothes dirty."

Amelia jumped up and hugged her sister. "Something to do," she exclaimed. "Okay, the ladder's already at the back of the garage so we only need to move it four or five feet. Easy, right?"

"Whatever you say, little sis." She laced Amelia's hand in hers and immediately let go. "Go wash those sticky hands, and bring me something to clean mine."

The girls had no more than gripped the ladder legs when the back door to the garage opened and Henry stuck his head outside. "Em, is Delia here?"

She could feel the guilt stinging her eyes. "I don't think so. Want me to find her?"

"No, you get in here. Jane, mind trying to find her?"

Amelia clapped. "You want me to come to the meeting?"

"I do," he said. "Jane?"

She sighed. "I can do that, anything other than this."

What luck! Amelia entered the garage and waved at the nine men and three women who sat in a semicircle. They were all people she'd come across in town, at church or the grocery store. Before them were pieces of cut-up cardboard boxes, a pile of thumbtacks, long wooden sticks, and permanent markers.

Henry sat in his chair. "Em, tell them what happened to you and Delia at the soda shop, when that boy kicked you out. Tell them who stood up for the two of you."

Amelia recited the story, a task she and her sister often performed for their dad recently. When she finished, the people looked toward Henry for verification that Gus had stepped in.

"I didn't believe it myself, but they've repeated the story so many times I know it's true," Henry said.

Amelia frowned at him. "It *is* true! It happened!"

Someone asked Henry why he didn't call for a picket of the place right after the incident occurred. "Lack of preparation," he gestured to the supplies, "and the reason why we're here."

"When will we respond," a church lady asked, "today?"

"If we're done in time. Texas LULAC rules state we can picket anywhere we're not allowed service as long as it doesn't turn violent or disturb the peace," Henry stated.

The members traded nods and began suggesting ideas for signs.

Amelia listened to their ideas, and realized no one sat down to start writing the words. "Papá, can I help? Por favor? I won't mess it up, I promise." She clasped her hands in prayer.

"Of course you can. Start in pencil so the words are spaced out the way you want them and then go over it a few times with a marker until the words are tall and thick enough that you can see the message from far away. Think you can do that?" Henry briefly touched her chin.

Always the perfectionist, Amelia jumped out of her seat. "Yeah I can!" Her knees to the cement, she began fanning the cardboard pieces out.

Jane returned to announce Delia left to visit a friend.

Once they started Amelia on a few phrases they focused on where to go. Restaurant names were tossed around, but Henry pushed everyone to think beyond the expected. "What else is around here besides places to eat and buy groceries?"

Amelia pulled her hair back into a ponytail and wondered out loud. "Get a haircut?"

He went to her and kissed her on her head. "Yes ma'am, the barbershop! Krejci's Barbershop on Main." He ran a hand through his hair. "I could use a haircut and I know Krejci, he's Catholic like we are, and an usher."

The others nodded in agreement.

Henry weighed his options. "He might cut my hair without a hassle . . . but I don't think so. It wouldn't be in his nature, especially if other customers waited. Gotta keep up appearances." He clapped. "Okay people, let's help my daughter finish."

"Dad, is this what you call a protest?"

"A silent protest, we're not going to be yelling or throwing fruit at the windows."

"Awww. Can I carry a sign, Papá? Please?"

"No, no," he said, "it might not be safe. You're too young. It needs to be adults, so they'll pay attention to us." He stacked another sign on the growing pile. "Whose spouses can join us?"

A momentary silence passed, then excuses started spilling out. Wives needed to take care of children or clean the house, and husbands needed to work to put food on the table. One man outright admitted his wife would be too scared to picket businesses for fear of getting arrested or enduring drastic measures against them, and then no one would be around for their kids. Others agreed.

Amelia knew what this meant. Her eyes brightened when her father made eye contact with her. “I’m going to go change clothes.”

“Just this once,” he told her.

Another lady called out, “Invite your hermanos y hermanas!”

She ran through the house with her announcement while she chose a dress. Jane and the older two of the six brothers, Bobby and Alonso, tagged along and raised their numbers to sixteen.

Henry instructed the group on their cues. “I’ll go inside alone and ask for a haircut, you all wait in the car. If he obliges, I’ll head outside and let you all know to come out so you’re not stuck waiting. Otherwise I’ll give a signal and we’ll pile in front of Krejci’s windows.”

They drove to Main Street and parked a few blocks away from the barbershop. Amelia watched and waited with her siblings. *That old man better not hit my father,* she thought. She watched as her father faced the man and their mouths moved for a few moments. Then the old man shook his head and looked at the floor. She observed sadness on the man’s face, remorse. The setup wasn’t unfolding the way she hoped it would. She wanted drama.

Bobby broke the silence. “Why are we here? I still don’t understand. Dad wants to get into a fight with that white-haired man?”

“Dad’s asking that man for a haircut, expecting he’ll say no because he won’t serve Mexicans,” Jane offered. “They’re not supposed to do that. The people with us, they’re all for making sure businesses in this town understand that we know they’re not supposed to say no because of our color.” She pointed down the street to the courthouse. “Today, a lawyer is fighting in there for us. Mexican people in this county should have the right to sit on a jury. Equal representation.”

Henry stepped outside the barbershop and lifted the forefinger on his right hand and circled it in the air. “Round ’em up!”

“Showtime,” Jane clapped. “Alonso, pop the trunk.”

Amelia piled out of the car with the rest of them. “I can’t believe it’s happening!” She bounced and danced a little jig as she chose her sign. “Yes!”

The width of Krejci’s barbershop storefront spread no farther than fifteen feet, enough for the LULAC group to stand side by side.

People from the Edna Theater, Winn’s Cafe, The Eatery, and William’s Pharmacy and Soda Shop began pointing through their windows, while others went outside to get a better view.

What started out as excitement morphed into equal parts nerves and curiosity for Jane, who withered a bit at the stares, but not Amelia. She held her chin high and her shoulders straight. To Amelia, her strong stance personified confidence and inspired her to find more inside herself. The moment empowered her.

Henry Cruz was the same. Proud and strong, he stood on the curb and lifted his sign a little higher than everyone else. The people on the street seemed to identify with him.

Amelia overheard a passerby say, "They're probably doing this hooey because of what's going on over at the courthouse."

Jane puffed out her chest and spoke out to the people. "That's exactly what we're doing. This is for Pete Hernandez."

Suddenly a boy walked past with his hand locked in his mother's, someone Amelia recognized. His name was Dave Grimland, a boy she met on the fairgrounds the year before. They struck up a friendship for a time and bartered items: he asked for popsicle sticks and gave her fancy pencils in return. Dave needed the sticks for his log cabin, and she had nine siblings who loved eating popsicles.

He brought her pencils that differed from the normal golden-yellow octagon shape with the pink eraser; these were olive green and smooth, with a bright purple eraser shaped in a triangle. They even smelled better than normal pencils, sweet like warm cinnamon.

Dave and Amelia's eyes met as he passed. They waved to each other. His mother noticed their acknowledgement, and she tugged her son the other way.

Amelia wondered how someone like Dave perceived their silent protest. Would he talk to her the next time they crossed paths? Would his mother allow it? What if they *did* cross paths again and he asked her lots of questions that she didn't know how to answer?

Krejci hobbled outside, a balding man with wisps of white hair and wiry glasses hung over his nose. "Henry! I'll cut your hair, come on, but you have to send your people away." He addressed everyone on the street. "You all go home! I'm going to cut his hair, nothing to see here. Git!"

Bobby laughed. "We're not cattle," he said.

Henry lowered his sign. "Well, whatdya know! Fellas, I'm going to get my hair cut at this fine establishment . . . pack it in and take my kids home, will ya?"

The other LULAC members nodded and corralled the teenagers.

"Can I stay?" Amelia piped up. She yanked Jane's skirt. "I want to stay."

"Absolutely not," she replied. "Dad wouldn't want that."

Henry handed his sign to Amelia and squatted to her eye level. "I'm going to get my hair cut," he glanced behind her towards the courthouse, "and then I've got something to do. I'm going to be home later, okay? Thank you for being so brave. I couldn't have done this without you, mija." He lovingly nudged her on the chin and pulled her in for a hug, a rare occurrence in their family.

Amelia's eyes welled. Something about this encounter with him struck a chord. This moment felt bigger than the both of them, even bigger than everyone standing on Main Street. The earnest look in his eye, his carefulness. He showed affection to Jane, Bobby, and Alonso, too. She couldn't explain the feeling emanating from her father; it was just out of reach.

That evening the Cruz family piled into the main room to learn what happened after they left. Elvira, their mother, stood swirling a dishtowel in circles while their children took seats on the floor. She nudged her husband's shoulder. "Did you go?"

"Of course I did, they needed all the witnesses they could get."

Jane's head perked up. "Went where? To court?"

Henry held up a hand. "One thing at a time."

Amelia listened, but didn't quite understand the exchange. "I wanna know what Krejci told you."

"Yeah," Alonso chimed in. "Were you afraid old man Krejci was going to cut off all your hair? Oooh, or clip an ear?"

"No, we both knew that would've worsened the situation. That would've been a dramatic story though," Henry replied.

Amelia steered the narrative. "What did he say when you asked for a haircut? Was he mean?"

"Actually, no," he said thoughtfully. "He was remorseful, said he couldn't do it. When I asked why, he said, 'you're not white.' Once I sat in the chair we talked about church matters. He waited until his customers left and told me he commended what we were doing. Said dealing with customers can be difficult because no one thinks for themselves." He sighed. "They're going to know who we are, LULACs and the American GI Forum."

Jane raised her hand. "Did you go to the courthouse?"

Henry nodded and looked at Amelia. "I went to court today, as a witness for the Pete Hernandez trial."

Amelia thought of Gus and the strawberry soda he bought her.

He continued. "I was at Chinco's the night when everything unfolded. I butted into the middle of their argument, and they called me as a witness." His voice trailed off. "I needed a haircut."

Again, Amelia could sense she missed something her father said that her older siblings seemed to understand.

After bedtime, Amelia snuck out of the girls' room and crept down the hall towards her parents' room, where she heard them softly talking about the day's events.

"I met the lawyers," Henry whispered. "They said Shannon ran them out of The Eatery with some muscle. And they found a sign at the courthouse."

"Looks like every business in town received the word except for the courthouse, serves them right," Elvira giggled. "Restaurants were yanking signs left and right. They say these lawyers might be big time."

"They do say that."

"What do you think?"

Amelia listened for her father's response.

"From far away the men look hardened, tough; you can tell they've stayed up nights thinking and spent their days fighting. But they carry hope, light, you know? The moment they turned to me their faces were genuinely welcoming. They care about us because their families are just like us. The rocks on the mountain are sharp and the climb is steep, but you can tell they're not going to quit," Henry said.

"What about the shiny one?"

"Shiny?"

"They say one of them stands out, that there's something about him. Like a movie star," Elvira said with wonder.

"Ah yes, his name is Gustavo, and it never hurts to have someone like that. He's as tall as a ladder, majestic, but down to earth. I suppose he does have a shine about him, like a spotlight is positioned near him always." Henry paused.

"Some people are like that," she said.

"You know, in thinking back, I left something out about the barbershop. Before I left, I apologized for the crowd I'd gathered outside. He told me not to worry about it, then said, 'but you know I'm going to have to throw out these scissors, right?'"

CHAPTER 13

CHARGED WITH MURDER WITH MALICE AFORETHOUGHT, PETE HERNANDEZ WAS handed a guilty verdict by the jury.

Two guards approached to lead Pete out, and Gus lingered too long, watching him limp away on his clubbed foot. The day they met, Pete asked the lawyers to take a long hard look at his leg. He called himself a gimp. He told them no one would treat them badly if they didn't take the gimp's case.

Pete couldn't move quickly, and one of the guards guiding him out didn't bother to adapt to his slow gait. He slipped and tried to hang on the guard's arm, but the guard jerked back and Pete nearly fell. Both guards unsuccessfully tried to hold back laughter.

Guilt rose like a lump in Gus's throat. *We are responsible for that man*, he thought. *His suffering is our own, my own.* Gus glanced at Lenora and realized her heart broke for her son, which deepened his own sorrow. She made the sign of the Cross before following Pete out of the courtroom. *Was it wrong to go forward with an appeal?* Gus stifled the thought.

"Amigos!" Gus said to John and James after they waved goodbye to Lenora. "Might we have a drink before we part ways? I will be heading back to San Antonio to try and swoon my wife so she'll let me make love to her one last time."

James shook his head and John answered for him. "No, I believe we are too tired for the normal antics." He put a hand on Gus's shoulder. "He and I both have wives we'd like to be with this evening, and I don't know about you, but we don't have the money to be spending on drinks."

He persisted. "I have enough whisky for the three of us, and I didn't buy this bottle. It was a gift."

"Yeah, right." John shook his head more briskly. "To be honest, I'm a little irked with you. That mess about the translator, did you think it necessary?"

"He said it first!"

John groaned. "Why did you have to act like that? We're not trying to start a sword fight in the middle of a courtroom; there's going to be no room for bravado like that going forward."

James laughed uncomfortably. "It's only the beginning, JJ, don't get bent out of shape yet. It's too early in the case and too late in the night to go that route."

"Aye, sí, but we probably lost the possibility of quashing the moment you started talking down to him," John said.

"Mi amigo, I know you remember we spoke of this, but we NEVER had a possibility of winning that motion. Today wasn't about that. It was about setting the tone. I wanted them to know *we* know what we're doing, and we're not going to let anybody walk all over us."

"Asking if we speak English," Gus added sarcastically.

"The appeal process has already begun," John finished. "I won't continue this. Amigo, we're knocking on the door of fatigue and we have a drive in front of us. There's nothing much else to talk about, except the one thing I already know you won't talk about."

"Which is?"

"Bringing another trial lawyer onto the scene," John took a deep breath while James walked away to start the car. "I think our case would benefit from it."

Gus kicked at a rock near his car. "It's Carlos you want to add to the case."

"Just think about it, it doesn't have to be him," John said.

Gus didn't open his mouth.

"Hermano, you know the difficulty will double and triple from here. Instead of it being the Chivas that doubles and triples, let it be the lawyers. Besides, we are dedicated people who do amazing things. We're undoubtedly going to have more cases come our way at my firm, and I have my hands full as it is."

Gus wanted to tell him not to run for national LULAC office, if time was so important, but chose not to. He simply nodded.

James honked the car horn, and John clapped Gus on the back. "You are still the leading matador, don't forget that."

He waved as the two drove away into the night. Private drinking sounded more fulfilling anyhow, so Gus reached for the Chivas bottle he'd tucked underneath the driver's seat. Self-pity dipped in depression never tasted so . . . tasty.

To Gus, John might as well have said they needed someone to pick up the slack, and trust between them was nonexistent. To Gus, John might as well have said, you're hitting the juice too hard and you will become unreliable. To Gus, John might as well have said, we're worried you'll cause a scene we can't back away from.

To Gus, he might as well have said: we want Carlos Cadena instead of you.

Somewhere inside him he knew those weren't the words spoken, but his brain had juggled those thoughts before. Ideas and fears married and mixed themselves into one big cocktail.

Time for home, he told himself. He uncorked the Chivas bottle (already half empty), and breathed in its aroma before gulping some down. If his nose could've fit down the bottleneck he would've done it, if only for a new experience, but instead he merely inhaled. He turned the car ignition, swigged again, and drove out of Edna still listening to his inner voice.

It wasn't that Gus didn't like Carlos, though he knew their peers and college chums believed that. Because the two worked differently and butted heads occasionally, lawyers in their circle thought of them as being pitted against each other. In actuality, the two looked out for each other.

Gus begged Irene to name their second daughter Carlita after Carlos; he believed the man deserved every ounce of respect and honor. Gus envied the fact that Carlos didn't seem to need praise to fuel him. Carlos turned away from excessive attention, and always hoped not to be noticed. *My behavior is the exact opposite*, Gus thought. *I clamor for attention even when there's none to receive*. He swigged again.

For him to dispel the notion that Carlos was his nemesis would mean admitting more than just respect. It would be admitting brotherly love, and Gus knew he didn't possess enough courage to do that. So the enemy rumor continued.

"It'll be me who has to ask, I'm sure," Gus argued to his reflection in the rearview mirror. "Who else would it be? Oh Carlitos, these Houston giants Herrera and DeAnda need an unassuming little giant in the courtroom. No doubt you can sway the vote and win the respect we need to win this case, because I mess everything up."

Gus laughed at himself. *Talk about licking wounds*, he thought.

He mimicked Carlos, "You just want to keep this case all to yourself because that boy's mom came to you, right? Be honest, Gustavo." He eyed himself in the rearview mirror.

Carlos would fit in perfectly with John and James. He imagined the three of them sitting among a pile of open books and debating over mugs filled with coffee, no liquor added. James had mentioned in passing how he'd love to take advantage of working beside a legal mind like Carlos.

James goes with the wind, Gus thought. *Sure, he'll have a drink with me now, but the second Carlitos blows in the weather will change, and the vibe ruined. They'll notice my glaring inadequacies and talk about me when I'm out of earshot*, he surmised.

At least Carlos will keep on stuttering, Gus comforted himself, *I'll have a leg up on him in that category*. He swigged once more at the bottle and re-corked it for future indulgences, only to find it nearly empty by the time he arrived in San Antonio.

He prayed for Mateo's spirit to dip down from heaven and be by his side. As he squeezed the bull's cape beside him a whiff of bull floated out, Gus assumed from the cloth, but hoped it wasn't his own bullshit he smelled.

CHAPTER 14

"BE HONEST," GUS SAID TO PATRICIA, "how often are you unsure of your skills? How often do you question your choices?"

The two made an effort to see each other when they discovered themselves simultaneously in the same city. That week, she needed to be in San Antonio for several interviews and he found her bed to be the perfect padding for a bruised ego.

She ground her cigarette out into the ashtray and propped herself on a few pillows. "In what area? The bedroom, in the arena, or in a group of people scrambling to talk to me? My skill levels vary with all the above."

"Rate them."

"Stellar, novice, and inept."

"Pats," he tickled her underneath the sheets. "Your style and technique, I bet it's improving all the time, but are you ever unsure of yourself? How do you know what to improve?" He looked at the ceiling. "Being a matador is a solitary quest with constant competition, and you're the first woman to do this. When do you stop the doubt that men try to put in there?" He tapped on his forehead.

The ends of her short hair dripped with sweat. "Give the uncertainty credence, then let it go." She cracked her knuckles. "During a dance, I clear my head. You take what energy the bull gives off and expand on it. Like Manolete said: there's no time to think, instinct takes over. Dancing correctly means you're an extension of the bull, but to do it, you have to let go."

Gus sighed. "It all sounds so . . . spiritual. I still want to know what it feels like to be in front of a bull."

"That can be arranged." She let out a throaty laugh. "What's it like to be in your arena? When you've said the right thing or executed the right move, how do you feel?"

He mulled on it, but didn't say outright that he didn't want to talk about it. "Can you believe it's been a month since I horned in on you?"

"Gustavo," Patricia said in a serious voice. "What's going on? Why did you ask about my self-doubt? Is this because of you losing the trial?"

"No, it was intentional, we're appealing."

"So, what is it?"

"It's been weeks since my colleagues asked me to find someone to join the team, but I'm stalling."

"In finding or asking?"

"I've found, not asked."

"You don't want to? He's an enemy or something?" She lit another cigarette.

"Some have called him my nemesis, but he's not. To be completely honest, I have a hard time asking for help." He pulled the sheet from her body and pulled her closer to him, but bruises on her legs caught his eye and stopped him cold. "Pat! Is that from me or the bull?"

She lightly pinched him. "Is there a difference? Ignore those, and take this," she handed him her cigarette. He reached for her again and deftly, she pinned his hands above his head and straddled him. "Why would some call him your nemesis?"

"Take the cigarette back." His features softened as he wrapped his arms around her. "This is why you are so stunning."

"Answer me."

Gus groaned. "We're opposites, we argue sometimes, but we have a real respect for each other."

"Hmmm, and you are a stubborn man."

He cleared his throat. "Assume it's one of my stronger traits."

"We're passionate people, and when something or someone puts what we do at risk, the offense we take is almost always personal. Do you think he's smarter than you?"

"No, not necessarily," he answered.

"Does he hold court better than you? Can he sway a crowd?"

"Actually, he's not the greatest. He stutters when he's nervous. So you can imagine what that does for a crowd."

"Do you think he's better than you?"

"Never!"

Patricia tried to blow a smoke ring. "I'm not seeing a problem here. Is there a question I should be asking? Will you need to grovel?"

He nuzzled his head into her torso. "No, it's not that. If I have to ask does it mean I'm not doing a good enough job? I get insecure at the idea. A voice in my head keeps repeating the question."

"You just said he can't talk worth a penny, so he wouldn't replace you, he's in addition to you." She pinched his ear. "Your feeling of inadequacy is self-inflicted, you know this, correct? Are you intimidated by him?"

His face flamed. She'd hit it on the nose. "More like I'm intimidated by the idea of him being intimidating." Gus tried distracting her by burying his face in her neck.

She exhaled. "If this man is your bull, when you charge at him, here's a tip," she said. "Don't look at his horns, position yourself at your endgame and let the cape do its job."

"Do you believe I'm passionate?" He stuck his head beneath the sheets.

"Of course," she said breathlessly. "When you're compelled to do what you love, regardless of the shit it puts you through, it crosses into the realm of passion." She yelped out, then giggled.

"It's true," Gus said, while kissing her. "The law is my motivation for living."

"Everyone brings something different to the table. Keep working on your craft and you'll be fine." She cried out again. "Worry about what your role is in all this, and work hard at what you're doing right now."

His head popped up from the sheet near her feet. "My role? In what? With the case or in this bed?"

Patricia picked her head up and stared deeply into his eyes. "I referred to your current act, but yes, the case as well."

He obeyed, until suddenly she spoke out.

"I know you have a wife. Before I opened the door I looked through the peephole and saw you hide your ring in your jacket pocket," she said with a soft face. "I don't mind; it doesn't matter to me, but in the past you've hinted at wanting something more, so I needed to address it."

"She asked me to stay away before you and I met. I never came home, and I forgot special occasions," he offered. "Ignorant, selfish, and drinks too much—that's what she thinks of me."

"That doesn't sound easy, but I like what we have right now. Let's continue in this way without pinning each other down. It sounds like we have some big things happening down the road." Patricia cupped his cheek in her hand.

Disappointed, he agreed. "Then yes, I do know my role in this bed. But you can't blame me darling, I want nothing more than to do what you're doing."

"You want nothing more than to make love to yourself? We can arrange that," she said with a mischievous smile.

Gus gently pinched her on the side of her stomach. "I want nothing more than to dance with bulls . . . and death, I suppose. So maybe playing with you is the closest I'll get, unless you can arrange it." He pulled the sheets over his head. "I know my role, I promise!"

Patricia's giggling filled the room again. "Yes, yes, I'll arrange anything!"

He sat up, brightened. "You've given me such a feeling . . . one more time and then I'm visiting Carlos tonight. No use in waiting now!"

CHAPTER 15

GUS KNEW CARLOS CADENA WOULD BE AT HIS OFFICE LATE INTO THE EVENING. He enjoyed the quiet at night because he didn't have to endure conversations. After calling to receive permission, Gus waited downstairs to be let in.

When he appeared, Gus opened his arms wide. "Carlitos!"

Carlos reciprocated the gesture with a smile on his face before unlocking the door. "Gustavo."

"Who else would be at your door this late?"

Known as one of the brightest and most detail-oriented lawyers his kind had to offer, Carlos struggled to be an extrovert, but tried his best when it became a necessity. People knew him to be reserved, and sometimes it came off as grouchy or frustrated, but his features could account for that, because he frowned when he listened. A short man, he had thinning hair, thin eyebrows, and a thinner smile, but wasn't considered thin by any account.

Some saw his shyness as a weakness, him included, but he used it to his advantage. Carlos listened. He heard what one did and didn't say, something that couldn't be said of Gus. His quietness could also be attributed to a stutter he sometimes had.

"I should've known you'd try to ss-ss-saunter into my building at this time, who else would it be? Most ss-ss-sane men would be finishing the dinners their wives cooked and tucking their children in bed," Carlos said.

Gus cocked his head. "I don't know if you don't know or you know and you're poking fun."

"Know what?"

"Irene and I are through."

Carlos gasped. "I had no idea." He stepped forward and hugged Gus. "Did you break her heart?"

"Maybe," Gus said. "I'm convinced it was a series of heart-breaking events over time. I want to make it up to her, but I'm afraid sooner rather than later I'd break her heart all over again, and I don't want to do that to her." Gus waved his hand in the air as if swatting a fly away. "That's all I'll say. What are you up to?"

"Just working. Ss-ss-studying." He leaned against the doorway. "I haven't seen you in some time."

"Have you missed me? I know you're trying to cover up that you're actually happy to see me." Gus hugged him again. "Aren't you going to let me in?"

Carlos groaned, but attached it with a smile. "Aye amigo, come in, you're right, I'm just trying to give you a hard time."

Gus chuckled and entered. "Why are you not with Gloria and your many children?"

When Carlos laughed, his belly shook slightly. "It's the silence. I spend all day staying attentive to other people, and it's the same thing at home with the kids. I need time in the middle to think for myself."

"Be careful. You'd miss it if you didn't have it," Gus warned. "It happened little by little and then before long . . . poof! Nada."

"Give her time," Carlos advised. "You've always been the one for her. I remember how she looked at you when we were in law school, I'm sure it hasn't changed much. Make her feel special. Spend time with the girls, that's the way to her heart."

"That's what I should've done. I think now it might be too late."

"Nonsense, give it time."

"Not important," Gus waved the topic away. "You said you were studying?"

"Sí, I've started courses again at our alma mater, but I'm thinking of transferring to St. Mary's for a fellowship. Been working with George for some time on cc-civil rights arguments." Carlos dropped himself into a club chair.

Gus flopped onto a nearby couch. "Good old George Sanchez? We went to lunch when I spoke at the Alba Club earlier this year."

Carlos scanned the papers on his desk and pursed his lips. "Can I ask, why have you come to bother me?"

Gus opened his mouth, then closed it, debating on how to go forward. "I was in Edna recently with JJ on a new case, and some civil residents politely nudged us out of a restaurant." His eyes glittered. "Of course, nudged is a kind word."

"What's new with that? Y Johnny? How is he?"

He scoffed. "Busy as usual. They want him to run for national office at LULAC."

"Well, good for him! It suits him well, he's vice president now." Carlos outwardly shivered. "All those speeches, and getting votes, it sounds horrible." He studied Gus. "It doesn't sit well with you, though, does it?"

"It would've been nice to have been asked." Gus didn't notice himself crossing his arms, nor the bitterness in his voice. His defenses were up.

Carlos bellowed. "You're not serious, are you?"

Gus puffed his chest out. "You don't think I'd be a dazzling president?"

"I know you're not that deluded. In no way can you afford to have your life put under a microscope, you know that."

"So says you!" Gus's chest deflated. "You're bruising my delicate ego."

"Be reasonable, Gustavo. I can never tell when you're joking." He squinted at him. "Back to the story, nudged out of a restaurant. How did Herrera take it?"

"Him and the boy with him, young man named DeAnda, they looked sad, and a bit frightened."

Carlos raised his eyebrows. "Y tu?"

"Quite the opposite, I'm afraid. Invigorating." He glanced around the office. "You don't have a bar, do you?"

"You know the answer to that, I don't have a *bar*." Carlos pronounced the word as if the idea was preposterous. "Besides, I don't like you when you drink."

Gus smiled. "That's a shame, because I like you better when I drink." He relayed the incident from The Eatery, which led into explaining the situation at William's with the Cruz sisters. "I don't know why such racism ignites me so."

"It gives you a reason to keep going. You wouldn't fight otherwise."

Gus considered this. "I see that."

"So, why have you been in Edna so much?"

"Ah, that's the Carlos I love, always looking at the bigger picture."

"It's the common denominator. What's the case?"

Gus described Lenora, Pete, and the details. "After Herrera's work with the Aniceto case, I think it calls for another go. Success through repetition."

"That's . . . risky."

"So I shouldn't do it?"

"That's not what I said. I'm merely suggesting it's an undertaking."

"I've got to do something big. I can't sit around waiting for Irene to come around. Besides, that mother came to me and I said yes. Plus those sisters, no one should grow up in a world where it's okay to talk to someone like that. And the men who backed him up! I suspect that town, like so many in the south, needs a social shakeup. I feel the call, Carlitos, I feel our race calling." Gus began to tremble.

"They're always calling," Carlos responded. "Isn't it the reason we studied law? To help our people, to be an example for them."

"So you think I should do it?"

Carlos smiled. "Always the little brother, aren't you? Aren't I the younger one?"

Gus held up two fingers to represent the two years between them. "Not by much, but you've always been the more mature one. I'm the risky one."

"If it feels right and you've got well-written arguments, I don't see why not. Does it light the fire inside of you?"

Gus studied his shoes for a moment, then turned his gaze back to Carlos. "It feels like the moment when caffeine from coffee hits you, like pure energy."

"You need to listen to yourself more often, that sounds like a clear message to me."

Gus tapped on his forehead. "Yes, but they lie."

"They?"

"The others who reside in my head. I don't want to say 'the voices' because it makes me sounds crazy. Please don't tell me I'm not the only one." The trembling continued.

Carlos frowned and brooded. "I have my conscience, my inner voice."

"Right, yes, my inner voice and its debater, the drunk one, my ego and my doubter. Plus the one solely about the law." Gus began to fidget with his hands.

"Hmmm, that sounds busy."

Gus exhaled loudly and clenched his fists. "The courts just refused our case, and we're going to appeal. They think no discrimination exists. The thing is . . . I think we're . . . or *I'm* going to need your help."

A long pause passed between them, neither looking at the other.

Carlos spoke first. "Are you asking me to step into your spotlight? I will do no such thing."

"No, no! You know how I get," Gus gestured to the air, "and now with Irene, plus the holidays are nearing . . . I don't trust myself. I shrink in winter. Honestly speaking, I trust you implicitly, Carlitos."

Carlos covered his heart with a hand. His heart aimed more true than Gus's and John's combined. "That means more than you can imagine. You know, I always thought Irene was too good for you."

"Only because you have a lingering crush," Gus jabbed. "But seriously, that's how I feel. You can help us in a way I cannot. Or JJ cannot."

"Aye, Gustavo."

Gus let the pause hang in the air. "What do you say, are you in?"

"I told Herrera yes, as long as you were okay with it," Carlos admitted.

Gus froze. "He called you? Herrera called you? JJ?"

"Sí, the Monday after they denied a re-trial. You didn't know this?" A long, long pause followed. "Mierda," Carlos studied his face, "you knew nothing of this."

"No!" Gus sighed. "No."

Carlos babbled on. "In terms of the brief, it turns out the work I've been doing with Dr. Ss-ss-sanchez is relevant, it's as if the case you s-ss-speak of would come to a head at the same time. Once I started my fellowship, we knew." He proudly smiled. "Why, I found out about the type of discrimination that runs rampant in the boxing sport, and it's going to ss-ss-seep through every situation you can think of, and a dozen more you can't."

Gus exhaled slowly, and set aside his anger for later. "In Aniceto's case, the judgment said Mexican people aren't a separate race, but white people of Spanish descent. We shouldn't try the separate race argument again. They stated there are two classes, white and Negro. And Irene said . . . something about us being 'separate and apart, though we'll always be a part of each other,' something like that."

"As if we, Mexican Americans, are a class apart from the white race," Carlos continued. "A third race, but one they won't recognize."

"So . . . " Gus said, "not another race, but another class within a race. Like you said, a class apart."

Carlos scrunched his eyebrows together in confusion. "If we're saying the courts recognize our people as part of the white race, at the same time we're still apart from them due to discrimination. We can mess with the semantics of it."

"Aye Dios mío," Gus said, "oh my God," he repeated in English. "You are so right, we'll hit from every angle."

Carlos clapped him on his back. "The brief with Sanchez is half complete, and it's simply waiting for facts to fill in the black spaces. I think it can help you all, and if you are okay with it, I will join your team. But if you don't want it, tell me now."

Internally, Gus struggled. He thought of the various fighters used to debilitate an animal in a bullfight. The banderillas and picadors on their horses helped weaken the bull so that the matador could show his skill without a hitch.

That's what Carlos and Herrera are for, Gus thought, *and DeAnda, they will be my primary tools in crippling this bull we call racism. Asking for help is what I need to do,* he realized, *Carlos knows his place, and it's me who needs to know mine.*

His mind raced on. *Show them the mental discrimination we've been consistently shown. Someday soon we will not be the minority, Gus foresaw, someday soon we will be the majority and teach the new minority what to think, just as they tried with us.*

"I want it," Gus mustered out. "I need your help, our people need your help. No matter what I do or say in the future, Carlitos, don't let me forget what I'm telling you right now. Belittle me when I need it, condescend to my manners when necessary," he pleaded. "Even when I am unaccepting, don't let me falter."

Carlos approached Gus and hugged him with force, a moment that lasted. "I will not. Send me what I need to further the argument and fill in the blanks, I will be waiting. I can help."

The two men were united in a way they hadn't been in some time. Their powers, like those of superheroes, doubled in intensity when joined.

"Yes," Gus said, feeling free and almost lightheaded, like one can feel after overcoming a fear. "This, I can do. Sí, se puedes."

He had no idea the depths of the hole he would soon fall into.

CHAPTER 16

"WE'RE ALMOST IN A NEW YEAR, Mr. Hernandez." Donovan stared at Pete from across a table and steepled his fingers. "Your team lost the first go-round, and now you've been transferred to Austin, where no one knows you. Except me. That's a list called 'facts you know.' But here's one on the 'facts you don't' list." He leaned in. "Your team is dropping the ball," he said in a singsong voice. "The deadline passed for them to file for an appeal, and they did nothing. Are you aware?"

Pete scratched his head and then slunk down in his chair as a male translator for the Jackson County Jail shared the news.

His reaction pleased Donovan. Matter-of-factly, he said, "Oh, yes. They've done nothing. Your Gustavo in charge is getting weak." He straightened his tie. "That's why I'm here." He cleared his throat. "Have you thought about changing your legal strategy? New lawyers?"

Pete merely shook his head, his eyes blank.

"Frankly, I want to talk about the racial issue."

At that translation, Pete sat up straight.

"Do you know the possibility of winning your case goes up if you're represented by a white man?"

He squinted. "Someone like you?"

"Actually, no. I represent a group of men who will find someone specializing in homicide to give you the best chance of being set free, or the best chance with the shortest term. We, or they, can find you a topnotch defense lawyer, ten times more qualified than the team representing you now."

"Gustavo?"

"The very same," Donovan snorted. "He hasn't been the most upstanding man to the people he's supposed to be loyal to. You need someone who will look out for you and think of what you need before you need it. Gus is only out for himself, and he can barely do that with class. I applaud him for taking a different route with your case, but that will do nothing but waste time. The men I work for would give your family financial stability during your jail stay, and provide whatever you need behind bars. Can your team afford to do this for you?"

Considering his words for a moment, Pete shook his head. "What are you offering?"

"Whatever you need, from an extra dessert or blanket at night to a whore hiding around the corner to take care of you while your fellow inmates are kicking the ball outside. I heard they won't move you to a bigger facility than here because no one wants to take care of your bum leg." The words tumbled out more easily than he expected.

"Foot," Pete corrected.

"Hey, if one foot doesn't work, what does it say for the other?" He chuckled, while the translator launched into an uncomfortable cough. "Kidding, I'm trying to inject some humor into the situation. I can get more handicapped accessibility here, a podiatrist, whatever. You think of something you want, and we'll talk about it."

"Go on."

"Same goes for anyone who lives, or lived, under the same roof as you in Edna. Groceries, doctor visits, winter coats, school supplies, gas money, anything. Think of this as a safety net. Maybe we could start a bank account and your mother could operate it. We'll figure it out."

One eyebrow lifted. "So you want me to hire you?"

Donovan shrugged. "Something like that."

"Fire my guys and hire you." The handcuffs clanged together when Pete tried to cross his arms. "Anything else I can do for you?"

Donovan snorted. "Tell me, has Gus been able to do any of this for you?"

"No, but he hasn't offered, and I haven't asked."

"Exactly my point. Pedro," he paused, realizing how silly the name sounded coming out of his mouth. He didn't let it be a deterrent. "Pedro, Gus may be adequate, but that's just it, he's adequate. Why would you stay with someone like him when you have these resources available to you? Before I came along it might've made sense, but now, how can you rationalize it?"

The translator's voice chittered with words one way, and then the next.

"You know what, white man? You can take your pretty boy offer and shove it up your ass." Pete shook his head. "I don't know where all that cash comes from, and I don't want to know. I won't trust you or someone like you and I never will."

Donovan stood up and pointed his finger in Pete's face. "You're going to regret this. Gus will not win for you, he's weak, vilely unprofessional, and nearly throws himself into histrionics when he doesn't get what he wants. It's atrocious. He'll say whatever he needs to get by, it's disgusting."

"You don't sound so bad yourself, amigo. Look in the mirror." He laughed. "I see you, your face getting all twisted and upset, you don't get told no too much, do you? I bet you grew up with money. Do you have a rich papí? Did you go to school with a bunch of boys? I bet you did." This time, Pete leaned in with a wicked smile. "See, I can read you rich *gringos*. It's not hard. How about you go back to wherever you came from?"

Donovan had enough determination to stay and try persuading Pete a few more times, but his argument ended when Pete spit in his face. Even the translator cracked a smile with that one. Wanting nothing more than to wrap his hands around Pete's throat, Donovan stood, thanked him for his time, and left his business card. Enraged, he climbed into his car and drove back home to Austin.

As he walked through the door he noticed a fresh Drambuie waiting in the foyer, left by Kiana, no doubt. The two had escalated flirting to the next level since the law party. He sipped and searched for her, finding her in the dining room dusting candelabras. Donovan snatched a few moments of appreciating her from behind without her noticing. The skirt of her uniform hugged her slim, round curves down to her knees. Whichever way Kiana moved, her hips shifted up and down. He liked how much more curvy she was compared to the girls he'd grown up with.

He fantasized about how heavenly it would be if he could take her right then and there, and they could be as loud as he wanted. No, nothing wrong with that at all, it's not like it would be forbidden by his parents, and hers too. Being shunned from society might be the best thing for them, then neither would have to answer to anyone but each other. He wondered if being with her for real would make him happy, or if playing the "shhh" game fired him up more than the act itself.

Donovan lightly knocked on the table to catch her attention, and when Kiana turned to smile at him, he didn't like it one bit. Unsure of where this feeling came from, he went forward to her anyway, and regretted it.

The rage he experienced earlier with Pete flared unexpectedly.

He tried his hardest to be kind with her, but failed horribly. He blamed her for making him weak, making him smile, but he didn't say a thing to her, he showed her instead. He gripped her wrists a little too tightly, and held her in place a little too long. He resented her for being there for him so readily, and he resented himself for letting her in.

Later, while alone, he went over what bothered him so much and couldn't put his finger on it. The smirk on Pete's face came back to him, along with his insults. The emotions from the day crept back up on him, and he imagined punching Pete. Donovan wondered, *what is happening to me?*

CHAPTER 17

DONOVAN WATCHED HIS MOTHER FINISH UP HOT TODDIES FOR HIM AND his father.

Cordelia Kincaid stocked up on Christmas decorations after the war and had accumulated a great deal. Naturally, she preferred the best. Steinbach nutcrackers, as tall as her knee and as short as her index finger, lined the shelf above the ivy-covered fireplace. A Christmas universe—complete with three villages—filled one side of the living room with neighborhoods, a downtown street, and an oversized nativity scene. Every piece she personally designed through the Putz brand and each was hand-carved from wood.

She was fond of her collection, but nothing made her more proud than the centerpiece of it all, the tree. She called it her Titanic because of its strength, sheer size, and inability to tip over, and despite pets, tipsy party guests, and a young Donny climbing to the top a few holidays in a row. The tree still stood mighty and unwavering, like a Kincaid.

Ultimately, the Christmas tree personified family to Cordelia, and her family in particular. Her husband Don represented the strong trunk holding it all up, Donny and Donovan branched the family out into the world, and lastly she, the ornament that turned an ordinary tree into a Christmas one. She thought herself rare and delicate like the handcrafted European glass ornaments she selected in West Germany, or the silvery ones made out of mercury glass she found in Poland one year on a trip. To further the symbolization, she requested her sons and husband find and cut down a towering specimen to further promote their bond.

Don and Donny always agreed to lie about how they attained the tree. It strengthened their bond, until Donovan joined them when he reached walking status. Within a year he'd snitched their methods to his mother, and they began leaving him at home the following year. He quickly became the sous chef to Cordelia's decorating. She taught him tree upkeep secrets, and he adopted her vision. By the time he turned ten he could erect an entire Putz village from memory.

She filled two mugs with steaming tea and handed them to Donovan.

The previous month, Don bought her a Silver Pine, one of those new aluminum trees from the Addis Brush Company, but Cordelia didn't like the artificiality of it. She called it a starved Christmas and stuck it in the library for him to appreciate. He found a box of cheap, metallic Christmas ornaments to hang on the skinny branches so it didn't look so bare, and that was that.

Donovan found his father staring at the same sad tree as he entered the library. "There you are."

His voice animated Don to life. "Do you think it upsets your mother that she goes through all the trouble of decorating in the main area, only for us to convene here in my study?"

"I think she's glad we're not disrupting her decorations," he answered, and lifted the mugs. "I have one for you."

"What timing," Don pointed to an empty glass nearby, "I just finished that one. Bring it here," He sniffed the liquid in his cup. "Are you sure this isn't made with your frou-frou whisky, what's it named?"

Donovan sighed. "You know what it is, Dad, the same as always."

"Ugh." He made a face. "I know, I know, Drambuie, the sweetest stuff on the planet Earth. I don't know how you stand it."

He sighed louder. "Did I catch you at a lousy time?"

There was a pause, then Don asked, "How is it that we're so different?"

"Is there something you want to say?"

Don eyed his son, measuring him. "You're suggesting I speak on it?"

"If we're men, yes, and if you're not too drunk."

Don laughed. "If we were men, we wouldn't have to speak on the subject."

"Need I remind you, the first comment came from you. I didn't come to talk to you about my liquor choices."

"Son, I'm not one for reading books and pontificating on *how* we do things signifying *what* we are, but you must see a correlation." Don held up a hand. "I apologize for my tone, but the fact that you sweeten your drink . . . you might as well tell me you still want to suckle at your mother's breast."

"What's that supposed to mean?" Donovan's face went beet red. "I'm no child."

He smiled and shook his head. "I didn't say that, don't do that. Stand up to me, don't whine about it."

"Riiiiiight, I'll keep that in mind." A beat. "You are drunk."

"How are things coming?"

"Suddenly, a pep talk seems harder to come by," Donovan edged out. He toyed with the paper square at the end of his teabag. "You haven't been around much lately."

"Been a little busy." Don eyed his son again. "I might as well tell you where I've been, you being nearer to the inner circle and all."

Donovan took care not to show how much the comment excited him.

"I've been on Sid's property mostly."

"Richardson," Donovan filled in, not knowing how to coax out a longer explanation. He knew enough about oil, and also knew making oil money wasn't the only thing going on at Sid Richardson's property. They shaped Texas history there. "Meet any famous people?"

"Of course." Don snapped his fingers with a raised eyebrow. "I should've gotten some autographs for you."

"Very funny. I've got more important things on my mind."

"That's what I like to hear! Pep talk?"

His father's declaration put him at ease. "More like advice." Donovan took a deep breath. "I haven't had the best of luck lately. Sure, the lawyers lost their case, but not with any help from me. Gus turned me down cold, and I visited the client last week. No go."

"Let me ask you something, did you expect either of them to say yes? I doubt your persuasive skills are honed that well."

"I don't know what I expected, to be honest. Horace said I should start approaching the other players on the team." He shrugged. "Trying to be proactive, I guess."

"I won't fault you for that. There comes a point where one needs to stop asking and start doing, that's the Symmetry way."

"What should I have done? I've got to start somewhere."

"Try approaching them later on down the road, those lawyers. If they have money it won't last long. They get desperate." Don peered inside of his mug, then poked his head out of the room and called for anyone to bring them fresh drinks.

Donovan sneaked a smile.

"I question your passion for this project," Don said.

The smile dropped. "Why do you say that?"

"A gut feeling. I've had them with many a candidate. It happens within five minutes of a challenge. It's in the eyes, after the reality of the situation hits them. Some have that ready-to-attack look; others maintain a control. I've seen panic before—a what-did-I-get-myself-into—but yours is a first."

Donovan saw the honesty on his father's face. He knew what he was about to say.

"Scared shitless, like you didn't know how to tie your shoes. Preston said you'd suddenly been dropped in the middle of a forest, then someone demanded you find useful objects to fight bears."

He ran a hand through his hair. "That's sorta what happened, I think."

"Most men act as you have your whole life, they react as if success is deserved and not far behind. Sure-footed. But you . . . you didn't want to be standing near us. Complete aversion."

"Oh. Wow. I didn't realize."

"That doesn't mean you can't turn it around. Just now, your self-awareness about being scared proved that. I need to see some fire in your eyes, a strength in your walk. Find that charm within you." Don grabbed his own groin. "Be big about it."

"Dad, you're drunk."

"So what, it's Christmas."

Kiana entered with a tray of whisky and placed it near the aluminum tree, which she eyed as suspect. Don asked her opinion of it, and with naiveté, Kiana said it looked naked, then glanced at Donovan. He did his best to acknowledge her answer without reacting, but it was that very behavior Don noticed.

He waited until she departed the room, then looked at his son grimly. "I coddled you like your mother would, telling you what you need to do, but I won't do that again. I will not sugarcoat it for you: In order to keep your foot in the door, you've got to go to extremes. But also know, I am not going to come to your rescue."

You never have, Donovan thought.

"I can tell this isn't going to be easy for you." He held up a hand. "And don't pretend like you don't know what I'm talking about. Your ignorance right now will piss me off. You must keep your mind on task and be strict with yourself. No truffles or trifles for you." Don glanced in the direction of the door. "This isn't a time to be sweet, on anyone."

Donovan's eyes widened with full understanding. He lowered his head. "I see what you mean."

"Are you going to be able to do this?"

"Absolutely. What is requested, can be fulfilled."

"This will make or break you. Remember that as you go through this." He tapped his glass with a fingernail.

Uneasily, Donovan said, "Merry Christmas. Dad." They clinked glasses.

"You too, Son, and a happy new year," Don sipped thoughtfully. "I tell you what, how about calling me Don? It'll probably take some getting used to, and I doubt you want to call me 'Dad' in front of other men. That might help in you finding your footing."

"How right you are . . . *Don*." The shared smile between them warmed him. "Can I ask, what did you do to earn your membership?"

"Uh-uh, you don't get to know until it's official. But I will say this: don't think I didn't have my share of distractions. It's all a test to see what you're made of."

Donny poked his head through the doorway. "My younger brother is made of horse-shit, as far as I know." His hair covered one eye and stopped just below his nose so he could still show his mouth curled into a smile from any angle. "Mom's playing Bing Crosby again and asked me to find you both. A 'White Christmas' indeed."

"Ever supportive," Donovan said, "and tactful."

Donny rolled his eyes as he took a few unbalanced steps into the room holding a beer bottle. "Say little brother, is a little lady coming tonight to be your date?" He glanced at the aluminum tree and made a face. "That's god-awful. Has an atomic bomb hit us already?"

"You said your mother called for us?"

Donny nodded, and set his sights back on his brother. "You didn't answer me."

Donovan shook his head lightly. "Horace might be stopping by."

"Oh, isn't that sweet, your best friend. How long have you two been dating?" He snickered at his joke.

"I'm not doing this," Donovan said to their father, and exited the room. He followed the sound of music and found his mother standing in front of the tree.

Cordelia gathered a handful of evergreen needles from the floor and inhaled them. "So warm and forest-y green. Darling, come sniff."

Donovan obeyed. "Who's coming this evening?"

She rattled off a list of names. "Not some of our regulars, I'll admit, but your father said it's business."

He spent a few hours sitting on the stairs, arguably one of the best seats in the manor when a party played out. Donovan watched his father's face soften as he shook hands with guests, then harden when he neared someone from Symmetry. He studied his mother's face, and did the same with Preston, who noticed and advanced toward him.

"Good boy! I hadn't seen you there, you might as well have been part of the scenery," Preston said. "I felt eyes on me and had to find the culprit."

Donovan laughed comfortably, and hoped the Drambuie helped with that. "Just learning."

Preston clapped him on the back. "Good to hear! How have things been coming along?"

Conscious of his smile evaporating, he tried some honesty. "I have some things in the works, but I'm not ready to talk about it right now."

"I can respect that." Preston looked to the people, then back at Donovan. "I will say, completing my challenge took me a little over two years. I learned so much about myself when I did the unexpected. If you need advice, I'm around." He closed the gap between them with a step.

Two years? Donovan could smell the liquor on his breath. "In my case, what sort of unexpected thing would you do?"

Preston finished his drink and made a sweeping gesture at the crowd. "Throw a party. Do you know how many intentions are hidden when one throws a party? Your mother is fantastic at it. Just look at this evening." He tried to drink from his glass and discovered it empty. "That's just me, everyone is different. Your dad would probably send a case of liquor."

"I don't know if that's unexpected," Donovan countered.

Preston's face grew inquisitive at his mention of Don. "I know your dad well, and he's probably using the same approach he did on your brother. Maybe even harder on you because Donny failed. Find your strengths, because none of us operates the same. It's not going to be one and done with your targets, it's a process of working them, visiting them, and finding a way to become valuable to them. Isn't it that way with everything? Women, especially," he scoffed. "My wife. My girlfriend. Just like Donny. I saw him trying to work one of yours in the library."

Donovan shook his head violently and felt his face go white. "One of mine? When?"

Preston waved a hand in the air. "You know what I mean." He pointed to the nearest maid. "One of *them*. Granted, they might give in more easily, but you still need to use some finesse."

"Excuse me sir, I need to use the restroom," Donovan said, and headed past the crowd for the library, unaware he caught his father's attention in the process.

The door to the library was slightly ajar, and he placed his ear near the opening, expecting to hear distressed noises. When he heard silence it worried him further. *What if Kiana accepted Donny's advances? What if?* He thought of his father using the phrase "scared shitless," and pushed the door open. A book flew at his face. "Hey!"

Donny turned to the door and smiled at Donovan, the evil look he knew well from childhood. As Donny walked past he grabbed the front of his pants in the same manner Don did earlier in the night. "When they want it, they want it."

Still fully clothed, Kiana slid down the bookshelf and sat on the floor as Donovan approached her. "Your brother is not like you," she said.

Panic and fury clawed at each other inside him as he squatted beside her. "What did he do?" He scanned her for clues, but found none.

"He kissed me and I pushed him away." Her hands shook as she gestured toward Donny. "He tried to talk me into it, and asked if you were the reason I wouldn't. He tried coming towards me again, and that's when I threw the book. Then you burst in."

"What timing," he said quietly. "What did you tell him? He didn't hurt you?"

She shook her head. "He stinks of liquor and cheese," Kiana said, her voice growing stronger. "His words ran together. He said he had a job to do."

"What did you say about me?"

She cocked her head back, indignation on her face. "I said nothing about anything." She straightened her apron. "I must get back out there."

"I didn't mean to say—"

"No. This is a price we pay." She walked out without looking back.

Donovan waited for all the guests to depart and joined his family in the main room. Without a word, he made a beeline for his brother. Donny attempted to stand, but fell back into the couch when Donovan punched him. Cordelia yelled out and ran to guard her tree in case a fight ensued, but the punch made Donny slide to the floor, passed out.

Don gripped the back of Donovan's arm fiercely and guided him outside to the terrace into the cold air. "Did you have to do that in front of your mother?"

"I wasn't thinking." He searched for words. "He was going to do something . . . stupid."

"Sitting in front of your mother and me, he wasn't doing much of anything."

"He'd already done something dumb. I wasn't going to let him take it further." Donovan began to pace. "One of our maids. It's not acceptable."

"The young one?"

"Exactly! Because she's too young."

"Hmm. Let me ask you something." Don waited a moment before delivering his next line. "What makes you think he hasn't already?"

Different expressions flitted across Donovan's face. "Her reaction, *Don*."

Neither said Kiana's name.

Don lifted an eyebrow. "I can imagine *they* can be quite dramatic when put in a tough spot. Defending their innocence and all that. Surely she's fond of you."

"What makes you say that?"

"Or maybe she's fond of you both!" Don said it brightly, as if it were the punchline to a joke. "The look on your face when you charged towards him," he laughed at the memory. "That's what I hoped for after we came to you. I saw a new son in there, alive with passion. You should get to know him."

CHAPTER 18

GUS AWOKE WITH HIS CHEEK FLOATING ON TOP OF A COLD BLACK SEA. He had passed out on the cold bathroom floor of his office. He struggled to his feet and went to the sink. In the mirror he could see a bruise forming on the right side of his neck. *How did I get on the floor,* he wondered groggily, *and how long have I been there?*

He flinched when a jarring knock sounded at his door. An envelope slid under it as a man's voice called out, "Urgent!"

The return address showed Judge Frank Martin's name. Instantly Gus was on full alert. What could the letter contain? He weighed whether he should make a drink before reading it, in case it was bad news. A wave of nausea swept over him as he ripped open the envelope with shaking hands.

Out loud, he read the letter by the Jackson County judge who had challenged his English. With each paragraph Gus's body stiffened. He took a few steps back to sit on his couch, once a bright orange houndstooth, now slowly turning brown from sloppy drinking, coffee, food, and pen marks. Like Gus, it seemed to be falling apart.

Dear Mr. García,

You called me a few days ago with reference to the Pete Hernandez case in Edna. I have since communicated with the court reporter, Mr. Otto Kehrer, and he advised me he has not received an order for a statement of facts from you or your team.

I presume you will want a statement of facts in some form, and in that connection I call your attention to the Session Laws of the 52nd Legislature, providing the attorney for the appellant shall file within fifteen days after the notice of appeal is given. The request is made of the official court reporter for the preparation of transcript of all or any part of the evidence desired, and shall specify the portions desired in narrative, plus question and answer form.

In view of the fact that Mr. Kehrer stays very busy he is not always able to get up a statement of facts within a few days, and if you desire a statement of facts in the cause mentioned above, I would suggest that you now make satisfactory arrangements with Mr. Kehrer for the statement of facts to be furnished. Particularly in view of the fact that over thirty days have elapsed since the motion for a new trial was overruled.

Yours very truly,
Judge Frank Martin, 135th District Court
January 16, 1952

He recalled Irene's letter back in August, when she asked him not to return home. *Now,* he thought, *this judge also chides my forgetfulness. Embarrassing, disappointing me.*

Gus wondered whether or not he had contacted the reporter, Otto Kehrer. *Did I think about it, but didn't follow through?* He racked his foggy brain. *What day is it? Was it the new year? Didn't I call the reporter directly after the loss? Or was it something I should've done?* No clear image came to mind. He tried to recall what happened at Christmas.

His trepidation grew as he scanned the papers on his desk and the floor, hoping to find any verification of a call. *Maybe one of the guys knows,* he hoped, but grew ashamed at the idea of asking John or Carlos, because it would be a confession of multiple blackouts. The pile of papers and scraps of notes grew messier as he shuffled through them looking for a clue.

He found a letter-sized envelope on his desk with Carlos's name on it that should've been delivered weeks ago, after they spoke on the phone. Boxes wrapped in silvery and gold paper and frilly bows—Christmas gifts for his daughters—leaned in the far corner of his office in brown paper bags . . . they too, should've been delivered weeks ago. Another demerit.

The holidays always carried an inexplainable heaviness for Gus, bringing on longer bouts of drinking than usual. The urge for oblivion was still strong. This time, he decided to forge ahead with work and dialed Victoria instead.

The reporter picked up on the first ring. "Otto Kehrer here."

"Mr. Kehrer! Gus García here. I'm from the Pete Hernandez trial in Edna. How are things down yonder?" His voice started to break.

"Ah, hello." A pause followed. "Mr. García, yes sir, things are busy over here. How about you tell me where you're located so I can send you a statements of facts? Call me Otto, please."

"Otto is a great palindrome name, just great," Gus blurted out.

"Uh, sure," Otto said.

"Did I call you already?" He cringed at asking the question, his voice cracking like a child hitting puberty. "I'm mortified I even have to ask, I just fired my s-ss-secretary because of her inefficiency at keeping tabs." *Was that a stutter?*

Otto drew out his words. "Not that I know of . . . actually, I've been waiting for your call."

"For the ss..." His cheeks warmed. "Ss...statement—" His cheeks turned a shade redder. *What was happening?*

"Statement of facts?"

"Yes, sss...s—" Gus took a deep breath. "We're appealing." With trembling hands he reached for the Chivas and poured a drink.

"Well, good for you," Otto said sarcastically. "Give me your office address and I'll get them to you as quick as I can. I wondered what took so long." He paused. "Unless it's not in the cards for you."

"Ah sir, it most definitely is," he said, feeling sheepish. "Things have been . . . *complicated* around here, especially with the holidays and all. And the secretary," he quickly added.

"I ran into Judge Martin last week, and your case came up in conversation. Gosh, I hope I didn't make things difficult for you, I know how tough he can be," Kehrer said. "Did he contact you?"

"How do you mean?"

"He sees potential in cases depending on the topic, and he tries to light a fire for lawyers like yourself, but not always in the most constructive way."

"He sent me a letter," Gus said, ashamed. "I'm over thirty days past due in filing appeal."

"Oh wowza, that's an honor. To be sent a letter, not to be past due. I'd feel . . . obligated if a judge sent me a letter a month after the case. He wouldn't do that for just any case." Otto paused again. "So, I'll have your request filled as soon as I can, sounds good?"

"Excellente," Gus said, "gracias," and then hung up the phone.

Gus counted the days since the retrial had been denied: December 15, until today, January 18. No matter which way he looked at it, it had been over a month. The judge mentioned it in his letter twice. He blushed again.

John's voice echoed in his head: Don't dwell.

He couldn't help but dwell. Stuttering like Carlos, why did *that* happen? Should he have imbibed more or not drunk at all?

Gus grabbed the paperwork he'd set aside for Carlos and walked to his office to deliver it personally.

The walk seemed to jog his brain a bit. About halfway there, a flash of memory stopped him: he remembered a trip to Mexico as a teenager, the first time he drank hard liquor with his abuelo.

The two drove in a day early, stayed at Evitarse, and ate dinner with Roberto. The following morning Gus asked Mateo numerous questions about which arena they would visit that day. As Mateo answered him, Gus noticed that his hands trembled constantly. At the bullfight, he produced for Gus a clear bottle the size of a cola and told him to take a small sip. Gus coughed for a full minute, but afterward his body hummed with joy. He noticed Abuelo stopped shaking after he drank some.

Now he realized his grandfather had been drunk the entire drive to Mexico. He couldn't put his finger on what was wrong at the time, but now things were becoming more clear.

CHAPTER 19

IRENE WAITED NOT SO PATIENTLY FOR GUS'S ARRIVAL BY STARTING VARIOUS chores around the house, then abandoning them mid-task. First the dishes, then straightening the girls' room, and then hemming a pencil skirt. She'd hardly started the last task when she pricked her ring finger threading the needle.

She sucked on her fingertip and switched to an easier project, brushing her hair. *Would he remember to show up?* She wondered. *What state would he be in if he did?*

Back in college Irene believed Gus to be the perfect man with a huge heart and ambition to match. He floated from group to group with a politician's ease and enough charm to get away with anything. She thought him to be gentle, giving, and his inner light golden and contagious. Men wanted to be like him, and women wanted to be *with* him.

She smiled at her reflection and hoped he would, too.

As time passed, Irene quickly learned that law drove Gus's life, even more than the drinking. She could compete with the bottle, but not with his frustration at his lack of recognition. Attention from others fed him in a way meat and vegetables couldn't.

Gus's top four: God, law, family, alcohol, and not necessarily in that order. Pretty soon though, the whisky won out because it didn't voice concerns or ask him to improve himself.

She hypothesized often about her life if she hadn't married him, or had kept him at bay longer. In college, women kept their men on a string—always wanting. But Gus, he knew the perfect words to utter and melt her heart. He had the ability to turn the conversation so smoothly, she hung onto his every word and said yes to everything.

Irene debated putting on the pendant he'd given her for Christmas the year before the last, in 1950—a simple gold chain clutching a jade stone. She wore it when she felt particularly fond toward him. He'd given necklaces to the girls as well: silver discs, nickel-sized, with their initials engraved on them. To say thank you, the girls hugged him over and over, and she hugged him in the dark, only to find him gone from their bed the next morning.

On second thought, she decided to leave the stone sitting in the box between her perfume and hairbrush. Jaded.

When the doorbell rang and ran to the door she jumped in her seat—a little too quickly, she realized—to let him inside. He was an hour late, and she imagined drunk Gus, or hungover Gus, unbathed, with greasy hair, a stubbled chin, and a disposition to matching his wrinkled clothes.

Instead, she found perky Gus when she cracked the door, his jade green eyes sparkling. The melting process within her began. His hair perfectly groomed and black as sin, his smile gleaming. In his hands were brown paper bags with what looked to be Christmas gifts inside.

"Irene," he said breathlessly, "my Reenie."

"Gus," she said, tempering her excitement, "mi Gustavo."

His voice quavered. "Is it me you still love? Am I the apple of your eye?"

She pressed her thumbnail into her palm to jar her back into reality. "Just because you may be the apple doesn't mean it's not rotting with a worm inside."

"Pero, mi amor, I thought you always liked my worm." A mischievous smile was his specialty.

Irene blocked his entrance. "No," she said stubbornly. "I am your wife, Gustavo, you will not flirt with me as if we were getting liquored up in some dark bar."

He took a step back. "You are correct, as always. I cannot help but, but to . . ."

"Be a smart-ass," she finished. "You can't help but be a smart-ass."

"Exactly," Gus said. A smile started on his lips, but he wiped it away and dropped his head, appearing embarrassed. "Can I come in?"

Irene turned away and let the door swing open. "Fine. Close the door, and join me at the kitchen table."

He obeyed. "Is something wrong?"

"No, I thought you'd like to sit. How are you?" *Not yet,* she thought, *it's not time yet.*

"Ragged. They denied us a retrial, and now we're working on appealing to the state courts."

Irene's eyes widened. "Wow. And you're the primary on the case?"

He matched her expression. "Seems so."

"Good luck, you will do well. Work hard. Be diligent." She squeezed his hand mechanically.

He sandwiched her hand with his. "How are you? How are the girls?"

"Good, good, we're good here." She thought she sounded fake, phony. "The girls are at a school function for the evening."

"You didn't ask me here to ask how work is going."

"I have not."

His face darkened. "I need to talk to you about a memory that resurfaced. I've been thinking on it for days. Do you remember me ever telling you a story about the first time mi abuelo gave me liquor? I was a teenager, up until that point it had only been beer. We were in Mexico at the time."

Taken aback, Irene looked at him in shock. "That's how you classify that bullfight? The first time you tried alcohol?"

"Well, I just put two and two together earlier today and I think he was drunk that entire trip."

Irene laughed in disbelief.

"Why are you laughing at me like that?"

"I just think it's funny you're worried about precisely the same issue I'm unnerved about with you." She crossed her arms.

"What are you talking about?"

"Christmas."

"I'm not sure what you mean. Christmas with you and the girls was grand."

"No, no it wasn't, Gustavo. You were drunk the entire time, don't you remember? You brought a ham when I told you not to, then became angry when you saw I had one. So you argued with me and tried to eat an entire ham at the dinner table, sloppily, I might add. Later, you ridiculed my gift choices for the girls, then unearthed your gifts . . . *from your office.* A stapler, some pens and folders." Tears formed at the corners of both eyes. "I didn't know what to say to the girls. Thankfully, this isn't their first time through this, so I didn't have to say much."

His mouth hung open. "No. I . . . I . . . that's not how I remember it."

"Of course not, you were drunk the entire time!" She screamed at the top of her lungs. "And you're here worried about something that happened twenty years ago?"

Gus went to his knees and held on to one of her hands. "I don't even know what's happening, please don't do this to me. The team and I, we're about to enter the next level. Our moves will be under a microscope, a spotlight. I need to remember where my home is," he pleaded, squeezing her limp hand. "I need to touch base with you."

She let out a shaky breath. "I can't do this right now, I can't take it." She forced herself to look back at him. "The girls, please, stay away for the sake of our girls. They're growing older, and have accepted the situation for what it is. If you come back to court them with gifts, even for a day, their hearts will take longer to recover when you don't return."

An angry look crossed his face. She jumped when he dropped a fist on the table. "Damnit Irene, please don't make this a repeat of what you did to me in August. Do you know what I'm going through? Your behavior is so . . . insensitive."

Calmly, she asked, "Can you get three steps outside yourself for once, enough to realize what you've put your family through?"

Gus banged the table again. "I'm not talking about you right now, I'm talking about me!" He studied her face. "See: no compassion whatsoever from you. You think this is easy, the road ahead of me?"

Her chest rose and fell in short breaths. "Minutes ago you were sweet as candy. Is this what saying no will get me?"

Gus stood up forcefully enough to tip the chair backwards to the floor. Irene saw panic fill his eyes, and she wanted to stay quiet, but words kept bubbling out. "The girls aren't tough enough yet, they've not been fully hardened by worry and strife. A father bouncing in and out of their lives on a whim: I do not want them to think that's what love is." A tear tumbled down her cheek. She tried to stay strong.

"What about you? Are you tough enough?"

"Apparently, I'm not." She lowered her head. Defeated, she said, "You're crushing me, Gustavo."

"You're the one crushing me!" Gus narrowed his eyes at her. "Does it feel good to act like a bitch in my time of need? What's that like?"

Irene looked at him, his face scrunched up and pissed off. She took a step forward and slapped him. "Get the hell out of here and shape up. I'm not going to talk about this with you anymore. You don't deserve it."

He walked to the door with his head hung low.

"Gus." Her voice changed, it went quieter, calmer. "You really need to come to terms with the way Mateo died. What you're doing to yourself is ridiculous."

CHAPTER 20

PUNCHING HIS OLDER BROTHER AT CHRISTMAS BROKE NEW GROUND IN Donovan. A rush of power burst through him, not only over Donny but over the entire world. Later, he sensed the same could be done with his Symmetry membership. He envisioned a version of himself that took control and got things done. A successful, professional Donovan, a persuasive Donovan who people wanted to get behind. His new year began with a promise to behave like that person, and the switch within him was that of a method actor.

It was time for him to approach the next name on his list: John J. Herrera. Rather than making an appointment, Donovan chose an ambush. He hoped catching John off guard might push him to make a decision he would've waited on otherwise. He spent the first half of his drive to Houston by preparing his offers, and the second half keeping his self-esteem high. He did this by reminding himself of his motivations.

Membership to Symmetry topped the list, that and his family's respect. He wished there was an option available where he didn't have to rely on other people's help for acceptance into the group. Hindsight told Donovan he jumped the gun and shouldn't have visited Gus right away, but his confident inner self said the day would be different with John Herrera.

He approached John's office building and waited outside. If they met on John's turf, Donovan assumed it would bolster John's confidence and dim his own, so he sat on a cement bench to study his talking points.

If John harbored the smallest seed of dislike toward Gus, Donovan felt he could capitalize on it without being obvious. The idea was to keep their meeting as lighthearted and off-the-cuff as possible . . . until the last moment, when he would reveal his offers.

Around noon, a tall and confident John walked out wearing a black overcoat that covered his clothes. Donovan noticed a take-charge attitude in his stride as he neared. He stuck out his hand to shake John's. "Mr. Herrera! I tell you what, it's a damn fine pleasure to meet you. My name is Donovan," he said in a folksy tone he hoped would fit the moment.

John smiled back carefully with a raised eyebrow. "The same goes for you, my friend!" As they shook hands Herrera pulled him in slightly and lowered his voice. "Should I know you?"

Donovan nodded. "A busy man like you, I'm not sure you would know me! But you will soon." He laughed, hoping to keep his last name a secret until the last possible moment. "Can I take you to lunch? I have a proposition for you and I'd love to get more than a few moments. Do you have time?"

"You've caught me on a solo lunch day, but I suppose I can manage a free lunch." John pointed down the street. "I frequent a restaurant nearby. Do you like authentic Mexican food?"

"You know, I can't say that I even know what that is!" He bit his lip to stop talking in exclamations.

"Great, I'll introduce you to some. Let's walk, it's only a couple of blocks, and it'll give you time to tell me a bit about yourself."

Donovan nodded, already caught off guard and out of his element. The fantasy in his head started differently: he hadn't weighed out what information to give about himself. "I'm a Kincaid from Austin." *There goes that,* he thought.

"I see!" John's eyebrows raised. "You heard about me how?"

"A peer, Horace Wimberly. I believe the two of you took some of the same classes at North Texas." The words tumbled out of him too fast, but he saw the effect they had on John.

His face softened at the mention of his alma mater. "A friend of an alum chum! How is Horace doing? Working with the attorney general, isn't that right?"

"He is, he is, ambitious as ever . . . and still short."

John laughed heartily at the joke, a boom that seemed to surround them. "Here we are," he gestured. "After you."

María, the woman who cooked, brought recipes from Mexico passed down through four generations. She greeted them at the door and received John like a son, who hugged her readily. Though the top of her head only reached a few inches above his waist, John treated her with the deference and admiration one would give a queen. She smiled, Donovan also noticed, with the same careful look John had given him earlier. "Who is this?"

"Donovan, ma'am." He bowed to her. "You have a beautiful establishment."

"Don't lie to me, young man," María chuckled, then glanced at John. "This place looks like a dump. It's about the food. Eat some of my cooking and then we'll talk." She walked away talking to herself.

"My table is back there," John pointed. "In the corner."

"Where the girl is placing cutlery and a martini?"

"The very one. Should she get one for you as well?"

"Might as," Donovan smiled, and signaled at the girl.

The two sat and John steepled his fingers between them. "Now. What brings you to me?" He squinted at him. "I've gone through it in my head, and I can't fathom what sort of help a Kincaid would need—who has a friend at the attorney general's office, I might add."

Donovan's eyes widened in response, and he quickly recalibrated his talking points. "To be truthful, part of this is about what we can contribute to you." He loosened the knot in his tie, then decided to remove his jacket. "My family, my mother actually, hosts various parties for my father and their friends." Donovan tensed at his mention of parties, and for the briefest of moments he could feel the pressure of his brother's face against his tightened fist. "A certain Christmas party in particular will interest you, where the guests can vie for large sums of money."

John frowned.

"That came out wrong." Donovan sipped hungrily on the martini placed before him, though he couldn't recall when it appeared. "My father and his associates set aside large sums every year to invest. Instead of holding interviews, they throw a party and invite a list of people or groups. This gives both sides an opportunity to meet under more jovial circumstances. The thing has grown so much that if one is at the top of the list the invitations are offered early in the year." He winked. "Which you are, by the way."

"Here it comes!" The men turned their heads towards María and two girls holding their plates of food. "My special dish," she flourished, "molé over turkey. Do you know what molé is, Mister Donovan?"

A flash of Kiana undressing before him interrupted his thoughts, causing him to lose his words momentarily. "Molé," he repeated. "I do not."

"It's a Latin dish, made from chiles, vegetables, nuts, and seeds," she said proudly. "This recipe has been passed down four generations."

"It's difficult to explain how it tastes," John said. "I urge you to try it. Hers is as authentic as you're going to get in the states. Well, in Tejas, at least."

"Yes, yes of course." Donovan looked deeply into María's eyes, attempting to communicate that her presence interrupted them.

She batted her eyes at him as if she couldn't read social cues at all. "Taste, taste," she urged.

Donovan spooned a small amount into his mouth. Bitter and hot on his tongue, it carried a certain warmth he'd never tasted before. "Complex. I've never had anything like it."

María smiled and nodded. "I'll take that as a compliment, coming from you."

John chuckled. He paused a few beats before continuing. "You mentioned a list."

"Your entire team, to be more exact."

"My firm?"

"No, actually. A civil rights case you're a part of, an appeal was filed recently, correct?" A thin layer of sweat began to form underneath Donovan's button-up. "The work has perked the ears of some rich men, and they'd like to meet the team. Plus spouses."

John wore his poker face. "Impressive. I had no idea we were on someone's radar. How did you, or they, learn about us?"

"Who knows? Probably from the same people who caught wind of Thurgood Marshall. The point is, you've been noticed. Now is the time to push forward and know you're being watched." He thought his laugh sounded shrill. "There I go again, saying stupid things. What I mean to say is, this is something worth working toward, because it could pay off." One pause turned into several.

"You're a busy man," Donovan continued, "but I'd appreciate if you'd spend some time thinking about it."

"I'm curious, how many cases are you personally involved with at your firm? Twenty? Fifty?"

"Closer to the second number. Why do you ask?"

Donovan shrugged. "I'm just trying to imagine how busy you must be. I noticed as well that you're running for national office?"

"In a few months." John's frown returned. "Listen, I'm not sure if it's your method or demeanor, but I'm beginning to find this encounter unsettling. I suggest we get the check and return to our starting point." He began to stand up.

"Wait, please! I'll come clean, please. I promise." Donovan signaled for two more martinis. "I'm in an odd position, a fortunate one as well, but odd all the same. Though I'm the man before you delivering a message from men who can bankroll your case all the way to the Supreme Court, I'm also working for the other side. I'm also the man offering you money or votes if you can get your head counsel to drop the case."

"What the hell are you talking about?"

The waitress placed the martinis in front of the men, but neither reached for their glass.

"Gus."

"Votes?"

"To win your presidential slot, if that's what you desire. LULAC, I think it's called. Or money. Whatever you prefer, the options are endless."

John stared at him in disbelief. "Who *are* you?"

"Like I said, a man in a rare position." Donovan studied his face and leaned in closer. "There's a reason you haven't gotten up and left. What's it like working with Gus? He's unpredictable, isn't he? I bet it's hard to place all your bets on him. Every time I turn around I hear about him making a scene in a courtroom. Maybe it's time to give him some rope, huh?"

Suddenly, María burst into the room shaking a finger at Donovan. "Okay, that's enough! I think it's time you pack up and leave my establishment." She turned to John. "Johnny, don't listen to this man one bit. He's the devil incarnate, and I can't believe you've sat here for this long." She turned back to Donovan. "Shame on you! You come to this man, a good man, to dangle dirty money and power, thinking it will elevate you. No doubt you're working with others like you."

Donovan watched her face turn red as she chided him. Her frustration turned into a fuel for the new Donovan, the one who punched his brother in the face. He simply smiled sweetly at her. "We can work in a deal for you too, María, don't be shy. All you have to do is ask. I could make your restaurant popular with my people in a snap. I could get you money to expand this place, better tables and chairs. Better ingredients."

María looked at John with a pleading expression, and he stood up. "I think it's time to walk back to my office, what do you say Mr. Kincaid?" He waited until Donovan stood, then said, "María, I wait for the moment when you forgive me for bringing in the wrong patron." She squeezed his arm and left them while ignoring Donovan.

"Mr. Herrera, I need you to know something," Donovan said as they walked out the door. For a moment he thought about what it would be like to admit his true motivation. He went so far as to open his mouth, but hesitated at the last minute and reminded himself of the plan. "I must tell you, I can't possibly move forward on my own. I need your help, and no one can do it but you." The new Donovan has no trouble with lying, he realized. "In reality, it'll only save you from some work. Either that, or you can put those precious hours to better use by finishing strong in your campaign and spending the next year serving your people properly."

John shoved his hands in his pockets and listened with an absent-minded look. "I've done some stupid things in my life, especially in my youth." He chuckled. "I used to drive a taxicab for money, and police arrested me for selling liquor out of the trunk. Can you believe that? My father was a sheriff at the time." He shook his head. "I almost lost the opportunity to take the bar and become a lawyer. All because I chose to do something stupid. From then on, I decided to look out for the stupid things that could end my career. This is one of those times."

Donovan laughed uncomfortably. "I understand why you would think that. Hold onto this, just in case. You never know what can happen, stress can annihilate a person." He produced his business card from the inner pocket of his jacket. "Keep thinking about the Christmas party. It would be a great opportunity to stay on track."

They arrived back at the office building quickly and parted ways with a handshake. Donovan mentally moved to his next plan of attack. He knew one of his tactics would work before Christmas arrived, because everybody loves the chance for free money. The image of Symmetry members shaking his hand and his father clapping him on the back flashed through his mind. *Everything will be fine,* he told himself, *just keep trying. Do it for the family.*

The Kincaids developed a bad blood for Herreras two decades prior, when John Sr., a sheriff, had arrested Donny, who was selling liquor out of his car. A teenage Donovan woke in the middle of the night to hear his father ranting on the phone. He snuck out of his room to overhear the events being told to his mother, who let out a wail upon hearing the news. Symmetry had been considering him at the time, but word traveled fast, and Donny's reputation diminished faster.

As it is with wealthy people, Cordelia pushed Don to scrub Donovan's record clean on paper, but the damage had already been done. They spent countless hours trying to rehabilitate Donny's image with jobs and community service, with no luck, mainly because Donny liked the high rush he felt when he broke the law. He found it liberating, being unable to live up to the family name.

The family vowed revenge toward anyone in the Herrera family. Donovan realized this was his chance to fulfill a familial obligation.

A tiny voice inside him pointed out that John may not be aware that his father arrested Donny, but he decided it didn't matter. Revenge was revenge, and the endgame was the goal.

He found physical solace with Kiana when he returned home to Austin. Their connection surprised him upon each reunion. Every time he approached her he expected their relationship had dissipated since the last time, but each time she accepted him with open arms. Kiana's presence reminded him of the old Donovan, the one who didn't lie or bribe to try and get ahead. Being with Kiana made him feel so good, he felt refreshed enough to trudge on, to become something he dreaded as he tried to get into Symmetry.

Time arrived for him to make another move.

CHAPTER 21

"GIRLS! IT'S TIME TO WAKE UP, SPRING HAS SPRUNG!" IRENE PUSHED APART yellow and white curtains in her daughters' bedroom to bring in the light. "The sun is rising and so should you both on a day like this."

"Moooom, please." Carlita pulled her blanket over her face.

"I know, I know." Irene ducked underneath the blanket. "But you girls were at school, and now your spring break is beginning." She leaned in for a kiss and her chocolate brown hair tumbled over her shoulders.

"Moooom!" Carlita made a spitting noise. "No thank you to your hair for breakfast."

Teresa, being the younger sister and always longing to be part of the action, got up and gently pushed her mother into her sister's bed. Irene tumbled in willingly, and the three fell into giggles.

"See now, this is how our day should begin," Irene pulled Carlita's blanket over their heads. "You have all week to sleep in if you so choose. But I want nothing more than to begin my spring gardening to the sounds of my daughters playing in the front yard."

Carlita rubbed the sleep out of her eyes. "Can we have pancakes for breakfast?"

"Yes!" Teresa jumped up and pulled away the blanket in the process.

"Well," Irene smiled, "that answers that. Get ready for the day and I'll get it ready."

Teresa raced for the bathroom with Carlita at her heels.

Irene felt joy as she heard her daughters fall into their normal morning bicker as she opened and closed cabinet doors to retrieve ingredients. "Today will be a beautiful day." She poked her head inside the refrigerator and spoke to the carton of eggs. "Today *is* a beautiful day."

Repeating morning mantras had become a routine since Gus stopped living at home, a decision she continued to wrestle with. The tension leaked out to the girls: Carlita grew moody more often, leading to arguments, while Teresa turned into a people-pleaser to attract attention. Irene knew her rift with Gus to be the catalyst, but it was the lesser of two evils.

She cracked an egg into a melted puddle of butter and added another. The yolk turned a bright orange as it bubbled around the edges.

"Mom."

Irene jumped and turned to see Teresa. "You scared me, love. What's wrong? You're still in your pajamas."

She nodded. The girl—not unlike Amelia—stood short with dark brown hair that fell past her shoulders. Her nightwear consisted of an oversized teeshirt that reached her feet and swallowed her whole, plus a pair of white socks. "Um, it got quiet after Carlita closed the door, and I started thinking." Her voice cracked. "About Dad."

"Oh, come here darling." Irene knelt on the floor and opened her arms. She smelled the eggs behind her. "Don't cry, little one."

Teresa's bottom lip quivered as she pulled herself away from her mother's arms. "When will we see him again?"

"Maybe this week, he knows you two don't have school." Irene tried her best to sound reassuring.

"Can we call him?" Teresa's eyes darted to the doorway as if she felt someone watching her. "Or, can I? I don't know if she wants to talk to him."

"Of course." She tucked a lock of hair behind Teresa's ear and whispered. "Does your sister make you feel guilty for missing him?"

She nodded sheepishly.

"Don't feel badly, my sweet," Irene said. "We'll find some time early one morning to call when your sister's still sleeping. It'll be our secret."

At this, Teresa's eyes brightened some. "Yes." She went back to her room.

Irene found the eggs slightly overcooked, but still salvageable. The yolks stared back at her, hardening like a pair of questioning eyes. "Today will be a beautiful day."

She lifted the pan on one side and tucked the spatula underneath the eggs. The move was supposed to be seamless and easy; slide them onto a plate in one movement, no problem. Instead, she jerked when a drop of grease hit her forearm as she pulled the spatula out. The utensil punctured one of the eyes and yolk dribbled out over the egg white.

The oozing reminded Irene of the time Carlita came home from school with a busted blood vessel in one eye. Dark red veins near her pupil spidered out and slowly took over her entire eye. Carlita cried out that her brain was dying from the inside out, but Gus calmed her down by convincing her she might gain superhero powers after healing.

"Mom," Carlita said. "What are you doing?"

"Overcooking eggs." Irene decided the eggs had hardened too much and dumped the plate into the trashcan. "Want to help me?"

Carlita approached the stove. "I will with the pancakes."

Irene came back to reality and smiled. "See, you're helping already."

Carlita studied her. "You're having a rough day."

She kissed her daughter's head. "I don't know what you're talking about, today is going to be a beautiful day."

"Yeah, sure mom, whatever you say."

"If I said yes, would that change anything?"

"Actually, yes." Carlita made direct eye contact with her. "It would help me see you're human."

Irene measured this. "Yes, I'm having a rough morning, but don't tell your sister. Still want to help?"

Carlita responded with a hug. "Much more."

Breakfast finished smoothly, and Irene cleared the table while the girls gathered what they wanted to take outside. Teresa took a small crate of toys and Carlita grabbed a book and her jumprope. They walked out the front door to find a wheelbarrow filled with sunflowers in six small pails. As they turned to Irene, they squealed at her attire. She wore an apron covered in a sunflower print with a matching ribbon on her straw hat.

"Wait, there's more!" Irene pulled out a pair of matching gardening gloves. "I couldn't resist." She attached the hose while Carlita went to turn on the water. Teresa went to splash her sister. "Not yet, you two. We can get wild later in the day."

The girls shared the hoe and rake to prepare the soil while Irene used a spade to take out patches of grass and weeds. The girls lost interest and switched to their activities once Irene began pouring compost.

Scents of freshly dug soil, grass, and compost, along with the sound of her girls playing, sent Irene to her happy place. She measured the spacing between each bunch of sunflowers and dug holes, taking her time. Occasionally she stopped to appreciate the weather and glance at the girls during their jumprope contest, then at the army of toys Carlita helped Teresa build when she lost said contest.

As Irene tucked the third bunch of sunflowers into the earth, she noticed the girls went silent. *They must be hungry for lunch,* she thought, and sat back on her feet to judge the time of day by her shadow. As she did, her shadow began to swell and double in size as if the sun had set in a matter of seconds. She turned around to see a woman blocking her light.

"Hello there," the woman said.

Irene took careful notice of the woman from the bottom up as she stood. The woman wore heels, about four inches tall, and a small pair of white shorts that stopped halfway down her thigh. Her blouse, a warm orange tone, clung to her skin. "Hello. Can I help you?"

The woman shook her dirty-blonde hair off her neck with a whip of her head and straightened her shoulders. "You're Irene, am I right? Irene García?"

Irene nodded. She gauged the looks on her daughters' faces. They both looked suspicious and worried at the same time. "It's about lunchtime, girls." They didn't move.

"You're the wife of Gus?" The woman's eyes sparkled.

Without breaking eye contact, Irene raised her voice. "Girls!" Carlita grabbed Teresa's hand and tugged her inside the house. "He's not here."

"Hm-mmm," the woman said. "I know."

The confidence in her voice straightened Irene's spine. "You know so much, and here I am, unaware of your name."

The woman flicked her hand in the air to show her indifference and a pair of newly manicured red nails. "Wouldn't you like to know?"

"Did I not make myself clear that I wanted to know?" Irene made a show of looking at the woman's feet. "Actually, woman-I-do-not-know, would you mind stepping onto the sidewalk? Either that or take off your shoes."

The woman flashed a fake smile and took a step backwards. "I'm here to deliver a message."

Irene took a step forward. "I don't care about your message, I want to know who you are."

"Patricia, my name is Patricia." She shook her hair back again.

The woman's demeanor changed the moment the name exited her lips, and Irene caught it. "I see." She saw a flicker of fear pass over the woman's eyes.

"We're in love, your husband and I." She puffed her chest out again.

Irene squinted at her. "And what . . . you're getting married?"

"Wha—um, yeah." Her hands clutched her abs as if a belly sat underneath.

"That is the universal sign for pregnant," Irene pointed out. "I think you meant to show me a ring on your left hand."

The woman looked down at her bare fingers. "It's going to happen," she said. "I thought you should know. We're going to live together and start a family."

Irene couldn't help but smile conspiratorially. "Gosh, I don't know where to begin. How do you fight bulls and keep your nails that length?"

The smug expression fell from her face. "I . . .I . . ."

"Yes, I know about you." Irene lowered her voice an octave; it became compelling, almost hypnotizing. "The matadora, sí." She took a step to the side, then another. "I know enough about you to know you are not who you say."

The woman quickly realized Irene was slowly making a circle around her. "You know nothing."

"Nor do you. You don't know my husband sleeps with more than one woman, and would never look to have another marriage, much less a child. You don't know how much he's told me about the woman you're trying to mimic, and how many ways you've gotten it wrong." Each declaration propelled Irene forward a step. She stopped. "Who sent you?"

After several tense moments, the woman weakly lifted both her hands in defeat. "Look lady, you're right, I didn't know what I was getting myself into. I got a phone call, but never saw the guy."

Irene cursed. "He gave you this address?"

She nodded. "Gave me the lowdown, wired me money." She let out a whistle. "I even asked for a little more info on that woman, *Patricia*, because he offered a pretty price. He said it wouldn't matter in the long run, but I can see it does." Another whistle. "Seriously lady, your husband tells you that much about the women he sleeps with?" She lifted an eyebrow. "Do you two get off on that sort of thing?"

"Not exactly," Irene said sadly. "Marriages mean different things to different people. So does compromise."

"Uh-huh, never been married." She pointed to the sunflowers. "Your flowers are pretty, I wanted to tell you that earlier, but I was trying to stay in character."

Irene nodded wistfully at the front yard. The sight appeared odd, three plants on one side and nothing on the other. "I choose them nearly every year because of their meaning. Sunflowers represent loyalty, adoration, and longevity. To this day I still see adoration in my husband's eyes despite his wrongdoings, and I am loyal to him for that. Therefore, longevity has become part of our language."

The woman's eyes widened. "Whoa."

"Are you sure you don't know anything about the man who hired you? I'm pleading with you here."

"Sorry, wish I did." The woman snapped her fingers. "They should have a machine by the phone that tells you the number someone is calling from. Bet that would help in a lot of situations."

"Bet it would." Irene turned to the house as the woman walked away.

"Hey lady. Your husband."

Irene spun around. "What about him?"

She pointed to the sunflowers. "Does he know about that flower stuff? Why you plant them?"

Irene shook her head. "He's never asked."

CHAPTER 22

GUS SHARED THE STORY OF IRENE'S STRANGE VISITOR TO CARLOS AND JOHN AT a meeting. "I'm not being paranoid, but someone is out to get us. Or me. Or this case. I haven't decided which." He drummed his fingers on the table in front of him when he spoke.

"I think you mean some-*thing*," Carlos responded. He waved over the breakfast bowls before them. "Have some fruit, eat a taquito, a donut. We have a deadline to meet in less than a month. I'd say have another cup of coffee, but I think you've had enough." He reached for a glazed donut and bit into it happily.

John nodded.

Gus lightly banged his fist on the table. "This is no joke. Have either of you come across anyone odd or suspicious?" He whirled a finger around in a circle. "In this office, has anyone said anything to you? Cadena, you need to be serious with me. Herrera?"

"I am being serious and I think you're acting silly," Carlos said. "Whether someone is or isn't after you shouldn't bother you in the slightest. Things of more importance need your attention." He tapped the top of his desk with a forefinger. "This case, for instance, whose deadline is in June. Herrera, you've been quiet, how about you weigh in on this?"

John smiled widely. "I can't help it. How long have the two of you been married?" He bit into his taquito. "If you both would like me to step outside, I'd be glad to do it."

Gus scowled and grabbed a taquito from the small pile. He hadn't shared his encounter with Donovan yet, though he knew it would prove his paranoia, not a lack of it. He squinted at John while he unwrapped the paper from the tortilla. "You didn't answer my question."

John pulled the skin from a banana. "Was it not rhetorical? You say you're not paranoid, but I don't believe you. Your eyes flit about every time you mention it. Really, Gustavo, you keep this up and I might find cause to worry." He shifted in his seat, afraid to tell Gus about Donovan for fear of worsening his condition.

"Hear, hear," Carlos agreed.

Gus alternated his gaze between the two men. He saw the doubt growing in their eyes, the questions they held back, similar to the looks his daughters gave him before he moved out. A gut feeling arose in him that someone was lying. He bit into his taquito and stared at Herrera. "You still haven't answered my question."

"I've been bombarded by all sorts of people in the past few months, odd and otherwise. Everyone seems suspicious." John paused. "With that being said, I know of nothing suspicious. Only odd."

"Speaking of," Carlos feigned a cough and raised his glass of orange juice. "Can I just say again, congratulations, Johnny. National LULAC president is quite an accomplishment for your résumé. The upcoming year will be filled with surprises and I'm proud to be making history with you."

Gus gripped his orange juice glass tightly and raised it reluctantly. "To the future." The clink their glasses made triggered the urge to drink. He scowled.

John shifted in his seat, evidently unable to enjoy the win. His gaze continued to wander, thinking of Donovan Kincaid. "I guarantee this won't affect my work with this case."

"Of course not," Carlos waved the thought away.

"Actually, I was wondering that," Gus jumped in. He unconsciously squeezed the taquito in his hand. "How do you know it's not going to hinder your work here?"

John and Carlos traded looks. "I don't, but I'm choosing to think a little more positively," John said. "It's one of the reasons Cadena joined. And I hoped word of our case would travel farther and have more meaning behind it with my win."

Gus tensed. "Oh, so your victory validates our case? *My* case?" Chunks of egg and potato fell onto his shoe.

John raised his voice. "Is there something we need to talk about? I didn't think it would come to this, but here we are. You're obviously holding something in." He snapped his fingers several times. "Out with it."

Gus knew his thoughts were foolish. It wasn't as if he wished the LULAC presidency belonged to him. The constant travel would bore him, and representing the club night and day would exhaust him. It was the idea behind the win that he longed for. Men approached John to run for office, he didn't choose it for himself. People wanted . . . him. Furthermore, a large group of people elected him at a conference with other LULAC members. Gus craved the influence and power John possessed, but he refused to admit it. Plus, the win; he ached for a win like that. Then there was Donovan. He threw his hands up in the air. "I'm dealing with things. I need some fresh air."

John and Carlos stayed silent a few minutes after Gus left the room for fear he'd reenter while they spoke about him. Carlos spoke first.

"Be honest. Do you think someone sent a woman out to Irene to get at Gus? I don't see what good that would do now. He's been out of the house for nearly a year." He nibbled on a strawberry, then reached for another taquito.

"I agree," John said. "But to be honest, I think it actually happened." They laughed to lighten the mood. He cleared his throat. "Is he this paranoid all the time?"

Carlos nodded, painfully embarrassed to be doing so. "Not all the time," he corrected. "It comes and goes." He bit into the taquito with fervor and spoke in a muffled voice. "The drinking has worsened, but he's going through a separation. It's about Irene."

John raised an eyebrow. "Have a crush, do we?"

"Stop. I'm just saying she's a difficult woman to move on from."

He leaned in. "Let me be honest. I *was* approached by someone who asked me to stop the case or switch to head counsel."

Carlos chewed more furiously until the egg, cheese, and potato turned into mush. He swallowed with a loud gulp. "Ah, so this is what paranoia feels like. Who was it? What did you say? Was he trying to bribe you? We could press charges."

"I don't know who it was, he didn't reveal his name to me, and I couldn't get it out of him," John lied. "Probably a peon representing big names too cowardly to show their faces." He shook his head. "I didn't want to tell Gus after the way he behaved earlier. Should I?"

"It's probably best to refrain," Carlos mumbled. "Gus has an imagination that can grow like a cancer." He glanced at the door. "Should we worry about this?"

John debated on whether to share about the Kincaid Christmas party invite, but footsteps approaching the door interrupted him.

Gus reentered the room and walked straight to John. "I'm sorry, I'm losing my mind. You never flaunted this in my face, you never tried to make me feel inferior, that was all my doing. I don't wish to be in your position, being president of LULAC is something I don't have the attention span for. You're being recognized for your hard work, and you deserve to celebrate. I desired the respect and recognition, that's all." He looked at Carlos, and back at John. "I can't help but be paranoid because of the situation we're in, and I understand I need to focus my thoughts on other subjects. God knows there's plenty to think about."

Carlos clapped. "Yes! This is what we need. Take charge of yourself for all of us."

John regarded Gus's apology with some skepticism, but the option to trust him seemed like the less dramatic choice. "I accept your apology. Let's not make it a habit, bueno?" He placed both hands on Gus's shoulders. "You are head counsel, you hear me? No one in this room can get out of you what is needed except you. We each have cases and people who depend greatly on us, and for you, that is Pete Hernandez and his case. Let's not let him down."

Gus nodded, biting his tongue the entire time and drawing blood.

Getting their appeal granted meant everything to Gus. Time was his biggest enemy, the waiting for something to happen made every moment drag. Drinking ticked the seconds away faster, and passing out from drinking sped up the hours. He knew he attacked his problem all wrong, but it was the only way he knew how to fight it.

CHAPTER 23

REPRESENTATIVES FROM LULAC AND THE AMERICAN GI FORUM TRAVELED TO San Antonio to discuss the next steps after they learned the Texas Criminal Courts denied the lawyers' attempt to appeal. Trying for the Supreme Court meant money, time, and support—all rare jewels for the men.

John spoke first. "Is now the time? We didn't appeal Aniceto's case to the state court, but do we want to with Pete? What variables have changed or improved?" He swallowed some water.

"There's talk of Thurgood Marshall doing it, why can't we?" Gus looked at their cocked eyebrows.

Dr. Victor Gonzales from LULAC spoke up. "It's a lofty idea. But first off, they have more funds. Do you realize, on the whole, his supporters are likely to donate three times as much money as ours will? If we lose . . ."

"I know without a doubt we're ready for it," John said. "Though the terms might've been better with Aniceto, we've got the experience from his case to help us to the next level."

"Not to mention," DeAnda interjected, "Aniceto didn't want to go to the next level because one, he didn't want the attention, and two, ten years in jail wasn't a bad deal to him."

Gus spoke. "I will admit honestly that Pete doesn't want to go forward either. He doesn't want the attention. Or rather, he's tired of what he's already had to deal with. On the other hand, we must take the risk now and strike while the iron is hot. The topic is heavy on people's minds." He swirled a golden tumbler so the ice clicked together.

Everyone saw him pour the Chivas into it. The activists traded uneasy looks with one another but said nothing.

John noticed. "So time to strike, then." He raised his glass to Gus.

Carlos raised his glass of soda.

Gus lifted his tumbler to them both. "Exactly," he replied. "We will never be younger than we are now. Carlos, you're at the top of your game and can mince words while constructing an exquisite argument that I will do my best to match. John, you have the clout and hopefully the fundraising skills to fire our rocket to the moon!"

Carlos raised his glass. "It sounds as if our lead speaker will be able to dice words as easily as I! Your tongue flicks silver as you speak, Gustavo."

"I'm merely saying I have utter belief in my partners, and believe the argument solid," Gus said. "We will convince the animal to bend to our will and listen. We will be cunning in our story and hypnotize them in the arena."

A group hip-hip-hooray notched up everyone's mood. Maury Maverick Jr., known by his last name, was a fellow lawyer close to the team. He suggested they move down the street to La Mancha to drink a few. Maverick bought everyone a round, and the more others drank the darker their conversational tone turned, full of worry and doubt about one particular issue.

Many of them spoke to John about it. He found Gus sitting alone, drinking and staring at the wooden table in front of him. "Everyone is worried about how much you drink."

Gus waved him away. "I drink so much today because the courts denied us, and you should too." He gestured at their acquaintances. "They should as well."

John lowered his voice. "I'm not talking about now, I'm talking about your drinking problem. Just because you want everyone else to drink doesn't diminish the way your drinking looks to those same people," he hissed.

"Calm down, mi amigo, you sound angry." Gus sipped at his whisky.

"Must we add liquor to our budget? How much of your talent is born of that brown liquid you hold? What might you sound like without it?" John arched an eyebrow.

Gus laughed. "Do you mean liquor isn't a part of our budget already?"

"God knows a spotlight will be on all our lives, and reveal every problem any of us has. What will they illuminate in you, Gustavo?"

"JJ, I'm joking. You'll be glad to know liquor is a part of my personal budget, so no need to worry." Gus staggered a bit. "Let me say though, one might say I'd know my way around an arena or a courtroom better if I drank!"

Some of the men who gathered near them laughed at Gus's joke, egging him on to continue.

"Besides, what do you care? Is it because the national LULAC president is scared for his image? Are you going to revoke my membership?" Suddenly, Gus began to feel guilty for what he said. He wanted to go back to what he was doing before John approached him. He wiped the jokester smile from his face. "How about instead, you just leave me alone? You came to me."

Gus swiveled his chair to face a different wall. He went back to thinking of Irene before they argued; she took the time to share the story of the strange visitor, but nothing more. He thought of one of the sweeter times they spent together, when she told him they'd always be a part of each other, but needed to be apart. Something more than the wordplay and emotional content of the statement struck him, but he couldn't pinpoint what.

Unbeknownst to Gus, Maverick gestured for Carlos to sit in a corner of the bar before asking Gus to join them.

Before Gus could start bringing out his persona, Maverick held up his hand. "Oyes Gustavo, I need to say something and I didn't want to do it in front of everyone. Carlos is here to support you. Your drinking—" His voice cut off as he appreciated a voluptuous woman who sauntered past them.

Gus did the same, but Carlos didn't look.

The woman entered the bathroom and brought Maverick back. "Jokes are jokes, agreed?"

"I concur," Gus said. "We all have a joking nature. Except for Carlos."

Carlos smiled and sipped his soda.

"Claro que sí. Pero, personally, I'm worried about your intake. You and I have known each other for years, enough to see the ebb and flow of our personal lives."

"Stop shitting on me, what are you getting at Mav? You're slick, but I am just as slippery. Just tell me," Gus egged on. "I think I already know, but I want to watch your lips formulate the words. Speak."

"Your whisky, amigo," Maverick sighed. "It's always been normal for you to drink, but in the past six months it's escalated, don't you think?"

"I try not to think when it doesn't have to do with this case. Damn, you're killing the mood, Mav. Is it you who's truly worried or did they put you up to it?" Gus scoffed. "I'm sacrificing myself for something important, don't you know that? Sacrifice means something." For the briefest of moments Gus wondered where he'd heard that saying. "This is my sacrifice. You of all people should know that."

"Gustavo! The sacrifice only means something if we win. How can we guarantee winning? Everyone will say you drank your way through, which isn't how you want to be remembered." Maverick shook his head. "This isn't bullfighting, my friend."

"What do you know about it?" Gus spoke quietly.

"This is coming from me, not from any of them. I know Irene kicked you out, so is that the root of the problem? Do you need a place to stay? Where have you been sleeping? I'm asking in earnest."

Gus frowned. "No, I don't need a place to stay. I've been staying at a motel," he lied. Anger began to build in him. "No one would've dared ask mi abuelo to watch his drinking."

"Oh no? How many cases was he working at a time?" Maverick jested. "Look, I know you want to drink your nights, but your cutoff for nighttime is happening earlier. You may not think this, but it changes your day. Some people have the luxury of doing nothing because they don't have the gift. But you, mi hermano, you have the gift. Drinking is only slowing it down."

Gus smirked.

"I'm not with you every moment, only you are. Maybe I'm wrong about all this."

"I'll be the first to admit, yes, I drink more than usual, but it's not abnormal for me to do that. It doesn't worry me. Does it worry you?"

Maverick nodded his head, slowly, with a speck of sadness on his face.

"Amigo," Gus said. "I don't get sidetracked because people of my kind are being killed for being in the wrong place at the wrong time . . . and when I say 'my kind' I don't mean just grown men and women, I mean children too, the little girls and boys who are murdered for being 'in the way.' If people choose to be more interested in my drinking than the injustice going on, I think we have another problem right there."

"I'm pushed on by the same shit! I'm on edge trying to stay on top of everything." Maverick ran a hand through his hair and lifted his hands in the surrender position. "Fuck, Gus, this case is going to intensify any issues you already have, we all know it. I know you know it too, but I don't think you're prepared for it."

"I asked Carlos to join our case! What more do you want from me?" He paced in the small area next to their table. "My drinking isn't what we should be focused on, my drinking is what's going to give me the longevity to see this through." He blew a raspberry into the air and squinted at Maverick. "If you guys are worried about me now," he pointed, "you better hold on to your hats. The volume is turning up and you all can kiss my ass. Carlos eats to deal and no one tells him he's eating too much. John is obsessed with attention but no one intervenes on him."

"Gustavo . . . " Carlos interrupted.

"When I drink, it all makes sense. I feel unstoppable. So try and stop that." He punched the air and kicked his right foot into the cement wall. An urge flared in him to hit harder, so he did. His foot seized and all his senses focused on the pain. A tension released in his chest, and frustration drained out like he'd yanked the plug from a bathtub. He let out a ragged breath. Everything inside of him flip-flopped: where he was strong, he instantly turned weak.

Maverick stood up. "You all right man? I can't tell what's happening to you right now, you look confused. Shit. Hey, sit down right here, and I'll be right back."

But before Maverick could walk away Gus had him by the shirtsleeve. "No, no, stay please." His face turned stoic as his insides crumbled. "I don't know if it started with Irene, I really don't. Thinking about it is what I avoid because that's what would send me over the edge." He gestured to the men. "You all are able to maintain a family and keep your wife and kids happy. I can't seem to do that."

Gus positioned a barstool against the wall he kicked, sat down and lifted his throbbing foot on another barstool. "Bartender!" To Maverick: "Would you like to send anyone else my way? I'm holding open office hours."

Without speaking, Carlos pulled a barstool near Gus and sat down. Maverick walked away.

Gus drank more, possibly harder, to spite the people around him. He'd spent the previous months with a nagging sensation of forgetting something without knowing what it was. It tore at him, and yes, he drank more Chivas to forget that feeling, but it never helped him remember what he forgot. He thought of Irene once more, and her advice for him to get over Mateo's death, but he didn't know where to start. He found the memory irretrievable.

Even when he tried imagining his abuelo in a coffin, a macabre undertaking, to be sure, nothing threaded itself into the thought.

CHAPTER 24

AS GUS DRESSED FOR THE DAY, A KNOCK JARRED HIM OUT OF HIS SENSE OF calm. He plunged two bottles of Chivas into a mass of crimson cloth inside an open desk drawer. As he opened his office door he found Carlos on the other side. Blocking the doorway as best he could, he continued buttoning his shirt.

"S…s…say, is there a revolution occurring in here?" Carlos lifted a paper bag with grease stains on the side.

Freshly showered, Gus tucked in his crisp, white long-sleeved shirt and put on a solid cobalt blue tie to match his navy-blue pants. "My little giant," he said to Carlos, "now that you're here the revolution can begin! You and I can do the job ourselves, can we not? I'm rearing to go."

Carlos beamed at him. "Ah, mi amigo, when you present yourself in this light, I know without a shadow of a doubt we are truly unbeatable."

"I can feel your spirit," Gus said. "When you present yourself in the same light, we can understand each other until the end of time." He pointed to the side of his legs. "I wonder if I could get away with embellishing the sides of my pants?"

They laughed together. "Then you must shorten your pants like a matador as well. We don't want bull horns scraping at your legs." Carlos shivered.

"Can I ask, why are you here?" Gus made sure his face held no trace of kindness.

"I'm here to escort you?" A guilty look passed over Carlos. "You know why. This morning is important."

He patted him on the back. "Which is why I'm prepared!"

"How's Irene?"

Gus slyly smiled. "I think if you're wondering, you should check in with her."

"Yes, yes, I'm actually wondering about you, but you didn't let me get to it."

"Are you . . . concerned about me, or Irene?"

"Come on, you're clearly hurting. This must be about her."

Gus's face hardened. "I don't want to talk about it. Now's not the time to go soft, I can't afford it."

They headed for Carlos's office building.

As they walked, Carlos spoke. "I'm going to spend the weekend with mi familia before this preparation *really* gets underway," he disclosed. "I need to let the girls know what I'll be doing, and the speed I'll be doing it in. You should think about washing your head out one last time." He tapped on the side of his head.

This struck Gus oddly, and it aroused the sensation that he'd forgotten something. Again. He couldn't pursue the thought because they reached the office, where the others from the previous night were eating breakfast.

A man from the American GI Forum spoke. "Men, I know we can talk about this until we're blue in the face, so I'm going to start the discussion about the situation before us." He gestured towards the main lawyers. "Because of the work done with Aniceto in Fort Bend County and the appeal to the Criminal Courts, I think it only right we take this case the next step up. If we don't, the inaction in and of itself will be considered an action." He lifted his coffee cup. "This is a long time coming, and once we start going at that level, even if the writ isn't granted, sooner or later we're going to get the right case through at the perfect time."

Maverick nodded. "What we're really saying to the people is we're willing to do what it takes for however long it takes, and we've got the resources to do it. I know everyone will do their part to funnel money to the cause."

"We'll never find the perfect case," Gus said. "It doesn't exist." He paused for dramatic effect. "Any time wasted waiting on perfection is an exercise in procrastination. We must fight now."

The others took notice of the attention Gus grabbed. Because of his look and confidence, they responded.

John approached him and clapped him on the back with a huge grin. "I think you've just reminded us why you hold head counsel, because you're the best at bullshitting a crowd. We're going to need the fearless disposition of a matador, and then add the force of the bull."

Carlos spoke up. "Hermanos, the road starts, we have ninety days to file, starting ahora."

John clapped once. "With that, I have an announcement to make. We have a chance at finding a donor . . . if we attend a Christmas party in Austin with our spouses to make our case."

Gus frowned, and Carlos spoke. "More information, please. Who is throwing this party? What is going on?"

"It's hosted by the Kincaids, at their manor. They like what we're doing and want to meet us," John explained. "I'm not going to say no to money, especially oil money. We can always say no."

"I'll think about it," Carlos said.

"They want all of us, not just the three of us. Spouses too."

Gus said nothing, but tensed at the Kincaid name coming out of John's mouth. His dread reached an all-time high thinking…no, knowing…that someone was out to get him.

"If it's okay with everyone, I'd like to get to work," Carlos said. "I suggest Gustavo does as well, and in order for that to happen, it's time for everyone to leave." He stood erect, with a look that told others to get out.

Gus nodded as a statue might.

Carlos addressed him. "I know you think I'll be keeping tabs on you, but I'm too busy for that. I have work up to my ears and I, as well as our colleagues, will trust you are going to take care of your end. But I'm here for you in case you need anything."

Gus managed to say, "What do you mean by that?"

"You have this expression like things are about to blow." Carlos cocked his head. "But I see fear, too. Like you know you're doing something wrong, or someone is doing something wrong . . . I can't put my finger on it."

Gus opened his mouth again to speak of Donovan, of his mistrust towards John, and of his gut feeling that they were marionettes on a stage being controlled. But nothing came out, he didn't know where to start

"How are you suffering?" Carlos asked. "I see it on your face Gustavo, but I don't know where it comes from. Is it Irene?"

Gus took a deep breath, thankful for the out. "Yes, sure, this is about Irene."

"Will you invite her to the Christmas party?"

"The holidays . . . " Gus looked away, "the holidays are hard."

"Why the holidays?" Carlos furrowed his brow trying to understand.

"That's the worst part," Gus admitted. "I don't know why, I just seem to suffer. The togetherness, the carols, the joy, something about it makes me want to—"

"Don't say it," Carlos interrupted. "Just don't say it."

He nodded.

"The way you talk, it sounds like you need support, someone like Irene." Carlos left a long pause. "Call her."

"Have you spoken with her?" He knew the answer, he always knew Irene to be the answer for Carlos. "I want you to admit it."

Carlos lifted the phone receiver and offered it to Gus. "Yes. She's expecting your call."

As Carlos walked away, Gus lifted a middle finger to his friend and used the other hand to call Irene, who answered on the third ring. "It's been months."

"It has."

"Have I stayed away long enough?"

"I suppose." She left a pause. "I hear you need a date."

Gus paused, realizing the world around him. John told Carlos about the Christmas party before he announced it to everyone, far enough in advance that Carlos had time to call Irene and convince her. They left him out of everything.

In the end, he decided to go along. "Be my Christmas date, Reenie, I need you. An early Christmas. All the wives are going. Let's impress rich oilmen. Have pity on your husband."

"Whose party is it?"

"The Kincaids."

Irene breathed in sharply. "And you all are going? To Austin?"

"Still trying to raise money, we need some oil money. They invited us."

"Sounds like a lion's den."

"I'm sure it is, and all the more reason for you to escort me! Besides, it's only a party, and I hear they go to the nines. Please? I'll pay for a new dress."

"I'm shaking my head because I don't want to deny you, but you know my answer. I know you know it, I don't understand why you have to put me in the situation of saying it to you."

Gus breathed in sharply. Hadn't Carlos convinced her? What was he to say now? "Your answer is no," he said, realizing it as he said it.

"Yes . . . it's no," Irene said with a lack of vigor. "No," she repeated, but stronger. "No Gustavo, I will not go with you to this party. You must tell our friends I'm sorry for my absence. I'm sure they'll take you under their wing and make sure you don't embarrass yourself."

Gus hung up on her.

CHAPTER 25

NEARLY EVERYTHING ON AND WITHIN THE KINCAID MANOR REMINDED GUS OF the main reason he harbored an aversion to Donovan's life in college. Each item his eyes landed on spoke to a wealth Gus knew he could never achieve in a lifetime.

A butler stopped him in the foyer. "Your coat, sir."

Gus didn't like the idea of shedding a layer of armor already, but knew it to be the polite thing to do. As he wriggled out of it, he asked for the location of the bar. The idea of alcohol calmed him.

"Whisky," he said to the bartender. "Do you have Chivas?"

"No brown liquors, the white carpet," the bartender said. "Mrs. Kincaid doesn't like stains from big parties. So no brown liquors, only clear." He straightened his white jacket and lifted his chin.

"Well, shit," Gus blurted out. "Where does that leave me? Drinking vodka, rum, and what else? White wines?" He scanned the countertop as his anxiety increased.

The bartender nodded. "Champagne, Prosecco, too, plus silver tequila, Japanese sake, and gin."

"Ah, sí se puedes! I'll have a gin and less tonic to start." He knew better, but reasoned the desperation from not drinking at all would be worse than an unfamiliar cocktail.

"Gin and less tonic?"

"With less than it normally carries."

The bartender darted his eyes about the room to see if anyone watched their conversation. "Anything else?"

"A handgun, if you have it," Gus added, half joking, half serious.

The bartender's expression of relief broke the tension.

Gus found himself looking for Donovan. People near him began stealing glances when he ordered a second gin and less tonic. He felt foolish when he made a gun with his thumb and forefinger towards the bartender. "Thanks, it's a big night."

He briefly weighed the consequences of sneaking the quarter bottle of Chivas from the car, then shook his head and downed the first entire gin and less tonic. A voice he recognized spoke out above the crowd, and he grabbed his new drink and followed it.

"The average is twenty-five dollars," Maverick explained to a group of people, "from one club totaling ten people. I wish we could see the sort of money Thurgood does."

Gus noticed all of his peers each had someone, just as he feared. He also noticed Maverick spoke to people in their circle, and not anyone financially prepared to bankroll them to the Supreme Court. Judging from the looks on their faces, Gus correctly assumed no one wanted him there. He reached for another drink from a nearby tray and looked for Donovan again.

Tony, a leader of LULAC, said with his wife, "It all sounds great. You should add a bit about its national importance."

"Yes! Then I'll mention the Texas boys: Carlos, John, and Gustavo. We're glad the state courts denied us, we've got bigger fish to fry!"

The other wives murmured to each other in excitement.

Gus mumbled to himself. "I thought *I* was lead counsel."

"Like all things, we just have to keep working at it, chipping away at it little by little," John said to another group, and acknowledged Gus with a nod. He approached him. "No one case will change people's minds, but we have to let them know we're here."

"Little by little," Gus said sarcastically, and took another drink. The ice clinked against the glass and he focused on the vibration, momentarily becoming fascinated by it. He could feel the gin kicking in.

John spoke quietly. "We should be on our best behavior."

"Why? I don't see anyone here who hasn't been here before," he challenged. "Where's Sid Richardson? The main Donald Kincaid?"

This time he spoke through clenched teeth. "His name is Don, for Donovan."

Gus saluted him. "Yessir, mister LULAC president. Or should I call you my liege?"

John's eyes turned to slits.

"Awww, poor JJ," Gus baited. "Do I sound too snide for you?"

A fellow activist leader heard the exchange. "We need nimble minds who are ready for anything. Gustavo . . . you up for the challenge?"

Gus crunched on his ice. "I'm up for any challenge, always and forever." He studied the man's face. "What are you referring to when you say we need nimble minds, ready for anything? We don't know each other well. What do you imply here?"

"Stand down, soldier. I know Carlos and JJ have been writing and raising money for the case, but you are the smooth talker, the orator." He pointed to Gus's glass. "What if you have too many of those, what would happen then?"

Gus opened his mouth to answer, but Carlos stood by his side and hissed at him. "Stop this instant."

"Enough of you," he groaned, and saw a small plate with sugar cookies shaped like stars with blue sprinkles nearby. He picked it up and shoved it in Carlos's chest. "Calm down. Eat these."

"I see Preston Armstrong," John said. "I'm going in."

A few partygoers wished him luck.

Another activist spoke in his place. "He's just worried about the case. I know I am. He's showing concern and we just want what's best for Pete and la raza. Our people."

Gus guffawed. "Pete? No one here cares about *Pete*." He swung his glass and his eyes turned to slits. "None of us. Does anyone know how he's doing? Who's spoken to him last?" He spat on the carpet. "None of us."

Carlos spun around and walked away.

Nearby, a woman whispered. "Irene isn't here. Don't you all think that has a hand to play in this?"

Gus downed his drink and scowled at her. "I heard you, don't think I didn't hear you, just like I saw you laughing at me earlier." His head filled with defensive responses and his sight blurred. Bitterness, jealousy, and loneliness made him dizzy. He noticed the woman still looking at him. "Who are you?" he roared.

Cordelia Kincaid rushed to him when Gus spit onto her carpet and asked him to stop immediately. She put on her best party face and spoke carefully, laying on a thick southern accent. "Gus? How about we put you in the guest room for a little while, what you do think? Doesn't that sound nice?" She pulled the glass from his hands. "Come this way, I'll save you some food, I promise."

"Well, hello there." His attention turned. "What's your name? Do you come with the house?" His words slurred together.

Cordelia led him away from the group. "Actually, I do. Call me Cordy."

"Cordy . . . Cordy." His face twisted with thought. "Does that stand for Cordelia? Are you Donovan's mother?"

"I am." Her demeanor softened almost immediately. "I have the perfect bed for you to find your bearings in. It's only a few feet away. Come with me."

"Everyone is talking about me," Gus whispered conspiratorially. "I know it." He focused on her face. "You're probably going to complain about me soon. They're going to sneak to Washington without me, you watch. They don't have the *cojones* to tell me to my face."

"What a silly thought! Hush now, you've just had a little too much." Cordelia led him to the nearest bedroom and reminded him numerous times that a bathroom could be found a few feet away. "I'll bring you some food and coffee."

Gus mumbled into a pillow until he passed out. A moment later he ran to the bathroom to vomit, hugging the toilet and calling out for Irene.

The group moved near the room to stay near Gus. John joined them to share his rejection.

"Armstrong said no. And then," he raised his voice in mock excitement, "we saw Gus happen from across the room. Armstrong said he's too much of a liability. Cheers." John said.

"Three sheets," Carlos pointed to the bedroom. "He's in there."

"I'll wait until my term is over to murder him, I promise." John smiled. "I'm angry with him, but he's in an unfamiliar house. We all are."

"JJ, you're not your brother's keeper, and he is not your brother," Carlos said. "Gus is a big boy; he can take care of himself. Have a cookie."

"Tell me about it." John shook his head at the offer and frowned. "I thought you were going to help him stop all that behavior."

Carlos shrugged. "Yes, but, I'm tired of worrying about it. I waste too much energy on it. To be honest, I don't care what he does when he's not working on a case, a man can do what he damn well pleases. Irene not being here broke his heart, but it's one problem among many. You all have to give him the benefit of the doubt. We all have our iniquities."

"What a new song you sing," John commented. "How lucky he is to have you. Next thing you're going to tell me is he spends our money wisely."

Carlos turned his head away.

"Tony can vouch for me. LULAC has been on my ass about it." John spread his arms. "Why do you think we're here?"

"You take a break JJ," Maverick offered. "I see another one, I'm going to do the pitch."

Another topic quickly took over. The wife of one of their own addressed the crowd with a clear voice and sipped on a flute of champagne. "I read this study last month, doctors are starting to regard drinking too much as an addiction, which would be considered a disease. Did anyone see that? They might be able to cure such urges, aside from assuaging them. Jorge," she asked her husband, "didn't you read the study, too?"

"I did," he answered dutifully. "But I took it as an idea more than a hypothesis. No hard facts, only the statistics gathered and correlated." He sipped on his champagne and avoided eye contact with his wife. "It's all still new."

John shook his head. "Nonsense, that sounds like psychology talk to me. I've known Gus far too long. That man," he pointed, "as charming with people as he is with his words, doesn't want to stop drinking, plain and simple. Gus likes to drink, and he doesn't want to stop."

Gus listened to them all. *They don't want me on the team, they see me as a liability*, he told himself. He suddenly regretted not taking Donovan's offer when he had the chance.

John poked his head into the room and saw Gus with his eyes open. "Mierda."

Gus sat up. "What are you doing here, scrounging for more ammunition?"

John closed the door behind him. "Listen."

"Don't say a word." Gus crossed his arms. "I heard what I heard."

"You burst out right at the wrong time and I was trying to close the deal."

Gus popped up. He needed time to process, but reacted instead. "You've always been jealous of me, haven't you? All this time."

"What are you talking about?" John laughed. "Don't make me laugh. Your petulance is becoming annoying."

Gus pulled a file from his mind and read it out loud. "Where do I start? You're the uglier version of me. When we went out during the Bastrop case, you hated it when the women flocked to me. I mean . . . look at me . . . and look at you." He swiveled to face John and an arm hit a crystal vase filled to the brim with water and roses. It crashed to the floor. "You mimicked me and started a firm after I did, then stole all my clients and closed me down. You didn't want to run for LULAC office and win that damn presidency, but did it for fear they might ask me."

"Such delusions," John shook his head. "I've had it with you, my little golden matador boy. You are a bullshitter, not a bullfighter." He took a step forward and sat on the bed so they could see each other eye to eye.

Gus struggled up and lurched past him and into the crowd again, nearly losing his balance on the way. One man caught him by the arm.

John appeared behind Gus. "Amigo, maybe you didn't lie down long enough. You should head back into the room awhile," he advised. "Don't let them see you like this."

"You get the hell away from me," Gus demanded. "I want to get out of here."

Maverick rejoined the group. "Escort him out now. Gustavo, you can't handle this."

"I can handle another!" Gus said. "Somebody, DeAnda, pour me two fingers of whisky, neat."

Maverick put his hand on Gus's shoulder. "I'm not talking about the juice, you can handle that more than any of us. I'm talking about the work, you can't handle it. You need to sleep more tonight, my friend. You sound like a fool, and you might've ruined our chances."

Others chimed in agreement with Maverick.

"He already has," John interjected.

"None of you believe in me, I know what you all think of me," Gus wailed. "I could hear you in there. You can go to hell, all of you," he yelled. "None of you think I can do this, but none of you are better than me."

The room went silent while the women carefully stepped back. Their husbands tightened a circle around Gus.

"Get him out of here," John demanded. "Find a muzzle."

"Step to it!" Gus screeched out. "All you minions, follow your leader!"

He twisted out of their grip, but more replaced them, making him dizzy. Suddenly, he knew what he had to do. He zeroed in on John, who'd taken several steps away from them.

Cordelia called out from above their heads on the second level of the mansion. "Stop him!"

Gus saw Donovan standing beside her, a smile curled on his face. Gus threw a punch at John, missing him completely. John stepped to the side to dodge the punch. Gus tried again and lost his balance.

Cordelia screamed as Gus fell into the Christmas tree, her sacred tree. It enveloped him for a second, then seemed to push him back out. He gripped onto the branches for leverage, but fell backwards to the floor, taking the titanic tree down with him. It crashed into the glass coffee table as ornaments leaped off the tree. Everything broke into pieces on impact. A plug yanked off in the process, and a string of lights whipped through a handful of champagne flutes. They tipped over one by one, like dominoes.

Cordelia's first scream was an attempt to halt Gus, but her second scream was a surrender. "Leave, everyone leave this instant!"

Maverick, Carlos, and DeAnda moved the tree to the side and carried Gus outside to Maverick's car, where he proceeded to throw up on their shoes.

Gus sat up in the car after they angled him inside. With a brief lucidity, he said, "You all have a tenacity I don't have. I'm beginning to think as a result, I'm not handling the pressure well enough."

Carlos patted his head. "Rest your head, my weary friend. Enough loco for now."

"That's just it," Gus gushed. "I *am* loco, more than any of you will ever know. That's why I know I might not make it, or just barely make it to the finish line. Our writ hasn't even been accepted, and I'm already killing myself—that's how I know I'm not built for this the way you all are." Then he dropped back onto the seat and passed out.

Maverick made the sign of the Cross in the dark as he took in what his friend said. He turned on his car. Sober thoughts of a drunk mind? He said a prayer to God and asked for Him to keep an eye on them all.

CHAPTER 26

DONOVAN GLEEFULLY WATCHED THE ENTIRE SCENE UNFOLD FROM THE SECOND story balcony, but it tore him up when his mother fell into despair. Everything happened as he plotted, which gave him joy, but the consequences took it all away.

It started when Gus entered the party. The wrinkled clothes, wild hair, and slumped posture: it humanized the man. *He looks tired*, Donovan thought when he walked in, *an empty shell.* The clear liquor seemed to aide in his decline as planned, but the acrimony from the other men was a surprise that gave Donovan pause. He waited for the satisfaction that came with the knowledge of imminent success, but guilt sprouted in its place.

He believed his mother's reaction to the falling tree was dramatic, perhaps even comedic. Denied on both counts. Her piercing wail filled him with shame.

Then the attempted assault. Donovan hoped the alcohol would drive Gus to cause a scene, but this? He tried convincing himself it didn't matter, the fault belonged to Gus, but he knew better. His conscience was the thing separating himself from his brother and father. Feelings were inconsequential to them, something to be glossed over. But not for Donovan, he reacted to the plight of others differently.

Sometime later he headed downstairs, believing everyone had departed. Instead he heard arguing outside and hid himself to hear more.

John removed his jacket and threw it to the ground. "I don't have time to babysit that spoiled man. Not after the way he talked to me. I can hold my temper for only so long."

"Calm down JJ, I don't think that's the main issue." Carlos picked up the jacket. "He's a caged animal who's been poked too many times. Any of us might do the same in that state."

"The main issue is the alcohol. The main issue is Gus himself. Too much ego, too much alcohol, and he loses all sense of responsibility. That's when he spends our money," John added.

"Not true," Carlos pointed out. "He does that when he's in withdrawal, Gus buys new clothes, new things. I think he drinks so he'll stop spending."

"I really don't care, to be honest," John spat out. "I don't have time to figure out the cause. He needs to be cut out of the money loop. Period."

"I don't have the time either!" Carlos began shifting the weight on his feet. "I don't know about you men, but I'm currently working on forty-seven cases. Not to mention Gus and I live in the same town. This is your first time experiencing an outburst like this, though I admit it's gotten worse." He shook his head. "Sometimes he drinks and becomes productive. Razor-focused. It's not always a problem."

John exhaled noisily. "It's become irreparable. Come off it Cadena, I'm not going to start comparing who works more." He groaned. "You must find complaining energizing, or satiating, at the very least."

"Excuse me? You come off it!"

"It exhausts me hearing you complain about him, but you do it so often you must find a worthy payoff somewhere in the process." John smiled sweetly at Carlos. "I'm only saying it may be enough for you, rather than fixing the problems you complain about."

"Now I get to be the one to take him home." Carlos let out a stream of Spanish curses before retreating to his car and driving away.

Donovan watched as John turned to the house and stared in silence for a few minutes after they drove away.

John cleared his throat. "You still there?"

Donovan pushed open the door and stepped out. "Come inside and let me fix you a drink."

Neither spoke as Donovan poured and served. They stayed in the main room near the fallen Christmas tree.

John pointed at it. "Can I do anything to help?"

"No, we're going to leave that to my mother. She's devastated right now. Her spirit needs to settle." Donovan tried to chuckle, but it came out flat. "It may be just a tree to you and me, but it's so much more to her. A symbol of our family."

"It smells good."

"It smells like my mother's despair. Gus's too, since we're talking about it."

John nodded. "I'm going to cut to the chase: I'd like to talk further about the terms you offered me a few months ago. After tonight, I think I'm ready to go forward."

"I can see how you'd arrive at that conclusion."

"It's for preservation of the case and the people involved, it can't go down because of one man. I care for my friend, but he's gone too far." He pointed down to the carpet. "The aftermath of his behavior is like those shards of glass caught within the fibers. Ornaments shattered in the immediate circle," he pointed to the tree, "but the pieces fly farther than you expect, and hide upon landing. You pick up the pieces, you clean and clean. From one angle the area appears devoid of debris, but take a few steps to the side and a dozen bits shine and catch your eye, just waiting to break your skin."

Donovan waited, dreading more. Excuses flooded his mind.

"I'm probably not making too much sense," John filled in. "Let's talk business. I say yes, and then what happens?"

His response was a shrug. "Do you want to take over the case?"

"An emphatic no," John said. "I'm there to provide information because of my previous work, Carlos is the man for that."

"I am NOT making an offer to him." Donovan smiled.

"He already turned you down?"

"Not exactly, but I'm sure he would." Donovan wondered how much to tell, and decided to keep it short. "We have history, that's all I'll say."

"You went to school here?"

He gave a thumbs up. "Want another drink?"

"No," John said thoughtfully. "We should get back to the matter at hand."

"Of course. I suppose you need to get everyone to vote him out."

"Honestly speaking, what about money? I only say something because you said I'd be compensated, and I only say that because the case could use the money if I take over." He shrugged. "Or it may stop entirely."

Donovan panicked, realizing he hadn't thought this far along with his plan. He suddenly wanted their conversation to be over immediately.

Having John take the helm meant the case would still have to be stopped, not just Gus. Donovan saw his journey stretch further and his future move farther away. "There's no money," he lied.

John made a show of looking at the interior of the manor and cocked an eyebrow. "No money?"

"Well, not like that." He struggled with the right words. "The offer has been rescinded," he finished. "I want to say more, but I will not."

John locked eyes with him, a frustration building up behind his eyes. "You waited this long to say something? When did this happen? Wait, don't tell me." A long silence followed as he began to pace.

"Don't do this to yourself," Donovan warned.

A knowing look came across John's face. "No one in your circle was going to donate, were they? Tonight was a farce, you wanted this to happen so everyone could see. You expected Gus to do what he did."

Donovan's smile curled wickedly. "Did you really think my people would back yours? I needed a patsy." He scoffed. "Besides, you said no long ago."

"Am I the only one you approached with this mess? I'm not, am I? Who are you working for?"

"Who doesn't matter," Donovan snapped. "Just know the deal is off the table. Therefore, without a reason for this," he gestured a circle between them, "you can get the hell off my family's property."

John left without another word.

Ashamed and surprised by his actions, Donovan turned and reentered the house. He spent the rest of the night picking glass out of the carpet and attempted reconstructing what ornaments he could.

CHAPTER 27

DAYS LATER, FLASHES OF THE KINCAID PARTY STILL HAUNTED GUS EACH MORNing when he woke. The first day brought the sounds of that night. He buried his head into an office couch pillow and cringed when the shatter of glass ornaments colliding with a glass table filled his ears. Remembering the cry from the woman who lived at the manor made him groan like a foghorn.

The second day he recalled the feelings from that night. The basic emotions—anger, confusion, embarrassment—ripped through him, especially when he couldn't pinpoint why he'd been angry or confused or embarrassed. By the third day the memories bubbled more clearly to the surface and Gus remembered the words that caused some of those feelings, especially at the end, when Carlos deposited Gus at his office building.

"Where's my car?" Gus had demanded that night. His foot slid when he stepped onto the curb. "Did anyone hear me?"

"We've made arrangements," Carlos responded quietly. "It'll be here tomorrow."

"You better not drive it to Irene's. You'll really see me angry then."

Silence, followed by a sigh. "Gustavo, I'm worried your failing marriage is having a negative impact on everyone, but you worst of all."

"Here you go again," Gus slurred. "Is it already time to intervene with me again? You're telling me I'm a failure?"

"I'm saying your marriage has been. I think the split between you and Irene has had a bigger impact on you than you think, not to mention this case. I think you drink as much as you do because you don't believe in yourself. You're sabotaging yourself," Carlos said. "We all want you to succeed more than anything. We want you to be your best every moment of the day."

Gus sneered and looked out into the night sky. "I don't see anyone else here."

"Only because they all can't fit in my car! I'm hard on you because I know what you can do. You don't know how good you are, if you did you'd never doubt yourself a day in your life." Carlos let the comment hang in the air. "Do you know what I'd give to be as confident as you are in the courtroom? I start stuttering and lose credibility in the process. When I'm frustrated with you, it's mainly because I can't do what you do, and I hate watching you sully your talent by being drunk as Pepe Le Pew." He lowered his voice again when his wife stirred in the car. "You waste your talent, you waste so much, you waste it all."

A knock at his door jarred Gus into the present time. He covered his face with his hands. Realizing he couldn't bear to face the day alone, he persuaded Patricia to spend a day or two in San Antonio before the new year began. He opened the door and found her holding a new Chivas bottle.

Gus groaned. "Why did you bring that? I have more than enough for the both of us."

"I didn't bring it, I found it outside your door." She checked the bottle. "No note." Patricia reached out and patted him. "Let's get breakfast and go to a hotel." Her eyes brightened. "Better yet, let's get breakfast AT a hotel. I can only stay for a night."

"That's probably best," he replied. "Our deadline is at the end of January, and the days are ticking away. As is my life."

She shushed him. "No words, not yet. Get some clothes, we'll talk about it with Chivas in our coffee."

CHAPTER 28

AFTER A LONG NIGHT OF DRINKING AND VENTING TO PATRICIA, GUS DECIDED to drive to Mexico and attend a bullfighting festival she mentioned. He found himself thinking about quitting the drink, but also discovered he didn't want to quit at all. Thinking about his next drink kept him going, and besides, to quit now might do more harm than good. He heard his abuelo say that phrase a few times. Drinking stirred the brain up with new ideas.

As he drove, the argument he had with Irene a year ago kept nagging at him. When she mentioned getting him to come to terms with Mateo's death, Gus found he couldn't remember the date of his passing, nor the reason. At first it hadn't bothered him; he forgot things all the time and simply assumed he'd remember the date when it came around.

As time passed the answer didn't come to him, and he didn't want to ask Irene because he could see it pained her to talk about it. He hoped going to a bullfight would spark his memory.

The entire drive to Mexico his grief seemed like a heavy rope pulling him forward. He recalled his last memory with Mateo. Wasn't it at a bullfight? He couldn't find a fully formed impression.

His mind traveled back to the Christmas party again, and something Carlos said afterward. *I wish you'd start making an effort to be good rather than merely wanting the appearance of goodness.* Gus felt humiliated when Carlos said it.

Thinking of his abuelo brought a dread to his soul, followed by a flash of guilt with no apparent origin.

Gus chose the Arena de Matadors so he could spend more on booze, and stay at Evitarse as usual. Cheaper arenas charged less for tickets and cut costs with less cleaning and few renovations. He paid two dollars to sit near the front row, a bargain, and arrived early enough to walk the arena's small outside perimeter, an inadvertent habit. It had the feeling of a familiar place, but Gus couldn't put his finger on it. It wasn't too much to assume his abuelo took him at least once.

He could hear Mateo and the bulls calling out to him, so Gus answered the call. Just the small victory of understanding himself a little on the drive down lifted his spirits enough to propel him on his journey. He slowly circled the exterior to visually check the wooden beams and poles for sturdiness, inspecting for architectural red flags and listening for creaking up above, of which he heard on all sides. A bad sign.

Almost certain he'd been there before, he entered the stands and circled the inside, checking a final time for any cracking or other signs of the outer structure crumbling. Nothing looked quite familiar, but the familiar feeling still held him. He was stumped.

The fences lining the arena reminded him of a boxing ring with its rubber band sides, one push at the right angle and it might bounce back or topple over. Gus swore the wood went wobbly as he looked for a seat, and his stomach turned. Another creak told him to slide down a few seats so he obeyed, and as he took in his surroundings the splintered edges of the inner arena stood out where one too many bulls had connected with its edges.

A group of eight, mostly drunk, loudly ushered themselves into the stands near him. People seated nearby clutched their belongings or ducked out of their way because they randomly burst into laughter or yelled out undecipherable words to each other. A particular man stood out to Gus. He wore a crimson-red long-sleeved button-up shirt, black pants, and a wide smile bordering on maniacal. Clearly the most intoxicated one out of the group, he swayed as if he stood on a boat and stayed out of the conversations. Gus learned the man's name was Miguel, and the longer he watched the easier it became to see his grandfather standing there. They wobbled the same when trying to find their balance.

He tried to think back, how much alcohol would he see Mateo consume in an afternoon, or simply on the long drive over? As a child he didn't notice, or care, he was too enthralled in the show. Besides, Mateo had Gus drinking as well.

His grandfather could drink beer all day and still look sober, but with liquor, it became a different story. He remembered the fire grow in Mateo's eyes when the liquor settled, he looked for a confrontation, a reason to misbehave. He tested his limits, and Gus learned from him to do the same.

How much could he drink before getting sick? How much did it take before Mateo snuck away? How long before someone noticed a child was drinking beer?

Gus paid little attention to the first match of the day and gave his attention to the rowdy group, particularly to the drunk man in the red shirt. A big-bosomed woman seated in front of them turned around and caught the man's eye.

Suddenly the memory of the chesty woman with the yellow ribbon woven into her braid jumped into his mind. He caught a glimpse of her at his first bullfight, and over the years he would see her hiding at the back of the crowds, always turning around right before Mateo reached where she stood. *Could it be,* Gus thought, *did Mateo go to her every time?* The first time a matador almost died, Mateo fed him beer. He did the same thing the second time, and the third.

A clear memory stood out. She wasn't there the last time, and Mateo looked incredibly depressed as a result of her absence.

The man in the red shirt tripped. The sound of it brought Gus back to the present, and triggered another memory. Mateo fell like that once—when, when was that?—and behaved just as the red-shirted man had, tripping and falling on his way down to the front while waving his beverage around with abandon.

As time passed, the man in the red shirt began to yell out obscenities and insults to the matadors and other people in the crowd. He then proceeded to start an argument when one of his friends booed at a matador. "What do you know? You aren't any better than a bull's balls," he hissed.

The man's rants brought his friend to his feet as the third match began. They started shouting at each other and stole attention from the bullfight. People in their section chose sides and cheered on the men fighting. They wanted a show, and didn't care how it was achieved.

As the scene unfolded, the pit in Gus's stomach grew. He switched his attention to the arena.

There, it appeared the matador lost the animal's attention to the fighting in the stands. The bull charged erratically at the matador, and a picador only managed to prick its skin, which pissed the bull off even more. Gus knew, suddenly and without warning, what would happen, but he could do nothing to stop it.

The bull charged, and caught the matador off guard during a veronica twirl, causing the cape to flutter out limply. The animal slid several feet past the matador in the dirt, and began another charge. Unprepared, the matador ran towards the nearest fence to duck behind, which happened to be directly in front of the section the man in the red shirt stood.

The bull picked up speed and rammed into the fence. Just before it collapsed on him, the matador made a last-ditch effort, balling up his cape and chunking it—a move to deflect the bull's attention. The bull directed his horns at the cape and the wall. Miguel and his red shirt still faced the edge in awe and full drunken enthusiasm. Panic didn't set in until the wall parted with a loud crack.

A woman screamed, causing the crowd to fall into a panic. The animal found its new target and charged one last time. A bellow came from the man in the red shirt, a sound that scared Gus to his bones. He couldn't look away. The bull charged into his brain and a flashback exploded.

A gray-haired Mateo took a sixteen-year-old Gus to his last bullfight in 1931, but he didn't know it would be their last. The teenager was going to buy a car soon, and from then on he'd drive them to Mexico. Mateo laughed, nodded, and ruffled the boy's hair. Everything felt ceremonial during that trip.

He chose the Arena de Matadors. Hours into the bullfighting, a drunken Mateo started arguing with a man, who welcomed a fight. Before he walked toward the man, Mateo handed Gus a small bag of pills. The men tussled, their bottles crashing over the wall. The sound grabbed the bull's attention and it began to charge. Without hesitation, the animal crashed into the wall, backed up and crashed again.

In retrospect, Gus remembered that Mateo wasn't alarmed.

Until the wall collapsed.

Mateo was far away, and a young Gus knew he couldn't get there in time. They both knew it the moment they caught each other's eye.

Mateo and the man crumpled with the wall's pieces and spilled out toward the bull and their deaths. It unfolded in one gasp. Even though a teenage Gus was fast, dodging through the spilling bleachers with ease, it was no use. People's cries and wails pierced the air and chorused around him as he dug through the rubble. Several people were trapped under the debris, and other men joined Gus in the ring to try to free them. Gus didn't realize that he was screaming, too. His grandfather called out to him, the bulls called out to him, and he did his best to answer the call.

But then an image suddenly filled his mind, something true he'd forgotten amidst the chaos. Right before the wall collapsed, Mateo gave Gus a look of contrition.

And jumped.

When he reached him, his abuelo had a contented expression on his face, unconcerned about the blood oozing out of him from various gashes and cuts. Gus blocked out the insanity surrounding him and cradled Mateo's head in his lap. "I'm going to get you to another bullfight, Abuelo," he cried to him. "Next year it's my turn. Plus the year after next, and the year after that, it's my turn to take you to the bulls."

Mateo reached out to try and hug him, but he had no strength. "Sí mijo," he agreed. "Whatever you say goes."

Tears blurred Gus's sight as he watched the life leak out of his grandfather's dark brown eyes. "Why? Why does it end like this?" he cried out. The bull, immobilized by banderillas, moaned. The stands had fallen apart in an eighth of the arena, and Gus's whole life hung in that one section.

"This is the way it's supposed to end." Mateo tapped his forehead, and reached out to Gus and tapped the side of his head. "This bull has finally won. It's your bull now." Gus wept while Mateo tried to console him. "Don't cry, we're going to be together forever, we'll never be apart. If you want to be happy, do everything in your power to get happiness. If you want it, you'll get it."

It all happened right before the holidays. Gus realized this was why he binged on alcohol at the same time every year without knowing why.

Gus remembered himself as a boy running from the panic and chaos, weeping and gasping for air. He opened his eyes in the present to see the man in the red shirt was still alive, with people around him praying.

A rumbling slowly grew in volume, an unrecognizable hum from people in the arena praying in monotone. Praying in tongues. As he breathed in the scene before him, Gus realized he didn't want to see any more of it and found the nearest exit out of the rickety arena. His understanding was as clear as water. He'd found the March day in 1931 he'd misplaced, the day he'd chosen to forget.

"I repressed it completely," he said out loud to himself.

Too much drinking followed after a bout of uncontrollable crying. Hours later he woke up in his car to a woman knocking on his window asking if he was okay. When she moved away from the window Gus saw the Evitarse sign.

He staggered in to find Roberto reading a magazine behind the counter. "Gustavo!" He exclaimed, to which Gus slipped to the floor.

Gus mumbled Mateo's name over and over. "He died, he died here." He muttered incoherently until he passed out. "He jumped . . . did his sacrifice mean something?"

"It has finally happened," Roberto surmised. "You remember."

A shot of whisky and a glass of water met Gus's eyes the next morning, along with a headache full of the memories from the night before. He sat up to notice a familiarity about the room before laying down again. When sleep didn't return he searched for the items from earlier and found them on a flimsy end table, the same one where Patricia graced him her personal information from years earlier. A note leaned against the water, with a scribble from Roberto asking him to go downstairs whenever he woke.

As Gus descended the stairs he noticed it carried a new runner, a dark plum with large faded sunflowers going down the middle. Suddenly a memory swooped in from 1931: Evitarse didn't have a stair runner. He remembered because he slipped going up and down the stairs that night and the following morning the day after Mateo died. Gus hit his head twice, in the front and the back, just enough to help him along in forgetting his memory around the event of his beloved grandfather.

The truth is, what could've given him a concussion twenty-two years prior didn't do as much damage done by the amount of pills and liquor in his system at the time. They dulled his pain instantly, but the force still altered his mental state in the short term.

Roberto forbade him from returning to Texas by himself. He forced the teenage Gus to stay the night and wait for his mother to drive to Mexico. She hadn't arrived by morning and Gus waited in the lobby rather than going back to the room. Waiting simulated pure torture.

As he currently rounded the corner, he caught wind that he was about to sit in the area of Evitarse he hated the most, the place he pretended wasn't there, the lobby. Three people stood in line waiting for Roberto's service while he finished with the one standing before him. Roberto waved and pointed to the couches. "Wait for me."

Gus nodded, turning to the lobby. It contained a simple enough layout: two couches with plastic green plants on all four sides sat facing each other, plus a coffee table sandwiched in between. Technically, the lobby was only half a room because it had two corners, one with two chairs, and the other with a coffee station. He avoided the couches for the time being and went to the corner with caffeine.

The station consisted of a wooden pushcart Roberto placed in the corner thirty years ago. As tall as Gus's waist, it measured the width and length of a kitchen sink. On top, a coffee pot, a container of instant coffee, instant creamer, sugar, a package of filters, plus paper cups no taller than a human fist, and the machine holding a coffee pot stained amber on the bottom half. The pushcart contained a drawer with napkins and plastic spoons.

He looked up to see two customers remaining.

Gus stared at the extra pot and noticed it had a jagged hole on one side in a crooked shape of a star. *It sits there as if useful,* he thought, *as if it can be fixed. Clearly Roberto noticed it, but doesn't bother discarding it. What about the other people who've made coffee for themselves? Haven't they thought to throw it away? It's taking up room and no one does anything about it,* he thought. *Just like me.* When he couldn't find where to fill the unbroken pot with water he discarded the idea completely, and decided to sit down instead. Still two to go.

Gus chose the couch facing a side exit door, the same one he sat on twenty-two years ago. The windows across from him took up the entire wall, and revealed a set of stairs outside with a worn bicycle leaning against them. He remembered waiting for his mother on a couch similar to the one he sat on now. He remembered memorizing every detail so as not to go mad thinking of Mateo. Now, he needed to recall those details.

He concentrated on the room as it was. The couches were a rusty reddish brown back then, but the coffee table was the same: rectangular-shaped with deep gashes on all four corners and a top stained with coffee rings. Back then, Roberto owned a black cat he called Mi Amor, who basked in the sun and liked to catch rats. Gus could also see in his mind's eye through the mullioned window where a cage with two chirping canaries inside was suspended from the stairs. Mi Amor spent most of her day watching the canaries from the window. Gus felt caged in by

Roberto, like the birds, when all he wanted to do was take flight.

One customer left.

The grief of losing his grandfather hit him suddenly in a wave of heavy sadness. Back then, thinking of Mateo's body in rubble amidst other bodies became too difficult to bear, especially when his only task was waiting. He'd gripped the keys in his pocket and fantasized about running away from Roberto and Evitarse. Mateo's car was *right there*, he reasoned.

I would've never driven home, Gus realized to himself, *I would've driven to Tasca and learned how to make silver jewelry, or I would've gone to Cancun to make money working on the water's edge. Or*, he thought, *I would've stopped on the side of the road twenty miles from Evitarse and cried alone, until my body shook.*

Gus opened his eyes when he felt tears rolling down his cheeks and found Roberto sitting opposite him on the other couch. He pointed at him. "You sat there on and off all day checking on me . . . "

"You didn't say a word to me all that time, nor to your mother," Roberto filled in. "Six people died that night, including Mateo. The funerals were in Mexico City," Roberto said. "But you, you . . . "

"I didn't go," Gus whispered. The words fell out of his mouth as if the memories had been present all along. "I wouldn't acknowledge his death, so I forgot it instead. I dragged it out all this time."

"You went mad, dazed as hell. You lost yourself." Roberto shook his head.

"I stole some of your liquor. And I found the pills he gave me." He pointed at the stairs to the rooms, gasped, then covered his mouth. "I brought back women. I forgot that earlier."

"Four to be exact," Roberto filled in. He raised his chin proudly. "I covered the whole thing up. Your mom didn't need to know how her son became a man."

"Not a man." Gus shook his head with regret. "I couldn't get it up, I cried with all of them—coiled up like a little boy."

"One doesn't have to sleep with a fleet to earn manliness. You had your own funeral to start grieving."

"I didn't," he said. "I didn't, my heart and soul stayed soiled from that day on. To keep him with me." Tears fell.

A few more moments passed as Roberto looked at him expectantly.

"Do you remember what else you did?"

Gus dug into his memories and came up unsuccessful. "I have no idea."

Roberto sighed. "I thought you might remember."

Gus searched more. "Nothing."

"You pretended to me that he was with you when you visited alone." He stood up and began to pace the room. "I'd been waiting for this moment hijo, for you to realize. For years you stayed here after bullfights and acted like he was with you, but not beside you. Every time you tried paying for the room, you said he was still in the room or outside in the car," Roberto said.

"No, that can't be," Gus denied. But in his heart he knew it was true. He collapsed to the floor and bawled. His grandfather called out to him, the bulls called out to him, and so Gus answered the call.

"Year after year you lied to my face," Roberto said. "Or at least that's what I thought. It clicked for me one random year, you'd convinced yourself he'd been beside you all along: he'd never gone anywhere, he'd never fallen into that arena. You still kept coming to bullfights, but you stopped talking about him. Only when I mentioned his name did you talk about him, but always lies. Years later you straightened up and talked about him in the past tense," Roberto said, "but you and I never talked about that night and all the denial after."

Gus crumpled to the floor. He remembered it all, all the worlds he'd constructed in his head crashed together and exploded inside of him. Every time he blinked he saw a reflection of himself in front of the fireplace: empty, lost, and fucked out.

Roberto opened the coffee table between them and produced a bottle of Chivas Regal and a shot glass from underneath. He poured Gus a drink, who gulped it hungrily, then reached for the bottle.

The loss, a scarred-over gash, released a grief Gus hadn't known. The depression that consumed him tapped him on the shoulder to remind him it had never gone away. The alcohol fed its appetite. After he gorged on a few more shots, the tears again ran down his face. "He . . . died . . . mi abuelo . . . " Gus looked at Roberto. "You, Roberto, you were here . . . to console me . . . all those years ago."

Roberto began crying and nodding his head. "Sí mijo, I was here. The bullfight happened, the wall fell down, and you drove to the hotel afterwards, after . . . Mateo died. You were so . . . how do they say? Stricken with grief? I thought you might've forgotten the whole thing the moment you left for home by yourself. You were only a teenager."

Gus began to feel, eerily so, his past and present clash and combine. He pointed to the mullioned window. "In the morning I watched you pour water over the tiles outside to wash away the grime and dirt from the night before. It felt like you washed away his blood from my mind. That evening, just before mamá arrived, you did it again, you filled up a pail with water and threw it out over the tiles. I imagined the water making a path to the drain and disappearing, just like my memories of that night."

The tears flowed from both men's eyes and Gus could feel the sorrow and guilt take over him, thick and viscous. He decided, right then and there, that this understanding of his loss would be the thing that resurrected him from the Gus who kept him down.

CHAPTER 29

AMELIA ROUNDED THE CORNER TO MAIN STREET AND TOOK AN UNEASY BREATH as she eyed William's. As she plodded toward the business, every fiber in her being tensed and signaled her to turn around and head home. Standing on the street and collecting her nerves to ask for aspirin at the pharmacy just happened to be the last thing she wanted to be doing at that moment, but she literally drew the short straw when her mother requested headache medicine, and not one cousin or sibling volunteered to accompany her. Everyone wanted to stay at the birthday party.

Colorful piñatas hung from trees promising sweet candy, while the aroma of her mother's enchiladas had just started to spread. But duty called, she demanded aspirin, and the nearest adult promptly snipped four straws in half to accommodate the eight children nearby. Everyone stood in a circle and picked straws. Amelia groaned when she lost, and someone—she didn't know who—shoved some money in her hand.

As she approached the door she noticed a teenage couple standing near the front. The girl cried softly while the guy consoled her, but she kept turning her head when he tried to cup her face in his hands. Though she didn't know the reason for her weeping, Amelia knew something beyond the front door of William's caused her sorrow, and it felt like a foreshadowing. She reminded herself the quicker she started, the quicker it'd all be over.

The bell sounded, announcing her entry to the soda jerk and his one male customer eating ice cream. Amelia's eyes darted to the ground and they granted her wish to be ignored as she took the few steps toward the pharmacy. She could hear teenage girls giggling, and she saw two girls sitting at the counter behind the cash register, each smacking gum. Cracked on one side, a wide mirror hung above their heads to help them pick up on activity in the far back of the pharmacy.

Amelia hid herself behind an aisle and watched the girls for a few moments. She liked how they piled their hair into a loose bun atop their heads, it looked so nonchalant, yet intentional at the same time. One girl twisted a fallen tendril around her finger absentmindedly while the other flipped magazine pages.

Suddenly, the girl twirling her hair widened her eyes in excitement. “Oh my god, turn it back a page.” She tapped at a picture. “Do you know him? He’s my favorite.”

The other girl leaned in. “Ricky Nelson? Don’t think so.”

“The definition of dreamy,” said the first girl. “He starred in his first movie last year, *Here Comes the Nelsons*.”

The second girl nodded appreciatively. “Not bad.”

Amelia felt a small familiar jealousy growing within her. She wanted them to invite her to gaze at Ricky Nelson; she wanted them to teach her how to effortlessly gather her hair into a bun like theirs. It didn’t seem fair that they drew the long straws in life. Just once, she wished to be looked at as a white girl. Amelia glanced up at the mirror above and saw a tiny version of herself crouched behind an aisle longing desperately for other people’s lives. The crack on the mirror appeared to sever Amelia’s reflection in half at the torso.

She knew these were pipe dreams. She’d peeled herself away from her family to walk to William’s for aspirin, and it was a difficult enough task without staring at girls she knew she could never be like. Finding the right medicine and paying without being made fun of was her number-one goal. In her preoccupation she didn’t notice Gus nearby.

She became engrossed with finding the right product. Her lips moved slightly as she tried to make out the syllables and find the right brand. Occasionally she mumbled to herself. She chose a box, turned it around, studied it, then placed it back on the shelf. She did this to three more boxes before deciding to ask for help, the one thing she didn’t want to do.

Amelia turned to the counter, took a deep breath, and took two steps toward the girls, not knowing Gus watched her.

Both cashiers wore name tags on their shirts asking how they could help. One tag said the wearer’s name was Hannah, the other said Ava. Hannah lifted her head first and released the skein of hair she tugged on. “Yah?”

This was the part Amelia dreaded the moment she drew the short straw: her pronunciation of aspirin. She found some words she still had problems with, and she couldn't stop thinking about how much the word made her think of a sprain, like an ankle sprain. "Do you have . . . um, where is the ass, the ass," she stopped. "I need ass-sprain." She tapped on her forehead. "Medicine for headaches."

At this Ava lifted her head with a smirk on her face "The ass?? The ass??" She began to giggle.

Amelia imagined she could reach up and pull a rope that would let Ava drop through the floor.

Hannah stifled a laugh while she reached into her hair and pulled a pencil out. The bun uncoiled into a fluffy mess around her shoulders. "Okay, now, what is it that you want?" She formed a bubble with her gum and popped it with a forefinger. "What is it you want? I don't understand what you're saying . . . repeat it for me?" She spiraled her hair back up and stabbed the pencil back in.

Amelia exhaled noisily. She debated leaving and walking farther down the street to the grocery store, but she knew the scene would unfold all over again. "You take the medicine when your head hurts."

Ava giggled. "Kinda like the way my head is starting to hurt right now, I bet."

Hannah leaned forward. "Hmmm, I'm not quite sure what you could be talking about. Now tell me one more time, what is it you need?"

"A sprain, ass-sprain?" Amelia's voice faltered.

Hannah laughed and glanced at Ava. "Isn't it annoying when people can't talk English?"

Ava nodded and rolled her eyes. "It's like, learn it, or go back to where you came from."

At this, Gus stepped forward and interjected. "Okay, I think we all know what this girl needs." He held out two boxes of aspirin to Hannah. "Ring those up for me, will you, sweetie?" He turned to Amelia. "Don't worry about paying these girls here, I think you've paid enough."

Amelia's eyes glistened with tears, but she held them back for fear Hannah and Ava would see. She shot out her hand to clasp Gus's hand, and he held it tightly. "Thank you."

"Gus," he pointed to his chest, "García."

She wiped away a tear before it could spill onto her cheek. "Mr. García, will you please walk me out?" She spoke to the tile floor in a meek voice, and her breathing fell into rapid short breaths.

"Of course."

Hannah held out a small paper bag with the two aspirin boxes. As Gus grabbed it, Ava began to smile and clamped a hand over her mouth to hide it, but a giggle escaped.

Amelia's gaze shot up, her eyes hot and burning. "It's not funny." She lifted her chin and felt it quiver slightly. Her hand gripped Gus's more tightly.

"No, it's not funny, is it?" He tapped a fingernail on the counter. "I wonder if your mother taught you to behave like that."

The smugness dropped from both of their faces as Gus and Amelia walked out onto Main Street. They turned the corner together to the same spot where they met the first time. Gus quickly ripped into a box and dumped a fourth of an aspirin bottle into his palm. He shoveled them into his mouth and swallowed without water.

Now outside and thinking more clearly again, Amelia began to take notice of his appearance. His hair, shiny from grease, shot out in all directions. The black button-up shirt he wore sagged to one side, and his black pants were covered in dust. She watched as he tore into the bottle and sighed with relief as if they immediately worked, which she knew they hadn't. "Are you okay?"

Gus smiled. "Physically, no, but mentally, I'm okay." The smile grew wider. "I think I'm growing up."

She cocked back her head. "Still?"

"Always."

"My dad said you lost your case here."

"An intentional loss. We appealed, lost that, and now we're petitioning to the Supreme Court."

"What happens then?"

"Then we hold court in Washington, DC. It's the highest we can go. If we win, we get to retry the case."

Amelia eyebrows lifted. "So you start all over again?"

"Something like that."

"Sounds like a long road." She squinted at him. "Is that why you look like that?"

Gus laughed and scratched his head. "Yes, I guess you could say so. When things get stressful one can put a lot of pressure on themselves. Raising money, things like that." He pointed inside the building. "What happened in there?"

Amelia weighed the question. "I hate buying medicine for my mom. I don't know how to say any of the words."

"Then you have to ask someone if they carry the product," Gus filled in.

Her eyes brightened at him. "Yes! Then I get embarrassed, and then they usually make fun of me and all I want to do is tell them off, you know? But then all I do is cry. I don't know what to say or how to say it."

Gus shrugged his shoulders. "So learn. Then you don't have to ask anyone for help anymore. But you need to face your fears so you know how to overcome them. That's a lesson I just learned recently. The more you do it, the easier it becomes. You did a good job of standing up for yourself, and it felt good, right?"

"It felt great!" She looked out into the street. "I gotta go home, there's a birthday party at my aunt's house. Do you want to come?"

Gus fingered his shirt and glanced down at his pants. "I'd love to, really, but I need to get home myself. Plus, I'm not very presentable right now."

"They call you the shiny one. I heard my dad tell my mom."

He laughed uneasily. "I don't feel too shiny right now."

Amelia rushed into him and gave him a hug. She didn't know why she suddenly felt compelled to hug him, but it felt right as she squeezed. "You smell like a barnyard animal."

"Yep, that feels like an accurate depiction."

Amelia accepted Gus's offer for a ride to her aunt's home, and her comfort with him grew. She sniffed a few times openly and glared at him. "I found the barn."

"That's the thing about smells," Gus said. "At first you think it's intolerable, but after awhile, you get used to it. Soon enough you can't even smell it anymore."

She sniffed again. "Why would you want to get used to a smell like that? It's like saying I'll get used to attitude from girls like that if I just wait it out." She shook her head staunchly. "No way. If someone like you is telling me not to give up, there's probably someone telling them the same thing. Nobody quits." She turned to Gus and noticed a tear falling down his cheek. "Did I say something wrong?"

He reached out and squeezed her hand. "No ma'am, not at all. You said the perfect thing."

Amelia waved at Gus until his car disappeared around the corner and from her sight. An epiphany struck her as she turned to her aunt's house and walked to the backyard. She wanted to raise money for Gus and mail it to him. He moved her. He was the shiny one, like people said, and she could feel his light reflected off her.

The trees behind her aunt's house were Amelia's favorite thing. Sprawling and tall, they lined the backyard, providing breeze and shade for whatever barbecue or Easter egg hunt her aunt hosted. Swings and tires hung from the strong branches and held most of the younger family members, including Amelia. Her aunt planted a large oak in the corner of the property with the initials of every family member, and saved space beside their names in case they married. She built a fire pit in the middle of the backyard with a circle of large flat stones around it for people to sit on.

Three picnic tables covered in a royal purple tablecloth connected underneath two intertwined trees, with white napkins and plates lined up on each side. Subtle worked the best for adult birthdays. Beautiful decorations hung from the trees. The grandchildren, all twelve of them, constructed different types of streamers. Each one arrived at the party with a new pattern. Strings with buttered popcorn and bright paper links with candy glued on wove into branches and draped over the picnic tables. One string used pretzels and the orange cheese crackers shaped like stop signs; another used cereal.

Off to one side near a clump of trees a volleyball net waited for players. Among the trees hung hammocks for passionate and/or drunk family fans, perfect for napping. Two piñatas hung from yet another tree clump near the back door of the house, one a bird and another a cat. A semicircle of chairs surrounded the piñatas, each one from a different set. One chair had a mismatched leg; one was backless; another had only one arm; and another's arms were from different chairs. On the clothesline a string of newly washed clothes whipped slowly in the wind and dried themselves under the sun. Aluminum pails filled with ice and beer waited to be emptied and then refilled. A garden sprouting with new flowers lined the back of the house.

Amelia made her way into the kitchen. It smelled of seasoned beef and cumin, her mother's enchiladas, rice and beans. Four women, her mother included, ducked and bobbed around each other in perfect harmony without colliding. They babbled about where they would travel if they had money and didn't pay attention when Amelia began opening and closing cupboard doors.

She found a mason jar perfect for holding quarters and nickels, a used envelope, and a marker. Carefully, she wrote the word DONATE on the backside of the envelope and taped it to the jar. At first she placed it on a counter and thought it would be good enough. She left it alone and went outside to play with her cousins. She returned an hour later to find three quarters.

After dinner Amelia put it on one end of a picnic table and sat with it as a volleyball game started. She shook the jar and the coins clinked against the glass to catch people's attention, but still nothing happened. People tired of playing volleyball and passed by the table, but only three relatives dropped in some change, bringing her total to two dollars. Gus's words urging her to speak up crossed her mind, and she decided she needed to go out and ask for donations. This way, the act of asking would become easier the more she tried. At this point the sun had set, and friends began to join the family. They also brought beer and liquor.

Amelia found herself lucky with the females. She walked up behind them and tapped on their shoulders. When they turned around she batted her eyelashes and held up the jar, sometimes shaking it. "Will you donate for a good cause?" She received three more quarters almost immediately.

As she made the rounds in the backyard she noticed certain members with a glazed look in their eyes. They arrived already drunk, she decided. She avoided them for as long as possible, but she didn't realize they'd started to find her bothersome. One in particular watched Amelia bounce from person to person.

"Hey there, you there," he said. "Why haven't you come to ask me to donate?"

Amelia stopped suddenly and turned around slowly. Meekly, she said, "I don't know who you are."

The man took two steps toward her and knelt on the ground. He stuck out his hand. "My name is Frank."

Frank wore a navy and red plaid button-up shirt and faded blue jeans. He held a beer bottle in his hand and his breath stunk of beer, as did his ratty beard.

Amelia smiled thinly and nodded her head. "Hello, Frank." She turned to walk away.

"Hold on, now wait a minute," Frank said. "Don't leave so quickly."

Amelia glanced at the faces of some of her relatives, waiting for one of them to interrupt them. They smiled at her and urged her to go on. She stared at Frank but didn't speak.

"Now, why do you keep asking everyone for money?"

"I'm asking for donations," Amelia said.

"Okay, but why? Who or what are you raising money for?" He took a swig of his beer and burped loudly.

"A friend of mine." Her voice went quiet. "He's trying to make it to the Supreme Court." As the words came out of her mouth Amelia realized she didn't really know what she was saying. She merely repeated what Gus told her.

Some of her relatives immediately realized who she was talking about. One of them asked her for verification. "The lawyers for Pete?"

"Yes." She looked into the faces of her family near her. "The one they call the shiny one."

They knew who she spoke of and had their own things to say about Gus. "I heard he's a drunk," said Frank.

"I've heard that too," chimed in one of Amelia's aunts. "He can barely hold down the job he's been given."

Betrayed and shocked, Amelia needed to know more. "Where did you get that information?"

The aunt shot back. "Why do you care so much? You're just a child, you shouldn't be worried about those sorts of things anyhow. How do we know he's actually your friend? How do we not know you're just trying to get us to give you money?"

Amelia's chin quivered. Half of her wanted to turn and run inside the house, yet the other half of her realized this was another opportunity for her to stand up for herself. Her voice strengthened with every word. "Because I'm saying it right now. He's my friend, and Delia knows him too."

"Speaking of your sister," said Amelia's mother, "why don't you go find her and play with her?"

Frank laughed. "Your friend is representing a criminal. Pete Hernandez is a criminal. He shot Joe, we all know it."

A man's voice: "I think it's a little more complicated than that."

Amelia turned around to see her father. She smiled brightly at him.

"It is!" The smile dropped from her face. "But I don't know enough to explain it."

"You don't have to explain. Frank here wouldn't understand it anyway." Henry reached into his pocket for a roll of dollar bills, peeled one off and dropped it in the mason jar.

Frank scoffed. "She's got to learn what she's getting herself into."

"Maybe that's exactly what she's doing," her father answered back.

Amelia felt her father's energy enter her body, and her heart swelled. She realized speaking up wasn't something that suddenly became a part of her; she would need to gather her courage time and time again to speak up when something didn't feel right, or wasn't right. Frank wouldn't be the last. She eyed him as she went to another uncle nearby and stuck the mason jar under his nose. "Would you like to donate to a good cause?"

"Go away and play with your sisters," he said, and pointed at Frank. "I agree with him, leave me alone. Go away and play," repeated the uncle.

"Yeah," Frank added. "Go away and get pregnant or do something useful." He laughed and looked around for others to laugh with him. "Take off your shoes while you're at it. Woman should be barefoot when they're pregnant."

Amelia became incensed and turned to her father. She whipped back to Frank and stared at him for a moment. "Why don't you go away and make some babies? I hear that's all you're good for."

Her comment elicited laughs from her family. Henry stepped forward and patted Frank on the back. "Looks like you got put in your place by my girl." He leaned in closer. "Don't ever talk to her or any of my daughters like that again, or it'll be me putting you in your place."

Amelia went to bed that night flushed and feeling daring. She wanted to take those feelings with her into the next day and the next. For the remainder of the month she went into town to ask strangers for donations and was able to understand the issue Gus fought for. After a few months, Amelia mailed him twenty-five dollars.

She learned over time the person she really helped was herself, and it started to become enough for her. Frank apologized, saying he drank too much and would've never said something like "go out and get pregnant" if he was sober. Amelia eyed him and said she doubted that was the case, but thanked him for helping her learn to stand up for herself. She knew it was something she'd keep with her the rest of her life.

CHAPTER 30

AS LONG AS GUS STAYED BUSY, THE REVELATIONS IN MEXICO ABOUT MATEO didn't paralyze him. The looming deadline to file the writ helped. The other lawyers on the team completed their work and sent it to his office for compilation. He typed up the forms and triple-checked every page, soon quelling his peers' fears about his work. He made sure not to share with them his epiphanies, and didn't intend to until after they met their deadline.

Gus connected with John over the phone on Monday afternoon, two days before the writ deadline. "I'm proud of myself, John. This is crazy. I can't remember the last time I've felt this way. The paperwork is ready. I'm going to go through it one more time before I mail it out." He took a deep breath. "Honestly, things are going so well I'm waiting for the other shoe to drop. Do you know what I mean? Am I being ominous?"

John laughed heartily. "I think yes, but don't forget this amigo . . . you're the one wearing the shoes. Don't walk yourself into a disaster. Turn the other way."

Gus laughed with his friend. "I will try to do that."

"You've always been wearing the shoes," John said. "That's why you have me to remind you!"

"I forget to ask people for help," Gus said. "I forget to ask people about the reality of things when I'm unsure about it."

"Someone from the GI Forum, not sure who, will be over with the money to file by the end of today or tomorrow morning. He said he'd be sure to bring you a hot meal if you were in the mood for it."

Gus turned grumpy. His voice turned gruff. "Oh, it is payment for my work?"

"Sure, why not?" John matched his voice. "Are you hungry or not? When's the last time you had a hot dinner?"

"At this point a hot dinner would spoil me," Gus said bitterly. "I need to suffer. My work needs to be my food, my air, my blood."

"Aye Dios mío." John exhaled loudly. After a long pause he said, "When's the last time you saw Irene?"

Gus blew a raspberry into the phone receiver. "Good old Ireenie? We spoke before my showing at the infamous Kincaid Christmas party, but I haven't seen her since."

"What about the girls? Didn't you celebrate Christmas with them?"

Gus shook his head and glanced at a large brown paper bag full of gifts. "Intentionally or unintentionally, I keep forgetting to schedule a visit. I'm experiencing déjà vu."

"Kept forgetting or putting it off?"

"Same thing," Gus said somberly.

"Aye, after what happened at the Kincaid's, how far are you going to let this go? What doesn't cross the line for you?"

"I'd never miss a trial because I'd been drinking. I'd never steal or physically hurt someone to get what I want." He imagined how the situation might elevate, weighing what lines he'd already crossed. A picture of a bank burglary flashed through his mind, the one where the robbers hold bags with a money symbol on them and tiptoe in and out of the building. "I'd never pilfer money intended for a case."

"Now you've planted a seed of doubt."

"The point is: I know I have a problem and I'm trying to do something about it. If I didn't know better I'd think you were trying to test me."

"Who, me?"

"Well, thanks for calling!"

"Come on, García, if you're already at an end point, take a break and try to see your girls . . . all three of them."

"We'll see." He paused. "If it matters, I would've rather you not bring up my family at a time like this."

"Nonsense," John said, unbothered. "You're being a wimp right now. Buck up, we're almost at the next resting spot before we get to the finish line."

"You buck up," Gus retorted. "Demanding I buck up . . . you buck up." He hung up without saying goodbye, still muttering to himself until someone knocked at his door.

"Hello," a man dressed in white said when Gus opened the door. "I'm looking for a Gus García? The lawyer Gus García?"

"Yes, right here, I'm Gus . . . Gustavo."

"Sign right here," he requested, holding out a pen and clipboard. He reminded Gus vaguely of the soda jerk in Edna. He handed him an envelope and said, "Have a good day!"

Inside, Gus found two hundred dollars. The cost for filing the writ was ninety dollars. A note inside said: Not sure if you have to drive to DC to file; you weren't the only one drunk on Christmas! The extra money should help for gas, in case.

Three hours passed as Gus triple-checked the paperwork and planned his route. He stretched out on his couch, but couldn't fall asleep. His mind replayed the day's events, pausing over his conversation with John, especially his comment about using trial money.

Doing what he swore he wouldn't turned out to be quite easy. He saw himself walking down the street, purchasing a bottle, one bottle—maybe two. Nowadays, he could finish the bottle in one long sitting. He was golden.

Gus took the money envelope and went straight to the liquor store. He bought two fresh bottles of whisky. When he concluded the purchase and received his change, he sang a ditty he made up on the spot: *Mister Chivas, Mister Regal, makes me so feel fine.* The man at the cashier gave him an odd look, but Gus didn't pay him any mind.

It all happened too fast. He walked out of the store, pivoted back inside without a second thought, and bought himself an entire case of Chivas.

CHAPTER 31

CARLOS'S HEART JUMPED WHEN IRENE SWUNG OPEN HER DOOR. ALL OF HIS stress and uncertainty went up in smoke.

"Mira, Carlitos! I wondered when you'd show up." She lifted her mug. "After I finish my coffee I was going to call Gloria."

He waved the idea away. "She's with the kids."

"I thought two was enough," Irene commented. "But ten! Come in, come in." She opened the door wide.

"They keep her busy, and I'm always gone." Carlos stepped inside.

"I know that life. Do you drink to ease the pain?"

"Not a drop," he patted his stomach. "Too many calories." He blushed when she giggled. "Gus is here, right?"

"Of course. He turned up smelling of whisky and going on about a deadline he'd forgotten, all gibberish really. Would you like some coffee?"

"Aye Dios mío, I hope not, and yes please."

Carlos loved his wife Gloria for her maternal instincts to care for and nurture him and their children. Yet, if Carlos were to crush on someone, it would be Irene. He found her sensual and devilishly attractive.

In college, Carlos and Gus were friends, but Carlos met Irene first. They studied together and went out on two dates before she met Gus, and ever the competitive man, he stole her away soon after. Carlos relied on friendship to develop a relationship, while Gus relied on lust. He convinced himself Gus looked better standing next to her than he did, and Gus never let her go, despite the other women he peppered into his life.

When Carlos met Gloria, he found they fit together seamlessly. She had children from a previous marriage, nine to be exact. Gloria understood, like other women not as stunning as Irene, how to deal with disappointment and being put second on occasion. So Carlos married her, kept his crush to himself, and kept the Irene sightings to a minimum. Only in rare times such as now did he find his feelings hadn't changed much.

Irene set his cup of coffee on the table with a small plate of cookies.

"Could I get a glass of water? No ice," he requested. "Where's Gus?"

"He's in the living room." She went back to her own coffee.

Carlos found Gus splayed out and snoring on the living room floor, with a glass of water and a white hand towel beside his head. Gus's expression appeared serene, something Carlos hadn't seen in some time. Gus seemed thinner, and his face and skin sagged. He felt a bit of pity for his friend before he nudged Gus's foot with his. "Gustavo."

Gus stirred, but only to roll to the other side and return to sleep. He farted and a leg darted out that hit Carlos.

A rush of frustration suddenly stung him, so to be spiteful, he splashed water from his glass in Gus's face. Gus popped up gasping for breath.

Carlos leaned down and began yelling. "Yesterday was the deadline and you missed the deadline? Is this true?"

Gus dried his face with a throw pillow. "I think so."

"*You think so?* Why? What happened for it to come to this? I blame myself you know, for trusting you when I knew I shouldn't have!" He nudged him with his foot again. "Clean yourself up and come to the kitchen when you're done."

Irene tsk-tsked. "You didn't throw that water in his face, did you?"

"Damn right I did!" He took a sip of coffee. "If enough money was in the budget I would've suggested we hire a babysitter."

"Aye Carlitos . . . "

"He missed the deadline, and I find him here with you out of his mind. I'm only glad there's still time for me to fix it."

They heard Gus curse out loud. He walked in with his black hair matted on one side and a stain on his shirt. Sheepishly, he said, "My briefcase isn't here."

Carlos stood up so fast his chair tipped over.

"Irene, did I bring my bag when I came here?"

She shook her head. "No mi amor, you arrived with nothing more than an open heart."

His face flushed. "I screwed the pooch."

"How the hell are we supposed to find it?"

"Let's not panic just yet." Gus ran a hand through his hair. "You yell at me and we waste time finding it."

"So instead of getting the work done first and then drinking to celebrate, you had a drink and forgot to finish the work!" Carlos trembled and screamed obscenities at Gus, calling him names. "We trusted you! I trusted you! Herrera said he talked to you over the phone, and what the hell happened?" He didn't wait for a response. "Wait I know, *you* happened," he said sarcastically. "The *bottle* happened."

"Carlos, ya," Irene stepped in. "Enough."

"No!" Carlos stomped his foot.

"No Reen," Gus dropped his head in surrender. "He's right. Carlitos, you are correct. Everything you said, it's all correct."

"Just shut up," Carlos snapped. "Shut up!"

Gus's face said it all, and he buried it in his hands. A flood of obscenities came out of both men.

"La Mancha, that's where it's got to be," Gus said. "I went there on Monday afternoon, or was it Sunday night?"

Carlos gasped and lunged at Gus. "I will feel your neck between my hands!"

Irene grabbed Carlos by his collar and pulled him back. "Enough! You will not attack your partner. It's not going to help anything. If you knock him out, how are you going to find the briefcase?"

Carlos regained his self-control and straightened his tie. "Do we need to call every woman and bar in town to find your briefcase? To find our work?"

Irene cleared her throat. "I resent that, Carlitos."

"My apologies, it's just . . . Irene, this isn't your fault." He pointed to Gus. "But you . . . you!"

She lifted her chin. "Don't treat me as if I'm so naive. You think I don't know what you're going through with him? Welcome to my world. Gustavo has always cared more about his work than his family, and now we see he cares about drinking most of all." She smiled down at Gus. "But I worry about him, I can't help it. I see this man, my daughters' father, crumpled up on the floor. He came to me last night baring his heart and apologizing for his wrongdoings, and that's all I needed to hear. I knew something big would happen with the case, but something big happened in my own home. All those words he uses to charm others, manipulating through coercion, I realize the person he's tricked the most is himself."

Carlos, stunned, looked at her. "No wonder you fell for him so fast."

Irene turned to him with rage pouring from her eyes. She pulled her hair back in a rubber band she kept around her wrist. "Don't you dare say that to me, you don't know us. You never knew us, you never wanted to. Let me give you a quid pro quo. You want that briefcase so bad, go out and find it. I'm going to take care of a sick man."

Carlos laughed. "He's not sick, he's self-indulgent!" He pointed at Gus and looked Irene dead in her eyes. "We're not done with him yet. Pete Hernandez isn't done with him yet. If they don't throw the writ out because it's a day late, it's going to be a long year."

Irene followed Carlos to the front door. "Don't blame me for taking care of him."

Carlos spun to face her. "He WILL NOT stay here, he's coming with me. Gustavo! Put on your shoes, now. You didn't make deadline, so I will be your father and force you to deal with the consequences." As Gus obeyed, Carlos continued. "I convinced the boys to keep you as head counsel. They didn't want to, you know that? I told them to leave you alone about your drinking."

"I screwed up," Gus replied, "but I'm not going to take a tongue lashing from you all the way there. I'm still a damn man. So get it out, whatever you feel you need to say, get it out now." He bent down to tie his shoes. "You didn't want the accolades that came with being in my spot, is that it? Even though I've given you opportunity after opportunity for you to take charge."

"I don't want this case! I never wanted this case!" Carlos's voice boomed throughout the house. "This case was brought to *you*. Lenora visited *you*. Finish what *you* started! If you didn't think you had the balls to finish this, you should've said something a long time ago. I never trusted myself trusting you!"

"I told you this, but you didn't want to listen," Gus said quietly. "You never wanted to listen."

"Shut up Gustavo, no one feels sorry for you. Except Irene. Every one of us—John, James, myself—we're so damn busy with our own work and family life, we didn't want to take the time to divvy up your tasks. But no one has the man hours to learn how to drink the way you do. We didn't do the math." Carlos clenched his teeth. "Where's the other glass of water? I want to pitch that one in your face, too."

"I drank it."

"Like you do everything."

"Yes, my little giant, get it all out!" Gus stood, energized. "Tell me how horrible I am, and how juvenile. Don't forget though, don't forget I fight with more demons than you've ever come in contact with. Your life is perfect with your intact family and your aversion to alcohol. Pretend to behave like you know my woes."

Carlos scowled. "Like you know mine."

The men didn't speak once they piled into the car, nor during the drive into the heart of San Antonio towards their offices. Sure enough, Gus had left his briefcase at La Mancha and Petee kept it safe.

Carlos dug through the bag and pulled out the papers. He flipped through the pages with a mixture of shock and confusion on his face. It was wrong, everything was wrong.

Gus read his panicked face. "What? What?"

"This is typed, all of these pages are typed." He stopped flipping through the pages and sent Gus daggers with his eyes. "I could punch you right now. These are supposed to be printed!"

"For the love of God," Gus said. "I couldn't find a print shop, and when I did, it cost too much."

"Really Gus, how much time per day do you spend being a self-saboteur? Do you take classes, or are you just going by the seat of your pants!" Carlos jumped off the barstool and took the pages with him. "You stay here, I don't want you coming with me anymore."

"Thank the Lord," Gus responded. "My home is less than a block away. And I need something to drink after spending that much time with you." He leveled his eyes at Carlos and took a step closer. "You are no better than a hangover, Carlos. You make me regret every choice to make myself happy, to help me get through one more night." He waved him away like a mosquito. "Go, and leave my bag."

CHAPTER 32

AS CARLOS WALKED OUT, PETEE LEANED AGAINST THE BAR AND POURED GUS A whisky. "Bad night?"

Sarcastically, Gus said, "Whatever gave you that impression? I'm a failure and all my coworkers know it."

Petee laughed. "Gustavo, when you're done with your pity party, you let me know, yes? The cot is free for the night. I'll give you first dibs since you brought me the bottles of whisky."

"Sure." He smiled weakly and sipped his drink. "You've given me so many free drinks, I thought I could do something nice for you for a change."

"Want to tell me what happened?"

Gus shook his head.

Petee slid down the bar and received drink orders from a pair of women who'd just sat down, a brunette and a blonde. He called out to Gus, "Want one more?"

"Maybe," he answered. As Gus sized up the women he realized his unwillingness to be alone yet, on a cot or in his office. Being alone led to loneliness, which usually led to desperation, which inevitably culminated in self-destruction, and he couldn't afford it. Plus, the quieter his surroundings, the more he sank into remorse about what he had done in the past few days. He'd been glad to argue with Carlos because it pushed his guilt away.

He shoved it from his mind once more and scooted past the two bar stools separating him and the women. "Hello ladies," he said cheerfully, "how are we doing this evening?"

Maria and Mary behaved as a unit: they mostly spoke in unison and finished each other's sentences. "Fiiiiine." Mary tucked her brunette hair behind an earlobe with a long red nail, while Maria brought her drink to her mouth and sipped from a straw.

"I come here all the time and I've never seen you two in here before. Are we celebrating a birthday, a breakup, a boyfriend?" Gus started to feel more like Gus and back in his own skin, despite his matted hair and rumpled clothes.

They giggled and shook their heads.

"Could I interest you both in a drink back at my office? I don't have enough money to buy drinks, but I'd like to talk to you two more." When their eyes smiled at him, he knew he had it in the bag.

Maria cocked her head and crossed her legs. "Where did you say your office is?"

"Less than a block from where we are right now."

She shook her head. "I don't think so."

Mary's armor had softened until her friend rebuffed Gus's advance. She straightened her posture, but reached out and touched his forearm. "What's your phone number? I'm not saying I'm interested, but I might be."

Gus patted his pockets and wallet. "I have some business cards in the back room." He saw Mary and himself rolling around on the cot in a quick flash. A naughty smile eased onto his face.

"Oh really?" Her eyebrows stretched up as she glanced at her friend. "How about you go and get one for me," Mary coyly asked.

He opened his mouth to ask her to join him, but Maria hadn't moved a muscle. She raised an eyebrow at Gus and he wiped the smirk from his face.

"Sure," he said, "I'll be right back."

By the time he returned, only Petee stood shaking his head and polishing a beer mug with a towel. The blonde and brunette were nowhere to be seen.

"I'm sorry, man," Petee consoled. "One talked the other into leaving. I don't think they liked you or me." He cracked a smile.

Gus shook a fist in the air. "I would've had success if I'd showered."

Suddenly Mary walked back in and toward the bar. "I forgot my purse," she said to Petee, and acknowledged Gus.

He took it as a second chance and stepped up to Mary immediately. Brazenly, he reached out and tucked a lock of hair behind her ear. "Glad to see you again," he whispered.

Mary jerked back. "Whoa," she said, "what are you doing?"

The smooth smile dropped off his face. "I don't know. I'm sorry, I thought . . . "

"You thought what? Because I didn't rebuff you more strongly you thought you had a chance?" She put a hand on one hip. "Like I was coming back for you? A woman saying no isn't something you're used to, from the look on your face. I was trying to be nice, jackass, so we could leave." She found her purse on a barstool. "You both have a great night."

A few beats passed as the men watched her walk off. Petee laughed and turned to look at Gus. "She's spicy. I like it." He popped his towel at him.

Gus shook his head. "I'm not laughing."

"You're not, huh? Why not? Did she cause you to lose your shine?"

"I've messed up a lot in the past few days with work. Now I've got to strike out with a woman? It couldn't have come at a worse moment." He ran his hands through his hair, dejected. "I'm going to take my drink and lie on your cot back there."

In that moment, a large group of young men and women entered La Mancha dressed in cheap suits and holding briefcases and bags. Both Petee and Gus simultaneously sighed out loud. Gus knew what it meant. Petee needed help. He walked himself around the bar.

"I'll pour shots and get beer; you do mixed drinks?"

Petee clapped Gus on the back. "Thank you, you don't have to."

"I know."

They took orders: a blended scotch, two gin and tonics, four beers, a root beer, a margarita, and a screwdriver.

"Law students?"

The one who ordered a blended scotch said yes.

"I'm a lawyer myself," Gus said.

Blended scotch sized up Gus momentarily and rolled his eyes. "Sure, okay."

Suddenly Gus forgot about his appearance, his wrinkled, coffee-stained clothes, flat hair, and stubbly chin. He hadn't shaved since he'd gone rogue. "I promise."

The one who ordered a beer raised an arm. "Prove it."

"Just finished a writ of certiorari for the Supreme Court." Gus proceeded to go into a detailed explanation of the case, the approach, and by the time Petee brought the mixed drinks to the table he'd earned their respect.

Petee began another round of drinks while Gus leaned behind the bar and watched the group. The guys loosened their ties and the girls crossed their legs, allowing their pumps to dangle off their toes while they sipped their drinks. Within minutes the one who ordered a gin and tonic raised his hand to order another round of drinks, just as Petee predicted. He handed Gus a tray. "Here, take this to them," and Gus obeyed.

The margarita sipped on her second and offered some to the one who ordered a screwdriver. "It's the perfect balance of sweet and sour," she said.

Screwdriver tasted it, whistled, and hit the table with his hand. "Damn, nigger! You make one mean margarita."

To Gus, time slowed to a stop. The comment shocked him like he'd been electrocuted. What made it worse, the young man's friends behaved as if he'd done nothing more than give Petee a compliment.

He saw Petee's glass slip and shatter on the floor. "Who the hell are you talking to?" Petee threw his towel in the sink and rounded the bar. Gus darted in front of him.

The blended scotch spoke out. "What is going on?"

The root beer and margarita squealed as Petee neared with clenched fists. He kept repeating the phrase, "I'm not playing around!"

Gus maneuvered himself in front of Petee and threw out his arms, but Petee pushed him into a nearby table. Gus took a deep breath and spoke as loud as he could from the bottom of his gut. "TELL YOU WHAT! HOW ABOUT EVERYONE STEPS OUTSIDE?"

As the group filed out, Gus located the key on Petee, blocked him from the front door, and locked it the moment the last person exited.

"Gus! You gotta let me through, I'm not going to take that kind of mess from some kid like that." Petee was panting and had begun to sweat through his shirt. He pushed up against Gus but didn't move him.

Gus held up a hand. "You're better than this. They didn't know what they were saying. I would say ignore them, but I know you're not going to."

"So let me through!"

He dangled the key in Petee's face. "I'll give you the key, but you have to allow me to leave first. Given what I've done here recently, the difference between giving in to a fight or trying to stop one isn't much. If you don't do it for your career as a business owner, do it for me and the Supreme Court."

Petee's anger ebbed away, and he slumped into a nearby chair. The people continued down the road. "It's never going to change," he said, and pointed outside. "Their parents said shit like that, and grandparents, and their grandparents' grandparents."

"It will change someday. That's one of the reasons why men like me fight, in the hope that those judges believe it will change."

"When?" Petee's voice cracked. "When will it change? How soon?"

"Soon," Gus managed to answer. "We just have to work at it, a little at a time, chipping away at the perceptions of people like them. A good beginning is to heal ourselves."

"My grandmother used to say if we healed ourselves properly the pain others inflict won't hurt as bad."

"Your grandmother is an extremely smart woman."

"I know, right?" Petee smiled and shook his head regretfully. "I wanted to punch the one who ordered a screwdriver so bad."

"When I said it will change, I didn't mean they would stop that sort of behavior," Gus said. "I meant that we all might start doing more to outsmart them and make them stop."

CHAPTER 33

GUS FELT MORE OBLIGATED TO THE TEAM AS IT NEARED, GUILTY FOR NOT FOL-lowing through in January. He helped his partners edit their arguments in case the Supreme Court granted their writ. He studied the words and read them out loud repeatedly. The practice became second-nature, he'd repeat the phrase—deliberately, systematically, and willfully excluded, and deprived of equal protection under the law—while he showered, ate, drank, and sometimes while he made love. Overcoming the passion in the words and making them an extension of himself took some time, but the process of getting there burned the hours.

The obsession led him to Austin, to the Texas attorney general's office. Gus reminded himself that Donovan worked at the office of the Chief Disciplinary Counsel. His office would no doubt be a dead end, which led him to the state office. Luckily, an old schoolmate, John Ben Shepperd, sat in the big chair.

Gus and JB were born in the same year, 1915. JB graduated from the University of Texas and married his wife Marnie in 1938. He received his law degree in 1941, the same year as Gus, and Governor Allan Shivers appointed JB secretary of state in 1950. While representing the Democratic Party, JB gained the Texas attorney general position in 1952, and became so popular he served a second term. The line "Freedom is not free" is attributed to him.

Bile rose up in Gus's throat when he arrived and faced the Niels Esperson building. Gus thought about his own building, and jealousy spread over him like the sweat dampening his shirt as if it was summer instead of spring. He took a few steps and stopped momentarily to take in the skyscraper. It was a familiar demon, his full-fledged jealousy toward a schoolmate who'd climbed so high his office was located in a building like that.

"Do you have an appointment?" JB's secretary lifted her left eyebrow slowly, as if a string tied to it was operated by someone floating above her. "Mr. Shepperd is finishing up a small meeting with someone right now."

Gus managed a suave smile. "No problem, I can wait." He openly showed his appreciation for her perky chest. "What's your name?"

"Suit yourself, it's almost lunchtime." She settled back, opened her top drawer, pulled out a nail file, and peered at her nails. A buzzer went off at her desk.

A voice boomed out that Gus assumed was JB's. "Nancy, have you left for lunch?"

"Not yet."

"Sam's leaving right now," the voice continued. "He should be passing your desk in three, two, one. Did it happen?"

A man with blonde hair dressed in a khaki suit swung a brown briefcase as he exited, just as the voice predicted. Gus touched the woven leather on his own briefcase.

"Not bad, Mr Shepperd, a one-second difference," she judged. "I'm headed out, but you have a visitor."

"I'll meet him up there."

Gus kept the suave smile. "Ah, Nancy."

Nancy smiled at Gus apologetically. "Sorry it's so slow right now, we get this way right before lunch. Can I get you anything? Water? Coffee?"

Gus shook his head and blocked the hallway as JB neared. Though a few inches shorter than Gus, he took those inches in his shoulders. Short, chestnut brown hair covered his head with a slight curl. He wore a fitted three-button navy suit with a cornflower blue tie. Gus thought him sharp.

JB recognized Gus immediately with a huge smile, but joked as he squinted his eyes and used a hand to shade the light. "Holy hell, is that Gus García? What is the fine honor I have of seeing you at my office? Is it my birthday?" JB turned to Nancy and winked.

"God, I hope not," she laughed.

"Come on back to the office," JB requested.

Jealousy flared in Gus again as he went further inside. The room's image was polished and chic, Gus thought. Pictures of his family, hugging and happy, waited at just below eye level when he sat down. JB's desk was sleek with a pane of glass covering the top, and he could see the state seal underneath. To his right a wide bookshelf held more pictures, a set of encyclopedias, and countless books and binders, also with the state seal.

"Let me fill in the blanks for you," JB piped up, "hot damn, huh? I'm still getting used to it, and it's been three months."

"Yeah, something to that effect. You've made it big, JB." Gus scratched his head. His jealousy began to show, and it could go downhill rapidly if he didn't stop it now. A joke! He needed a joke to fill in the blanks. "I can see this hasn't stopped you from balding at your temples there."

JB rubbed them. "Always the witty one . . . can you imagine what I'll look like at the end of my term?"

"I don't want to think about it," Gus grinned. He studied JB's face and noticed imperfections. His eyes were dark brown with bags underneath. He had bushy eyebrows and long ears, but the dimple on his chin softened his cornfed appearance.

"I see you're married now."

"Yes, that's Marnie, we married in '38 after law school. Twin daughters," JB tapped on a frame, "Marianne and Suzanne, what a handful. Plus my junior, we call him JB now."

"Beautiful family." Gus scowled at his canned response. "What's it like raising a boy?"

"You'd really have to ask Marnie," he shrugged. "I want to say more work, but it may be because of the two-for-one special."

"Christ, is that what you call it?"

"Behind closed doors." A smile curled on his lips. "So Gus, I'd ask about your family, but I know you're not here to talk about that. Let's talk shop. Now, to be truthful, my assistant has taken over most of the grunt work and I'm overseeing it. I'll be presenting, naturally, but he hasn't finished yet. I think he's here, though, and it might help to have him sit in."

"Why not?"

Moments later Horace Wimberly walked in. Gus immediately thought him to be the white Carlos. Gus saw nothing extraordinary about him. JB introduced them and filled in Horace about the impromptu meeting.

Horace's eyes widened. "I know who you are!" He paused to glance at his boss as if asking for permission to speak further. Horace turned back to Gus and put on the hint of a sneer. "You know there's no precedent for your case, right?"

Gus raised his eyebrows at his forwardness. "Let's get into it, shall we? How long have you been practicing law?"

JB held up his hands. "Let's not get off on the wrong foot already. Gus, Horace is passionate." He held up a hand to cover his mouth from one side. "Plus a little bit of a goodie two-shoes."

"I can see that." Gus winked.

Horace, clearly ruffled, straightened his back. "Fine, I can switch gears. You want people of Mexican descent to sit in juries for equal protection, but do they speak English? Isn't that the point of weighing in on a jury?"

"It's one tine on the fork. My men and I, we've fought for education, equal work rights, voting, and this. That's enough to scoop you up an entire meal," Gus said. "Just because the majority speak Spanish, in every community there are upstanding people of my color who should play a part in the judicial process."

Horace scowled. "Your color? Heads up, you don't look like them."

"Exactly my point," Gus snapped back. "I'm still them."

"You're all considered white. Isn't that enough?" Horace wiped the smile off his face when he caught a glimpse of JB shaking his head. "I mean—"

Gus clapped. "I didn't realize we were white! Let me withdraw the case. Thank you, Horace, for informing me of that clause. JB, you've got one hell of an assistant here . . . "

JB stood. "Now look, everyone needs to calm down."

"Who said we wanted to be white? My people want to be recognized, not glossed over." Gus stood. "Why can't your race broaden its horizons? I can tell you went to a segregated school."

Horace flinched as if Gus slapped him. JB sat down.

"Let me tell you something," Gus continued. "I'm sure you read about the bathroom sign incident in Edna at the county level."

"I'm sure I did," Horace said haughtily.

"Right. I'm going to give you the front-row-seat story. This town, this county, swears up and down there's no discrimination. But every time I drove down there I experienced racism or saw it second-hand. I watched as two brown girls, one more light-skinned like me, had service denied to them because of their color. A waitress, backed up by men in the town, asked my associates and me—dressed in suits—to leave a restaurant 'for our safety,' when they were more worried about their own safety. The Mexican school is filthy, the electricity doesn't work, and the desks fall apart when you sit in them. Still, they swear no discrimination is acted out. So you can imagine our surprise when the very courthouse we're fighting in has a sign directing 'colored men and hombres' to use the downstairs bathroom. That doesn't sound like we're classified under the white race to me, even if a lawyer like yourself hasn't come to that realization yet. That's why I'm fighting. That's why I'm here." His body strummed and buzzed as he sat down. Fighting the good fight felt better than drinking, fucking, sleeping, everything. *You're going to do just fine*, Gus thought to himself. *Or was it his grandfather's voice?*

"I see your point," Horace barked back. "But your guy murdered the other guy, he's guilty."

"Not the point," both Gus and JB said in unison.

"Try again," Gus offered.

"I bet most of the people you're fighting for aren't even citizens." Horace crossed his arms and nodded his head like he'd struck a blow.

"Do you know why that is? All those years ago, their land was simply overrun by your ancestors, who thought they knew best. Borders were moved without any discussion. How is any of that right, or fair? Why should we take it sitting down? There's no precedent for the case, because we're going to be the precedent, because men like Thurgood Marshall are going to make you all see the truth. We'll hit from every angle and then really be on a roll." He gripped the handle of his briefcase.

"No," JB stood again. "Don't go." He faced Horace. "Son, I think it's time you went back to your office. We'll talk later."

His face turned red. "Mr. Shepperd, I—"

"Not now, please, you are dismissed."

Horace squinted at Gus before he closed the door.

Gus and JB said nothing for a moment, staring directly into each other's eyes. Suddenly, they broke the ice and began laughing. JB spoke first. "I'm sorry for his behavior. I like the passion, but I don't like the values behind it."

"It's soothing to know it'll be you fighting on the other side," Gus declared.

JB threw up his hands. "Hell, I agree with you, I'm only going to do my job here, and I know what your endgame will be, should be, especially with Cadena and Herrera on your team." He placed a hand on Gus's shoulder. "We're always comrades, yes?"

A bit reluctantly, Gus raised an eyebrow and smiled. "I suppose so."

CHAPTER 34

"HE'S A POMPOUS ASS IF I'VE EVER MET ONE! WHO DOES HE THINK HE IS?"

"What lawyer isn't a pompous ass? Isn't that a class for first-year law students?"

"Gus García is a haughty man who thinks he has the ability to change the world," Horace said. "If I wasn't standing next to my boss, I don't know what I would've said to him."

"He's determined, I'll say that." Donovan looked around them. "I don't see anyone out here today."

Gus became the hot topic in the early morning the moment Donovan and Horace arrived at the Colorado River. Horace repeatedly kicked a log as he shared the details of Gus's visit. His volume grew until his face turned red. Donovan listened patiently and injected humor where he could to placate his friend.

"I see a couple, a man and woman. Don't you see them?" Horace pointed. "Dark jackets. I should've met Gus earlier, I could've involved myself more in his demise. Do you see them? They're making out right now."

"Don't worry, he's doing just fine on his own, but he keeps scraping by on dumb luck." Donovan spoke in a low voice. "Oh yeah, I see them now."

"Did I hear a tinge of disappointment? Or was that remorse?" Horace studied his facial expression. "You're not behaving the way I expected. You should still be beaming from the party. I'd be smiling to myself every minute. Aren't things going to plan?"

"We'll see what happens." Donovan paused, not wanting to be entirely honest. "I will say this: I find conducting someone else's demise takes a toll on the mind."

Horace reached out and patted his shoulder. "The finish line isn't far away, just push through. Think how different your life could be in a year's time."

"This process has reduced me," Donovan admitted. "I've done things I'm not proud of. I lied to my father, or more accurately, I lied to a senior member of Symmetry. It's not the way I wanted to do things, and worse, I'm afraid of what it means about me. Why I lied."

"What did you lie about?"

"Dad, or Don, told me he heard me talking with someone in the house after the Christmas party, but gave us some privacy. Asked about it. John Herrera—"

"Wait! Tell me the truth first."

The woman screamed at the man and pushed him, and they began an argument. Horace suggested they walk nearer to the couple, and Donovan agreed. The two joked about how they might be preventing a murder, and it lightened the mood between them. Finally, Horace urged him to continue.

"I don't want you to react like that woman." Donovan exhaled. "But I'll tell you because you're you." He exhaled again.

"That bad?"

The woman yelled out to her partner about respecting her privacy as they walked closer.

"Gus's meltdown caused his people to argue after one took him home. I think that's what led to John staying. He changed his mind and wanted to knock Gus off the case."

"That's good, right?"

Donovan nodded. "In theory, but it didn't pan out that way. I told him the offer no longer stood and implied Gus's behavior at the party was part of my plan. The next day, when my father approached me about the outcome, I found out he had seen us speaking." He shook his head, instantly regretting what he was about to say. "I told him John denied another offer from me."

"What took you so long to tell me?" Horace went through a range of emotions as he comprehended what he'd been told. His face contorted with confusion, then morphed into clarity. "I see what's going on here. You're giving up, and you've one-upped yourself by choosing the coward's way out with a liberal bleeding heart."

"Don't say that. Understand what I'm trying to say here. I can see the anger spreading over your face. I panicked, then covered up my steps, and then I didn't want to talk about it. To be honest, I thought maybe I'd wait and see what he'd do. Then he turns around and shows up at your office."

"A minute ago you worried about how this would make you look, and what it says about you. I don't think being in Symmetry interests you anymore and you don't want to admit it to anyone, especially yourself. You lied to both sides so it wouldn't reflect badly on you!"

The couple embraced and let out a laugh. They began to kiss.

"You're wrong." Donovan shook his head and lowered his voice. "If you'd been at that party you'd know where my anxiety came from. I had to hear my mother cry, and try to soothe her for something I caused."

"A small sacrifice to achieve your goal." Horace didn't care about the couple anymore. His voice elevated slightly with every question. "You felt guilty? You grew a conscience? If that was true, why didn't you communicate that sentiment?" He tilted his head. "Hmm, I know why! Coward."

"Who are you turning into right now? What's wrong with you?" Donovan noticed the man pull a flask out of his jacket pocket and shared it with the woman. "Just as we heard them, they can hear us."

"I really don't give a damn," Horace blurted out. He waved to them and they returned the gesture. "Have you forgotten how we met? Has it occurred to you I've been by your side your entire life and thus, probably know you better than you know yourself?"

"Baseball, we met playing baseball," he said, not seeing the connection.

"We never played an inning; we met on the bench avoiding playtime. We bonded over being too yellow to quit. Do you see what I'm saying? It became easier to lie to our parents in order to keep them happy. That never changed with you, you've clung to that idea of yourself and not given anything else a chance. You're too yellow to quit, instead you're going to sabotage yourself so it'll do the quitting for you."

"Wrong again! I gave it a chance, I gave it a fucking chance!"

"And?"

Donovan's posture slumped. He laughed weakly. "Turns out I don't want to be that way for the rest of my life. It's only going to get easier, and I know I'm going to die a little more inside. I think I can actually have a chance to be happy, and I don't want to ruin it for myself."

They shared a silence lasting several minutes and stared at the couple, who'd begun removing their clothes. Each took one more swig from the flask and ran to the water and jumped in. They screamed with laughter the entire way.

"Donovan, have you met someone? Is this why you're talking like that? Because you're planning on settling down soon and getting married?"

He allowed a few minutes for contemplation before answering. "I hadn't put much thought into it. Maybe. Most women want too much. I said that because I realized there's still a shot for me to be happy before I go too far."

Horace let out a snicker and shook his head.

"Why do you laugh like that?"

"Everything has been laid out easy your entire life, down to your height and stupid fucking blonde hair. The boarding schools, the money, the manor, all due to your last name," Horace said. "Part of it is due to your brother messing things up and making you a shoo-in. All that, and yet you've always found a reason to complain. I waited for you to turn into your father once you graduated, but it never happened. You have a law degree, but still haven't passed the bar. You invested money wisely and until recently, never needed to work. The only thing you've done like your father is fuck the help."

The woman let out a laugh and whispered to the man.

Donovan whipped his head to the side. "Why would you . . . I haven't . . . " He glanced at the couple. "Hi, sorry, don't listen to him, he's having a tantrum right now because he's jealous of the life I've led. Don't mind him."

"I'm not jealous of you. I think you're dumber than you look." Horace kept his focus on Donovan.

"Come on, let's turn around."

Horace chuckled. "Don't worry, anyone with help does it sooner or later. I get it, that's why they're there, aside from serving you—"

"Now hold on, that's a damn lie." Donovan's emotions spilled out with his words. He pulled at Horace's coat for him to speed up his pace. "That is the most debased thing I've ever heard. It's not like that at all."

Horace stopped in his tracks. He pointed at Donovan. "That, that right there. I knew it when Donny told me about you two, that you had feelings for her. It's the youngest maid, right? God, I hope it isn't her mother."

"Just shut up, you don't know anything." Donovan looked down and noticed his hands curled into fists. He turned to notice the couple redressing.

"Look at me!" Horace walked in a circle. "I'm a short, fat man no one pays attention to until I open my mouth, and I've made it to the attorney general's office by mimicking men like your father and his friends. I don't mess with women. I don't drink or gamble. I try to get better everyday. I run this metaphorical race and I'm sweating every step, my inner thighs and arms are chafing, I'm going as fast as I can, and no matter what I do, do you know who I see ahead of me? You. It makes me sick."

Donovan glanced behind them uneasily. "They can hear you."

"I don't care! Let them hear us! You're so hung up on other people and what they think, and then when it comes to this crush on the maid, you don't care at all."

"I have no choice but to worry about other people's perceptions of me, and sometimes I want to do for myself," he snapped.

"*That's* what you choose? I'm stupefied. You stupefy me, even now, and I know you. Wouldn't you want to do absolutely anything to succeed? Wouldn't you claw your way to the top by any means necessary? If that was me during your Christmas party I would've followed Gus out while his friends carried him. Then I would've grabbed his shirtfront and pulled his face close to mine and let him know I was the conductor of his shitty life." Horace grinned at the idea and his face flushed with color. He unzipped the light jacket he wore. "Did it just get hot out here?"

Donovan watched his friend's excitement grow. He saw greed for power bubble through him. It gave Horace life, he liked it. In that moment Donovan knew he'd never feel that way, and realized he didn't want to. It frightened him seeing Horace give into it. "That's how I should feel, whatever it is you're experiencing right now. It should feel good, but it doesn't. Your ambition is too much for me."

"Yeah, well, maybe yours isn't enough," Horace shot back.

"I didn't mean it like that, but you're right, and I've been shit for not saying something. My inaction kept me underwater for longer, and that's my fault as well. Where Symmetry is concerned, my ambition doesn't reach the level they need. It's up to me to be honest about that."

"Eureka! Man, Kincaid, I thought you would've learned that lesson by now," Horace said.

"Being a Kincaid brings such high expectations, it weighs me down. People know who I am and want big things from me. There's a lot of pressure to reach that standard and stay there. Everywhere I turn someone wants something from me."

"Fortunately, you live in a big house with lots of secret hiding spots," Horace said. "But to be honest, I don't want to hear it. It's time you figured that out."

Their conversation stayed on their minds long after that day. Suddenly they couldn't remember the reasons for sustaining their friendship and wondered how they'd stayed united for so long, forgetting it was their differences holding them together.

CHAPTER 35

"MONTHS AGO. HE CAME TO TERMS ABOUT HIS GRANDFATHER, BUT I'M UN-aware what terms he actually reached," Carlos explained to John over the phone. A ham sandwich and two oatmeal raisin cookies sat before him uneaten. "This has happened before. He remembers things and then he drinks the memories away all over again. The cycle usually lasts a year."

"Does this worry you? I can't believe he's let this get to him the way he has," John said.

"Don't let your realizations about Gus ruin the good fortune our case has been granted."

"No, no. Gus and I haven't spoken much since the three of us met earlier this year. We spoke on the phone a couple of months ago and he hung up on me when I told him his behavior hurts our people more than himself. You know Gustavo, he just needs time and he hates looking weak. Plus, he does such a fine job of avoiding or lying to me that I never know which way to go."

Carlos cleared his throat. "I'm sure he thinks something similar of you." He pulled the corner of his white bread to inspect the color of the ham. His stomach growled.

"Yes, but we know the derogatory things Gus probably thinks about me aren't true. He's sophomoric."

"It's funny how everyone thinks Gus and I are at odds all the time because I complain about him openly, while here you are, intolerant and bitter. I don't mean to sound short, but—"

"Maybe you suffer from a little of that yourself," John filled in.

Carlos chuckled. "There's a little truth to everything we say."

"I will continue to avoid him. Quite frankly, so should you."

"You do enough for the both of us. I choose not to pity him, because

Irene does *that* enough for the both of us. But Gus needs someone like that now. To date, he's working the biggest case of his life." He began tugging a raisin from the cookie it clung to.

"So you have a soft spot for him."

"Johnny, we both know I have many soft spots, but now is not the time to start discussing it," Carlos joked.

John scoffed. "You know, I wonder if a tiny part of me would've been relieved if they didn't grant our petition. This is one of the best things to happen to our careers, but thinking of Gus's penchant for hating the holidays is giving me a horrible, eerie déjà vu feeling."

"Don't let it bother you. If he's sorted through whatever he needed to, then maybe we won't have that problem this year."

"This is Gustavo we speak of. Whatever he's sorted through won't suddenly be solved."

Carlos paused and rewound his train of thought. "You're not wrong about that. But I made a joke about money in the budget for a babysitter, so I found one for free."

"You're kidding me. You found someone to watch over Gus?"

"Who better than the one person he should be grateful for? Irene's been getting used to the idea for a couple of weeks. She owed me for not being his date to Austin last year, so I had Gloria speak to her and give her a little guilt trip about it. She'll take care of him and watch him until it's time for us to go to DC. If she changes her mind at any time, Gloria and I will do it by paying the kids to babysit him. I'm not about to go through a version of the past two years, even if it means treating him like a child."

"Does he know we're going to argue in front of the Supreme Court?"

"Not yet, I'm about to walk over to his office right now. In the meantime, plan a trip with DeAnda to come to San Antonio."

"Will do. Talk soon."

They hung up. Carlos broke a cookie in half and took a bite. After a few chews he spit it into his wastebasket. He chose not to share with John the fatigue he experienced from visiting Gus and never knowing what he might walk in on. Carlos never admitted to anyone that he checked in on Gus often because he didn't want to take over the case himself. He was far too busy with his own schedule.

On the short trek to Gus's he wondered what he might find this time. Would he find him dead or half-dead? He stiffened at these ideas. *This case will be over soon,* Carlos told himself, *and Gus will have to be responsible for himself.* He imagined a life as someone more grand, like a Supreme Court Justice. Wouldn't that be something? He knew his stutter would be with him always, but he wouldn't allow it to stunt his future.

Carlos reached Gus's building and took the elevator upstairs, creeping inside as if on a jungle safari trying not to arouse any predators. He quietly recited a prayer as he neared the door, which swung open a few inches. He said another silent prayer as he pushed the door open all the way.

The office faintly smelled of vomit, moldy clothes, food, liquor, and shaving cream. Gus snored with his head sagging to one side, shoeless feet propped on the desk, with a hole in each sock. Four Chivas bottles sat on his desk, none of them full or empty. Pale squares were on the wall where his degrees had once hung, and he found them shoved into one corner of the room, the top one with its glass cracked. Balled up papers were strewn about the room. Pictures on Gus's desk that he knew were of Irene and his daughters laid face down.

Carlos sat in the nearest chair, and saw Gus's shoes by the door of his office, a pair of polished black leather loafers with tassels. He didn't have to look to know how worn out the soles were, just like Gus. The man did his best to show a polished appearance, but underneath—where it mattered—he was falling apart, hanging on by a thread.

What would it be like to be in his shoes, Carlos wondered. *To have a failing marriage, plus an over-demanding case, not to mention living out of his office? What about the feeling of knowing how much he disappointed his daughters?*

To Carlos, Irene shined like an angel. He didn't blame her for his friend's situation; he blamed Gus. Irene would've never made him leave if she didn't feel he deserved it, and she needed the relief.

His eyes traveled to Gus's face and lingered on the sallowness in his cheeks. Dark circles half-mooned under his eyes, and his chest moved so slightly he wouldn't have known he was breathing if it wasn't for the short raspy snores escaping from his mouth. The situation had worsened since January. "He's wearing himself thin," Carlos mumbled. "He's dying." The truth of it made him unbearably sad. It almost felt like grief.

Gus stirred. "Cadena," he croaked. "What luck have I stumbled into for this visit?"

Carlos did his best to cover up his sadness with a smile. "The luck of Washington, DC!"

He sat up straight in his seat. "It happened?"

"We got it."

Gus laughed and ran to Carlos. As the men embraced, Carlos noticed that Gus's laughter subsided and thought it sounded a bit like weeping. He pulled Gus away from him to look at his face. "What's the problem? Does this not make you happy?"

Gus paced around his office a few times and pulled at his hands. "Whatever happiness I felt from your announcement has vanished." He glared at Carlos. "You know what the problem is; you're looking at it. The winter season is coming, and we know what sort of binges that can bring." He resettled his chair and it whined at him: *Squeeeeee.*

"You make it sound like it's an epic battle of the century."

"It kind of is, no?" Gus gave a half smile. "Trust me, if you were in my shoes you'd understand."

"No thank you. I think being in my own shoes watching you do this to yourself is almost as bad."

Gus shot up out of his chair and began pacing the room. "I can't stop myself. Sometimes I drink to make the voices go away, sometimes I drink when I'm bored. I drink when I don't want to eat, and other times I drink to make the food go down. When I tire of all that I go to the bars and do the same thing with women." Tears streamed down his face. "When I don't drink, I think of Irene and my girls, of Pete and what he must be going through. I think of his clubbed foot, I think of the day his mother burst into this office asking for my help. I wish she'd gone to you first." He wiped his cheeks. "Back then it was the last thing I wanted."

Carlos boomed out a laugh. "Preposterous! What good would that have done? You'd still be in this with me, and Herrera, too. You may not have been first chair, but we'd still be in this together. We need each other. None of us can do this alone."

Gus shook his head. "Maybe I shouldn't be a part of this at all. Maybe the people who wanted me off the case should get their way, and maybe the team would receive so much more donation money if people knew I wasn't a part of the trio."

"Maybe. But I tell you what: I don't feel like finding out, not so close to the finish line." Carlos walked to Gus's coffee maker and began preparing a pot. "We have three months to prepare, so we've got a lot of work in front of us. I'm getting more into the Sporty case—the boxer—and you should work on your presentation. John and James are planning to drive to us soon," Carlos said. "We just need you to get through the holidays."

"Hermano," Gus said, his voice cracking. "What is your family planning for Christmas?"

He heard the desperation in his voice. "We're staying home and not doing much of anything. Trying to save money for my travels. I still have more work with my UT fellowship," Carlos paused. "If Irene will allow it, would you stay at home for the holidays? I'm not entirely sure if she's said yes, but Gloria has been talking to her about it. We could celebrate Christmas together this year."

Gus's face brightened for a moment before the expression fell off. "If she'd have me, I would stay there for the rest of my life."

"I don't doubt it, but one day at a time." He reached out and patted his hand. "I think she'll have you, as long as you keep the holidays drier than the first prohibition. Call her, yes? I'll stay right here, it shouldn't be like last Christmas. She'll give you some stipulations, you'll say yes, then I'll take you to lunch and we'll celebrate properly with some good food. Without drink."

Gus nodded. "As you wish."

"This case is yours, Gustavo, it always has been. You'll see." Carlos pointed at him. "Do not doubt it: we believe in you one hundred percent. But I know enough to know it isn't enough. You have to believe in yourself, that's what we need. Believe in you, your words, and how you present your words. Find your self-control and possess it wholly."

Gus exhaled raggedly. "This case is killing me."

Carlos breathed in sharply, worried him admitting the truth out loud would make it ring true all the more quickly. Gus sighed, picked up the phone receiver, and dialed home. Carlos pressed a speaker button. The men listened as her velvet voice answered the call.

"My love," Gus cooed, "your voice is like a cool song to my ears."

"Gustavo. Is Carlito with you as well?"

"He is." Gus looked at Carlos for confirmation to continue. "I . . . I . . ."

"Irene," Carlos spoke out. "I hope this day finds you well. Have you thought about our proposal? Has my Gloria prepared you properly?"

"I know the holidays are nipping at our heels," she said. "I knew the moment she stepped into my door that her request involved you, Gustavo. I just don't know how I feel about it." Her voice went low. "I have half a mind to take the girls and visit my parents instead. I could leave the house to you."

Gus laughed sarcastically and reached for a Chivas bottle, Carlos slapped away his hand. "You might as well buy me another bottle while you're at it, then. Living in that house alone is worse than no house at all."

Carlos reached across the desk and pinched Gus on the arm. Quietly, but strongly, he said, "Shut. Up."

His demeanor changed instantly and his voice went meek. "Lo siento, I'm sorry." He looked out the lone window in his office. "You know this is how I get when I feel scared. I don't trust myself to be alone. No one should trust me when I'm alone. And I'm always alone."

"Aye Gustavo, this is not the time to be silly. You don't *want* to be alone." Irene chided. "You'll drink if I say no, and you'll drink to celebrate if I say yes."

Gus smiled at Carlos. "See, she understands me."

"She understands you *too* well." Carlos spoke into the phone. "Irene, this is no normal circumstance. I'm not saying you lack compassion—I understand what he's put you through—but I am asking you to look for some because of our situation."

"I know, I know. This is difficult for me too." She took a deep breath.

Gus pleaded with her. "I won't drink a drop, and if I do, you can kick me out right then and there."

"I'll hold you to that." A few beats passed. "I've spoken with the girls and of course they want you home. But they want you present, in the moment. They don't want to hear you on the phone yelling at people, or sleeping when you could be spending time with them. They want to see *you*, not drunk you."

"What else do you need?" Carlos nudged Gus's arm. "This is the time for your rules. Though I should be concerned with Gustavo, I'm more concerned with what you need and want through all this. I will be indebted to you forever if you can keep him clean."

Gus nodded but said nothing.

They heard her breathing over the phone. "I want you to know I've always wanted you, but now not in the same way as before. No alcohol: no Chivas, no beer, no wine, nothing. You follow that rule and the girls and I will help stave off your holiday blues."

"I can do that," he agreed.

"Can you? I will search your things everyday, I will check every nook and cranny whenever I feel like it, okay? I swear to it, Gustavo," Irene said. "I will request to smell your breath at any moment it strikes my fancy, and you must obey me. Do you say yes to my requests?"

"Reenie, I say yes to all these things. As long as it's okay that when you request to smell my breath, I'm allowed to kiss you." Gus winked at Carlos, who rolled his eyes and shook his head.

She laughed. "I think you know the answer to that. You'll never quit, will you?"

"I will not," he said defiantly. "That's one of my best qualities as a lawyer, and especially with you. I cannot wait to be in front of you and bask in your beauty. I will never quit with you," he repeated. He cleared his throat and held up a pair of crossed fingers to Carlos. "How early can I come home, can I spend Thanksgiving with you three as well? I think the Christmas decorations will be out on the town by then."

"Sí, Gustavo, of course you can."

Gus went to Carlos and hugged him tightly. They chose a taco stand near Gus's office building for lunch.

Gus shook his head and bit into his taco. The stuffing spilled out the other end. "Wow, I can't believe we made it. It's been two years."

Carlos nodded. "You'll work every day. Memorize your stuff, work on your inflections and pauses, your gestures. Don't deviate from the plan. If Irene will let you, stay with her until we leave for Washington and you will be in tip-top shape, I know it. We will work out a plan after Thanksgiving."

"Look at you rescuing me and buying me a meal." Gus reached out and clutched Carlos's hand. "I cannot thank you enough for trying to take care of me. I hate you for loving me so much, do you know that? I'm so up my own ass half the time, I never think to stop and say thank you. So thank you."

"You're welcome. It's not just about what you are to me, but what you mean to all of our people. Our race." Carlos stared out into the sun. "May His will be done."

"Today is the twelfth of October," Gus stated. "Did you know that? It's El Dia de la Raza, the day of our race, our people. Yes, this we can do. Sí se puedes."

CHAPTER 36

JOHN CONTACTED LOCAL LULAC PRESIDENTS IN TEXAS TO ASK FOR DONATIONS, because people were donating in small amounts. He found clubs responded with small totals as well, because they knew Gus would have access to the money. Word cycled around that he couldn't be trusted, yet no one denied the power his words demanded in a courtroom.

Albert Armendariz, a pale man with wavy brown hair, carried the honor of being the reigning national LULAC president after John. He respected the way they fought for civil rights and made moves that stirred up controversy. After reaching out to other officers on his board to start a drive for donations, Albert diverted the money set aside for scholarships that year and gave it to the trio. The amount totaled nearly fifteen hundred dollars.

Albert understood the urgency for sending the money post-haste. If the lawyers didn't pay in full to the Supreme Court the case would get kicked off the docket. They had a month at most. Albert took matters into his own hands and some presidents followed his lead.

Pete Tijerina, the president of a San Antonio LULAC club, diverted their funds from scholarships as well, though he didn't come under the same scrutiny as their national leader. Albert's move enraged the board, and talk of possible impeachment began to circulate, but it didn't come to fruition.

Gossips said the lawyers should've taken a pauper's oath to file with the Supreme Court and waive the fees. Gus shot back, calling those men Monday morning quarterbacks. Coulda, shoulda, woulda.

Surely, the trio discussed, the three million people of Mexican descent could help, and countered back with what the NAACP had been doing for Thurgood Marshall's case. Gus stayed in trouble for insulting his critics, calling them posers, bird-brained, and well-heeled clowns, while they responded, calling him a wino, a God-complexed child, and a mooch. Though some people saw Gus as brave and brash, others called for him to resign from the case for fear of giving others the wrong impression about Mexican American people.

Worried the backlash would send Gus into a drinking spiral, Irene called, looking for him to return home early that day, but was too late. She found him angry and drunk in his office, ranting about the lack of support from their own people. Irene decided right then and there that she would detoxify Gus, even if it didn't last one day past the Supreme Court.

Her mother agreed to take in the two girls while Gus went through withdrawal. Sick for days, he wailed or screamed his nights away until he vomited himself to sleep. Irene changed the sheets every day, heavy from his excessive sweating and smelling of his sickness. The period lasted three weeks: it was the middle of December before his health returned.

Irene's motivation came from the idea that she could give Carlita and Teresa a Christmas they had wanted for years, one with a sober father and a happy mother. Upon letting him back home she immediately dismissed the idea of happiness knocking at their door again. She knew the moment she left him alone he'd find the drink again, and she'd blame and berate herself.

Once the storm settled, she allowed the girls to live at home again. From there, the common family goal was to steer Gus toward work and taking care of himself. Irene pushed him to spend his free time with their daughters whenever the chance for a break arose. With her in charge, the family clicked just in time for Christmas season.

Gus realized how much money could be saved when he didn't buy whisky, so he used it to improve his image instead. He bought two tailored suits, both pinstriped; a steel-gray overcoat and matching scarf, plus new shoes and fedora with a crimson ribbon wrapped around it. He decided against a new briefcase and kept the two-toned crosshatch briefcase instead. Irene bought him new ties.

Their cohabitation took a turn for the better and pumped up his self-esteem immensely. Though she still denied him in the dark, her presence gave him the energy of a warrior, a king for their people. At the end of every day, without her laying a finger on him, she let him know of his worthiness. She reminded him of his strength in opposition, his passion for persuading people, and his fearless nature in going all the way for a win. To fight against white bigots, at a Supreme Court level, she'd tell him, is to strike them in their hearts and jugulars simultaneously.

Gus thought of alcohol the moment his eyes opened in the morning, and his hands would tremble in response. An urge to find whisky would quickly turn into panic, leading him to ask Irene for distraction. She taught him how to wrap the sunflowers if a freeze came along; he learned crafts with his daughters, and they taught him how to sew buttons on their clothes. Irene put him on house arrest, and he loved every minute of it: one, because it distracted him, and two, because it told him she still loved him enough to try. This in turn, made him love her in return.

The family reached Christmas happily, attending church weekly and preparing dinner together most nights. To see the smiles on her daughters' faces doubled and tripled Irene's joy, but to see her husband healthy gave her the most happiness. Gus walked stronger, he gained a few pounds, his hair looked blacker and thicker, and his eyes regained the green sparkle that had attracted her in the first place.

Gus whispered sweet things to her when they passed each other in the kitchen. He said feeling her breath on his skin felt like heaven, and he'd believe her if she said the world stretched flat. He asked her to stay with him always and if she agreed, his future would never darken. Her smile was like electricity through his bones, and he swore he'd live forever if she stayed with him. Irene never answered his pleas, except to squeeze his arm as if there might be hope.

On New Year's Eve day she woke to a bloomed rose and a proposal from him to take her out to an expensive dinner to say thank you for nursing him back to health. A steak dinner in the best restaurant San Antonio has to offer, he asked, and she said yes. Irene wore her best dress, a deep emerald green color to match his eyes. It fitted at her waist but billowed out at the sleeves before tightening at the cuffs. Gus wore a slate gray suit with an old black overcoat he found in his closet.

Gus reserved a round booth big enough for eight people, to give them some privacy. People recognized him as the big-time lawyer and went to introduce themselves, congratulate him, and shake hands. Some tried purchasing him a drink, and every time he denied, Irene scooted an inch closer to him. The adulation he received inflated his ego, but he didn't allow it to go to his head. People continued their introductions throughout dinner.

Irene noticed his voice turn gruff when people interrupted, yet it softened at their compliments. When he turned his attentions back to her his voice lowered, almost like a purr. Every few moments she reached out and squeezed his arm or lightly ran a hand through his hair just above his ear to show him support. She found herself falling for him again, because she saw the old Gus she once knew.

When the main course arrived she buttered his bread first before her own. At this, Gus scooped up a hand and kissed it to say thank you. Irene blushed, surprised that she blew a kiss back at him so freely. She laughed at his jokes while he charmed everyone who glided up to them.

It all changed when the waiter traded out their empty plates for coffee and cheese plates.

Gus looked deep into her eyes with an expression of complete generosity and appreciation. "It's been nearly two months since we've been together, and you've done so much for me, I don't know what position I'd be in if you hadn't let me back home. I'm utterly in debt to you," he said, while petting her hand.

His smile is perfect, she thought, *and his eyes truthful.* "I feel safe with you." A lump rose in her throat, causing her to look away. She touched a hand to her eyes, felt tears, and reached into her purse to find a tissue. It slipped to the floor, and Irene ducked her head underneath to look for it. After a few seconds she heard a raspy woman's voice.

In a bedroom tone, she said, "Hello, Gustavo."

"Well, hello yourself."

It all happened so fast. Irene jerked up instinctively and bumped her head lightly because she forgot she sat under a table.

"Reenie! Are you okay, my love?" Gus ducked his head under the tablecloth.

She waited for him to join her under the table—she wanted him to—but he didn't, despite the concern she heard in his voice. Irene poked her head out and saw Gus smiling to a woman with pale skin and short pixie hair. She thought her hair looked awfully manly.

Suddenly she realized the real Patricia McCormick stood before them.

Even more disgusting to Irene was the way Gus gazed at her. In one glance she could see the two clearly missed each other and cared deeply for one another. She saw familiarity between them. Her faith in him plummeted, as if she had fallen into an opened drain under the table, and nothing but suspicion bubbled up in its place. As she climbed back into her seat Gus turned to her.

"Is everything okay my love? Did anything fall out of your purse?"

She shook her head. "It's under control. Who's this?" Irene heard her voice go shrill. She turned to Patricia. "Who are you? You don't look like a lawyer."

Patricia wore a blood-red pant suit the color of a matador's cape. She glanced at Gus when Irene mentioned a lawyer. "Lord no! Not my style." She stuck out a hand. "My name—"

"Oh, her profession is more daring than that." Gus interrupted, and stood. "Irene, I would like to introduce you to Patricia McCormick. She is the first female bullfighter and hails here from Texas like us. Isn't that wonderful?"

"You don't look the way I thought you would've." She smiled at Gus apologetically. "How glorious that must be for you, Patricia, to be able to mold a career around something so juvenile as killing animals." She heard the curtness in her voice.

"This is my exquisite wife, the mother of my girls, olive-skinned, long-haired, angelic-faced Irene," Gus gushed, with one eyebrow cocked. He looked at Irene. "Are you thinking of that woman who approached you last year?"

Irene nodded, embarrassed.

Patricia took a step back. "Did I do something?"

"No," Irene said. "Well, yes. Yes and no. Patricia McCormick, I'm sure you know enough about my husband to know the case he's been working on."

She nodded uncomfortably.

"Yes, well, he's been paranoid someone is out to get him, other than himself."

Gus stiffened at this.

Irene became more comfortable with every word. "Last year when spring began, my daughters and I," she glanced at Gus, "*our* daughters and I, we spent some time outside, they playing and I gardening."

"The sunflowers," Gus said sweetly.

"The sunflowers," Irene repeated in a bitter tone. "A woman walked up to me at my house and among other things, told me she was sleeping with my husband. She claimed to be you, but I knew it wasn't. Nonetheless, I'm not fond of you."

"Well," Patricia paused, "how nice it is to meet you, Irene, you're a beautiful woman. I take it you're not willing to shake my hand."

"I still know how to be a lady." Irene reached out and shook it.

Gus looked from woman to woman. "It's nice we can all be so understanding and get this on the table." He leaned into Irene and whispered. "I'm so sorry."

"Don't instigate this further, I beg you." Her hands clenched under the table, she wanted to say so many things to both of them. *I see the way you look at her. Why do you feel the need to say hello in front of me?* Irene impatiently tapped her fingernails against her glass of water, enough for Patricia to notice.

"Look, I can't apologize enough. I thought your marriage was over . . . and I can see that it's not," Patrica said urgently. She gestured a connection between her and Gus. "This is not romantic. It's convenient."

Gus whipped his head up to Patricia with a shocked look, but immediately replaced it with an expression of confirmation at her comments.

Irene noticed. "Patricia, how long have you been in Texas? Do you fight here often?"

"I practice in Texas occasionally, but Mexico was the place to be until I could travel farther." Patricia cleared her throat and glanced at Gus momentarily. "That's why I came to say hello, I'm leaving for Spain in a few weeks." She made solid eye contact with Irene. "He and I haven't seen each other in a long time, I assure you."

Irene scoffed. "I'm sure that's not true. Darling, you look like you're in a state of shock."

Gus's eyes widened. "How wonderful for you, Patricia," he managed to mutter.

Irene blushed and she excused herself from the table to use the bathroom. She thought of how many times she denied her body to Gus, never thinking about him being able to find it somewhere else. With a good-looking husband like him, she chided herself in not expecting women were going to fling themselves at him. *How long can a man wait for intimate relations? Not long,* she answered herself.

As Irene washed her hands in the bathroom, Gus and Patricia stared at each other.

Gus hissed at her. "Why did you come to our table? Then announce that in front of her?"

Patricia softened her gaze. "I saw you and I couldn't help myself. I didn't know she was under the table, for Christ's sake."

"I need to see you. I'm not drinking right now. My mind is clear."

"Good for you."

"Can I see you?"

Patricia's gaze turned hard. "Fine, but let me ask you this: if she wanted you, would you still want me?"

Gus's face went blank. Irene returned before he could answer and slid into her seat.

"I must be going," Patricia said. She nodded at both of them. "Irene, I'm so sorry for coming up to the table, it's not right. Apologies."

Irene lifted her chin. "Maybe it was best so I could meet the real you." She turned to Gus. "Maybe someone *is* out to get you." She looked back at Irene. "You courageously approach bulls for a living, and my husband is something of a bull himself. But let me be clear about something. I'm not a matador, so don't give me *your* bull."

Gus smiled and looked down into his lap.

Patricia lowered her head. "I deserved that." She left them alone.

Irene's face fell and a tear rolled down her cheek. "You're always going to have someone, aren't you? Alcohol isn't the only thing you can't stop."

"Don't say that. I feel ashamed enough already. Everything was going so well."

"When did you two meet?"

"In Mexico," he mumbled. "A couple of years ago."

Her eyes widened. "Have you seen her fight before?"

The waitress brought them cake, a dark brown, nearly black square of cake with a dark chocolate frosting. A drizzle of chocolate sauce spiraled on the plate. The couple dug into their dessert and their conversation went quiet.

Irene waited for Gus to say more, but he kept his head down and continued eating. It saddened her. She knew the truth in her heart. She was an option, a first option, but still nothing more than an option. The more she pondered over it the more sense it made: what did she expect to happen when she requested he live elsewhere? She recalled the way women outwardly flirted with him in front of her; why wouldn't he take one up at their request? "She's here in San Antonio to see you, is that right?"

Gus coughed. "Nonsense, she has family here."

"Ah, I see. This is how you're going to do it."

Gus scooped up Irene's hand again. "You are my everything. I am a stupid man who makes mistakes constantly. I feel like the world is on my shoulders." He kissed her hand. "You know how I get, I'm like a dog an owner cannot train. If you allowed it, it would be you and only you."

Irene smiled sweetly. "You have something more important than us, so I will choose to say nothing. We will return to this subject at another time." She leaned into Gus. "If I'm not mistaken, your tongue is turning silver. I suggest you close your mouth in case it's contagious."

CHAPTER 37

GUS NOTICED A SEPARATENESS IN IRENE AFTER MEETING PATRICIA. SHE SPOKE in short answers and moved slowly, as if she wore an overcoat filled with sand. Watching her brought some of Gus's guilt back and he wanted to drink, so he took it upon himself to leave the house and give her space.

He contacted Patricia, and she suggested the Menger Hotel in San Antonio, her treat. She took charge, picking him up and driving them to the hotel. Though he inherently felt something off with her, lust distracted him from thinking further on it.

"They have air-conditioning," Patricia said to him. "They added it several years ago."

"Huh? Oh yeah, that's great. You do know it's rather cold out here, yes? AC not needed?"

She smiled widely and winked an eye. "I do, but I get this warm feeling inside me when I look at you." She reached out and squeezed his cheek.

Distracted, he turned his head. "Lord, don't tell me where." He opened the hotel front door for her and noticed a bike parked nearby with an empty birdcage hanging off one side of the handlebars. A container of birdseed sat inside a bundle of shredded newspaper.

As they settled into the hotel room Gus settled into Patricia's familiarity again. She brought a comfort to him like a confidante, yet they didn't speak or see each other often over the months. Within an hour of arriving they stretched out tired and naked in bed and decided to order room service. Pieces of their clothes were strewn about the room in random spots.

"My treat," she offered.

"By all means. Lord knows I couldn't afford any of this." Gus spread his hands out to their room. "Lily-white walls and blood-red curtains," he lifted the duvet up over their heads, "a comforter as red as your lips. Two long-stemmed roses in a vase standing tall and proud. Air-conditioning! A basket of fruit!"

Patricia laughed into her pillow. "The bathroom isn't up to par, the mirror has a tiny crack down the middle of it, going all the way down. Plus, I smell something. It's faint, but there. What's that smell?"

"I don't smell anything."

"It's off, I can't put my finger on it, but it's off."

"Stop trying to change the subject, I need to tell you something." He lifted one of her hands and kissed it. "I thank you for saving me," Gus said solemnly, desperate for connection. "Thank you for taking care of me."

"You've had it tough." She kissed him on his forehead. "If I suffered, you'd do the same for me."

Gus looked into her eyes and saw tenderness, he felt it. Undeniable. "You're falling in love with me, I can see it," he said softly. His face turned serious and hers did the same. "Don't worry," he soothed her. "I am, too. You're not alone."

"Hey—"

A knock sounded at the door. "Room service."

"Stay there, I've got it." Gus dressed quickly and answered the door.

A young man with a crooked smile pushed in a cart filled with plates covered in silver domes. Before leaving the room he verbally listed their food as he placed the dishes on a nearby table.

Gus began setting them on the table. "Why did you approach Irene and me that evening? I look at all this food on the table and my mind went back to that night. It changed our trajectory. Hers and mine."

Patricia stuffed spaghetti into her mouth. "Hmm?"

He filled a glass halfway with water and sipped on it as he gathered courage. "I wanted to puke, Pats. I think I'd been looking for an eject button." He pulled the eggs towards him and turned the plate upside down over his spaghetti, the eggs plopped over the pasta and broke the yolks.

"To be truthful, I thought you dined with someone new. I hadn't heard from you. I saw the plate beside yours, but assumed it was a colleague, or a new woman." She went quiet as she chewed. She shrugged. "I don't know, maybe I did notice it was a woman ducking her head under the table as I approached." More chewing. "You're not blaming that outcome on me, are you?"

His heart warmed. "You love me."

"She still loves you very much. Your wife. You know that, right?"

"Of course I do," he said sadly. "But she stops herself from giving me love, barely showing it. She's still the epitome of kindness, which makes it all the more difficult to do nothing, it breaks my heart all over again. She and I have crossed no intimate borders. Aside from her allowing me to kiss her on the cheek occasionally, the waters have been left uncharted since I moved back in."

Patricia sniffed the air. "Do you smell that? I still smell it."

"Are you saying I'm full of shit?"

A smile crept onto her lips. "Yes and no." She reached across the table and squeezed his hand. "She dried you out."

"Which is exactly why they've stayed uncharted! She nursed me back to health without an expectation of reciprocity. Irene and my daughters got me through the holidays a sober man. It's a miracle." He sighed. "That's when I knew I still loved her."

"You've always loved her. I didn't think it ever stopped."

"It hasn't. She kept me at bay, yet helped me prepare for my big day doing whatever was needed." Gus sighed again. "She's a miracle who won't have me anymore. If we win, she might."

"So you're never drinking again?"

"Let's not get carried away," Gus reassured her. "One day at a time. I'm holding off for as long as I can, it's the best I can do."

"Thank goodness. I wanted to give you one of your gifts." She rubbed her feet against his. "It surprised me when you didn't order any Chivas, I've been ready to spoil you with a brand new bottle in my bag. I forbid us both to drink it now, but winning the case is a perfect reason to crack it open and share with your friends."

Gus frowned. "You purchase us a hotel room, and then you give me gifts? What's going on here? Why are you being so generous, yet so harsh? I can't read you."

Patricia licked her fingers and sat back in her chair. "This is my year, or rather, I'm going to make it my year. I've received a small advance from Henry Holt and Company in New York to write an autobiography centered around my bullfighting, and they're funding a trip to Rome and Spain. I'm going to meet some of the greats and learn from them. I'm hoping to find a matador who will be willing to vouch for me so I can rank up. I came to some conclusions about my future, and I wanted to celebrate with you."

"Wow." Gus sat back in his seat. "Wow. That's amazing. Pretty damn great."

Her face narrowed. "Is it emasculating when you think about me fighting bulls?"

"I haven't thought about it. In the position I'm in now, I think it's sexy. Powerful. As a result, and this is just my opinion here, you give yourself up freely because of it. That allows you to allow me to be myself." Gus stood up and flung himself on the bed. He looked up to a cottage cheese ceiling. "Irene keeps dangling carrots over me and puts up so much red tape. I understand I've done her wrong in too many ways to count, and some unresolved pain has built up, but still. She's the mother of my children, she's got to know a part of me will never stop loving her."

"Would you like to ask her to join us in bed tonight?" She placed her chocolate cake by the bed and retrieved a white robe from the bathroom.

"Is something wrong? I've just said you allow me to be myself and I don't have to work at anything to be with you. I don't know about you, but I think that's a gift. I'm glad you halfway like me enough to want to spend time with me." He winked at her and pinched her leg.

"You're really good at making things about yourself, did you know that?"

His smile vanished and he sat up straight.

She grabbed her bag and pulled it to the bed. "Let's not be cross. There's not enough time between us for that." Her hand plunged in and retrieved the Chivas bottle and a small package wrapped in black paper. "I found this for you during a quick trip to Spain, it looked like exactly the item you needed to remember me by without being conspicuous. Here, take it." She tossed it at him.

"You went to Spain?"

"To find somewhere to live."

"I'm going to need to remember you?" Questions shot through his head as he tried to make sense of the present moment. He saw a bit of red as he slowly unwrapped it. "I thought I could visit you when the case is over. In February."

"Sodden with alcohol?"

"Let's hope not."

Patricia continued as if she hadn't heard him. "I just wanted to say thank you for the time we've spent together. I know it hasn't been much, but it's been enough for me."

Gus glanced at the bottle uncomfortably. *Something is happening*, he thought. *A misfortune so late in the game, it's a cruelty*. He regretted speaking so suddenly. "Tell me about your trip."

"I visited a few arenas and fell in love with the culture and the level of seriousness there with the sport. It's the right place for me to be if I want my career to continue going up." She pointed to the package. "They sell items by the tons at big arenas and set aside a huge area for them. I found cheap trinkets and upscale items, too. That was a little pricey, but it had you written all over it."

The wrapping paper fell away, and the soft, red material unfolded. "It's a tie." The color of red seemed to match the curtains and the duvet they sat on, a deep shade with bits of black mixed in. A brown bull nestled at the bottom of the tie at the thickest part, embroidered in brown with bits of gold. But instead of it standing at attention like one would expect, the bull sat on its hind legs looking dazed as if its skin had just been pricked. When Gus brought the tie closer to his face he noticed tiny spots of red on the bull's golden brown back.

"Do you like it?"

"This is beautiful. I didn't know you cared this much . . . " He pressed the material to his chest. "I will treasure it."

Patricia said suddenly, "I need to say goodbye, Gus Gustavo."

He gasped. "What for? Because you're leaving?" He brushed her cheek with his backhand. "That's not necessary. I will be here when you return." He tried to remain calm, but the look on her face said she'd been preparing this.

"Leaving is a part of it, but I don't know when I'll be coming back. You don't want anything to hold me back or make me feel obligated to come back home, right?" She touched his cheek in the same manner he did her.

He pushed her hand away. "I don't understand. You say this as if you're never coming back to the States. I said I would go to you when I'm done here."

Patricia shook her head briskly. "I don't want any ties here that aren't familial or professional. It will hold me back . . . because I've developed feelings for you."

Unconsciously, he began to crumple one end of the tie. "I can wait forever, I don't mind, just to know you still care."

"Think about Irene," she reminded him. "Don't you want to be available to her when the time comes? Your whole mind, body, and soul? I will always care, you should know that by now."

Gus stood and began to pace the room. "Don't do this. Why are you doing this to me? What did I do to you to deserve this?" The messages from his brain alternated between anxious acceptance and angry denial. "Please don't do this. I swear, when I win in DC you're going to be sorry."

"I already am," she said. "When you win—and you *are* going to win—people are going to want so many pieces of you. Your situation might be just like mine: experiencing a win on your own may help you realize you don't need to depend on anyone but yourself."

He roared his words. "Do you not know what I've been through in the past few years?"

She lowered her head and took a deep breath. "By whose hand Gustavo? No one but your own."

He fell to his knees. "The experiences you've given me in and out of the arena have been more than one man can dream of. Don't you know it's helped me through? What can I do for you?"

"Win," she simply said.

"I can go to you the day after we present. Spain, Rome, wherever you go." He clasped his hands. "Please," he begged. "Please, at least let's wait."

"It's too late now, it would be nothing but false hope. Desperation doesn't look good on you."

Gus suddenly realized he smelled something, the something Patricia spoke of earlier. The scent was slightly acidic, like sweet garbage. He left her in bed to track it, and it led to the welcome basket full of fruit. At the angle he approached it the fruit appeared shiny and perfect, ripe and round, but as his vision curved around the basket he noticed the spotty white-green mold taking hold and rotting from the inside. "Irene and I are getting a divorce," he blurted out. Though not entirely the truth, it felt right when it spilled out. It was like the apple in the basket, a symbol of wholeness and life, but when seen from every angle showed its true form. "I found the stink."

Patricia walked to the table and picked up the hamburger with one hand. She sauntered to the basket of fruit. "It's funny, I hardly even smell it anymore." She took a huge bite from the burger and a piece of lettuce flopped out. "Do you really think telling me about a divorce would change anything?"

"She did it for the girls, but it's irreparable, no matter how we feel. It hurts too much. This hurts too much." He ran to the bathroom and shut the door behind him.

Patricia ran to the door and knocked repetitively. "It's because you're sober, don't forget that." She tried the door and found he hadn't locked it.

Gus leaned against the counter with his back facing the mirror. Tears streamed his face, but he made no noise.

"I'm so sorry." She stepped forward and hugged him. "This makes it all the more dire, don't you see? You need someone to repair you and make you feel whole, and I'm not going to have more time. You'd be my side man, and your ego wouldn't allow that. You couldn't hold down a job, and if you did, I might move in a moment. Or what if I get hurt in the ring?"

"What if, what if, what if?!? Is that going to stop you from going forward?"

She went quiet. "I believe I'm going forward in a big way. I didn't say I couldn't live without you, I said it's time for us to do that very thing. I don't feel trapped, and I don't want you to feel trapped. I'm going wherever the wind takes me. I don't want to be the reason you can't see your family. The moment you needed to place blame you'd put it on me. This is why you keep tripping up, because you won't take accountability for your wrongs." She hugged him harder. "Let it go."

Gus cried on her shoulder. He cried for his guilt, his fatigue, his inabilities, and the fear that these would hurt him in the near future. He wept for his mother, his daughters, and his grandfather, he wept for his race. When he finished and Patricia's shirt was soaked, Gus looked at himself in the mirror. The crack that started at the bottom and ended at the top divided their reflection in two and sealed their fate.

He watched as she leaned forward and whispered in his ear. "Let's do this like soldiers bunkered together in a war. We'll go forward by the seat of our pants and charge the opposition like we're the brave bulls."

Gus dried his eyes. "We've been embroiled in fights, me for my people and you for womankind."

"You see, you do understand." She gripped his shoulders. "Look them in the eye, let them know you mean business. Look into their soul, you'll know what to say."

"It will be different. Intimidating."

She shrugged. "Same as the arena for me. But isn't that why we do it? We have to step out of our comfort zones and not lose ourselves in the process. You cannot lose your personality in the courtroom, that is what makes you and it will help you win favor. Hold on to it tightly and take it as it comes."

Gus wrapped his arms around her and gripped her torso.

Hours later they finished and Patricia rolled over to sleep. Unable to mimic her, he stayed up all night staring at the Chivas Regal bottle she so carelessly left unattended. When sorrow overcame him he stared at the ceiling to think about the days that followed. He dwelled when he knew he shouldn't. Drinking used to help the minutes go by faster and drowned the anxiety that idleness brought. Without the drink the hours and minutes stretched on forever.

Gus went to the desk and opened the drawers until he found the Menger Hotel stationary and a pen. He proceeded to write, and wrote from his heart until the words flowed and every sentence he scribbled felt like poetry.

CHAPTER 38

GUS LEFT FOR WASHINGTON, DC, SHORTLY AFTER PATRICIA SPLIT WITH HIM, and to his detriment, he made some decisions that angered his associates. He booked them rooms at The Mayflower Hotel, one of the most popular political playgrounds since its erection in 1925.

The men congregated in the large hotel room and took in the sight before them. On the table sat two metal buckets big enough to bathe a small child in. They were full of bottles of beer buried three-quarters deep in ice. Two bottles of champagne also sat chilling in their own buckets on top of the bar, with a lone pitcher of water at the end. Plates of meats, cheeses, and fruit surrounded the champagne.

John's face turned as red as if he'd applied blush to his cheeks. He walked to the metal buckets and pulled out a bottle to inspect. He laughed sarcastically. "Just answer me this one question, Gus," he whirled around to him, "are you nuts? If that's the case, that you're insane, please tell me now. I wish you would've mentioned something earlier, but there's still time."

Gus shifted on his feet. "Don't be silly, I thought we could finally use a celebration."

A blood-curdling shout came out of John. "What in the hell were you thinking, getting a room at The Mayflower? What in the hell is wrong with you? Do you think the donated money came with a note that said: Spend on whatever you want?" He began to pace the room and his face turned more scarlet.

The men who accompanied John and Carlos walked out of their hotel room without saying a word.

Bewildered, Gus stood in front of his peers wearing a gray and white pinstriped suit with a pale pink shirt and a matching pocket square. He'd expected someone to compliment him on his choice. "I'm afraid I don't understand what you mean, I prepared this for you all to celebrate. For morale. I don't understand why you're always so frustrated and angry at me. I don't understand it, I really don't. It's actually very upsetting."

Carlos took a step froward and held up a hand. "That's enough, you two act like children when the other doesn't do what you want. After these next few days we can all take a break from each other and get back to our normal lives. Doesn't that sound nice?"

"I am not a fucking child," John spit out.

"More like a bulldog," Gus said. "Men, this is The Mayflower Hotel, do you know how many greats have stayed here? This hotel is becoming one of the most popular hotels in the United States." He spread his arms wide. "Coolidge held his inaugural ball in the Grand Ballroom. Greatness has slept here. Those things can only be good for the road we're about to travel. Plus, we're only five minutes away from court."

John pointed at Gus. "I fear we won't have enough money to get home." He pointed to the fireplace. "We're paying money for that golden gilt, and it's everywhere."

"This is where I repeat FDR's most famous line, and I think it would behoove you to think about that right now. The only thing we have to fear is fear itself. You know, I'm really getting tired of you pushing your weight around like this and trying to make me feel bad about something I did for all of us. I don't see how that makes me a villain."

"I know I've said this before," Carlos said to Gus, "but I could really slap you right now." He went to the pitcher of water and poured himself a glass.

Gus began to smirk. "Did you bring two sets of white gloves that we can slap at each other? I don't think either of us is in a position to mar our faces, especially mine." He hoped for a laugh and received none. "My God, men, I didn't drink anything. I haven't done anything wrong."

Carlos gave Gus a warning look. "I know you get this way when you're nervous, when you think failure is following behind you with matches and lighter fluid, but now isn't the time to act like this. You're not alone right now, you have two people standing in front of you who care about you and care about this case as much as you do." He took a drink of his water. "Johnny, say something to your friend, please, I don't know what else to say."

"I don't have anything to say," he spit out.

"Have a glass of water," Carlos offered John. "I can see you're getting angrier, too."

"Have a beer," Gus said, still smirking.

John suddenly had enough. He widened his eyes and took a step closer. Before any of them could speak, he lunged out and punched. His arm shot out into the air and a throaty growl came from him.

Gus dodged him in enough time and pulled John onto a couch and to the floor. John pushed Gus away.

"Get him away from me!" John yelled. "Don't think I won't try again to punch your lights out!"

"I'd like to see you try!"

Carlos ran forward and stepped in between them. "Enough! I'm pissed off too, but now isn't the time for all this, wouldn't you both say?" He put his attentions back to Gus. "Amigo, what made you think: yes, I think I'll spend more money that we may or may not have? What led you to that conclusion, please tell me?"

"I purchased some things I thought you men would enjoy after the long travels, we've all worked so hard . . . " Gus straightened his clothes.

"Yes," John interjected, "some of us more than others."

Gus stared at him. "Why do you choose to be so angry? What is wrong, what has happened? I still don't understand. Why be physical? What have I done to you?"

"Your taste, though classy, is expensive, and too expensive to pretend like it's affordable," Carlos said. "I don't think it's something you'd deny, but it may not be something you understand, either."

"I'm sure we can return it," Gus said, trying to remedy the situation. "Here, let me connect with the front desk."

"That's not the point!" John threw up his arms. "You still think yourself above the rim, you find yourself floating over everyone, when you're not tripping over yourself. We said our race would be watching, but you think every pair of eyes will be watching you."

"They're already watching us, don't you see that? Anybody with a decent pair of eyes or ears will be keeping an eye or ear to the pulse of this case. I spoke with Thurgood Marshall the day I arrived. He said because our case is so close to the date of *Brown versus Board of Education*, the press will be swarming!" He walked to the nearest window to look out of. "I don't think of only myself above the rim, we're all above the rim. If we don't assume that idea we'll be cut off at the knees. The biggest arena is yet to come, and nine bulls will waiting for us. We have to think we're more than we are, we have to risk everything to get something at this level. All eyes are on us, that's why I hired the publicist . . . "

"A publicist?!!" John screeched. He looked at Carlos with wide eyes. "A *publicist*? I can't deal with him anymore. Screw this shit. I'll see you boys later." He pointed a finger to Gus. "I've always stuck up for you, friend. I've offered excuses for your stupidities. A *publicist*!" He slammed the door when he left.

Gus turned to Carlos with open hands. "I can do nothing right."

"Just . . . just don't spend any more money. Don't drink. Stay silent, worry about your craft, and try not to piss anyone off. I know it's the weekend, but you should be able to do that, yes?" Carlos didn't get a response. "We're so close, Gustavo," he pleaded. "Don't kill it now."

Gus went down to the lobby to clear his head. A beer bottle materialized and balanced on his right shoulder, held by a man he didn't recognize with the group. He didn't accept the beer.

"Off to a shaky start, huh?" He rounded the couch and sat to face Gus. "I'm Abel Cisneros from the Wharton radio station. We've covered the case since it started." He sipped from the beer he brought for himself. "Aren't you going to drink that?"

"Um . . . thinking about it." Gus stared at the bottle. "Tell me about yourself. Did you catch a train here?"

"Have you heard about the segregation at our local theater?"

"Another sign, correct?"

"That's right, to sit up in the balcony. Wharton donated a huge amount of money with the stipulation I got to tag along." He spread his arms. "So here we are!"

Gus realized after the fact that he drank from the bottle without thinking. His hand gripped it more tightly. "Here we are," he repeated. He finished the bottle, then chose to go back to the room.

Before he went to sleep, Gus pulled out an envelope from his suitcase with his name and address written in a red pen. Gus opened it and pulled out a note with creases from him folding and refolding it. The words inside were written with the same red lettering. He read it aloud using whispers.

Dear Mister Gus García,

Hi there, this is Amelia Diaz from Edna, Texas. Do you remember me? We met at the ice cream shop here in town and again in the pharmacy. You helped me learn how to pronounce the word aspirin, because the two girls at the front were making fun of me because I can't speak good English. Enclosed (I learned that word yesterday) you will find twenty-six dollars and fifty cents. I remembered you said in order to get to the top in Washington, DC you need money, so I thought I could help in some way. I asked all of my family and then got the courage to ask people in our community, too. Some people helped, some didn't. I know important things probably cost a lot over there, but I think you should use this money to buy a celebration beer. Or wine, whatever you like to drink. My mom always makes me spend money on things I need instead of what I want, and I don't think you should have to do that.

I just wanted to say thank you for helping me see that every Mexican man doesn't have to be like their father or uncles, or their friend's fathers. Not every man has to be drunk all the time, some of them can wear nice suits and fight for people like us who can't do it for themselves. And girls can do it too, girls can stand up for themselves and share their ideas without anybody telling them to shut up or go out and get pregnant because they think that's what's going to happen anyway. You've helped me see that, and I hope I've helped you see something in yourself as well. I hope you get to the top and stay there.

Love, Amelia.

CHAPTER 39

GUS WOKE UP ON THE FOLLOWING DAY IN THE SAME MENTAL PLACE HE WAS in the night before. Like a sullen child, he ignored most of the men and decided to work and eat in the hotel lobby. To prove a point, he went to bed early that night, letting them know he wouldn't be looking for a bar.

He slipped out the next morning, found the nearest church for mass, and took himself out for a frugal breakfast. Returning before noon, he looked for his colleagues, but found no one. He didn't know they went looking for God as well.

Gus left The Mayflower again to find another cheap meal, while John led the men to a nearby grocery store and brought sandwich food back to the hotel. Five in total, they stood in a line constructing sandwich after sandwich until they made enough for seconds. They aimed for a light-hearted conversation, but couldn't reveal much more than anxiety and tension. Any topic inevitably looped back to the case, and no one could do anything but worry about Gus.

Abel left the living room to take a shower at the same time Gus slipped back inside the hotel room without making a sound. Immediately he overheard his colleagues talking about him.

"We're already hiding money from Gus, aren't we?" Carlos asked the group.

No one answered him, aside from a few who lowered their heads in a guilty fashion.

"Hey," he lifted his hands, "I'll be the first one to tell you he's horrible with money and we're so close to the end. But we need enough money to get home. I'm the one asking here, we're hiding money from him, yes?"

"Yes," John stressed, "I can say LULAC has requested Gus not know what they send us. I told them it was fine."

The LULAC representative nodded to confirm. "This is people's hard-earned money. We wouldn't be able to look them in the eye if someone squandered it."

Gus thought about the Kincaid Christmas when he'd been liquored up too much, the first time he heard them gossiping about him. The hurt felt the same. He entered through the back bedroom and ran into Abel dressed and combing his hair.

"Hey again," Abel said. "Want to get a drink in the downstairs bar? Those men aren't that much fun. Brilliant, but not electrifying. The room is filled with angst about tomorrow."

"They *can* be boring."

"I'm itching for a drink, it's still the afternoon. Join me?"

"Why not?" Gus took the rest of his personal money he'd tucked away in his suitcase before they left the room.

As they passed the front desk, the manager called out his name and held out a Chivas bottle, explaining someone called to pay for a bottle to be delivered to him in his room.

"What luck! Abel my man, looks like we don't need to pay for drinks." When he asked who ordered the bottle, the manager couldn't say, except that a man called.

The two drank two each before Abel excused himself to use the bathroom.

The whisky in Gus woke up his drinking cells. He wanted more, and didn't want to do it sitting in a hotel bar with a man he barely met. The town called out to him, yet still promised him a good night's sleep. *Other men might need to dwell over the big day,* he told himself, *but not you. You need to be free.*

He didn't know his alcoholism would be an old friend who greeted him with longing and satisfaction at his return.

The bartender promised to keep Gus's bottle back behind the bar until he returned. He found a bar called Court Reporter, located near the main area of the Supreme Court and its buildings. The bar tended to house lawyers, reporters, and court workers who'd finished their day. Gossip stayed inside the bar; ironically, everyone knew the Court Reporter to be an off-the-record space.

On a weekend afternoon the bar filled with workers anticipating the week to come. The moment he stepped inside, he felt comfortable. Men and women lounged in their suits with loosened ties, and slung their jackets over wooden chairs. The women looked equal to their male counterparts, and Gus thought Patricia would fit in nicely there. He imagined Irene sitting beside him, but she didn't fit. She would've hated a place like this.

In women, he liked new and exciting, women like Patricia who, though in looks would never seem like his type, turned out to be an equal. But Irene represented home, epitomizing warmth and unconditional love. He realized he missed her greatly.

After staring at his whisky a full five minutes, he brought it to his lips, first smelling it, then drinking it slowly and holding it in his mouth momentarily. It felt like molten lava traveling down his throat.

He continued to think about Irene and her long, dark hair, her loving eyes like sugary almonds smiling at him. He missed that. Whereas Patricia's curves were tight and bruised, Irene's curves were soft, and only marred by his kisses.

Just as he shook the thoughts away, a women with short brunette hair, green eyes, and olive skin entered the bar. She caught his eye in the dim light and sat near him. Gus found it shocking how much she looked like Irene, but with some of Patricia's features. Her smile invited him and warmed his belly as much as the liquor did. When she ordered a whisky, Gus decided it was time to introduce himself.

Her name: Veronica. She bought him a drink and asked him questions, slowly prying his life story out of him.

"Yes!" She raised her fists in victory. "I heard about your case, *Hernandez versus Texas.* Social injustice is becoming more prevalent up north compared to down south." She took a hearty gulp of whisky. "Wow, so you must be on pins and needles right now."

Gus nodded and raised his hand to the bartender. "Another round, please."

"Do you mind me asking . . . why are you out right now, then? You argue the case tomorrow . . . what are you doing here?" She looked deep into his eyes like she wanted to pry out his soul.

"I . . . I . . . I don't know," he sighed. "I think a couple of hours ago I was trying to avoid my coworkers, but now, sitting here talking with you, I'm thinking I should abandon my life and we should run away together!"

Veronica's laugh sounded like it would be easy to fall into. "I've found facing your shit is always a better outcome than running away from it.

Besides, you've made it this far, why not get to the finish line? Whether you place first or not, at this point you've reached the last race." She lifted her glass. "Go for it."

"Yeah, okay, why not? I'll go for it."

They clinked drinks and downed them. Neither of them noticed when the sun started to set.

Gus ordered another round. "My grandfather always said happiness can come easy if you truly want it. It's about choosing to be happy in any position you're put in, because everything is in your head. It's the kind of happy other people become envious of because it radiates off of you. I am finally starting to truly understand what he meant."

With that, Veronica launched forward and kissed him. Gus kissed her back. They kicked back their whisky and walked to her car, quickly deciding to neck again. When they finally unglued from each other after half an hour, she asked if he wanted to return to her apartment.

They burst inside, falling over each other. Gus tried to be in the moment and enjoy it, but found himself out of practice in seducing a woman. She took the lead, and his mind wandered. He found himself hearing the voices of Pete, Lenora, his colleagues, the Victoria reporter, Shepperd, his assistant, Judge Martin in Jackson County, and the LULAC clubs complaining about him. Suddenly he felt like the entire Mexican American race called out to him, needing him, and he wasted time fumbling around with a woman's bra.

Veronica moaned while undulating her curves underneath his hands, but his body wouldn't respond the way she wanted it to. She groaned out in frustration.

It wasn't happening. His face flushed with warmth. "Shit, wait hold on."

Without malice, she reassured him. "Don't worry, it's okay." She climbed off him to put on a robe and went to light candles. She opened a cabinet to reveal a new Chivas bottle.

"It's not. But I need to go anyhow."

"Oh, please don't. Tell me what you've been going through," she requested as she poured. "I'm fascinated with what your life must be right now." She put the glasses on a tray and added a pack of cigarettes and matches from her purse.

When she set the tray between them, Gus saw The Mayflower Hotel insignia on the matchbook cover. "Hey," he pointed, "we're staying at that hotel."

"I occasionally hold interviews there." She lit a cigarette.

"Speak, tell me your story," she instructed him. "A long version, an abridged one, I don't care, just lay your troubles down at my front door. In getting to know you I can tell you hold a huge burden on your back, like Atlas trying to balance the world." She took a long drag and exhaled upwards.

Gus glanced at her, doubtful of her honesty. Who in their right mind would be interested in his story in the middle of a Sunday night? In the end he didn't question it further, because he wanted to talk about himself, so he began. She said nothing, simply puffing her cigarette until she put it out. As he spoke, Veronica listened while she lit matches, one by one. She studied each flame until it burnt out, or the flame crept too close to her fingers. Only once more did she light another cigarette, then continued to light matches until they ran out. Gus decided to stop talking, realizing he could've spoken forever.

"The spirits of different kinds of people," she started cryptically, "are like the flame of a match. No two are the same, nor do they burn at the same speed. Some last long enough to reach my cigarette and light it, but don't carry the same beauty as the short-lived flame that flares up high and shines bright. But the short-lived flame doesn't make it to my cigarette in time, it runs out of steam."

Gus agreed.

"The inconsistencies of a match flame can explain our behavior as human beings, and the sort of impact we have on others."

He furrowed his brows. "I suppose so."

"Pretend we just entered a cave," Veronica said, and flipped over to her stomach. "You light a torch, same as me, but they don't burn the same. Your flame is so bright and so loud, for a few seconds we can see the entirety of the cave, and where our way out begins. Another's flame doesn't shine as brightly, but can assist us in putting one step in front of the other to get us to the way out. If we only had one torch, at some point we'd be bumping around in the dark." She paused for a few beats to let the idea sink in. "It sounds to me like your coworkers are the longer-lasting flames, and you are the bright light in the night. You will show our race the way, but you may not be able to do it for very long."

Her words spoke to his heart so deep that he became dizzy, suddenly had to sleep, and all the while dreaming of the morning's events. But he convinced himself, as one sometimes does, that he possessed all the time in the world.

Still drunk, Gus stirred a short time later. Thin rays of blue light streamed through a window, and he noticed she still slept. His senses tingled with the importance of the day ahead, and he was grateful the alcohol blunted his anxiety. He closed his eyes and snuggled into her back, waking her up in the process. Veronica responded as the sun came up, and they connected physically in a way Gus hadn't experienced in a long time.

Despite his partners' pleas, he felt he had no one to answer to but himself, and though frightening, he abandoned himself to the moment. He felt a brazen confidence that he could do as he pleased, because in the end nothing mattered anyway. He relaxed into a limbo of whisky and forgetfulness. When the feeling wore off he felt fuzzy and small all over again, and he hated it. He closed his eyes to make it go away, and the next time he opened them the clock on the wall said nine. They were to argue after lunch.

"Nonononono!" Gus exclaimed. He sprang into action and crashed into her dresser. He found his clothes draped over a chair. "Wasn't it six in the morning a moment ago?"

Veronica stretched. "We fell asleep, but I don't know at what time. Post-sex trance. Come back to bed." She smiled sleepily.

He smiled back. "I wish I could . . . but mierda! Thank you for," he looked around, "this," he gestured. He shot out of her apartment without saying another word and ran several blocks to The Mayflower with half his clothes flying behind him.

Would they be waiting for him? Probably not. He'd need to explain himself, then thought it best not to. Excuses shot through his head, but all were worthless. He couldn't cut it with this type of pressure. His colleagues' voices screamed in his head, foreshadowing a similar reaction when he walked through the door. The idea came to him to act more intoxicated than he was, so he could explain less.

John and Carlos yelled the way he expected. The activists in the group threw him in the shower and threw soap and shampoo on him while Gus stayed quiet, trying to block out their shouting. Carlos pulled Gus's suit out of the closet, plus his socks and shoes. He prepared the tie with a Windsor knot.

"Carlos, you will do this alone," John said. "It's time for Plan B."

"I will not, Herrera, I will not. I can do what I've primed myself to do, but the passion, the persuasiveness, you know I cannot achieve that. Why can't you do it? You've held national office."

"Who will be the puppet master then? No one knows the filing system DeAnda made for me. I know where every document is, I can find what you need in three moves or less."

"I can do it," Gus croaked out.

They ignored him and continued as if he wasn't standing feet away from them. John wrote up Plan B months ago, because he expected Gus to be drunk from the pressure and wanted to be ready for anything.

Gus separated himself from John and Carlos to dress in his three-piece black and white pin-striped suit he'd saved for the big day. He added a red rose to his lapel and thought of his abuelo. He heard them bickering about him in the adjoining room. The lingering alcohol shielded him somewhat from most of their comments, but the words he heard from John hit him like a taser, stunning him into silence so that he was unable to stand up for himself. He briefly thought of calling downstairs for the Chivas he left at the bar.

Gus joined the others reluctantly. He snapped his fingers. "My muleta, I want to take it. For good luck. Abel, would you mind holding it for me?"

"You will do no such thing!" John leapt for the cape. "I will not have you or any of us walk into the Supreme Court smelling of bullshit. I won't allow it."

"Not if it calms me? It aligns me."

"I've never seen you aligned," John said.

Gus internally prayed for Mateo's spirit to be with him in his time of greatest need as he checked himself in the mirror and smoothed out his eyebrows before they left the room.

CHAPTER 40

THE *WASHINGTON POST* INTERN TRIED TO KEEP UP WITH HIS MENTOR, BUT HIS long strides couldn't match her short, quick steps. She was in the middle of a crowd of other reporters and photographers swiftly streaming toward the courthouse. "How do you go about this? Do you call one of their names out? Or talk to the three of them in general?"

Veronica's dark hair whipped in the wind and nearly snapped his face. "What are you talking about?" She didn't break her pace or turn around. Her green eyes stayed on the steps ahead as she gripped the tape recorder tighter in her hand.

"I'm just curious how you're going to approach the lawyers," the young man said. "Do you know ahead of time what you're going to do? Are they expecting questions before or after? Will they give a statement?" He nervously yanked at his jacket sleeves to get them over his cuffs.

"It depends on what sort of access you can get, but your brain," she tapped the side of her head, "should be prepared for both. Read their body language and go with the flow. Above all else, be fearless in your approach." She stopped to give him a glance. "I suppose I don't need to tell you that, you being a male and all. Anyone else is a minority." She turned back. "Once you find the best entry, charge in."

"Who will you try to talk to first: Cadena, García, Herrera?"

"Always go for the one who talks the most, they give the best quotes. Personally, I'm going for the showy one. In Texas they call him the shiny one." Her fingernails clicked on the tape recorder impatiently.

Veronica zeroed in on Gus the moment the men arrived, and flashes from the previous night came to her suddenly. The man *is* dashing, he dresses smartly, she said to herself, and he can put away the liquor. He suffered, that much she could tell, but it was a private suffering, like self-flagellation. The possibility that he liked suffering occurred to her, but she brushed it away to speak above the crowd. Her voice resonated in the chilled air amongst her mostly male cohorts on the Supreme Court steps. "Gustavo! Mr. García," she yelled above the crowd.

He focused on her. "Please, call me Gus," he said, and removed his eyeglasses to show her his own green eyes. He raised an eyebrow at her when he saw who spoke.

"You three are about to be the first Mexican Americans arguing a case in front of the Supreme Court. How does that feel?"

"Pete Hernandez is obviously guilty of murder," a reporter beside her interrupted. "Jack, from the *New York Times*. Why do you want to fight for a murderer?"

Jack stood close enough to Veronica that she could elbow him in his side.

Gus flashed a smile and answered in a clear, crisp voice. "This isn't about guilt, sir, nor should it be. It's about awareness and equal representation. I believe your associate was getting to that. Until you interrupted her." He looked at her. "Please, continue."

"Yes, Veronica," Jack mimicked. "Please continue."

"Why thank you, Jack," she smiled with sarcasm, and looked back at Gus. "You will be fighting a case for Mexican Americans to be recognized as a distinct class within the white race. Why do this? Why fight?"

"How can we not?" Gus gave them another smile with double the charm. "If we have been blessed with a brain, bravery, and mental toughness, how can we not? If we see segregation and discrimination in any form, blatant, everyday, or unconscious, how can we not see the need to speak out and fight?"

John and Carlos traded shocked looks and agreed with their partner out loud to the reporters.

"And here's an answer to your first question, Veronica," continued Gus. "It feels stupendous to be one of the first, and know this now: surely we won't be the last. We want everyone to fight the battles of our people, of our race, and we have been the first chosen by God for that fate."

Another reporter called out. "What if you lose this battle?"

"So what?" John spoke up. "We'll keep fighting. We won't stop."

"My associate is correct. Discrimination calls for us to keep going, so when racism stops, so will we," Gus announced. "This case will be a burst of fire in a dark cave, giving everyone a glance down the path," and then he looked directly at Veronica. "We must keep the flame lit within us, whether it be large or small, short or long-lasting, so it can illuminate the steps we must take to get to our goal."

She gave him a small, almost imperceptible nod as the other reporters swarmed the men with questions. She scribbled her notes and kept her eyes on Gus as they finished their statements and filed into the Supreme Court. She looked for something, anything, in his eyes, but saw nothing more. Concentration and confidence emanated from his face. He was in control. When he finally did look at her their rapport seemed to dissipate, and her spirits dipped slightly. She didn't expect to connect with him so fast, only to lose it all just as quickly.

The reporters started up the steps while Veronica hung behind, making sure to be the last to enter the courthouse. She veered off to the side and found a phone she could use during the lull before court began. She dialed a number.

The first ring was cut short when a man's voice answered. "What happened? Tell me now."

"I spent the night with him," she explained. "He left still drunk."

"Perfect."

"Yeah, but I met him on the steps just before they entered, several moments ago. He looked to be in perfect condition. Everyone has entered and they are taking their seats."

"And? What happened last night? Where's his mind at? How long were you with him?"

"A lot went on last night, and he seemed unfazed this morning. The eye contact he made, I don't know if you're going to get the outcome you're looking for." She spoke her next statement softly to soften its blow. "It's almost inhuman, superhuman, maybe? I don't know. He spoke with clarity, and it didn't strike me as a rehearsed statement. Plus, I got the distinct feeling he used me, rather than vice versa. I can't explain it." She paused. "It's the Supreme Court. Whatever lawyers end up there will have something to say, no matter what's happened before that."

The man cursed. "He'll never quit."

"Of course not, he's obviously a man with a mission. Passionate, but paranoid. He has a purpose, he's just wading through some shit to get there." Veronica laughed. "Of course, he's got men like you trying to sneak in an uppercut or two."

He sighed. "I'm just trying to do my job."

"Sure, sure." She paused. "Will I get my money? I did everything you asked, I did my job." Her throat released an unintentional snicker.

"Of course I'll pay what I promised. Maybe what you two did will make its way through by the time it's his turn."

"Just what sort of monster do you think you're fighting here? It's funny how in every story the bad guys always think they're the good guys. I guess that's what keeps them going." Veronica noticed the crowd in the main area began to thin out. She glanced at the time. "Look, are you still not going to give me your name? What if the funds don't come through? What do I do then?" She paused. "I'm a journalist, I have ways of finding you if it comes to that. Texas is not that far away. You have sixty seconds to answer." She counted down the numbers and reached forty before he spoke.

"Kincaid."

"Kincaid? Is that the first or last name?"

"Call me Donovan. Or Don. Yeah, Don. My name is Don Kincaid. The money will be in your account by the end of day."

Veronica nodded. "This fight you think you're winning, all of it is inevitable and not in your favor, you know that, don't you? I'm sure it's not something you sit around and think about, but I know people like you will fight it every step of the way just to postpone the inevitable, but it's still inevitable."

CHAPTER 41

DONOVAN RETURNED THE RECEIVER TO ITS CRADLE. HE COULD STILL HEAR VEronica's voice after he hung up. She spoke correctly; he could feel it in his gut. Working with the men in Symmetry had become a burden, a heavy force dragging him down. The more he tried to take control of the force the harder it pulled, insisting he surrender.

Through comments, conversations, and reactions to the world's evolution, his father ingrained in him that status and money mattered, for as long as he could remember. It was the foundation the Kincaids operated on. He learned to believe his race was more blessed than others. Until Kiana.

The events he secretly hosted during Christmas started putting things into perspective. Some of his motivation drained out of him that night, and his guilt flared when he thought about the total amount of Chivas he anonymously sent to Gus over the past two and a half years. It all felt so wrong, and he wanted a chance to start over.

Donovan leaned back in his office chair and it whined at him for the first time. *Squeeeee.* He knew the path before him and what must be done. As he descended the stairs his feet became leaden. Dread held him back. Thinking of Kiana gave him strength.

He knew where his father puttered around at lunchtime. He found Don in the library standing with his back to the door, an open book in his hands. Beside him on a small table, an ashtray held a burning cigarette next to a glass of whisky with three melting ice cubes. Donovan entered quietly and circled the room several times, scanning the books.

"Why are you dallying?" Don spun around. "I hate it when you hover." He studied his face. "You look troubled. Out with it."

Donovan took a deep breath, still gathering courage.

"Spit it out, you're wasting time. *My* time." Don turned a page.

Donovan exhaled. "I'm bowing out."

Don looked at him sharply. "Take a seat, son, there's no need for rash decisions. Have some of my drink, I'll get Kiana to fetch us more."

He shook his head. "No, we're not doing that. I'm not doing that. I've not succeeded in my task, and I've done nothing but cause sorrow. I'm stepping down."

"You mean you're quitting." Don snapped the book shut.

"I don't want to waste anyone's time. *Your* time. Preston's time. It's not for me," he admitted.

His father sat on a couch and patted the seat beside him. "Come. Sit."

Donovan hesitated, then decided to join him. "We don't have to get into it. Let me go gracefully."

Don's laugh sounded like a cackle. "I'll do no such thing!" He patted his son's knee. "Just because they're in front of the Supreme Court right now doesn't mean time has run out. You didn't flip the case into our hands, and that's all right. There's still time before the verdict. I bet Horace can definitely help."

"I'm not sure about that. He won't risk his job for this." He eyed his father warily, thinking it odd that he tried to be reassuring.

"Well, there's still ways, we'll think of something."

"Not without an invitation." It occurred to Donovan, without pity, his father's feigned friendliness meant he needed him to stay.

Don leveled his eyes with his son's, a look that said they were in this together. "I don't understand why you're thinking that way, they haven't even presented yet. Gus could still perform badly. I'm sure he drank last night."

His father's camaraderie made it momentarily difficult for Donovan to continue. "Actually, he did, I made sure of it. I bribed a contact in DC, a reporter, to spend the night with him. She pretended to like whisky so he'd find her more attractive. I just spoke with her. He left her place ripped, probably like he did when he spent Christmas here." The remorse returned.

"Good man! Now I call that clever thinking. Cheers to that." Don lifted his glass and took a sip. He frowned. "Why do you still have that face on? I'd call that success right there. No need to be a quitter." He nudged the glass toward him.

Donovan nudged it back over. "This past year or so has been a learning curve for me. I'm not going to talk about my feelings, I'm just going to say I'm not made for this life. I don't want it. I'm not . . . wicked enough to enjoy this sort of thing."

Don nodded slowly. His voice came out low and calm. "Is that what you think this is about? We're not the mafia, and I'm a little bit taken aback that you'd suggest such a thing." His expression hardened.

"Maybe not, but definitely we're gangsters of a different kind." Donovan paused. "Actually, you all ARE similar to the mafia, but without the guns and drugs. I haven't killed Gus outright, but I've been helping him toward a slow death."

"How liberal of you. Do you hear yourself right now?" Don stood and walked to the doorway. "This is ridiculous. Kiana," he called out, and rang the nearest bell.

Donovan heard her voice answer him, but didn't see her.

"Be a dear and fetch my son and me more drinks. Drambuies all around! He's going through a crisis." He shut the door behind him. "Did you tell Armstrong you quit? This can all be retracted."

"No, I'm telling you; I'm not backing down from this," he said firmly. "Do you know how long it's taken me to come to this decision? Bribing that woman in DC, I thought I'd try one last time. I still wanted to help Symmetry."

"Don't say our name out loud. You don't deserve to say it out loud." Don's eyes turned to slits. "I should've expected this from you. You've always been this way. I knew it the moment you tattled to your mother about the Christmas tree all those years ago. She's the one who taught you about your feelings. You should've been a girl."

Donovan winced as if he'd been slapped. At the same time his father's reaction gave him the strength he needed to forge ahead. "I never regretted doing that, even though you and Donny tried to guilt me into feeling that way. Watching Gus ruin her Christmas tree and knowing I played the conductor is what started to bring me back to my senses and see the truth. Or my truth, at least."

"Give me a break."

"So this is how it goes, huh? I don't do what I'm told, and you bring out the big guns to cut me down to size."

Don shrugged with an expression that said he couldn't care less. He looked at Donovan like one would a clump of dirt on the bottom of their shoe. "I'm just speaking the truth. *My* truth, I guess you could call it. I have thoughts too, you know, I'm not a careless devil like you might think, though I know I act like it. Fathers don't stop having epiphanies when they have sons."

"Oh yeah, and what's yours?" Donovan managed a chuckle. "You look just like Mom right now, all self-righteous."

Don ignored it. "I thought you'd learned some tricks from me as you grew up. You spied on us enough. I'd see the longing on your face, you wanted to be in on the secret. I recognized it on some of our newcomers, a desperation for acceptance. As time passed I realized it wasn't our secret you wanted to be in on, it was any secret. You wanted to belong."

A knock sounded at the door and Kiana slowly entered with four drinks on her tray. "I brought more than required sir," she said to Don, "to finish the bottle." Her eyes flickered toward Donovan, but they lowered to the carpet when he returned her gaze.

"I like your initiative," Don said. "You can go now." He pointed at her as she walked out. "Learning you had a thing for her revived my hope somewhat."

Donovan noticed she hadn't entirely exited the room before his father spoke about her. He looked at his father without speaking.

Don took a large swallow without offering up a "cheers." "Until I learned it dragged on and on. Until I caught stolen looks between you two and realized you had *feelings*." He said the word as if it disgusted him. "Remember, I'm adept at that sort of behavior. I perfected it."

"How could I forget, dear Father?" Donovan hoped his retort dripped with as much sarcasm as he intended. "As you've implied, I'm my mama's boy."

Don looked at his son with a certain softness. Usually, said softness came with something terrible not far behind. "You are a failure, you always have been." He spoke with an unsettling steadiness. "You've finally confirmed my assumptions. Donny is the troublemaker, and you are the predictable, boring one."

Donovan thought his Drambuie a little on the sweet side. He figured Kiana probably sweetened it with extra honey. Normally, he would've thought it just right. "It's not like you've ever been helpful. You never stopped Donny from messing with me. You let him be a burden and acted like you didn't notice."

"Who do you think asked him to fuck with you? Let me clear up the confusion, dear son, it was me. I needed to test your loyalty and keep an eye on you. I knew Donny could do both." He leaned in. "I should make him follow through with your little girlfriend just to teach you a lesson."

"This is all a futile fight, you know that, don't you? You may be able to stop men like Gus and John here and there, but it's impossible to stop the movement. They'll just fight back harder and smarter. You're wasting your time." He stood. "This is why I didn't want to sit down, you'd spin me into your web again."

"That's what you think," Don said. "I've got a meeting with a man named Richard Welch Jr. next week. He's interested in the way we operate, and maybe taking it national. So we're not stopping, sonny boy, we're going to do what we can to look out for the good of our state, and soon, this country."

"Well, good for you." Donovan wanted to say more, but decided against it. "I don't want it to end like this. The sort of man you're looking for, you can find it in Horace. I said earlier he wouldn't risk his job for this, but only because he'd prefer it be him who's offered a chance. He'd go the distance."

Don glared, gripped an empty crystal glass, and threw it across the room. "Do you know what it's like to have two failures for sons?"

"It's you the one who has failed me." Donovan paused for at least a minute. "I understand I will lose you as a father, and I'm willing to risk it. I know my mother will risk making furtive calls and visits to let me know someone in our family supports my decisions. The thing is, *Don,* I'm glad to get away from you, away from this. I let my issues with Gus cloud everything because I wanted to make him fear me, fear us." Donovan looked at his father's hand and realized blood dripped from it onto the carpet. He took a step forward.

The bleeding hand shot out, showing he'd been clutching a piece of glass. "Don't take another step towards me, you mean nothing to me. You are the biggest disappointment."

Donovan sighed sadly. "So are you, *Father*. You've been the biggest disappointment to *me.*"

Don gave no answer. Instead, he grabbed Donovan's glass and flung it across the room. It crashed into a shelf of books and left Drambuie drops and shards of glass in its wake. "That's for you," he pointed a bloody hand at Donovan. He reached for the third glass, still full, and threw it at the door. "That's for your vapid mother." He gripped the last one and threw it down into a glass coffee table, which shattered into pieces. "And that's for your stupid, fucking brother!" Don's roar thundered through the manor; the entire household froze at the fury in his voice. When the glasses ran out, Don started flinging as many books as his anger could reach.

"What about the first one? The first glass you threw, that one was for you, wasn't it?" Donovan shook his head. "You've created all this. We are Kincaids modeled by your forefathers and their father's fathers. All these broken pieces belong to you."

Don screamed again, but this time it sounded full of pain, like a man in anguish. Donovan slipped out of the room unnoticed, but stopped when he heard his name from a familiar voice.

"Donovan."

He turned to see Kiana. She stood with her hands clasped in front of her. As he went to her she opened her arms wide and wrapped them around him. Acceptance and love filled him. Another sound erupted from the library. Donovan thought surely his father had moved on to the encyclopedias.

He turned back to Kiana. "Run away with me. I'm done with all this." He spoke in a rush. "My bags are packed, and I'm headed up north. I've been planning this for some time. I have my own money. I can take you away from this and take care of you." He paused for a breath. "I'll go without you, but I want you with me. I'm in love with you. I didn't have the courage to realize it before, much less say it. But I'm saying it now. I love you, Kiana. Will you be my lady?"

Kiana reached up and put a hand against his cheek. She smiled at him as the sounds of Don's personal holocaust continued in the library.

CHAPTER 42

THE LAWYERS CROSSED THE BRONZE DOORS INTO THE MAIN CORRIDOR, THE Great Hall. Busts of previous Supreme Court Justices circled the perimeter of the room, looking down at the courtroom they once inhabited. The moment wasn't lost on the men. They felt the veneration and humility a Christian might experience upon entering a cavernous cathedral.

Gus sucked in all the air his chest could take, then exhaled slowly. The reality of what was about to happen sobered him a bit. "This is happening. This is not a dream. We are here."

John quietly whistled under his breath. "Everything we've done so far has come to this."

Carlos stayed quiet and allowed his colleagues' long legs to increase the distance between them. For him, speaking ruined the moment. Silence truly allowed room for it all. He knew that day would be a history-changing moment, whether the ruling would be in their favor or not. But if they did win . . . dear God, if they did.

Gus nudged John. "This makes me feel like I'm walking the plank."

"You're always walking a plank of your own design," John spoke under his breath. "I'm beyond livid for your behavior this morning, and no, you're not going to speak today."

Gus said nothing, mainly because they walked through the east door of the Great Hall into the expansive Court Chamber, which swallowed him whole. His eyes searched the high ceiling. "Dreams fly high in this institution," he whispered to himself.

Horace and JB came into view as they found their seats. In that moment, life began to make sense for Gus. He did it all for the presentation, not the paperwork. It all came down to this, and now the moments he'd been waiting for: to talk, to persuade, to prove. Besides, he believed himself to be at his best with a light steep in Chivas.

He turned to Carlos and noticed the man tried controlling his legs from bouncing, to no avail. Carlos tried distracting his nerves in several ways, he rubbed his hands together like he was cold, he flipped a pencil around his thumb, he scribbled nonsense on a piece of paper. Gus reached out and squeezed his hand.

Carlos jumped slightly. "What?"

"Your hand is clammy."

He snatched his hand back. "Yes," he muttered.

"We're here," Gus said evenly, and leaned closer to his ear. "I'm ready, I can speak, let me do it."

"No."

"No matter what, we're here. Let's make the best of it. I'm the best of it."

"I will not," Carlos emphatically said. He squinted his eyes. "Hand me that bucket."

"I will do no such thing. We are sitting in the chamber of the Supreme Court. Go to the bathroom. Will you let me speak?"

"No."

Gus sat back. "Then you do not get the bucket."

"Can you imagine what we went through when we woke up to start the most important day of our life and you weren't there to do that with us? We changed the whole game p-p-plan," Carlos stuttered. "If you'd been where you should have and taken this seriously—"

"Don't be so dramatic. Calm down. Your nerves are showing, and I don't think you're ready to do this. I say this with all the support I can muster, you cannot move mountains with your words loaded up on anxiety like that," Gus whispered.

"I'm not going to throw our team into confusion by sharing your plan with them."

A moment passed, then a glint showed in his eyes. He sighed and did an about-face. "It's not my time, but it is yours. If I don't make a decision to let you fly now, I fear you never will."

"Carlitos? Are you about to be my little giant?"

"Be ready to speak when the time comes. Just be on your toes so you know when that time is. Herrera won't stop you, how could he? The most he would do is tug at your sleeve." Carlos gripped Gus by the arm. "Open your soul, speak beautifully the things I want to say. Charm them and sway them with your words. Help them understand our plight."

John put himself into their line of sight and hissed, "If you two don't shut up I'm going to do something I might regret later."

Suddenly the marshal's voice rang out. "The Honorable, the Chief Justice and the Associate Justices of the Supreme Court of the United States. Oyez! Oyez! Oyez! All persons having business before the Honorable, the Supreme Court of the United States, are admonished to draw near and give their attention, for the Court is now sitting. God save the United States and Honorable Court!"

The Chief Justice Earl Warren, a man with white hair and thin-rimmed gold spectacles, entered through his door, while nine men, dressed in long black robes, filed in and filled their seats on the raised mahogany bench. Photographers knelt underneath the bench with over-sized cameras angled toward the empty lectern in the center.

Their entrance seemed to have a trance-like effect on Gus. He slipped into a calm state and took it all in. A matador knows nothing if he doesn't know his environment. Gus looked up and around. *Nine bulls,* he thought, *and my comrades and I are the three matadors set to slay them with our words.*

The images sculpted into the frieze on his left caught his attention. Three women he knew well: Divine Inspiration, Wisdom, and Truth. As he gazed into their likenesses, he saw himself and the men who currently sat beside him.

Truth held a mirror in one hand and a rose in another. John represented the good and bad of truth, and as a mirror image of Gus, they behaved as symbols of pure truth, but with thorns.

An owl perched on the shoulder of Wisdom. Carlos embodied the idea of knowledge and stayed vigilant to forever learn more.

Divine Inspiration held the scales of justice, the law of the land and God's law. Gus felt his relationship with the law was the only woman he stayed true for. Without the law, Gus knew he would be nothing.

Chief Justice Warren called the court to order. John spread out documents in front of them in a three-by-three square displaying nine stacks of data, ready to locate at any given time. Carlos stood and addressed the justices with a barely perceptible stutter. Each side had been given thirty minutes to present their case.

Gus tuned him out and thought about what started all of this. He recalled when Lenora walked into his office and he accepted the case out of a sense of obligation. He imagined Lenora on her knees, praying for a win and another chance for her son.

The image of Pete behind bars made guilt wash over him, and Gus began to panic. Sweat formed on his brow, and he pressed his hand against a small bulge where a flask filled with whisky nestled in the inner pocket of his jacket.

It would be so easy to excuse himself to a bathroom and empty the contents into his mouth. Liquid courage would flow into him, like the can of spinach did to Popeye. Deep inside he knew it would be a complete betrayal of his associates, even though it would be a quick fix.

Don't think of Pete and Lenora, he told himself, *this is not the time for that.* Go farther back, travel back in time to find the reason, the real reason he knew fighting for equal rights would be his mission in life. It happened so many years ago, the first time he truly fought for his own rights, back in high school. But against whom? He could see a shadow in front of him, but couldn't think yet who it belonged to.

A voice broke through Gus's thoughts. "They call 'em greasers down south, don't they? Aside from you men today, I don't know if I've had the pleasure of knowing what a Mexican American is." The judge's candor clearly came with respect, not sarcasm.

"Nor did I," another said. "Are they citizens? Do all of you speak English down there?"

The word *greaser* stopped time and transported Gus to a day when a man called him a greaser. His high school principal. A week before graduation, the principal, a tall man with a blonde combover, called Gus into his office to let him know he wasn't going to award him the scholarship that came with the honor of valedictorian.

The principal stated he didn't want to waste the money on a greaser who, though smart, probably wouldn't amount to much due to his last name. He commended him on the way he spoke English, but didn't assume his skin color would take him far. The principal thought Gus would want to know something like this before he entered a world full of disappointment. He told Gus he should be happy and feel lucky that his brown skin wasn't as dark as the next person's. It might help him find a wife easier, the principal commented, and maybe a better job.

Gus grew up in those moments and became a social activist right then and there. He took in the principal's words, studied his face, and vowed to himself never to let anyone threaten his future. His grandfather taught him never to let someone like that bring him down. *You'll remember me,* Gus told the principal, *you'll remember me because I'm going to be something someday, and you'll remember this moment right now. You won't forget you denied me the scholarship I earned. I won't go gently away. I will be recognized.*

Gus suddenly perked up. He understood his time stood before him.

"Your Honor, Justice Warren," he said, and stood up. "Gus, no . . . *Gustavo* García, if I may address the court."

"Your Honor," Carlos said, "I cede the rest of my time to my colleague."

Justice Warren nodded and Gus took the podium. He took in a deep breath and acknowledged each of the bulls before him by looking into their eyes. Nine white men of a certain age sat before him, each with whitening hair. They took Gus in, their expressions stoic, and waited for him to speak.

"More often than not, a Mexican American, stuck between two races, finds themselves struggling to be seen, and the ones who came a generation before us learned life is lived best when one is left alone. In essence, it causes us and our brethren to live life in the shadows, and inexplicably, we try blending into society like the melting pot this country is known for." Gus paused and felt a surge of power go through him. "In the act of blending in we ultimately fade away, and lose ourselves in the process, thus becoming invisible." He lifted his head, and with a great deal of humility, he said his next sentence. "Nothing is worse than the feeling of slipping away, whether it be one person or the idea of one, entire race."

Gus gestured to JB Shepperd and Horace Wimberly. "These gentlemen will try and persuade you that Mexican Americans are not discriminated from Anglo-Americans, and further still, they will attempt to say both are one in the same race." He tapped his foot. "Nothing could be further from the truth.

"Take Staff Sergeant Macario García: this man, Mexican-born in 1920, unrelated, fought in World War II and earned a Medal of Honor. His parents moved their family to Texas in 1923, and he was drafted into the army in the year 1942. Upon his arrival back into the country that he fought for, Macario was denied service at a restaurant in Richmond, which, mind you, is a town that houses a large number of Mexican Americans, located just miles from Houston, Texas. Instead of blending in, he argued with the owner until police were called in to arrest him. His case, fought by a colleague of mine, would've been won had the case not been dropped after a year of postponement. I say to you, Macario García was discriminated against."

Gus shifted his weight slightly. "A mere three years later, in 1948, Felix Longoria's remains are found in the Philippines after a volunteer mission at the end of World War II. They are shipped back for burial in a Three Rivers, Texas cemetery, where his ashes are promptly rejected. This is a cemetery where the 'Mexican' section is corralled off with barbed wire. The director denies the use of the chapel to Felix Longoria's family, due to disturbances related to the burial of other Mexican soldiers. One of the other reasons, the director stated, is that the whites wouldn't like it. After prompts began by the American GI Forum, plus telegrams and letters, Senator Lyndon B. Johnson responded with an offer to arrange a burial at Arlington National Cemetery, which the family accepted. I will say to that, that the remains of Felix Longoria were discriminated against.

"In response, Your Honor, to your question from earlier, yes, they call us greasers down there in the south, they call us wetbacks, and they call us eons worse than that.

"When those names are unleashed, it's implied that person is someone who crossed into America illegally: an immigrant. That's why the name wetback, because our backs have become wet from swimming across the border. The unmitigated truth is this . . . my race never crossed the border . . . the border crossed us." Confidence doubled and ignited the rebel inside him. "My people, the Mexicans and Mexican Americans, have been citizens for generations. My family is and was from Texas when it was Mexico . . . and Spain, and France.

"I've had relatives who've lived in Texas longer than Sam Houston. And yes, the Sam Houston I speak of is the wetback from Tennessee," Gus said. He withheld a smirk, and grew happy when he heard one or two snickers behind him. The interest in the faces of the bulls before him urged him on.

Gus sipped on a glass of water. "The line was drawn on those relatives, and the rules changed before them without much say, and with much war. Cubans, the Spanish, people from the Dominican Republic, Brazilians, all experienced forms of discrimination and what's more, each country has a distinctive cultural richness no one else can reproduce, just like America's melting pot of the Caucasian, Latino, African American, and Asian people.

"Yet, a disconnect remains. We are still a democratic work in progress." Gus paused to look each justice in the eye and let his comment sink in. "I say that because Mexican Americans, specifically, are considered unequal, just as much as African Americans are. Government systems, restaurants, schools, and pools—the way these organizations operate—prove it. Segregation through discrimination is a common, disgusting practice, and it's evident that this calls for a change.

"It's not decent to believe one person's life weighs more than another, a judge larger than all of us combined awaits that sort of decision. What I know is this: our contributions may differ greatly, but we are all equal. I tell you, this decision before you will change your children's future, and their children as well." Gus took a deep breath to gauge their reactions, and saw the men hung on his words, waiting for him to continue his verbal spell.

"Spanish and English schools are segregated for four grades. The Mexican American school fails its students in many ways. The school is kept in decline to deter Mexican American children from continuing their schooling. And when a mother attempts to enroll her child in the English speaking school, is told that even though her child can speak English fluently she must still take her child to the Mexican school. What else is this but a deterrent to continue school at all?

"The Constitution recognizes two races, Caucasians and African Americans," Gus air-quoted the word *two*, "and currently, I guarantee you there are clearly three races in the southwestern part of the United States. Who knows when there will be more? This understanding hasn't reached this far up north . . . yet . . . but it must be known that Mexicans Americans are a class apart from the Caucasian race."

Lightbulbs flashed from the photographers kneeling underneath the Supreme Court justices.

"The attorney general," he pointed, "John Ben Shepperd, and Horace Wimberly are here simply to prove to you what's already written on paper by Caucasian men like yourself." Another pause. "But I'll give you an opposing view. Caucasians stole America from the Indians long ago, and turned it into *their* country made by *their* people, and molded their America for their children. I'm asking you to look beyond that and envision something more than black or white. I'm asking you to recognize and understand the cultural richness of all classes and shades in between, and grant them equal rights."

A box sat to one side of the judges with a dormant red light and a lit green light during his speech. Somewhere toward the end, Gus didn't notice when the red light flicked on, signaling his time to stop, nor when the marshal called out to stop him. What happened next became folklore.

Some say the power went out, some say the justices became so enamored of Gus's speech that no one saw the red light flicker on. When Judge Warren finally noticed it and spoke up, he ended up letting Gus speak longer anyhow. This, in and of itself, was a battle won for Mexicans and all brown people—that words from a person with brown skin could entice and hypnotize an audience so much that they openly admitted how impressed they were.

The opposition argued that no discrimination occurred in the south, and isolated incidents of discrimination and segregation were just that—isolated. In no way did such incidents represent the people as a whole, and they never would. They stated Mexican Americans have already been treated equal and no one has ever worked against that. In no way would anyone ever rebel against the government to push the agenda that superiority belongs to one race. The Constitution spoke of two races being equal, and that statement should be respected.

Gus turned exceptionally quiet when the day ended, as if he'd performed an exorcism of himself with his words. He imagined a golden phoenix crafted by the sun. It burst from the ashes in that moment and ended his cycle of self-destruction. The justices appeared to be moved, the people around seemed to be impressed, yet he couldn't deny something still sat before him unfinished.

Sunlight washed across the Supreme Court steps when they exited. They stopped for a picture, and John pointed to Justice in the frieze over the building. "The balance will be in our favor, friend, and if it isn't, we're going to keep on going regardless."

Gus's eyes wandered to the Three Fates on the front of the building—three goddesses in Greek mythology responsible for the destiny of all people and things—known as the weavers of fate. One wove the thread of life, the second measured the thread, while the third cut the thread. He couldn't help but wonder which sister sat within him. He also couldn't help but imagine himself being chased by a pair of shears looking to cut his thread of life. Their fight inside the Supreme Court, would it be the measure of his life? If the fight ended today, what would happen next?

As he drifted in his trance Gus felt a pair of hands clasp his shoulders. He turned to find they belonged to John. "Amigo," Gus said.

"Amigo," John returned, "can I speak to you privately? I'd like to do it here with the sun setting on our day, and I want to walk away from this with a clean slate and an honest heart."

All Gus could do was nod.

John removed his glasses and slipped them into a jacket pocket. "Amigo, I owe you an apology for my behavior. I see now more than I ever had why you do what you do."

"You do? Please inform me, because I have no idea why. I realized only moments ago that it was me who needed to apologize to you. I should've never expected you to behave like Carlos, he's too tolerant."

"Nonsense, you did what you thought needed to get done and I can't fault you for that." John nudged him. "The way you were up there, that was a sight to see, especially after your state only hours ago. The law lives in you. That's how my father operated . . . so honest and law-abiding every single minute of each day. Exhausting work, I tell you. How do you press the envelope so much, yet find a way to live?"

"Talk about exhausting work."

"Exactly," John smiled at Gus. "In that way, one could say I used to be a little envious of you. But only a little, don't let the idea get out of hand." John nudged him again. "What I'm trying to say is if I've been hard on you and as a close friend, I personally want to apologize for it. We all deal with stress in varying ways."

"Hermano, that means more than I can say." A lump rose in Gus's throat, then subsided. He gripped John's elbow fearfully. "What's supposed to happen now?"

John sighed. "Now is the time I tell you your paranoia hasn't been all in your head. A certain ex-schoolmate of yours by the name of Donovan Kincaid has been pushed by his family or a group of people to stop this case. People with money." He went on to explain Donovan's attempt at a bribe and John weighing the possibility of accepting it. "The Christmas party, all of it was a ploy. I got so caught up in it and so angry at you for wearing yourself down that I contemplating ruining all of our lives, and right before I took office. It's not hard to see I got wrapped up in my own sabotage by even entertaining the idea of communicating with Kincaid."

Gus went silent again, reached down to his sock and pulled out the flask of whisky. He downed it all at once.

Carlos suddenly approached the men and clapped them on their shoulders. "Gustavo! You're starting without us. Even I want to have a drink tonight. Let us eat, drink, and be merry!"

"I told him about Kincaid," John said.

"I never liked that man," Carlos commented. "A wishy-washy prick."

The men roared with laughter.

"It's time to move on," John said. "Literally and figuratively. Widen the lens. Dig deeper."

"I agree completely," Carlos said. "We've reached the end of the road and it's time to find the next path. This is just the beginning."

Gus shook his head. "How? I don't know what to do next. This case has . . . consumed me." He tipped the flask back again and remembered he'd already emptied it. "I'm not sure I like endings, because it means starting over again. I don't know if I can do it; I don't know if I want to do it."

"You will, give it time." John led him away from people. "Don't overload yourself by thinking about it now. Decompress."

"It depends on how you want to look at it," Carlos added. "If it's going to be a disaster, it will be. If it's a perfect trip to heaven, it'll feel like it."

"People will talk about this, about us," Gus said. "I wonder what they will say."

CHAPTER 43

CARLOS AND JOHN TRAVELED BACK HOME TO CONTINUE WORKING ON OTHER cases while Gus stayed to network and bask in the praise their work in DC afforded them. The three agreed to reunite in a week at a party being thrown in honor of their Supreme Court appearance.

Gus called to invite Irene. Though she didn't say yes, they fell into a comfortable conversation. She admitted the amount of jealousy that filled her when she met Patricia led her to the conclusion she wasn't ready to give up on him yet. He called her again in the evening, and again the following morning, midday, and evening without an objection from her. She requested he do the same the next day, and he obliged.

Irene allowed him to begin speaking to the girls again. He called to wake them in the morning and called to say goodnight at bedtime. During the day he described the grandness of the courthouse, the steps, the people, and how well the men spoke. The girls giggled over his stories and bombarded him with questions until he asked for their mother's ear.

The sun seems to be shining a little brighter up here, he reported to Irene, *the colors are sharper, the sights are grander, the air smells fresher, and it all reminds me of you. When you're near, my joy bubbles over. I see God in you, and it brightens colors and cleans the air.*

Irene blushed, thankful he couldn't see through the phone. We're thinking about you over here too, she responded.

He started professing his love to her by the fifth time he called, and asked her to think about giving themselves one more chance as a couple. Nonsense, she said, you're on a high from DC, worry about your girls. He suggested seeing Carlita and Teresa more often, and she said yes, it would be good place to start.

On the third day Irene confided to her mother. "He's been so apologetic lately, about everything. I worry it's just the shine from Washington and he actually doesn't mean any of it."

Her aged mother, nearly eighty, spent all her time sewing, reading books, and watching television. She sat in a rocking chair holding an unfinished quilt on her lap. She rocked back and forth, staring off into the distance. "Maybe he's coming around. But so what if he does?"

"This behavior is vaguely familiar," Irene pondered. "I haven't witnessed it in ages. You know how sometimes, when you're given gifts for no particular reason, it can mean the gift-giver feels guilty about something." She sat at her mother's feet and gently nudged the rocking chair back and forth. "Years ago, Gus did that a month after we said 'I love you,' and come to find out, he'd cheated on me." Irene nodded to herself. "He did that a few times before I began to catch on."

"Women in my day didn't receive gifts unless you married an oilman." Her mother patted her hand with reassurance. "Maybe he's fallen in love with you again and it's awakened his guilt. It can be a good thing. But will that matter to you?"

"Which means he still sleeps with other women," Irene filled in. "How am I supposed to be okay with it while raising two girls? How were you okay with it?"

"Your dad, your husband, all men—they can't help being men. Men are going to cheat mija, it's a way of life. You have to learn to deal with it. Who else is going to take care of you?" She laughed at the expression on Irene's face. She appeared to be clearly upset by her question. "Look at it this way, at least he feels guilty."

Irene shook her head until she felt dizzy. "These mixed messages, what am I to do with them?"

"I wonder if this is the way he's had you feeling all this time, giving you mixed messages."

"He has!"

She shrugged. "It hasn't been a problem so far. Why does it bother you now?"

Irene stopped at this. "Because I'm tired," she finally answered. "He's pulled me every which way and I don't want to do it anymore. I know I've said it before, but . . . " Her voice trailed off. "How am I supposed to know which way to go?"

Her mother tapped the left side of her chest. "Your heart knows the way." She reached out and clasped her daughter's hands. "I come from a world where we did nothing about these things, you know that. I'm not going to tell you to push him aside, the best I can do is give you options. My granddaughters are strong. They can handle anything."

Irene went home from her mother's confused. She knew she needed to break away, but she couldn't see it to be the best thing. A part of her missed him when he was gone too long and she hated admitting it. Bit by bit she began to realize a truth. She'd convinced herself over the years she needed him by necessity, and not necessarily for love. The girls needed a male figure, and she needed a man to support their family, to move the heavy furniture and reach tall places. But it wasn't the truth, the reason was solely and fully for love. She fought with the idea of it so much that to admit it would be total surrender, as if she plunged herself into the depths of an ocean without any hope of air.

Since the decision revolved around their daughters she asked for an opinion. Already knowing Teresa would leap out of her chair and yelp in excitement at the thought, she went to Carlita instead.

"Just see how you feel the next time you see him," Carlita said. "Really Mom, there's no reason to make up your mind ahead of time. That's something Abuela would do."

"Your grandmother is my mother," Irene countered, "and she never would've asked for my thoughts on her marriage with my father."

Carlita shrugged again. "Unlike her, you've always been open to new avenues."

"I have?"

"That's who you are, Mom. I've never not known you to be a different way. Dad can be…difficult, so no one would blame you either way."

She took her conversation with Carlita into account.

People turned to their radios and tuned in to hear Gus tell his story as one of the "country bumpkins" from Texas who made their way to the Supreme Court. Speaking in Spanish, he used the sort of voice that perked ears, even the ones not listening. While on the radio he inspired others to make their mark in the world by using education to fight back inequality, and thanked the people who donated money or prayers to their cause.

One household found themselves particularly moved by his words: his own. Hearing her father's voice over the radio caused Teresa to squeal so much she covered her mouth with a pillow. It rendered Carlita speechless as she allowed herself to be impressed by her dad.

Nostalgia filled Irene at the sound of his voice. She knew it well; Gus reserved it for public moments and meeting important people. Hearing the voice reminded her of the Gus she fell for, the one who could grab a room's attention at a moment's notice and hold onto it for an hour. She decided to attend the party in that moment, without telling him.

Her trepidation stopped her from going straight to Gus when she entered the party. Hundreds of people showed up to support the men, and it mattered not whether they succeeded. She slowly began to circle the crowd, and saw the nucleus consisted of Gus, Carlos, and John. Realizing she couldn't make her way to the middle, she joined a small group of people who started standing on chairs to see the action.

As she kept her balance it dawned on her how much pride she felt for what he accomplished. Gus made it hard on himself, yes, but he still made it to the finish line when it counted. She couldn't fault him for that, he reached his goals no matter the process.

Each man stood a small distance from each other, and attracted different types of fans. The businessmen, lawyers, and LULAC members went for John, trading business cards and taking turns vying for his attention. The intellectual academics who preferred Carlos formed a line and quietly kept to themselves, murmuring amongst each other. Irene noticed the younger adults and college students circled Gus, with decidedly more female fans. This made Irene uncomfortable.

When the crowds showed no signs of thinning after an hour she decided to go home and wait for Gus there. She descended from the chair and found the women's bathroom. While she used a stall, a voice boomed out on an intercom asking for silence while each man separately addressed the crowd.

Irene needed several steps to exit the room, but stopped when she heard Gus's voice. He stood just outside the bathroom door.

"I don't need to get up there yet," he explained to someone, "and besides, everyone heard me on the radio already, I'd merely be repeating myself. Did you hear me on the radio?"

Irene heard female giggling in response.

"I want to finish what I started saying," Gus went on, "I'm glad you two found me, I want to find more like you. We need youth on our side, and no one can resist a pretty face."

"Our LULAC junior club holds at least ten more girls who'd love to help out at any fundraisers and do what we could for the cause. Can we get your business card?"

Irene heard one giggle. "I'd like one, too."

"I have enough for ladies like you," Gus said, "don't worry about me."

"Ladies like us?"

"Special ladies. Special because I see God in you, in both of you."

Irene gasped as her heart dropped. A toilet flushed nearby, taking her future with it.

Gus went on, unaware his wife stood on the other side of the bathroom door. "It's true! Don't doubt me. One cannot fake such a thing, it's inherent. People are drawn to you and they don't know why. Well, I know why, your spirit glows like embers in a fire."

A woman maneuvered herself around Irene to exit the bathroom. She pushed the door wide, inadvertently giving Irene a video to the audio soundbite that came next.

Gus reached out and tapped on the chest of one of the women with his forefinger. "They're drawn to God, and he's right there."

When her doorbell rang at midnight, Irene knew Gus stood on the other side. She cracked the door open three inches.

"Are you drunk?"

"No, actually, they babysat me all evening so I wouldn't embarrass anyone."

She walked away from the door without opening it all the way. "I don't believe you."

Gus let himself inside. "Hello, my love. Aren't you going to say hello to me?"

Irene sat in a chair and gave him an expressionless look. "Hello, Gustavo."

He cocked his head back. "The girls are asleep?"

"They couldn't keep their eyes open," she lied.

He sat on the couch. "You're still clothed at this time of night?"

"I've had an epiphany, Gustavo," she announced.

"Shhhhh." He took a dramatic breath. "I need to share something with you and I want to say it before our world starts to crumble. I feel it happening already."

"Fair enough. You first."

"A paranoia filled me soon after I accepted the case, back in 1951. It felt like people were trying to sabotage the case. Or ruin me, I couldn't make up my mind."

"They're one and the same," Irene offered.

"Exactly. Turns out I was right." He sat back with a satisfied smile. "Now, this may be tough to hear, but I encountered a woman in DC the night before the big day, a reporter." He received no reaction. "She found me a few days ago to confess our introduction was intentional. A man I know paid her to interact with me and do whatever she could to help me make bad choices. Drink too much, sleep too little, sleep too late," he listed. "Detain me in the morning, turn off the alarm, hide the coffee."

"What did she do?" Irene found herself interested.

"All of the above, and more," Gus said proudly. "I still had the showing of my life."

"I don't doubt it."

"She was certain him hiring her remained the last cog in a large machine built to bring the case down and make me the number one enemy." He clasped a hand with hers. "I'm not crazy after all." He laughed when Irene lifted an eyebrow. "Finally vindicated, finally proven right! It took me to the other side of my sanity to find out the truth, but I found out."

Irene took hold of his other hand. "Was it the same man who hired the woman to play your bullfighting girlfriend?"

"Probably. I've missed you," he said wistfully. "I don't want to talk about things like that. It's over with her, I ended it with her before I left for DC." Gus tucked a lock of her hair behind her ear. "I can't help thinking about the vibe when I first walked in. I'm afraid to mention it for fear of arguing." He continued when she didn't respond. "There is no one like you. I've been a fool, I'm always a fool. You are a goddess in a land of mortal women. I've missed every part of you, every strand of your hair. I hear you in my head, you are my conscience. So many addictions ravage me, but you are my favorite by far, and the most healthy choice. No matter what I've been through, you've always been by my side."

"Yes," she said calmly, "and I think it's time I stop doing that."

"No, no, not again." Gus knelt at her feet. "What happened since yesterday to make you say this? I've fallen in love with you all over again talking with you this past week. I thought things were going well."

"They were, until . . . " Her voice trailed off. "I see God in you. When you first said that to me I felt like the only girl in the world. I watched as your face turned bright like someone flicked on a light within you. A light personified."

"Because of you," Gus whispered. "I'll always see God in you."

Softly, she asked, "Yes, but I'm not the only one, am I?"

His eyes skittered about like a page of text had been placed in front of him. "Were you there?"

"I was there." She wiped away a tear. "I'd stupidly convinced myself that moment was ours."

"It—"

"I. WAS. THERE. Stop lying to me." Her voice stayed calm and steady, yet strong. "All this time I thought I never knew what I wanted, because I didn't want to admit what I wanted. But today, you made that decision for me. I make excuses for you because I'm in love with you, because my heart goes pitter-patter when I think of you, because I want you to touch me when you reach out to try. Now that I know for certain you can't give me loyalty, I will not give you love."

Gus shook his head and backed up into a wall. He slid down and sat on the floor.

"I realize we're only together here because I stuck around," Irene continued. "I'm special, but not because you loved me most. I'm special because I stayed. I'm special because I bore you two daughters." Tears started to fall. "You are the sun, in your warmth I'm alive, and in your absence I shrivel. Now your rays are too much and my skin is sunburnt."

"Don't say this, please stop." He kissed her knees. "I feel like I've finally found some peace and I want to share it with you. Please stop, I beg you. Your words are scooping out my insides, can't you see? They're shrinking my soul."

"That is nothing more than your ego, Gustavo. You're an appetite and you don't even know it. I must let you go so you can feed on the world." Irene ruffled his hair. "You've come all this way and you must revel in it, you must live it with everything you possess. This is your time!"

Gus's face fell. He seemed to age a decade in the few moments of silence that followed. "What do you do when you feel like you can't go on living? Even when things are at their best and you still want to die, what do you do?" He began to cry. "On the way home from DC the color in life began to fade. I had experienced the most natural high, but like with any drug, sooner or later it wears off. Time slows, your body begins to ache, you thirst for water, sleep, normalcy. It's like they say, the problems you shoved away are waiting for you when you come back. Or in my case, you realize they still reside in you, paying rent and taking up space."

"What do you do when you feel like you can't go on living? You go on, Gustavo. You keep moving on." Irene shook her head. "I'm worried about you. What if you win the case? What would happen then? What sort of high would you fall off of then?"

He smiled angelically, calm. "If we won, I could die a tragic death and not feel guilty about it. I could go insane and it wouldn't matter, because I've done my part and it's time to pass the torch."

"Don't say things like that, it worries me more."

He laughed. "If we won, I'd keep working, mi amor, I'd retry Pete's case and others like his. It'll give me the push to keep on going. I promise."

Irene didn't trust him, but didn't know how to convey it. That was the thing about letting go, you also let go of the responsibility you believed held the relationship together.

She allowed Gus to stay home for another month in order to save enough money to afford a place to live. Organizations and universities called him to arrange for lectures, so he made money quickly. He stopped trying to request her love. He set her free. They found a way to tell their daughters that didn't cause pain.

Irene learned a broken heart could be the launching pad for something better in her life. The moment she accepted the truth the easier the process became, and in time it released her beautifully, like a butterfly emerging from its cocoon.

Irene dug up the sunflowers in the front yard and planted tulips that year.

CHAPTER 44

AMELIA WOKE UP EARLY WITH A SLIGHT FEVER ON THE FIRST MONDAY IN MAY, and her mother Elvira kept her home from school until it subsided. Amelia didn't want to stay home that day, mainly because she'd become accustomed to meeting a certain friend after school.

Since she shared her bed with three sisters, she took advantage of the extra space once her siblings left for school, and stretched out as far as her limbs would allow. She fell back to sleep in minutes and stayed asleep for hours. She dreamed she grew up to be a lawyer and worked beside Gus winning cases for equal justice.

Yipppppp! A voice ripped through the air and jolted her out of sleep. It sounded like her dad's. Clapping and her mother's laughter followed his exclamation. Amelia sat up in bed, slipped on a pair of socks, and followed the noise. It sounded like genuine happiness, palpable and infectious. She found them in the kitchen with the radio low in the background.

"Mija!" Henry ran to her and scooped her up. "What a sight you are, rubbing your eyes!" He kissed her on both cheeks. "Today is a wonderful day, and let me tell you why. Your lawyer friend Gus, do you remember him?"

Hearing his name shot through her like caffeine. A flash of a dream came back to her. "Mister Gus García?"

"The very one . . . " Henry swung Amelia around in a full circle and let her down to continue. "They won, they just announced it on the radio, the verdict is in. They won!"

Amelia beamed at her parents, never happier to have stayed home sick. She clapped and danced a jig with her father in the kitchen.

Elvira laughed at them, then pointed at Amelia. "You, come here." She placed her hand underneath Amelia's chin and on the small of her back. "You still have a fever, sit down at the table." She plopped an orange in front of her. "Eat that and I'll heat you some Campbell's."

Amelia expertly peeled the rind from the fruit and split it in half. She pulled as much white fiber from between the orange slices as she could before sticking a slice into her mouth. As she chewed she tried speaking. "If my fever breaks . . . may I go out for a little bit?"

Elvira frowned as she turned on the stove, then looked for a pot and can opener. "Why? What's out there?"

Amelia shook her head. No way would she share who she met with, no way. She stuck another slice in her mouth and chewed. "I just want to see if anyone is celebrating in the streets. Today is a wonderful day," she mimicked her dad.

"Yes, yes, we'll see," her mother said. The chicken soup began to bubble under the heat. "Vitamin C, something warm, another nap, and we'll see about you going out today."

Henry stepped up to support his daughter. "Today is a special day; history is being made," he purred to Elvira. "If anyone is celebrating, today would be the day they'd do it."

She playfully snapped a towel at him. "You don't think I know that? You hush, let your daughter recuperate from whatever is ailing her."

Amelia dutifully finished her fruit, soup, and drank a glass of water before heading back to bed. As she waited for sleep to come again, she thought of Gus and how happy he must be in that moment.

Knowing nothing about the dread that can attach itself to success, she saw only good things for him, filled with happiness and celebration. She knew it would be a step in the right direction for everyone to be equal, that much she knew.

As she slept, her mother finished making her husband lunch, then went to the couple's bedroom and pulled a small red dress out of her dresser. Ever since meeting Gus, Amelia had been requesting a new one.

Her mother chose a soft, apple red cotton for the new dress and personalized it by sewing black piping on all the edges. She snuck into the girls' room and checked on Amelia, who snored quietly. Elvira found Amelia's faded red sundress and replaced it with the new one. She returned to the kitchen, retrieved a pomegranate she'd been saving for herself, and began the careful surgery of peeling it.

Amelia woke for the final time that day, and as her eyes opened, she noticed a clear plastic cup filled to the brim with what looked like shiny, tiny, ruby red jewels sitting on the corner of the sisters' balsa wood desk. She went to the bathroom and brushed her teeth.

The sound of the toilet flushing caught Elvira's attention, and she poked her head around the doorway. "How you feeling?"

"I don't feel like anything is wrong with me. This morning my body felt heavy but my head felt like a balloon." She smiled sweetly. "Thank you for the fruit. I know it was special."

"It's a special day." Her mother returned the smile. "Get dressed, your brothers and sisters will be home any minute. I'm sure no one announced the reversal at school today."

Amelia decided to wear red and absentmindedly reached for what she expected to be the faded red dress. Suddenly, a soft texture and vibrant color made her aware of the new replacement. She marveled at the black embellishments, the side pockets, and pleats at the waist.

It fit her well. She rushed to the bathroom and stood on the toilet to inspect herself, since that room held the only mirror in the house. Pleased with her appearance, Amelia returned to her room. She went for the pomegranate seeds and popped a few in her mouth. The juice spurt out on her tongue, bright and tart. The size of the cup fit snugly in one of her front pockets and secured the precious commodity as she went out to meet her family, their cries of victory still filling the house.

Delia ran to her. "That man at the soda shop, do you remember him? The day I poured the strawberry soda over the counter?"

"Of course I do! He's my friend," Amelia said, "I ran into him again after we met him."

"He's important now . . . your hus-band," Delia teased.

Jane joined them. "They won! Those lawyers won in Washington, DC!"

"Gus," Amelia offered, but they jumped around too much to listen.

The family next door owned a television set, so Amelia's family decided amongst themselves who wanted to watch television footage of the men gathered in San Antonio and who wanted to stay home and hear about it on the radio. Amelia hoped to do neither, and persuaded her father to permit her to leave the house for a little bit.

Amelia walked the six blocks to downtown Edna while eating some of the pomegranate seeds, retrieving them one by one and spitting them out onto the grass when she chewed the juice out. Her fingertips took on a bright pinkish-red color and stained her fingers, but she didn't care. The payoff was the juice exploding into her mouth as her teeth popped the seeds.

As she rounded the corner into Main Street, she saw a small group of people surrounding the television store window next to the barbershop. Sure enough, they aired footage from downtown San Antonio, and she caught a glimpse of Gus shaking hands with people around him and lifting their clasped hands in victory before a large crowd in the park. She stopped for a moment and smiled.

Mexicans took up the majority of the group who surrounded the television sets, and they clapped each other on the back and shook hands. Amelia's smile widened as her heart began to sing. Not completely understanding the full implication of the case, she understood the simple joy in the faces of her people, and understood this was something big. For her, Gus truly became the shiny one standing among the men.

Amelia reminisced about their first encounter at the ice cream parlor three years prior. Entering the shop that day filled her with anxiety. Her little sister Delia's assertiveness shocked her, in the soda shop and on the street. She longed to someday be as forward as Delia, and now felt she'd reached a point in her life where she achieved that goal.

Amelia didn't notice until later that two men stood close to each other in the back of the group. They appeared to be unhappy and were muttering under their breath.

She thought to herself, *there will always be people like that, men and women who don't like it when other people advance. There will always be people who don't want things to change, who try to keep everything the same.*

She went out into the middle of the street where Gus brought her and Delia their strawberry sodas and began to spin and spin. From above, her dress looked like a matador's cape spinning above her head.

"Amelia? Amelia?"

She stopped dizzily to focus on the boy standing at the curb. "Hiya Dave."

Dave Grimland stood before her, wearing navy blue pants and a starched white button-up shirt. Holding a pencil case in one hand, he was bouncing a small red ball with the other. Dave smiled at her when they locked eyes. "I didn't see you at school today, is everything okay?" He stepped onto the road.

Amelia found her heart skipped a beat when he flashed a hundred-watt smile at her. "Everything's a-okay. I had a fever this morning, but it went down."

He nodded. "I noticed you because of your dress and the way you were spinning in it."

She fanned the dress out. "It's new."

"Taking it out for a test drive?" He grinned.

Amelia felt her cheeks go rosy. "Something like that."

"Well, it's mighty fine." Dave looked down to the pavement. "If you don't mind me saying, you look pretty in it."

Her face flushed with more warmth, because no one had ever said that to her before. "Are you here alone?" She scanned the sidewalk. "Where's your mom?"

"She's not here today. I went to the hardware store for my pa but couldn't find what he needed. I knew I'd be seeing you afterwards." When he shook his blonde hair, it lightened as it separated in the sun. He held out the pencil case. "I brought you these."

Amelia snapped her fingers. "I forgot your popsicle sticks this time! I'm sorry. Next time. I became so excited about the dress, and . . . " She weighed how to tell him the news of the morning, and then thought of the reason Gus needed to fight in the first place. "A big thing happened this morning with my family, so I've sorta been walking on air." She pulled the cup of pomegranate seeds out of her pocket and showed him. "You want some? I have enough to share. My mom gave them to me this afternoon. Break the skin and suck on the seed, but don't eat it. Spit it out when you've gotten as much juice as you can."

He popped a few in his mouth. "I've never tried them. A pomegranate, right? Say, those are good."

"I know, right?"

"Huh." He spit a seed out. "We could have a spitting contest."

She nodded brightly. "Let's do it!"

"We could walk down the street around the corner to sit down. Wanna do that?"

"Sure." Amelia couldn't think of anything else she'd rather do.

Dave took another handful and chewed on them. "How do you take them out? I can see your fingers are stained."

"Depends on if you're good at it. I do it carefully and pull seeds one or two at a time, but my mom breaks the fruit in half and uses a wooden spatula to get the seeds out. She spanks one of the halves until the seeds shoot out. It's less messy."

They walked the short distance to the corner and sat where a stream of water ran under their legs. Without saying much they dipped their hands into the cup and ate seeds.

Dave spit out first and gauged his distance. "Gosh, that's a lot of work."

Amelia shrugged. She spit out the seeds, some of hers reaching farther than his. "I guess so. The work is worth it to me, you know?"

He smiled widely at her. "I do."

Amelia gazed at Dave and a brief thought passed through her mind. Never in a million years would he have looked at a girl like her, or wanted to spend time alone with her. And never, ever would someone like him be smiling at her in the way he was right now.

She hoped that for every person who didn't want the world to change, there was a person greater than them who did.

EPILOGUE

WINNING BROUGHT MORE CLIENTS, WHICH GUS NEEDED TO GET HIM BACK ON his feet and find a proper place to live. As time passed, he began to believe the win in DC was first a gift, then ultimately a curse on his career.

The gift came in terms of new work and more attention, both of which he appreciated. The curse turned work into too much work, more than he knew what to do with. He found it hard to turn clients down, so he said yes to everyone. His wins declined, and scrutiny of his life increased. He received too much attention, and never found time for privacy. People always wanted a piece of him. He continued to drink.

The Jackson County jury reindicted Pete later that year, in September, and Gus took it upon himself to continue fighting for him. He represented Pete alone this time, and moved the case to Refugio County by October. They called for a new jury, and it contained two Mexican Americans. A second trial was slated for the middle of November, and Pete was found guilty again. Authorities transferred him to Harlem State Prison in Austin.

After Gus lost the retrial he hoped a weight would be lifted from his shoulders. He wanted to sleep forever. With Lenora, he drove to Austin to visit Pete and apologize, but he did something he wasn't expecting: Gus cried when Pete limped into the room and hugged him.

At the end of their catch-up session, Gus began to cry again. "Trying to get you freed was my biggest mission in life," he said, with tears streaming down his face. "It didn't matter whether we won, because we vied for your life, not a title or a win. It may have seemed different to you, but . . . " Gus pressed a hand to his heart. "I hold so much guilt inside when I think of you sitting in a jail cell. You need to know that."

Pete reached out to console him. "I can see it on your face, amigo. Don't keep these feelings caged in a prison, it'll cause you to kill someone," he said seriously. "A man's prison doesn't have to be behind bars. I learned that here." He tapped the side of his forehead and gave Gus a searching look.

Gus held his eyes, and for a moment, he thought he could see Mateo smiling back as he said, "I made it to the top, and I don't know if my sacrifice meant something. All I wanted was to win, be seen, and be remembered. I'm not sure if it was worth it, the way I feel right now."

Pete patted his shoulder. "You sound tired, friend. You need to rest. Keeping up with a man's life behind bars is nearly impossible. I don't know how you lawyers do it. The journey sounds like so much . . . work." He scratched his head. "When I'm happy, I'm happy, and when I'm upset, I'm upset. There isn't a lot of in between. I think the smarter you are, the more you have to contend with up there." He tapped the side of his forehead again. "No thanks."

Lenora came toward Gus and hugged him. Instead of soothing him, this made Gus cry harder. He wanted to curl into a ball and collapse onto the cold floor. He wanted it all to be over. Not just because he lost Pete's case, but because he admitted to himself that the loss of his marriage and the relationship with his daughters had become too far gone due solely to him.

In the following years, Gus never was able to get back on the horse and work at the high level he reached in 1954. That year turned out to be the best and worst year of his life. Clubs, groups, and lawyer's associations honored him left and right. He did his best to keep up with the law crowd, but it didn't last very long.

By 1955 he declined most of his invitations to law forums. Gus started a new firm to try and renew his career, but it fell apart soon after it began.

The drinking never stopped. He drank more, and longer, spending too much time forgetting about where he was and daydreaming about where he'd like to be. Appointments were fewer, and when one happened, he showed up tipsy and shabbily dressed. Living up to the image he'd created became more and more difficult.

Though he remarried, they soon divorced. He lost his house, his family, jobs, friends, associates, and he lost himself in the process. By 1960, Gus began working small jobs and asked for alcohol as payment.

He still made it his life's mission to fight a bull, as a matador would. To smell the bull rush past him, to feel the weight of a cape twirling between his hands and listen to the sound of its unfurling . . . that goal became his new Supreme Court, the thing pushing him to meet and reach his dreams. All he needed was one bull charging at him, the best high he could chase.

In 1963, Gus mustered up enough courage to face his biggest fear. He stood in a practice arena holding Manolete's muleta, the one item he still kept with him, and dressed in the finest clothes a bullfighter could wear.

As he strode into the arena's dusty sea, he kept his eyes on the gate the bull would enter from. Though no crowd watched him, he imagined his abuelo watching, with Irene, Carlita, and Teresa cheering him on. He saw Manolete there, and Patricia, too, clapping and calling out advice.

The door swung open and an overexcited bull entered. It looked angry, its nostrils flaring in the dusty air. It advanced slowly at Gus, grunting like a revved-up car engine. Gus glanced back at the fence he was going to run behind. He heard people erupting into a chant that sounded like the ones he heard as a child, when he barely reached his grandfather's waist. The sound put him at ease, and he grew confident of his moves with the muleta.

Gus drew himself up to his full height, and the imaginary audience went wild. He sashayed to one side and flipped his cape, then darted to the other side and turned around with perfect timing. His breath danced as his muleta whipped in the air. He'd been practicing for this all his life.

He tried another move and felt he rode the air like an ocean wave. He'd been so happy, doing what he wanted to be doing, and having people around him who appreciated it. He imagined executing the move in front of the Supreme Court steps.

Suddenly, water splashed in his face and pulled him out of his trance. The sounds of many horns blared in his ears. Gus fell to his knees and whipped his head around to face the headlights of a car.

This was wrong, he thought, *all wrong,* though he couldn't explain how. He gasped and turned the other way, thinking himself still under a spell. Instead he looked into the grille of one car, then another, and more still. The honking became more insistent.

A voice he didn't recognize sounded in his ear. "Sir? Sir! Can you hear me? I'm going to pitch more water in your face if you don't respond to me." A policeman came into focus. "Are you okay?"

He took in his environment. Some people had wrecked their cars in the middle of the street trying to avoid the crazy man waving a faded red blanket. Other people parked in the surrounding lots to watch the man as he danced about in the street. They believed him to be stark raving mad.

The policeman dragged Gus off the street. "Are you drunk?" He shined a flashlight into his face. "Where do you think you are?"

Gus shook his head and shaded his eyes with one hand. It all came into view, the cars, the people. "In San Antonio, and yes, I'm drunk. But just to let you know, everything is wrong with me. Nothing is what I think it is. It's all in my head." He began to laugh.

"Are you planning to hurt someone, or just yourself?"

Gus shook his head. "Just myself."

"Then come with me." The policeman pulled him to a park bench and demanded he sit. He pulled out his handcuffs, until a voice interrupted him.

"I've got this, officer, you don't have to worry about it."

A short, stocky Mexican man in a snappy suit met the policeman's gaze. "Carlos Cadena," he said, and stuck out a hand for the officer to shake. "I used to work with that man when he was a lawyer. I'm responsible for him."

"Yes sir, I've heard of you. You know who this guy is?"

"Absolutely. This man stood beside me in front of the Supreme Court in Washington, DC. Show him some respect."

"He wouldn't give us any identification, not even a name. Do you know where I found him?"

"I'd stepped away to get him some food. I had no idea he wandered too far. He's like a child, you see, but more like my brother," Carlos added.

The policeman surrendered Gus.

Gus looked up to Carlos as the sun outlined him and gave him a golden silhouette. "My little giant, my Carlitos," he praised. "Do you recognize me? It's your little bullshitter."

Carlos sat beside him on the bench and held out a hamburger and fries wrapped in newspaper. "Of course I recognized you."

Gus nudged him. "Look at you rescuing me and buying me a meal."

Carlos smiled wistfully. "Where did you go, my friend? I haven't heard anything about you in some time." He waved his hand in the air. "It doesn't matter, just eat, eat first."

Gus shook his head. "I have no idea where I went. Down a vortex?" His eyes watered and tears mixed into the salt of his fries as the two looked at each other. "I have no idea where I went, I was in my head, and that's where everything is, isn't it?" He trembled as he looked around him. He bit into the burger, then started crying. Food fell out of his mouth. "I'm a mess."

"We all are in one way or another, we're all damaged goods. Some of us hide it better than others, that's all," Carlos said.

"Sometimes I try to figure out how I got here, but when I think about it for too long it feels like my brain has been sucked up in a whirlwind and all my thoughts are tossed about." It surprised Gus when he found he had more to say. "Sometimes I'm just ready for it to be all over. Do you ever think about that?"

Carlos smiled sadly. "I don't need to hear you say that." Quietly, he asked, "Were you waving that blanket around like a muleta in the middle of the street? Or were you trying to hurt yourself?"

"I did wave a cape around, but I might've been trying to hurt myself, too. I truly started the afternoon believing my time had come to face a bull. Maybe my bull is a bull of death, just like mi abuelo's. Maybe." He laughed bitterly. "Mateo always warned me that I'd be happy if I chose to be, or I'd dance with the bulls." He tapped his right temple with his fingers.

"And here we are." Carlos took a breath and gazed out toward the park. "Looks like chipping away at the social issues meant some chipping away at our souls, huh?"

Gus bit into his hamburger. "Maybe you're right. Maybe Herrera was always right for saying it."

"I have a question for you, Gustavo. Do you think, if you'd been a flamenco dancer, or a bullfighter, you'd have done anything different in the way you lived your life?"

Gus munched on a handful of fries and looked up to the heavens. Feeling more like himself, he said, "Not one bit. No matter what, I would've always lived my life without doubt, regret, or shame."

Carlos tilted his head. "Come now, I think we both know that isn't true."

"I would never lie to you!" Gus widened his eyes. "I might've tried harder to do more, but the way I lived my life? I wouldn't change a thing, because I wouldn't have gotten this far otherwise."

"Amigo, I will agree that you haven't lived with much shame in your life, but without doubt or regret? I've known you to be nothing but." Carlos reached for a few fries and chewed thoughtfully. "Do not live in ignorance. Life is short, and you rode the ride hard."

"Maybe you're right; I may have lived life as a doubtful fool filled with regrets," Gus said, and smiled wide, "but I never will be the first to admit it. One thing I will be honest about: they say life is short, but if you get into the mix and ride life hard, it can be a long and tedious thing, regardless of the duration. The minutes and hours stretch out to eternity. As far as I know, there's nothing short about life. I think T. S. Eliot said something to that effect."

"When you put yourself in a mental dungeon for what you did or didn't do, I think that's what makes life long."

"Maybe you're right, but I don't know any other way." Gus stuffed a french fry in his mouth and watched the cars go by, listening to them honk. "I'll say this: if I'm in a dungeon of my own making, I'd be lucky to die on the streets of San Antonio, or any place in Texas. I'd be just as proud as a derelict as I would be a king."

AUTHOR'S NOTE

FROM WHAT I COULD GATHER, AFTER GUS RECEIVED HIS LAW DEGREE HE SPENT eight extraordinary years building up his career, leading to the SCOTUS win at the top, the pinnacle. I write that because I noticed in the same amount of time, eight years, he traveled slowly back down the ladder he climbed.

One can read about his short life in the few accounts available, or watch the PBS documentary, *A Class Apart*. The lack of information about Gus led me to use real moments in history and use fiction to link the stories in a more dramatic way. Since Gus tended to be theatrical in most things he took on, I figured taking liberties here and there would allow me to tell a full story.

The special features in *A Class Apart* imply that Gus may have had an affair with the first female bullfighter, Patricia McCormick. I imagined them meeting because I think he would've seen her as his equal. When I learned he obsessed over matadors and bullfighting, it seemed like the right thing to do.

After her bullfighting career, Patricia McCormick lived a long, ripe life into her eighties and never married or produced children. She was known as the first North American matador and fought for women's rights in the sport, though she never progressed past the novice level. Most matadors agreed if she'd been born a man, Patricia could've been one of the best bullfighters out there. She even used her grandfather's World War I blanket as a cape in her early years.

In the early 2000s she went through some tough financial times, just as Gus had. She nearly lost her apartment, but due to a fan's help she was able to get back on her feet. She briefly renewed her career, but not for long.

Patricia performed in hundreds of bullfights and was even impaled by a bull's horns, but it hardly bothered her. "I loved the brave bull," she wrote in her *Lady Bullfighter* memoir about the animal who impaled her. I'd like to think Gus was a brave bull she loved as well.

John J. Herrera came from one of the first fourteen families to settle in San Antonio.

A huge highlight of his life included his introduction of John F. Kennedy at a LULAC assembly at the Rice Hotel in Houston on November 21, 1963, hours before Kennedy's assassination. The speech was known as the first address by a sitting president to Latinos.

John J. Herrera's work is also the reason World War II Liberty ships are named after Latin American heroes. He organized fifty-three new LULAC councils in Texas, Arizona, and New Mexico, and received a lifetime honorary membership to the American GI Forum. He served as the twenty-first national LULAC president.

He died in Houston on October 12, 1986. He said he owes all of his success to LULAC.

After their SCOTUS win, Carlos Cadena went back to public law and served as the head of the San Antonio attorney's office until 1961.

African Americans entered a Woolworth department store to peacefully protest after not being allowed to lunch there at the counters. When things came to a head, Cadena instructed the chief of police that students who are peacefully protesting shouldn't be arrested. According to the press, all six major department stores in San Antonio opened their doors to equal rights customers, making the city one of the first in Texas to do so.

Carlos Cadena helped found the Mexican-American Legal Defense and Educational Fund (MALDEF) in 1968 and served as its president since the inception of the group. He was appointed to the Fourth Court of Appeals, first as an associate justice in 1961, and later became the first Mexican American Texas Chief Justice in 1977. He held the position for twenty-five years. He passed in 2001.

Gus C. García died in 1964 on a park bench in downtown San Antonio. He was forty-eight. His body sat unnoticed for several hours, and no one knew who he was for some time. At one point in his life, he actually was found dodging cars like they were bulls, and I tried to write it in a happier light.

Rather than dying because of his addictions and depression, I'd like to believe Gus died happy, that he was at peace.

I believe during the entirety of his life, the blessing of knowledge plagued him. He knew he had the potential to acquire more, do more, and it made him feel obligated to live his life as hard as he could to make *la raza* proud of his work, despite his personal shortcomings.

I think Gus knew what he did stirred the hearts of others, and it became a gift and a curse. He had good looks and charm by the busloads, but it came at a price. He used what he had to his advantage and went as far as he could, and it surprised many people along the way. A man like Gus could speak with an easiness others found daunting. It exhausted him, but he did it anyway.

I believe when death called out, Gus wanted to get a good seat for the action. He found a nice sunny bench to sit on, because Mateo would surely be the one to pick him up, no? I hope Gus answered the call with a smile on his face, finally ready to leave the world to watch over his colleagues as they achieved more and more.

July 27, his birthday, is known as Gus García day in Texas.

The *Hernandez vs. Texas* win was overshadowed by the *Brown vs. Board of Education* win, because it happened two weeks later, and fought gloriously by Thurgood Marshall, because the topic was still seen from a black and white perspective, and not a black, brown, and white perspective. I believe this story is just as compelling—and not just because of Gus's tragic end.

As for Amelia, she is a real person in this story, too. She grew up constantly learning to overcome her shyness and tried to be more than what others expected from her. Amelia Cruz married and bore four children, a boy and three girls. Two of those girls, named Millie and Jane, died all too soon. Later in life, Amelia legally changed her first name to Emilie, turning herself into Emilie Diaz. The boy, Robert, grew up to have a family, but oddly lived his life hard in the same way Gus did. I like to think they're drinking in heaven.

Amelia injected her ideas about life into her third daughter, also named Millie, and shared her childhood stories. That daughter ended up writing the book you're reading now.

After learning about their victory in May 1954, Gus gave a speech informing the public of what happened during their journey so it could be recorded for posterity.

Toward the end of his speech, he said this: "Using Texas as a barometer, we discover, for example, that, projecting our present fantastic birth rate into the future, by 1970 we shall actually be a majority of the population in this state. [Although this has not quite happened yet, it is projected to happen in this century.]

"Proportionately, the same thing holds true in all other states with a heavy 'Mexican' population. Thus, in spite of diseases which would seem to decimate our ranks, we are rapidly being swept forward to a position which will call for more responsible leadership, and for more effective participation in the everyday affairs of our society. This will be a problem which can be solved only by an intelligent program on the part of our organizations as well as by a more enthusiastic application of worthwhile methods by the state educational authorities.

"A final word of caution: do not place on a pedestal those whose fate it has been to fight your battles, We are not little tin gods . . . alas, alas, all mortals have feet of clay.

"Crusaders, at best or worst, depending on your point of view, are simply ordinary folk with little quirks and an inflated social conscience—and, perhaps, a Messiah complex. Most of all, try to remember this last bit of advice, which I express while having to resort to that moth-eaten cliche about don't do as I do, but do as I say: the right to occupy a respected place in our social strata can never be demanded; it must, of necessity, be earned."

ACKNOWLEDGMENTS

WITHOUT GOD AS MY BASIC STRENGTH, I WOULD BE A PUDDLE OF NOTHING. I thank HIM.

Now, to my mother, my mom, Emilie Diaz . . . it's happened. Long ago, you implanted in my head that I would do something meaningful, and somewhere down the line, I started to believe it, despite the naysayers in my head. I hope someday you know how much I've appreciated your support. This story wouldn't be so well-rounded if it wasn't for your childhood stories, not to mention your father and my grandpa, Henry Cruz. I still feel the goosebumps on my skin when I stumbled across his name on the witness list for the original trial. It still boggles my mind about how kismet this story is for me, to be writing a story that started in my hometown, and to have my grandfather be a part of it long before I came into this world. I can only hope I can stand up for our people in the future the way he did for Pete Hernandez in that dusty old bar.

To my dad, Robert Diaz, I've heard your prayers when you weren't noticing and know how much you pray for me. You're the one who taught me in college that I can be happy if I choose to be, because everything is in my head. It changed the way I looked at my world, and I thank you for that. I love you, old man.

To William E. Reaves and Linda J. Reaves: Linda and Bill, this book would not have come to fruition so quickly had it not been for the two of you entering my life. I'm forever in debt to you both for offering me guidance when I needed it most. If it wasn't for the nudge from both of you, I wouldn't have sent out proposals so soon, nor looked deeper into the themes of my story because of the questions you both asked. You two work as one person and made time for me at a moment's notice in the early stages, and I couldn't be more grateful. The help you've given is incalculable.

Thank you to Shannon Davies, my beloved Eric John Muelhman, Rene Barrera, Michael Brooks, Dusty Dust Buehring, Leslie Cruz, Kerry Karl, Crystal Diaz, Robert Diaz, Judy Lundy, Mary Ballin, Ina Hightower. You all have played vital roles in my life at one time or another while I worked on this project.

Finally, I want to thank the TCUP staff: Daniel Williams, Kathy Walton, Rebecca Allen, and especially Molly Spain for sorting through my endless emails. Thank you for taking a chance on me and giving me an opportunity. I hope to do you all proud.

If I forgot about you and you think you should be listed here, get back with me so I can thank you in person.